PRAISE 1

"The main characters are compelling. Foiled Silver has everything: humor, mystery, even a little romance. You keep reading as the excitement builds to a smashing and surprising conclusion!"

—Dana Newman, Executive Director,
Talbot County Free Library

"Susan Reiss captures the magic, mystery and charm of that quintessential Eastern Shore town – St. Michaels. Secrets lay hidden for generations among the stunningly beautiful estates along the Miles River. Can't wait for her next 'silver' adventure."

—Kathy Harig, Proprietor,
Mystery Loves Company Bookstore

"*Tarnished Silver* is a fabulous debut novel! Abby Strickland is someone I can relate to, my kind of heroine. I admire the way she rises to the challenges thrown in her path. She's a brave and loyal person whom I would love to call a friend (if she were real, of course). Susan Reiss is a great storyteller, and I'm really looking forward to more stories in the Silver Mystery Series.

—Kassandra Lamb, author,
Kate Huntington Mystery Series

"This series will transport you to the Eastern Shore of Maryland, but will remind you of whatever town has a special place in your heart—hopefully without murder. It leaves me wondering what other secrets this quaint little Eastern Shore town is hiding and I'm waiting for Susan Reiss to tell us."

—Barbara Viniar, Retired President
Chesapeake College, Wye Mills, Maryland

"This is a series that captures the local flavor of our area – St. Michaels, the food and the quirky characters who live here and visit. The descriptions of all the real places make me feel like I'm there. The mystery kept me turning the page. This is a series I recommend to my library patrons... and to you.

—Shauna Beulah, Branch Manager,
St. Michaels Library

SILVER MYSTERY SERIES BOOKS

Tarnished Silver
Sacred Silver
Painted Silver
Hammered Silver
Foiled Silver

FOILED SILVER

SUSAN REISS

INK & IMAGINATION PRESS
an imprint of Blue Lily Publishers

Copyright © 2019 by Susan Reiss
All rights reserved.
No part of this book may be reproduced in any form or by any electronic or mechanical means, including information storage and retrieval systems, without written permission from the author, except for the use of brief quotations in a book review.

This is a work of fiction.
Any resemblance to a person, living or dead, is unintentional and accidental.

Author Photo by Marie Martin

ISBN 978-1-949876-11-6 (e-book)
ISBN 978-1-949876-10-9 (print)

Website: www.SusanReiss.com
Facebook: Susan Reiss
Twitter: @Susan Reiss
Goodreads.com: Susan Reiss, Goodreads Author

*To D.N.
because you wanted to know all about
your favorite character, Dawkins*

TERRAPIN

A slow and plodding creature that some people believe is stupid, but she is a miracle of nature.

Protected by a diamond-patterned shell, she feels the vibrations of the land through her the body, barely an inch above the ground. She is free to raise a sensitive head to detect the rhythms of the air and elements all around her. The Turtle has existed for more than 220 million years and blessed with a lifespan of 40 years or more, it has learned much from Mother Nature.

The Terrapin lays her eggs on the shore, but as more and more of the Chesapeake shoreline is protected or reinforced by bulkhead or boulders, fewer and fewer natural beaches exist.

To a hungry Terrapin, a floating plastic bag may look like a jellyfish. If she eats it, the bag does not pass and she can starve to death.

CHAPTER 1

Always treat the Family Silver with care and respect. In its own way, it speaks of the elegance and position of the House.

"The Butler's Guide to Fine Silver"
Mr. Hollister, 1898

"Lorraine, the appraiser called to confirm—" I walked into the library. But Lorraine wasn't there. This was the place and time I usually found her going through papers, making phone calls, managing her different businesses.

Lorraine and I had fallen into a comfortable routine. She ran Fair Winds, an estate and working farm on the Eastern Shore of the Chesapeake Bay and I organized, appraised and completed her massive sterling silver collection. I think I got the better part of the deal since it included a cottage on the estate, overlooking the water.

But today, she wasn't where she belonged.

The windows in the room were opened wide to catch the breeze along with the scent of fall hiding behind the fading tang of summer flowers, corn crops and sea salt. Then I heard her laughter, like a tinkling of bells, drifting from the terrace. Things had changed ever so slightly but things were different since the arrival of Alex Conklin, a handsome package of charm and intellect.

"You're too funny for words," Lorraine called out to the man sitting on the terrace as she walked into the library. "Oh! Abby!"

I plastered a smile on my face, feeling like I had intruded on a private moment. Who was I to deny my dear friend a new companion and maybe a new love? Even though he was monopolizing her time.

"Yes, it's pesky me. Sorry to interrupt. Just wanted to let you know that the New York silver appraiser will be coming down to Fair Winds as planned."

"Oh, that is good to hear," she said automatically as she stood at her large antique mahogany desk flipping through papers.

"I put the list of silver pieces he will examine on your desk. The epergne is at the top."

"Uh huh," she said absently. This reaction was the opposite of her wild anticipation when I told her the tall silver centerpiece decorated with hanging baskets, cherubs and grapes might be worth almost $200,000.

Was she even listening?

"When I talked to him today," I continued. "I could have sworn he stuck his nose in the air when he said he would be amply prepared to inspect the pieces I've set aside." Lorraine didn't react. "Dawkins is helping with the final round of polishing." Still nothing. "So, we'll be ready when he arrives *next year*."

It was naughty of me to slip in that exaggeration, but it proved that the man sitting on the terrace was truly in her head and maybe her heart. I had to fight down the urge to march outside and threaten that if he ever hurt her, even a little bit, he'd face my wrath.

Instead, I said, "That's all. Just wanted to let you know."

I turned away to hide my face. It was probably bright red. Too often, my emotions flashed on my face like a billboard. To be honest, Lorraine deserved every ounce of happiness that came her way. Period.

"Abby," she called out as I reached the doorway.

I turned to see her face filled with excitement, the face of a woman falling in love.

"You are doing a wonderful job. It's hard working with experts from New York. Sometimes, they can be such snobs."

"Sometimes?" I blurted out and we both laughed. The world tilted back in place again.

"You know, we're having a meeting tonight to help Alex build some bridges in the community to make his *Chesapeake Haven* real estate project a success." She glanced down and moved some papers around on the desk a little with her index finger. "I was wondering if you'd come to the meeting. You don't have to say anything," she added quickly. "You've learned so much about this corner of the world, you'd be a great pair of eyes and ears to help gauge people's reactions." She looked up, her blue eyes bright. "You're someone I trust. Someone who has my best interests at heart."

Yes, I was that person and thankfully, she knew it. But my instincts went on alert. Did she want me to help gauge how people were reacting to the developer's ideas… or evaluate the developer himself? More than silver would be appraised at Fair Winds.

"Sure. I'll see you tonight."

If I had known what would happen, I would have locked her in her bedroom.

CHAPTER 2

There is a wide variety of pieces used in individual place settings that are collectively called knives, forks and spoons. Remember that each is a unique, designed for a specific purpose.

"The Butler's Guide to Fine Silver"
Mr. Hollister, 1898

JUST BEFORE THE meeting was to begin, I called Simon, my black Lab puppy, to the kitchen. Puppy? Who was I kidding? Simon was growing into a monumental canine. He skidded across the kitchen floor, straight to the small mountain of cookies. They were a bribe to stay quietly in the cottage for the evening. He wouldn't go out for his usual evening romp around Fair Winds with all the strangers coming for the meeting. They wouldn't be expecting a black shadow making a dash across the drive to chase a squirrel or lightning bugs. No, he was safer here.

Outside, the sun was inching toward the horizon. The air losing some of its heat. The late rays of sunshine filtered through the trees to create a golden glow around the edges of the leaves. A steady stream of cars coming down the drive made me quicken my pace. I took up a position in the hall by the foyer so I could see people coming in the front door and have a good view of Lorraine and Alex welcoming them. Lorraine was radiant in her silky cornflower blue dress with flowing sleeves and flirty skirt. Her highlighted brown hair sparkled in the light from the crystal chandelier overhead. Looking like the perfect couple, Alex stood beside her. His crisp monogrammed shirt, beautifully-tailored navy blue blazer and thick silver hair struck the right note of casual sophistication.

I arrived as my log canoe sailing buddy Charlie walked through the door. I rushed over to say hello. "Hey, what are you doing here?"

He looked around nervously. "Am I in the wrong place?"

"You might be. There's nothing on the agenda about sailing." I hoped my little joke hid my shock at seeing that wounded look in his hazel eyes that wasn't there when we first met. The tragic events at the Governor's Cup sailboat race were still haunting Charlie.

"Cute," he said with a dry laugh. "Maybe it's not on the agenda, but this development will have a big effect on the water. I want to find out what they want to do."

"Then you are definitely in the right place." I squeezed his arm and gave it a little tug. "Stand over here with me and tell me all about the people coming in. I don't recognize anyone."

As we tucked ourselves into a corner that gave us a perfect vantage point, he said softly, "You know, I'm out of my element here. If someone isn't a sailor, I'm not—oh, there's someone I know." He caught himself pointing and lowered his hand. "That's Jacob. He's making a name for himself as an environmental activist around here."

Jacob looked pretty conservative for an activist. Dressed in a flaxen-colored jacket of natural linen and clean, pressed jeans, he greeted his potential opponents with a polite handshake.

More people were tumbling through the door. But Charlie was

looking at someone standing under the arch to the dining room. "That's someone I don't recognize, but he looks familiar, sort of."

I followed his gaze and smothered a laugh. "He looks familiar, because he belongs here. That's Dawkins, the butler, house manager, staff supervisor—majordomo of Fair Winds. He opened the door when you picked me up to go to the yacht club and see the Governor's Cup trophy. Don't worry, he's harmless." *At least I think he is,* I added silently.

"Okay, but..." He turned toward me. "But trouble is coming."

I stood on my tiptoes, searching the crowd. Everyone looked rather dull. "Who?"

"I don't mean someone. I'm talking about something. Churning in the Atlantic."

I scooped my auburn curls that had escaped and pulled them back into the barrette. "The Atlantic? What are you talking about?"

"It's a tropical depression, but only two days ago, it was a weather wave rolling off the African coast. Now, it's spiraling into a closed system, building wind speed and drawing up moisture from the ocean."

"It's a tropical depression," I pouted. "How sad."

Charlie rolled his eyes. "Abby, that's the oldest joke in the book."

That was my old friend, quick with a comeback. Maybe he only needed some more time to heal. "I know. I'm sorry. I'm a little giddy tonight. It feels like a party."

He leaned closer. "I get it, but this storm—I think it's going to be a hurricane—it may not be a laughing matter. I have a bad feeling."

"Charlie, please don't be like those people on the weather channels, always trying to stir up anxiety about one storm after another."

His eyes stared into mine, making me a little uncomfortable. "This time, Abby, this time, I think something's going to happen."

FOILED SILVER

"Well, look what the wind blew in!" Ryan clapped Charlie on the back and gave me a peck on the cheek. "Charlie, these must be big doings to pull you away from the boats."

"Charlie was just telling me about the big storm coming." I wanted to sound unconcerned, but Charlie had said *hurricane*, a word that truly caused concern. I needed Ryan to say I shouldn't worry.

Ryan pressed his lips together and shook his head. "Charlie, you know better than to scare the lady. Abby, it will be fine."

While the two old friends laughed and talked together, I noticed a man walk in with a gawky young teenage boy wearing glasses. Curious, I slipped over by the table to listen in.

"... and teach Biology at the high school," the man said. "Edward Stephens here is one of my students. He's involved with environmental organizations here. Tell them where you volunteer."

I could just make out the words barely spoken by the bashful boy, *Pickering Creek* and *Phillips Wharf*, two local ecological projects,.

"I brought him along tonight to observe and learn how communities and developers can work together," explained the teacher. This is a great opportunity for him to see the process from the beginning."

Not sure how this meeting would hold the attention of a teenage boy, I returned to my observation post and waved when Dr. Rupert Phillips came in. He was a short man, a little roly-poly, but impeccably dressed. He would be a good resource for the group with a head full of information and pockets stuffed with facts about the Bay, Miles River and building restrictions. The matronly woman next to him was known as a professional volunteer. Reading glasses hung from a chain around her neck, ready, so she wouldn't miss a thing. She had probably driven him to the meeting.

Lorraine bustled around, greeting people she knew and

making introductions. She had high hopes for this meeting even though it was about real estate development, a dreaded topic here on the Eastern Shore that riled up people in ways that reminded me of the Civil War and the feud between the Hatfields and McCoys. I hoped it wouldn't deteriorate into a session of everybody talking and nobody listening. To me, it would be a success if she got out of the meeting alive.

It was an age-old clash of perceptions. People were attracted to this area of the Chesapeake Bay region for its natural beauty, variety of wildlife, fresh peaches, corn and succulent delicacies of blue crab, oysters and clams drawn from the salty waters. It was a lush area only hours from the traffic-choked, smog-ravaged, crime-threatening cities on the East Coast. And the last thing people wanted to see here was a cluster of cookie-cutter homes with more cars parked on the hard road surfaces that sent rainwater runoff into the Bay. It made no difference that the builders tried to design homes and community centers in the quaint, old-fashioned styles of long-established neighborhoods. More people meant more residences and businesses sure to spoil this pristine area that was unique and under threat already.

Usually, Lorraine would be at the forefront of the defenders, but she'd quickly discovered that Alex was a different kind of developer. Though she didn't like to admit it, the Shore needed to create more job opportunities for young people and families so it didn't turn into a massive retirement community with only nursing and patient care work available. Alex had told her that the Eastern Shore was primed to create cottage industries and attract high tech if it upgraded its infrastructure, built incubators and business parks. He was prepared to deliver a community where these workers would live, raise their families and take advantage of new opportunities. He'd taken the time to learn about the critical areas, threats to the natural habitat and the time-tested values and pace of this land known for its pleasant living. He'd proven he was willing to follow the rules and guidelines set down by the state and various foundations concerned with the environment and wildlife. Lorraine said he'd shown he would 'walk the talk' by the preliminary work done on the 189 acres he'd bought in the county. He had won her over and tonight, she was starting the campaign to win over the people in the community.

A rich, male voice whispered in my ear. "A good turnout, don't you think?"

Without turning my head, I hissed, "Stop that! It's rude."

Dawkins jerked back. Had I made my point, finally? He had to stop appearing silently out of thin air. It might be a good quality in a butler, but it was unnerving. At last, I'd found the word that would get under his thick armor. *Rude.*

Not one to gloat, I added, "Yes, there are a lot of people here. She wants me to observe, but I don't know how I'll keep them all straight. There are too many people."

"Don't try to keep track of every individual. Relax, watch and wait. The targets will show themselves. Now, if you'll excuse me."

Dawkins returned to his post and stood painfully erect in the foyer. Many of the larger estates and farms on the Eastern Shore had someone help with the arrival of guests, but Dawkins was in a class all his own. His well-developed muscles under the simple, tailored dark suit seemed a little unusual for a butler. Wasn't his heavy lifting limited to a seven-piece silver tea service? It was just another one of the curiosities that surrounded Dawkins as he politely directed people to the dining room for refreshments.

There, in the center of the large dining table, stood the massive silver epergne. Almost two feet tall, the silver centerpiece was dressed for a party. The vase at the top held lavish Peace roses, tawny yellow petals blending out to a delicate pink. Lorraine thought they might have a calming effect on the guests. Considering the possible clash between the environmentalists and developer, it was worth a try. Several men mumbled their disappointment about the absence of beer and mixed drinks. Dawkins had warned alcohol might fuel disagreements and disrupt the proceedings,

He shifted his eyes to the dining room, checking on things,

when he frowned a little. Was it my imagination that Dawkins look unsettled? I followed his gaze as an older man, short, rotund with black bushy eyebrows glided into the room. His jet-black eyes looked down his bulbous nose at a young server expecting to see only perfection. He spoke softly to the server and pointed toward the display of cookies. I frowned. He didn't *point*. Instead his hands moved smoothly this way and that, as if he was conducting a very small orchestra. His balding head had a fringe of black hair that looked too dark to be natural. His shirt was blinding white and starched stiff. His jacket was midnight black. If this was a Halloween party, he would have won Best Costume as an Italian restauranteur. I'd never seen the man before, though he seemed comfortable with the work. I'd have to ask about him later.

At the door, Dawkins stopped a man trying to walk a bike into the house. "Sir, it is inappropriate for you to bring your bicycle into the house. If you'd like to leave it outside by the—"

"No sir," the man shot back sarcastically. "I would not like to leave it outside or anywhere else for it to be stolen. Do you know what you're looking at, man?" The rider took a step away and balanced the bike at arm's length so Dawkins could admire it. "It's a Cannondale."

"Yes sir, I know I'm looking at a mode of transportation that does not belong in the foyer of Fair Winds. Now, you may either park it outside, park it by the back entry or…" The alternative of 'ride it away' was unspoken.

"Alright, I'm supposed to be at this meeting so I guess I'll park it in the back," he grumbled. "You have to guarantee it will be safe."

"I assure you things do not go missing here at Fair Winds," Dawkins gracefully motioned for the young man serving in the dining room. "But to raise your confidence, I suggest you chain it to a tree or whatever you do to secure it." He whispered something to the young server who led the man and his bike out the front door.

FOILED SILVER

More and more people arrived. There was a man in a business suit and a couple who looked like they'd just stepped off a golf course. There were too many people. How could I remember them all? Why should I? Dawkins was right. The important ones —the targets—would make themselves known.

Finally, Dawkins closed the front door and corralled the stragglers into the living room. Some admired, some feigned not to notice, the fine antiques, velvet-upholstered sofas and grand windows framed by lavish draperies. Designed for grand parties, it was now the scene for tonight's community meeting about a proposed real estate development. It was difficult to read Dawkins' angular face, but he seemed relieved when Lorraine rose to welcome everyone.

I needed a break to make room in my brain for my upcoming meeting with the silver appraiser. The man had an international reputation and Lorraine had talked his boss into sending him down to look at the epergne in the dining room. I believed I'd found a treasure tucked away in the attic. After polishing it carefully and doing the research, Lorraine and I agreed it was worth bringing the appraiser to Fair Winds. This was the week and I was getting last-minute jitters. I needed a little break.

I slipped down the hall to Mrs. Clark's kitchen to get my beverage of choice. There, I filled a dark blue glass with ice and poured in a tiny pitcher-full of cold-press coffee. It was the way to make a less acidic chilled beverage than using ultra-strong brewed coffee.

Dawkins introduced us to this special brew made by soaking ground dark-roasted beans in cold water overnight. By morning, the strained concentrate would appear in the fridge for anyone to enjoy. I balanced one-third concentrate with two-thirds cold water, added a splash of cream and voilà! Heaven, without the heat. As I took that first delicious sip, the walking Italian stereotype breezed through the kitchen, mumbling under his breath. What did Dawkins think about this man with the haughty attitude and silent butler's walk invading his fiefdom? I tried to catch up to him, but he evaporated the same way Dawkins often did. The answer would have to wait. I had to get back to the meeting which I hoped was proceeding without drama.

CHAPTER 3

The "Baltimore Roses" are the Kirk's Repoussé, the Stieff Rose and the Schofield's Baltimore Rose patterns. These floral or rose patterns are often confused with Stieff Rose – a unique chastened rose pattern.

– The Stieff Company

PEOPLE WERE STILL FLOWING through the door, welcomed by Dawkins. His use of the word *targets* unsettled me. It sounded like he was referring to a shooting gallery. But knowing Lorraine, the shrewd political animal that she was, these *targets* were probably key opinion-shapers. I settled back against the wall and followed his advice. I wouldn't try to keep track of everyone. I'd let the important ones emerge. The targets.

Finally, Dawkins looked outside, closed the front door and corralled the stragglers into the living room furnished with fine antiques, velvet-upholstered sofas and grand windows framed by lavish draperies so the meeting could begin. Designed for grand parties, it was now the scene of a community meeting about a proposed real estate development. It was difficult to read the man's angular face, but he seemed relieved when Lorraine rose to welcome everyone.

Lorraine was exuberant as she spoke. She had high hopes for this meeting even though it was about real estate development, a dreaded topic here on the Eastern Shore that riled up people in ways that reminded me of the Civil War and the Hatfield-McCoy feud. Everybody talking, nobody listening. To me, it would be a success if she got out of the meeting alive.

It was an age-old clash of perceptions. People were attracted to this area of the Chesapeake Bay region for its natural beauty, variety of wildlife, fresh peaches, corn and succulent delicacies of blue crab, oysters and clams drawn from the salty waters. It was a lush area only hours from the traffic-choked, smog-ravaged, crime-threatening cities on the East Coast. And the last thing people wanted to see here was a cluster of cookie-cutter homes with more cars parked on the hard road surfaces that sent rainwater runoff into the Bay. It made no difference that the builders tried to design homes and community centers in the quaint, old-fashioned styles of long-established neighborhoods. More people meant more residences and businesses sure to infect this pristine area that was unique and under threat already.

Usually, Lorraine would be at the forefront of the defenders, but she'd quickly discovered that this developer was different. Though she didn't like to admit it, the Shore needed to create more job opportunities for young people and families so it didn't turn into a massive retirement community with only nursing and patient care work available. Alex had told her that the Eastern Shore was primed to create cottage industries and attract high tech if it upgraded its infrastructure, built incubators and business parks. He was prepared to deliver a community where these workers would live, raise their families and take advantage of other opportunities. He'd taken the time to learn about the critical areas, threats to the natural habitat and the time-tested values and pace of this land known for its pleasant living. He'd proven he was willing to follow the rules and guidelines set down by the state and various foundations concerned with the environment and wildlife. Lorraine said he'd shown he would 'walk the talk' by the preliminary work done on the 189 acres he'd bought outside of town. He had won her over and tonight, she was starting the campaign to win over people in the community.

A rich, male voice whispered in my ear. "A good turnout, don't you think?"

Without turning my head, I hissed, "Stop that! It's rude."

Dawkins jerked back. Had I made my point, finally? He had to stop appearing silently out of thin air. It might be a good quality in a butler, but it unnerved me. At last, I'd found the word that would get under his thick armor. *Rude.*

Not one to gloat, I added, "Yes, there are a lot of people here. She wants me to observe, but I don't know how I'll keep them all straight. There are too many people."

"Don't try to keep track of every individual. Watch the total scene. Key targets will make themselves known. Now, if you'll excuse me."

It was too much to hope that there would be no drama or heated words at a meeting about environmental and real estate development issues. I heard the raised voices as I emerged from the quiet kitchen. Why do people say, *With all due respect*, then attack someone? Or *I can understand your position*, then pepper the person with comments that show they have absolutely no idea about the position. As I tiptoed into the foyer to better hear the discussion, I was so relieved that I wasn't locked into a chair in the living room somewhere.

With his calm, non-threatening voice, Alex recognized a quiet young man who had raised his hand. I craned my head around the corner to get a glimpse of the speaker. Jacob. His curly light brown hair was tamed by an elastic band at the base of his neck. The t-shirt under his jacket had some writing on it, but I couldn't read it. Jacob spoke respectfully. There were several raised eyebrows in the room. I don't think the older people expected a young, hippie-looking man to be so polite. So, they listened.

As Jacob warmed to his subject of protecting the environment and the sins committed by developers, his argument took an informed, but radical turn. "How do you propose to prevent the debris field from up north adversely affecting our area?" he demanded.

Alex said, "We have nothing to do with that."

"Oh, yes, you do. It's a problem created by people like you," he shot back. His verbal attack on Alex shocked me and I looked to see how Lorraine was reacting. Her well-mannered demeanor camouflaged her true feelings.

"And until you can answer those questions, sir, I guarantee you will meet a wall of resistance, a wall that will not yield." Jacob sat down in a gasp of silence. A few people around the room clapped. Next to him, a woman was incandescent as her adoring eyes beheld him.

The man with the scraggly beard called out in a raspy voice. "He makes good points about protecting the environment. We must recycle and reuse. I'd consider supporting your project if you did it on a small scale and built everything using recycled materials." There were some supporters of the idea in the group, though I speculated that most didn't have a clue what recycle-repurpose meant. The discussion was picking up steam.

A woman joined in. "It's not about recycling. It's about money, making all of us pay for sewer and water lines for the few people who will live in your *Chesapeake Haven*." She spat out the name of the development like it had a bad taste.

"I don't want my sewer bills going up!" one man declared in a gruff tone.

"Yeah, if you want—"

"Arnold!" A shrill voice, probably Arnold's wife, yanked him back in line.

Over the tittering, one voice boomed out. "You're going to inflict lasting damage to the Bay. What do you say to that?"

The room fell silent. All eyes were on Alex. No one else had made that straight-up claim, pointing a finger at one person. How would the developer handle it?

He was quiet, as he put a pensive look on his face. Then he acknowledged what everyone else in the room was thinking. "Well, that's quite an accusation." His tone was calm, almost a little hurt. "What basis do you have that I'll be inflicting lasting damage to the Bay?"

"You want to build hundreds of houses— I have no idea what the latest count is." An older man with a face that had seen a lifetime in the sun and weather got to his feet with a little hesitation that came from age. "Think of those houses as hard surfaces, because rain runs right off the roof into the gutters and down to the land. The point is, those houses need streets and driveways. All those hard surfaces mean runoff. Add in the landscaping that needs fertilizer and pesticides. All that runoff hurts the river and the Bay." He put his hand flat on his chest. "But don't take my word for it. He gestured to an attractive young woman seated next to him. "Ask her." He waved his hand, encouraging her to stand up. "Go on, tell them who you are."

The woman hesitated as she looked around the crowded room to find all eyes on her. She stood, glanced at him for some courage and addressed the room. "My name is Jackie Johnson, Dr. Jackie Johnson. I'm a limnologist."

A murmur went through the room. "A what?'

"A limnologist," repeated Alex. "Someone who studies inland bodies of water. Do you specialize in salt water environments?"

She gave him a smile of appreciation. "Freshwater and brackish are my specialties. I'm impressed that you're familiar with my scientific area."

Alex gave her a slight bow. "Thank you, but it shouldn't be a surprise. If someone is serious about working around the Chesapeake Bay, the largest estuary in the world, he or she needs to be familiar with limnology. And sir, your concerns are valid. That's why we need to complete the engineering studies before we talk further."

Lorraine jumped in while Alex took a much-needed gulp of water. "That's why I called this meeting. It's the first of many, I hope, so we can become familiar, with aspects like limnology, and we can go through this process together."

A shy young woman raised her hand. "Will there be jobs for local people?" Her accent, petite stature and ink black hair suggested her Mayan heritage.

"Yes," said Alex. He bowed a little at the waist in a modest gesture that was one of his endearing qualities. "But at the beginning, dear lady, and forgive me if I'm making an assumption, the jobs will be heavy construction work."

"I have a husband and two brothers," she said quickly. "They're good workers."

"Then they should put in their applications when we get all the approvals we need." He held his arms out wide to take in everyone in the room. "Hopefully, with your help.

Alex answered more questions and a woman responded in a sweet tone, "I see, then that's all right."

The door swung open and banged against the doorstop, almost denting the wall. In walked a woman who might have been 5'2" but she was stooped with age. Grizzled gray hair stuck out from under a worn old fishing hat. The shirtwaist dress of a tiny flowered print was not as clean as it could have been. At her waist, a clunky Swiss Army knife hung from her belt so she was ready for any mishap. Her black rubber and leather boots were laced to the ankle, wet and tracking mud on the marble floor. All in all, she looked like she'd escaped from a woodland fairy story. She took in the scene and marched into the living room as she pulled her left glove off her hand one finger at a time.

"Sorry I'm late. Guess my invitation got lost in the mail." She inspected Alex from his shoes to his face and held his eyes. "This is the first meeting about this project, isn't it?"

"You are correct, ma'am," Alex said formally, in an effort to take back control of the meeting. "This is our first meeting and—"

The woman turned to the people gathered in the room. "The

first meeting and, from what I heard outside, you're already caving in." She mimicked a high feminine voice, "Then that's all right."

She turned back to Alex. "We can have as many discussions as you want... as long as you understand..." She slapped the glove into the palm of her other hand. "We're not push-overs."

"You have me at a disadvantage, ma'am," Alex said gallantly as if he was at a garden party. "I do not know your name." I had to admire his composure under fire. He was here to establish connections and he'd met a challenge.

But the request for civility lit up the woman's face. Her muscles lost their tightness and she responded politely, "Mary Rose."

"Mary Rose," he repeated in a way that appreciated the sounds her name made. "Mary Rose... what?"

As if someone pulled the plug on a lamp, the light in her face went out and she snapped, "That's all you have to know. Mary Rose." She took another step closer and set her jaw. "I have a question for you, one of many." Her verbal gauntlet slapped him across the face. "You answer this one right and we can keep on talking."

He waited, unwilling to retaliate or back down. Mary Rose put her fists on her hips and spat out, "That man was right. What about the damage you're going to do? What about that?"

Alex held his arms out wide to draw in everyone in the room. "We are going to go through the process and everyone will have a chance to speak—"

"Hogwash!" bellowed Mary Rose. "You're spouting what some mediator told you to say. You have no idea about this land. You have no understanding whatsoever. This discussion is over!" She spun around and stomped all the way to the door, beating Dawkins to it. She yanked it open and she melted into the evening, crickets madly singing as the door swung shut behind her. Dawkins grabbed the door a moment before it closed, denying her the loud slam she wanted.

CHAPTER 4

Conduct a meticulous inspection of each silver piece. Anything that does not belong in the Family Silver collection should not be used. Set it aside for sale through a reputable broker.

"The Butler's Guide to Fine Silver"
Mr. Hollister, 1898

STUNNED BY THE THEATRICAL DISPLAY, I asked Charlie, "What was that?"

He ran his hand over his short dark hair and blew out a breath. "I've never seen her up close before."

"One time is enough for me. Who is she?"

"She's like Mother Nature incarnate. She's always watching the sailboats and log canoes to make sure we don't dump anything in the water. She yells at us, but doesn't do anything. She's harmless."

It was impossible for the meeting to get back on track after the raucous interruption and it was getting late, so Lorraine brought the meeting to a close. People chatted in small clusters as they made their way to the door when a man stopped their progress as he walked in against the flow. Mid-fifties, not fat, but fleshy, he was starkly sophisticated. His thinning hair was a suspiciously dark shade of brown, courtesy of his hairstylist? His casual clothes were tailored to make the most of what little he had. The fabrics were expensive and his slacks still had a sharp crease at the end of the day.

He scanned the room like a lord surveying his realm and zeroed in on one man. With shoulders back and chest out, he marched over to Alex and shook hands. "Alex, what can I say? The traffic! The bridge!" He shrugged. "We don't have these problems when we stay on the Western Shore."

With little enthusiasm, Alex clasped his shoulder. "Yes, but we're here now, Allen. This was an important step and a good one."

The smile froze on Alex's face and his eyes grew wide when he saw a woman walk into the room. She didn't really *walk*. It was more a *slink*. The effect took my breath away. She was petite, but used every inch her mile-high stiletto heels to command attention. Her flawless skin was the color of honey. The straight hair of shiny midnight black fell over her shoulders and down her back. Bangs, cut straight across, hid her eyebrows and set off her amazing turquoise blue eyes that focused on Alex, making him the only person in her world. As she approached him, the rosy glow drained from his face, replaced by the cold, hard steel. I moved closer to observe and eavesdrop as she planted herself in front of Alex.

"What are you doing here?" Alex hissed.

She laughed. A delighted laugh of triumph. "Oh Alex, that's no way to welcome someone you once adored. We've spent hours in a monumental traffic jam just to come and support this pet project of yours. And I've brought you this." She held a man's Burberry scarf. She raised her hands high to drape it around his neck. He bowed his head slightly, more of an automatic reaction than the warm acceptance of a gift. But that wasn't the impression garnered by another observer. Lorraine was taking in every move, every word. Her reaction of shock and hurt registered on her face.

After placing the scarf, she patted his chest softly. Waves of loving emotion rolled off her and enveloped him. "I found it in a drawer and knew you'd like to have it with the cold weather coming. It goes so well with your winter topcoat," she purred as she stepped away with a Cheshire Cat smile.

Instead of ripping off the scarf, he shifted all his attention to his partner. "Why did you bring her here, Allen?" he demanded.

The man shrugged. "You want me to sell these houses you're going to build out here and she is the best agent I have. You're always saying that you want the best for this project and Arabella is the best. Guess we'll have to ignore the fact that she's your ex-wife."

Ex-wife! And still around. I wanted to go to Lorraine, stand with her as she took in this scene. But the crush of bodies kept me from her. I wanted to clap my hands and end this drama after seeing her face, stricken with hurt, teary-eyed with disappointment.

"Yes," the siren proclaimed. "Only the best. We should toast the new project. It's tradition." She headed to the dining room as people scampered out of her way. One look at the pitchers of iced tea and lemonade made her nose wrinkle. She shot a question at the Italian-looking server in disgust. "Is this all you have?"

He looked down at the fine crystal pitchers and glasses and brought those bushy eyebrows together in a frown. "May I offer you something else, Signora?" His Italian accent was as thick as the darkest espresso.

"Of course." Her air of contempt was unnecessary. "Scotch. Single malt. Neat. Three glasses and put mine in a pretty glass."

How could Alex's ex-wife come into Fair Winds, act like the place was hers and order the staff around? This was so wrong. Like a coup. Why didn't Lorraine say something, do something? My eyes swept the room. Lorraine had disappeared.

I watched helplessly as the Italian gave her a quick nod and glided out of the room. He moved like Dawkins. Smoothly, silently and quickly. While she waited, the interloper ran her hand under her hair so it undulated in a wave down her back. She was performing and she had an audience. Some women tightened their lips in disgust and looked away. Men were tangled in the tendrils of sensuality she was sending out. I noticed that even Ryan was not immune. His face was lit up with interest. A stab of jealousy hit me. I wished the arrows I was staring at her were real.

The Italian breezed into the room again with three small crystal glasses on a small silver tray and served the woman first. She held the glass up to the light to examine its amber color. A smile played at the corners of her mouth.

"Really, Arabella," Alex said. "Fair Winds has the best of everything."

She took a sip and closed her eyes. She moaned so deep it was erotic. She opened those startlingly blue eyes and looked straight at Alex. "This time, you're right." She raised her glass. "To *Chesapeake Haven*." The woman knew how to manipulate Alex. He had to join in the toast. Together, they clinked their glasses and drank.

But the woman wasn't done. "At last, I'll have a place to keep Eagle's Talon."

Alex choked on his Scotch. "Your horse? You're bringing your horse to the Shore?"

Her face beamed. "Oh, yes. Here, he'll have a home again instead of moving around like a gypsy since you sold our farm. He's important, you know. We went to the Upperville Colt and Horse Show in June. That's the oldest running horse show for hunters and jumpers in the country and he was the Reserve Champion in the Hunter Division." She glanced around to the other people who were listening. "They have to jump fences that are three feet, nine inches, you know." She was a proud parent talking about a favorite child.

"Were *you* riding him?" Alex asked in disbelief.

She shook her head so her glossy black hair rippled like

flowing silk. "Oh no, I'm not qualified to ride him in such a prestigious event, but I'm still taking my weekly riding lessons." Again, she was proud, but like a little girl bragging to her father.

"I know," he responded grimly. "I'm still paying for them. In fact, weren't you supposed to lease him out to another rider last year to generate a little income? That was part of the case you made when you wanted me to buy him. When is that going to happen?"

She pulled her lean body up to full height and pushed out magnificent breasts. I wondered if he had bought those for her, too.

She crooned, "When we talked about buying a horse and leasing him out to other riders for six months or a year was a definite possibility. How was I to know that we would find Tally? He is special. I know every owner says that, but he is. I couldn't loan him out to someone for *money* and run the risk of him being ruined. I would never forgive myself."

Alex sniffed. "You care more about the horse than people. I wonder what that makes you." He put his glass down and walked away in disgust, right toward me.

"I'm sorry you had to see that. Where is Lorraine?"

I wasn't sure what to say. I made it vague. "I think she went for some aspirin. All the upset gave her a headache."

"I have to find her." He turned and his path of escape was blocked.

The man, who looked like a walking heart attack, thrust out his hand. "Stu, Stu Atkins. I think you could benefit from my expertise."

Alex ignored his hand, but gave him a weak smile. "Nice to meet you, but I'm afraid I— "

"I'm retired now, but I know development. This project is something I can get behind. It will bring big city living to the area on a small scale."

"That's good." The smile was gone. "But, I really have to—"

"Of course," Stu moved slowly out of his way. "I'll give you a call next week. We can bat around some ideas."

Alex pushed forward. The man, desperate to be taken seriously, looked crestfallen, then pulled another cookie out of his pocket and took a big bite.

At least Alex would find Lorraine, explain himself and hopefully, smooth over her hurt feelings. The meeting stirred up emotions and caused well-hidden opinions to bubble to the surface. I was eager to escape the highly-charged atmosphere. Dawkins would sweep the people out of the house, most courteously, so I crept away.

Outside, the evening air was refreshing without the scorching heat of summer or the chilly shiver of fall. The light of the almost-full moon created a magical view. After all the drama inside, it was such a relief to stand quietly, listen to the frogs and crickets and breathe in the clear air. That's when I heard raised voices from the terrace.

Actually, it was only one raised voice, ragged with tears. Lorraine. I wasn't proud of myself that I tried to listen. It was difficult to hear her words clearly except for the one question she flung at someone.

"How could you?" she demanded.

The response was muffled. I couldn't hear the words, but I recognized the man's deep, gentle voice. Alex. Evidently, he had found her and she was upset right down to her core. It wasn't the meeting. She'd beamed with pride every time she looked at him. It was the arrival of that woman and his business partner.

No, it wasn't right for me to eavesdrop. I walked out from under the oaks and focused instead on the sky that was a blanket of deep sapphire dotted with diamond points. It was the kind of evening that calmed one's soul and connected the spirit with the universe.

Until a gunshot rang out and split the world apart.

CHAPTER 5

If the House is in mourning, a silver locket containing a lock of hair may be worn as jewelry. It shall need special attention, because it often comes in contact with the fingers of the bereaved.

"The Butler's Guide to Fine Silver"
Mr. Hollister, 1898

THE LOUD GUNSHOT crushed the quiet calm of the evening and silenced the crickets. It reverberated across Fair Winds and rolled over the landscape. I froze in mid-step. I looked around. Nothing was out of place. All was as it had been only a moment before. Had I imagined it? I moved forward, taking one tentative step. Then another. Maybe it was only a truck backfiring. It made sense since many of the men around here opted for the loud roar of their trucks rather than the quiet of a muffler system. Nothing had changed around me. Except a small flock of crows flapped into the air from a clump of trees in a frenzy of caws.

I'd almost convinced myself it was nothing—that the evening would return to its feeling of serenity—when lights suddenly blazed inside and out... security lights. People scurried around amid screams.

The shot was real. Chaos erupted. People yelled. Someone sobbed. Lorraine. Dawkins. I took one step. Then another. Then I ran.

People tumbled out of the house and crowded around the place where Lorraine liked to sit. I couldn't see anything. They were all in my way. I ran faster. I plowed through a wall of people then, what I saw stopped me all at once. And stood in front of the man slumped in the chair. Alex. A scarlet stain drenching what was left of his shirt.

I turned to stone, unable to move. I could only stare. There was no breath to cry out. My heart broke for the man who lay dead. And the woman who would give anything to call out his name and summon back his spirit.

"Call an ambulance. Somebody, call an ambulance!"

A tall woman clenched her hands into fists and screamed. A chubby man grabbed his head as if to keep it on his shoulders as he stared at the body.

A deep voice boomed above the noises of upheaval and silenced the commotion. The voice of reason. Dawkins ordered, "Quiet! Everyone back in the house. NOW!"

His declaration demanded obedience. I was close enough to see his head movement, back and forth, scanning the area. I realized with a shiver that one shot could lead to another and another. I joined the others and stumbled toward the safety of the house.

"The ambulance is on its way. Now, please—"

"Look!" A man called out, making us all stop and turn. "Who is that?"

The glow of the dock lights threw the scene into sharp relief. Everyone focused on the impossible scene right in front of us. Only I couldn't believe what I was seeing.

Lorraine stood there with a gun in her hands.

"Lorraine, what have you done?" someone murmured.

A woman shrieked and ran in the house. Others charged after her.

But I walked toward my friend.

Her mouth opened wide. No sound came out. Her eyes fell to the shotgun in her hands. With a little yip, her fingers jerked open. The gun fell to the wooden dock with a thud and discharged.

The deafening shot sent people crouching to the ground, arms over their heads. A window in the boathouse shattered.

One man, Dawkins, ran toward the dock, toward Lorraine. Another figure followed him. Ryan. They must have believed it was safe to approach, so I too moved toward her.

Dawkins stepped on the weathered planks of the dock and held out his arms to Lorraine. I could hear the low drone of his voice, but couldn't make out what he was saying. She held out her hands. I thought she was reaching for him, but her eyes were locked on her hands. He moved toward her, but she stepped backward, away from him. He said something else to her and stepped over the useless gun lying on the dock, putting himself between them. He spoke again and she shook her head. Everyone around them stood frozen, not knowing what to do, overwhelmed by the violence in front of our eyes.

Wailing sirens broke the spell. We all started to move at once. People poured out of the house again as if the approach of the authorities made the area safe again.

In minutes, medical personnel swarmed over Alex's body. Police officers in dark uniforms moved forward, their bodies distorted by Kevlar vests and equipment in special pockets and hanging from their belts. Radios crackled in controlled alarm, but that was the only sound.

The lead police officer didn't yell like they do on TV. He was silent as he moved in the direction of the dock as he held his pistol in both hands, straight out in front of his chest, his eyes scanning the whole area. They locked on the tableau of Lorraine and Dawkins facing off at the dock. He quickened his steps in their direction. His movements quieted everyone as we watched in fascinated horror.

"Let me see your hands!" The officer yelled. "Let me see your hands! Hands up! Hands up, now!"

Terror twisted Lorraine's face. Dawkins spoke softly to her as if calming a skittish doe.

"Hands up NOW!" the officer repeated.

Slowly, Dawkins raised his hands. As if in a trance, Lorraine watched him and followed his lead, her chest heaving in great gulps of air.

"Officer," Dawkins called out. "There is no threat here. The only gun is on the dock, all cartridges discharged. We will cooperate fully."

"Put your hands on your head. Both of you. Do it now."

A second officer walked up with his weapon drawn. Together, the two officers moved toward the dock.

"Brice," Ryan spoke to the lead officer with his gun trained on Lorraine. "Officer Hayward, she isn't armed. We can—"

"Ryan, step back." The officer kept his eyes trained on Lorraine and Dawkins while he addressed Ryan out of the corner of his mouth. "You need to—"

"Dawkins was not part of this. He was with me when the shot was fired. Let him…" He took a quick breath. "Let them both lower their hands. We can work this—"

"Ryan, step back. I will not tell you again."

Ryan lowered his head and took a step away. The officer waited. With a sigh, Ryan came to me. "It will be okay, Abby," he whispered. "I promise."

It didn't look okay to me. One sound, one move and the skittish officer could fire. There was no question in my mind that he was well-trained and could destroy the woman standing with her hands on her head, shaking like an aspen in a mountain gale from fright, not guilt. Of that, I was sure.

The lead officer raised his chin. "You, ma'am, turn around."

With tears glistening on her face and her body shaking, Lorraine turned around. "Now, both of you, down on your knees."

An officer rushed forward with his weapon drawn and stood by the door to the boathouse. He took out a flashlight and shone it around inside. A moment later, he disappeared into the dark, the sound of his heavy footsteps vibrating through the planks. Did they think a shooter was inside? We all would be at risk.

"Clear," he shouted and I noticed that the lead officer's shoulders relaxed.

Dawkins slid down to the ground, his body under control, but Lorraine wasn't so lucky. Not only did she have years on Dawkins, her last time at the gym was decades ago. Her chosen form of exercise was walking which didn't build up much muscle tone. She bent her knees a bit and wobbled. She stood up quickly to keep herself from falling.

"Down. On. Your. Knees!"

The crowd of people who marveled at the home of this woman, who enjoyed her refreshments, who willingly listened to her considered arguments, watched in hushed silence. The humiliation was almost too much to bear. Some people averted their eyes. They had all seen the paramedics hang a blanket to hide the body mutilated by a single gunshot. This was now a murder scene. Everyone had the same unspoken question: Did she do it? Did she murder that man? Were they looking at a killer?

Lorraine's arms were at an awkward angle. She couldn't use them to steady herself, but she tried to comply. She bent her knees slowly and sank down until she lost her balance. A shoe came off and she fell against the wood with a cry. A gasp went up from all who watched. I took a step to go to her. Ryan's arm shot out to bar my way.

He was right. A bruised knee was better than a bullet. Please, I thought, please let her get through this without falling in the water or getting shot.

"On. Your. Knees." The office repeated evenly.

She pushed herself upright.

"Hands. On. Your. Head."

In a jerky movement, she raised her arms and laced her fingers on top of her head. I took a ragged breath, not knowing how this could get much worse. But the officer wasn't done.

"Now, both of you. Put one ankle over the other."

Dawkins managed the maneuver smoothly. Lorraine struggled.

The officer on the dock holstered his weapon and approached Dawkins with his handcuffs out and ready. With practiced precision, he swept one arm off his head then the other and cuffed his wrists behind his back. Brought to his feet, he hustled Dawkins away.

An officer, who looked too young to carry a gun, closed in on Lorraine. He grabbed her left wrist and pulled it down behind her back. She whimpered in pain.

"Easy does it," said the lead.

"Yes, sir." He moved her right arm down into position with a little more care and snapped the cuffs closed. He tried to lift her into a standing position, but Lorraine was so unsteady, she fell hard on her knees again.

The lead holstered his gun and moved in. "Easy, now," he said to the rookie. "Together."

They brought her up into a standing position and held her for a few moments until she was as steady as she could be with her arms secured behind her back.

The lead officer recited the Miranda Warning. I gulped down a sob. This couldn't be happening.

As they walked her down the dock, a figure in a white shirt that blazed against his mahogany skin charged across the grass. His face glistened with tiny beads of sweat. I almost cried with relief. It was the Chief. The chief of police would make things right.

"Take those cuffs off Miss Lorraine," he thundered. The officer hesitated. "That's an order."

The Chief walked up to Lorraine who was rubbing her wrists,

now free of the metal cuffs. "I'm sorry about that, ma'am. He was following procedure." He shot a steel-pointed look at the lead officer. "With a little too much enthusiasm." He looked back at Lorraine. "I do need to talk with you about what's happened." He linked his thumbs into his belt and planted his feet. "It has to be now … at the station in St. Michaels." He pointed to two officers. "My men will take you. I'll be there shortly."

"And we're transporting the man, too, Chief."

"Who is that?" the chief asked.

"I don't have his name. He's all dressed up in a—"

Lorraine breathed out the name. "Dawkins."

The Chief leaned closer to her. "Who?"

Hearing the name, he looked up to the sky and took a deep breath. Strangely, his reaction made me feel better somehow. He was looking for divine guidance to get him through this confused situation.

Someone had shot Alex. Dead. Murdered him. Lorraine had a gun, *the* gun, in her hands only moments ago. Of course, the officers had to follow procedure. Of course, they had to ask her some questions. But they didn't have to hurt her, humiliate her. I knew she could never take a life. It wasn't possible.

Then her words from the terrace echoed in my mind: *How could you, Alex?*

The words were almost unimportant. It was the emotion, the anguish behind them that hit me hard.

Could she?

NO! I gave myself a shake. What was I thinking? She didn't kill Alex in a fit of rage or anything else. She couldn't.

Could she?

First things first, he directed an officer to take Lorraine to a car for transport to the St. Michaels police station and the Chief walked away to get the scene processed and get the statements taken from all the people who attended the meeting, including staff and, I realized, me. It would be a long night. I just hoped I had the strength.

My heart ached as I watched the officers walk Lorraine around the house, her house. They wouldn't even let her walk through the home, to draw strength from her familiar surroundings.

A whiff of a familiar scent—clean, fresh with a touch of lime—touched my nose. I felt Ryan's arm slide around me, driving away my dark thoughts.

"Abby, come on," Ryan said softly. "She needs us now."

I leaned into him as we followed the officers walking Lorraine around to the front drive and the waiting police SUV. Dawkins followed just steps behind her.

When the officer opened the door of the car, Lorraine stopped, turned and looked around madly, searching. The officer gave her a nudge toward the backseat, but she pushed back, still searching. Something made me raise my hand high and wave. That's what she needed.

She rose up on her toes and yelled out to me. "Abby, Abby, call Bill. My lawyer. Tell him." The officer nudged her again, a little stronger. Her voice was laced with desperation as she called out again. "Call Bill. Number's in the Rolodex. Kitchen."

The officer put his hand on her head and guided her inside the car. And she was gone from my sight.

I lurched forward, hoping to see her through the tinted windows, but there was only my reflection in the darkened glass, my face strained with worry and fear. I realized that I should conjure up a smile in case she was looking at me. She had to know I was there for her. That I would do everything I could to make things okay.

"Step away from the vehicle, ma'am," the rookie declared.

"Please, can I go with her?"

The officer put rested his hands on his belt, not far from his pistol grip. "I'm sorry. This is a murder investigation. Step away from the car."

Murder. The sound of the word sent the chill of death through me.

"What can I do?" My voice was feeble.

"You could go down to the station and wait, but if I were you, I'd find a tall one," he answered, failing to hide a smirk on his face. "It's going to be a long night." His face hardened. "Now, step back from the car."

Fury rang in my ears. Ryan must have sensed it. He tightened his arm around me. It felt odd. I'd spent years making myself stand strong and alone, since I lost the women who raised me. But now, his strength wrapped around me, holding me up. And I leaned into it.

We both stepped away and watched helplessly as the police car holding Lorraine drove away from Fair Winds.

CHAPTER 6

The silver lorgnette, often used by the Lady of the House, requires diligent care. Polish the long silver opera handle, often rich with scrolls and flowers, with great attention to the patina which gives it dimension. The eyeglasses folded inside must be spotless.

"The Butler's Guide to Fine Silver"
Mr. Hollister, 1898

AN OFFICER EXPLAINED that we both had to give statements before we'd be allowed to leave and go home.

"I am home," I snapped. *And Lorraine should be, too,* my mind screamed. "I have to make a phone call before I talk to anyone. Thanks to you, I have to call her lawyer. If you think you're going to—"

"Abby!" Ryan brought me up short.

I was almost as mad at him as I was at the police. I turned and marched into the kitchen to place the call.

Later, Ryan made me see that I should stay at Fair Winds to be sure that all the people attending the meeting had left and without a memento. I polished off all the cold-press coffee Dawkins had stored in the fridge. It took the crime scene investigators a lot longer to gather evidence both on the terrace and at the boathouse than it did on the TV show *CSI*.

It felt like everyone relaxed a little after they removed the body from the terrace. But I found it hard to drag my eyes away from the spot where Alex had sat. How could such a thing happen, here at Fair Winds, the safest place in the world, our home? And in the one place where Lorraine and I ... and yes, Alex, liked to sit and chat? It was unfair in so many ways. A thought kept niggling at my mind. Would we ever sit here again? Innocent people went to jail all the time, didn't they?

Could she—STOP IT, I ordered myself. *She is innocent and I'll make sure that the person who fired that shot is caught. I promise.*

I kept repeating those words over and over while I paced around the house. A minister in a white clerical collar sat in a chair in the corner of the foyer in the sparkling light of the chandelier. He exchanged tentative smiles with a few people, but he sat lost in his own thoughts. He'd probably never been this close to a mortal sin. Thou shalt not murder. He was probably lost in purgatory about what to do: should he be a moral leader to the people who experienced this horror or should he follow his own instincts to run away? Great, now I was making up stories about the people hanging around Fair Winds waiting for their release.

I walked into the living room trying to calm down even to get my thoughts organized, so I could keep that promise when I noticed a man with the beard that needed a trim, strolling around, scoping out the little decorative accessories on tables and shelves. I made a mental note to keep an eye on him in case he decided to scoop up something and stuff it in his pocket. What am I thinking? That would be one stupid move with the police crawling all over the place. The man was probably trying to distract or amuse himself, that's all.

I walked out of the room, a bit disgusted with myself. I was seeing gremlins everywhere... except the one who fired the shot gun. I marched down the hall to the library, hoping to find a little comfort, maybe. Ugly yellow police tape crisscrossed the door leading out to the terrace where Alex died. I turned away and focused on this favorite room where I'd shared so many happy, eventful hours with Lorraine. We solved problems here. We shared bits of our past here. Everywhere I looked, there were signs of Lorraine. When my eyes went to her desk, they saw only a vacant leather chair. In front of the marble fireplace, there were only chairs and a settee, comfortable, but empty. That's how I felt. Empty. Lorraine wasn't where she belonged.

Fearful that I'd break down in tears, I headed back to the front of the house where most of the people were milling around. The bald, overweight man, who'd blocked Alex's escape to find Lorraine, juggled a handful of cookies as he hovered by an antique chair. I held my breath as he squeezed his bulk between its delicate arms. Nothing happened, thank goodness. The potential for drama didn't seem to end.

At the front door, Alex's partner Allen, his arm around Alex's ex-wife, argued with a police officer. "Can't you see, man, that this woman is overwhelmed with what has happened? I need to take her away from here. Get out of my way."

The officer didn't budge. He leaned in and said something I couldn't hear then motioned for another officer to take them both away. I was not interested where they were going. I wished they had never come.

I wasn't the only one wandering here and there. People were everywhere, moving around with little care for Lorraine's home. Lack of privacy or respect was another aftereffect of a single gunshot tearing open a man's chest. Keen to distract myself again, I noticed a woman leaning against the wall, nervously sipping a glass of water. She was making me nervous too. If she took one step backwards, she would bang into a painting with a heavy gilt frame. She was moments away from sending an expensive original to the tile floor. Enough damage had been done this night. I went over to coax her away to a safe distance from the painting. As I got closer, I realized she was the woman who gazed adoringly at Jacob, the man I'd labeled the Rabid Environmentalist after his tirade and threat against Alex.

Not wanting to appear too obvious, I opened the conversation with a couple of inane remarks. "Hi, are you doing okay? Do you need some more water?"

She looked at me with big doe-eyes filled with innocence. Almost breathless, she said, "No, I'm fine." She was anything but fine. "But you're very sweet to ask."

A hand touched my elbow. "Excuse me."

I turned to find the woman who driven Dr. Phillips standing next to me, her hands kneading what was left of some used tissues. "Excuse me, but did you see me when that poor man was shot? I was in the living room the whole time. Did you see me?" She didn't stop babbling long enough for a response. "You did see me, didn't you? You live here. They'll believe you if you tell them you saw me." She cast her eyes around us in a panic. "I have to find a police officer. I have to tell him I wasn't the one. I didn't do anything. I was in the living room the whole time." And she tottered away.

"Oh my," said Jacob's admirer. "This has upset people."

"Some more than others," I added.

"Do you think she'll be alright?"

I was more worried about this woman and didn't want to lose the chance to find out more about her. "Oh, I'm sure someone will know what to do and help her."

"Poor lamb," she murmured.

"Do I recognize you from the meeting?" *Really! If I was going to do any detecting, I'd have to get my act together and not sound so lame.* "Weren't you sitting next to that man..." As soon as I mentioned Jacob, the strain cleared from her face and her hands calmed.

"Yes, I was sitting next to Jacob, Jacob Morrissey. I'm his wife, Maddie." She extended her hand to me. "I don't believe we've met."

I took the hand, thinking how ridiculous it was for two

women to be shaking hands while the police were all around us, interviewing possible murder suspects. But I went along with it. "Jacob, yes, he was the one who was…" *Bad-mannered and offensive*, but I kept the words to myself and let her fill in the space.

She was nodding at me as if encouraging me to speak, but I said nothing. It was a little trick I learned from a homicide detective I respected. Suddenly, she burst out with the word she most wanted to hear.

"Passionate. Yes, Jacob is very passionate. That's one of the things I love about him. I love to watch him in action."

"Action?"

She nodded again. "Oh yes, he was in good form tonight. I thought he declared his position very well." *Offensive*, I thought again, *in more ways than one*. She beamed with delight. "As Jacob likes to say, to persuade someone to join your position, you have to push, hard. Go to the extreme. That way, when that person pushes back, you can engage in debate and score your points. Then, if you're skillful like Jacob is, that person will end up closer to your position than when you started. He calls it the Rebound Effect: Push people to an extreme so they can rebound and end up where you want them."

"Isn't that a little risky?" I asked. "People could dig in their heels and refuse to budge."

"Oh no, Jacob says sometimes you just have to do what it takes to help people think and do the *right thing*." She said those last words with a little smirk.

An officer interrupted her. "Ma'am, we're ready for you now."

"Nice talking to you." She said and followed him into the dining room, but I noticed her hands were shaking again. I wondered if Jacob had gone to the ultimate extreme and fired a shot.

Alone again, I felt drained. I hoped they'd call me soon. Guess they left the people closest to Lorraine and Fair Winds for last. The crowd had thinned out so I figured it would be soon. I should stay close, but I wanted to be quiet somewhere. The living room, where angry words were exchanged just hours ago, was peaceful, an oasis in the midst of activity. I sank into a wingback chair by the window where I liked to read and curled up. That's when the effects of events hit me, now that the adrenaline was no longer pumping. I must have fallen asleep immediately.

"That's no way to get your beauty sleep." A man's voice penetrated my foggy brain.

I awoke with a start. *Where am I? What? Why—* and the memories of what happened flooded back. I looked up, hoping to see Lorraine. Instead, I met the heavy-lidded ink-black eyes of Detective Ingram, homicide detective from the State Police assigned to Talbot County. "What time is it?" I moved to get up, my muscles firing off complaints to my brain. "Is Lorraine home?"

He patted my hand. "Take it easy. It's early or it's late, depending on your perspective."

It must be the middle of the night. His business suit wasn't rumpled, but he didn't look well put together. I glanced out the window. It was still dark outside.

"I know you like to follow investigations, but this one is a little too close to home, don't you think?" He glanced around the living room.

His feeble attempt at humor fell flat. "Lorraine?"

"She's still at the station with the Chief," he said. "You really should lie down in a bed. You don't have to worry about the team. I'm here now."

And for that, I was grateful. I knew this man. He was called in when someone was killed in Talbot County. It was his job to investigate and find the killer. And he did his job well. Even so, I squeezed my eyes shut and tried to will him away, will them all away from Fair Winds. I wanted to rewind the clock. But it didn't work.

"Abby, I'm sorry about what happened here. You know, I have to do my job."

"I know. If someone had to come, I'm glad it's you." That

pleased him as the strain around his eyes relaxed. I sat up. "What have you learned?" I asked urgently. "What did I miss?"

"Not a whole lot since I just got here a little while ago." He searched my face. Yes, I knew I was begging for something to grab on to. "Okay, I know a little about the incident. The victim was probably shot with a break action 12-gauge double-barreled shotgun, but we don't have the ballistics report yet." He looked down, not wanting to meet my eyes. "And I know that Lorraine—"

I jumped out of the chair. "She didn't do it!"

He caught my arm as I swayed, unsteady from lack of sleep and a flood of emotions. "Okay, okay. Easy does it. Sit down." He guided me back to the chair. I sank into the cushion and tucked my feet underneath me. "Getting upset isn't going to help anyone, especially Lorraine." He turned to a uniformed man standing in the foyer. "Officer, can we get a glass of water over here?"

The man paused for a moment, his eyes flicking from side to side, unsure of where to go. His training took over and he responded, "Yes, sir" with confidence and set off to see what he could do.

The lady who'd brought Dr. Phillips was still wandering around, desperate for someone to give her an alibi. "Did someone see me?"

Ingram followed my eyes. "Don't worry, I'll find someone to help her, too." Then he crouched down so he wasn't looming over me while we talked. "Abby, do you feel up to answering a few questions for me?"

"Sure," I shrugged. "But I don't think I know much of anything that will help you."

He gave me a little smile. "Let me be the judge of that. You're an excellent observer and I've learned to listen to you. You're not always right, but you usually give me a nugget or two I can use. After all, you may not know what you know."

I was grateful when the water arrived. I didn't realize I was so thirsty. Ingram dragged a chair over next to me so we could talk. And he began. "Think back to the meeting. Who was here?"

I looked around the room, once packed with people, now abandoned. "I don't know. Everybody."

"Okay, who was here and then left?" he asked carefully.

I took a slow, jagged breath and closed my eyes, trying to visualize the room.

"Was Lorraine—"

My eyes flew open. I was frantic. Ingram was trying to make me implicate Lorraine, my friend, my confidant, my ...

"There you are!" Ryan sounded relieved as he walked into the room. "I've been looking everywhere for you."

"Ryan!" I cried desperately. "I don't remember. Tell him that you saw Lorraine. Tell him that she couldn't have shot Alex."

Ryan looked stricken as he stood there. "I can't, Abby," he stammered. "I didn't see her."

I wanted to grab his expensive shirt and shake some sense into him, to make him tell the detective that it wasn't her. But my energy had leaked out of my body, leaving me exhausted.

"She must have been here." I could barely hear my own words. "She couldn't have shot him. She hates guns. Her nephew..." The room was whirling.

"Okay, Abby, that's good. You're helping," Ingram said, though I knew he was lying. He patted my arm. "Now, tell me what you did see."

"Nothing, really. It was what I heard." I told him how I was on my way back to my cottage and— oh no!" I swung my feet to the floor. "Simon! Simon is locked in the cottage." I jumped up. "I have to go. He'll be upset, frightened." I started to walk away, realized I was holding the glass, made a beeline back to Ingram, thrust the glass at him and scrambled out of the room.

I flew out the front door, panting, my heart racing. I saw the place where the police car had parked, where they put Lorraine in the back seat with her tiny wrists in cold metal handcuffs. It was unthinkable, but I'd seen it with my own eyes. Just as I saw Alex sitting back in the chair, his chest a bloody mess. If all that could happen, anything could. I took off at a run.

Seeing the light shining through the kitchen window reassured me, but only a little. If the police hadn't found the person who shot Alex...

I leapt up the stairs, crashed through the door and found Simon sprawled on the floor, snoring. He raised his head and cocked it to the side in that cute way of asking a question. I grabbed for the counter. Relief came with gulps of air.

With dramatic precision, Simon slowly stretched every muscle in his black, furry body like a rolling swell of the sea, then he swaggered over to me and sat at my feet. I dropped to the floor and wrapped my arms around him. Scientists say that dogs don't like to be hugged. Not Simon. He waited patiently while I hung on for what felt like forever, drawing comfort from him.

We both jumped when there was a heavy knock on the door. Simon launched himself at the door with an ear-splitting assault of barks and growls. To no avail. The person outside kept knocking.

Resigned, I hauled myself up using the counter for support, reached for the door knob, but paused. Police were crawling all over Fair Winds. A killer had struck only yards from my door. And the murderer was still free. I knew they didn't have the shooter in custody. Lorraine didn't do this awful thing.

Be careful.

CHAPTER 7

The silver quizzing glass, used to magnify items or writing, must be spotless for close examinations. Be sure the silver rim is holding the glass securely. It would not do for the glass to fall out during an inspection.

"The Butler's Guide to Fine Silver"
Mr. Hollister, 1898

I TOOK my hand away from the doorknob called out, "Who is it?"

At first, I couldn't hear over the barking. I clapped my hands once in front of Simon's nose, our hand signal to be quiet. Tentatively, he took two steps back, not sure he wanted to obey.

The voice came through the door. "It's me, Detective Ingram. Is it safe to come in?"

It gave me a little flash of pride that Simon had unnerved the big, bad policeman. I swallowed the feeling and opened the door. "Yes, but let him check you out first."

I stifled a smile when I caught him take a little breath then step toward Simon with his hand held out for a friendly sniff. Did he think the dog would bite it off? Well, maybe, I thought, considering how he spent his days chasing people who killed people.

I started my morning brewing ritual since I was feeling the stimulating effects of Dawkins cold press coffee wearing off. Dawkins.

I turned to face Ingram who was kneeling down to give my guard dog a tummy rub. "Did something happen? Is that why you're here? Lorraine?"

He shook his head and pulled himself up. "Still in custody. I understand her lawyer is arranging bail. I suspect the judge will agree, with conditions. The amount will be high, of course..." His eyes were filled with regret. "considering the crime."

It was clear to me that he didn't want to believe she could kill Alex. I didn't either though there were those ugly words I overheard from the terrace just before... No, I wouldn't even consider it. I went back to measuring out the coffee, decaffeinated this time to help settle my clattering nerves.

"What about Dawkins?"

"He was released, considering that several people saw him in the house when the gun went off," he said, relieved to shift the topic away from Lorraine. "Except he won't leave the station. Says he'll wait there until they release Lorraine."

I was almost afraid to ask, "Is she saying anything about what happened?"

He shrugged. "My questions only raised questions of her own. She said she was taking a walk, but I don't understand why she would be taking a stroll in the dark when her home was filled with guests."

He didn't know, but I had my suspicions. "Do you take cream? I can't remember," I said quickly, rushing to the refrigerator. I wasn't going to volunteer anything, yet.

"No cream, thanks. Mind if I sit down?" He didn't wait for my answer and sat down. He failed to hide a yawn. "I want to know what you know. What did you see and hear?"

"I heard the shot and ran to see what happened. That's all." I tried to act nonchalant as I took two mugs from the cupboard.

"It's probably more important to know what you saw and heard *before* the shot was fired. Most murders aren't premeditated. Those involve intricate planning. Many happen—forgive me for using a cliché—in the heat of the moment. Somebody wants to teach the guy a lesson, make him eat his words, retaliate because of hurt feelings, that kind of thing."

I handed Ingram his mug of black coffee, hoping he didn't see my hand shaking. It was too much to hope. His eyes rested on my hand and raised his knowing eyes to mine before he took the mug.

"Sit down and talk to me." He took out his small notebook and pen, ready to take notes. "Were you at the meeting of all the people... it was in the living room, right?"

I don't know why I thought I could hide things from Ingram. A film producer wouldn't call him handsome, but there was something about the way his face hid what he was thinking. His best weapon—what made him unique—were his eyes. Deep-set coal-black eyes could tear the truth out of a suspect. And now, they were looking at me.

I had no choice. Resigned, I sat down with my coffee. Simon curled up at my feet, giving me support. "I can't believe it happened here, right here at Fair Winds." With no warning, tears threatened to flow so I dug my fingernails into my hand to maintain some kind of control.

"It's okay, Abby." He reached out and laid his big, beefy hand on my fist. "What you saw tonight was terrible. It might help to know why it happened." I raised my eyes and searched his for an answer. "Not why this particular murder happened. We don't know yet, but why someone is driven to take a person's life."

I was ready to listen to anything that might help me deal with what I saw.

"A violent murder like this is the last resort of a person who is passionate, but feels ignored or insulted, someone who has a burning resentment and has kept that feeling locked inside for too long, maybe even a lifetime, with no means of relief. Then something happens. The cork pops. The glass shatters. Simmering fury explodes. And someone dies. My job is to find out who lost control and committed this act. And I need your help to do my job." He gave my hand a little squeeze. "Will you help me?"

I looked down at his hand on mine. In truth, the last thing I wanted to do was to relive everything. But how could I go upstairs and curl up in my bed with Simon and find any kind of peace. Whoever did this crime had to be named, had to pay for taking a life. But the horror of reliving it, especially in the detail that Ingram wanted... no, that was more than I could do.

Ingram leaned closer and I raised my eyes to meet his. "Abby, if it wasn't Lorraine who fired that shot—

"It wasn't Lorraine," I stated calmly, as a matter of fact. "She hates guns."

Ingram slowly shook his head. "That's what you may think, but she grew up on the Eastern Shore. Many of the men here want their daughters to learn how to handle a gun, even if they're taught behind their mothers' back."

I remembered that Lorraine had mentioned her father had taught her to shoot skeet. He didn't think it was lady-like for her to tromp through the woods on the trail of a deer. Her mother would never have allowed that, but shooting skeet was more gentile.

Ingram was waiting. "Go ahead. Tell me."

In a small voice, I did. "Lorraine knows how to shoot skeet. She practiced at a gun club last year for a charity competition."

"Did she use her father's gun, do you know?"

I barely moved my head. "Yes, I think so."

"That's good, Abby. It meshes with what she told me when she identified the gun. She said it was her daddy's gun. It has his initials on the stock. It's the same one found at the boathouse. Her prints are all over it."

"Of course, they are. She found it. Picked it up. We all saw her holding it. Her prints must have covered up... I don't know. I'm so tired."

"You're doing great, Abby." Ingram patted my arm. "I need you to stay with me a little longer. If it wasn't Lorraine, the person who did this is still out there and..."

He didn't finish the sentence. He didn't have to. I heard the missing words in my head.

And that person could hurt someone else.

"I need your help, Abby. You were there. I wasn't."

I looked back at his hand covering mine. It spoke volumes. *I will be here for you. I will comfort you. I will protect you. I will support you in every way I can. Trust me, Abby.*

I started at the beginning with the reason for the meeting: the development of a large plot of land with many new single-family homes, a nature park and a hotel. It still sounded to me like alien invasion from another planet. There were other people who felt the same way. I warmed to the topic as I realized that I could suggest several suspects to the detective—suspects other than Lorraine.

There was Jacob, the hothead who worried about ecological balance. There was Alex's business partner, who couldn't see his way clear to show up on time, to stand with him as he faced the angry locals. I tried not to sound petty, but I think I failed, when I added that the partner had walked in with Alex's ex-wife. That was awkward on so many levels. I wondered if they arrived late because they'd stopped along the way for a little—. Really, I should let the detective draw his own conclusions.

"Alex's partner is getting it on with the ex-wife?" His eyes opened wide and his eyebrows shot up in surprise. "That's awkward."

"Yes, I guess it is... or should be. It didn't seem to bother Arabella at all. What kind of name is that? It might work for a music box ballerina, but this woman was a panther stalking her prey."

Ingram narrowed his eyes in suspicion as he made a note. "Ex-wife, stalking her former husband? Maybe wanting him back?"

"No," I said quickly, wishing I had kept my mouth shut. "That's not what I meant."

"Doesn't matter. It's an honest observation, that's why I like talking over a case with you. But this time, it doesn't sound good for Lorraine. Jealousy is one of the oldest motives ever."

"But Alex was killed, not his partner," I argued.

"If it was the other way around, Alex would have been your number one suspect for killing the partner." Then I described the scene of the ex-wife putting the scarf around Alex's neck. It was such an intimate moment that I'd almost looked away.

He wrote in his notebook. "Maybe the ex-wife still had feelings for her old love, maybe she was trying to get back with him and the partner didn't like it."

Yes, I thought, that man belonged on the list of suspects. "And there was a gatecrasher. Her name was…" I closed my eyes seeing her so clearly in her floral print dress, rumpled fishing hat and muddy black boots. "Mary Rose. A character right out of a fairy storyteller's imagination."

"Lorraine invited her? Muddy boots and all?"

"Not exactly. She said she heard about the meeting, assumed her invitation was lost in the mail and came anyway."

"Was she civil? Some people who truly love nature aren't that peaceful."

I cleared my throat. "I wouldn't say that she was violent. She's an old woman, for heaven's sake, a really old woman. She got impatient with Alex and what he was saying. Called it hogwash and stomped out. I remember Dawkins wasn't pleased when he saw the clumps of mud she left behind."

"Okay, that's good." Ingram made notes. "Who else?"

"Wait, you're including Mary Rose as a suspect?"

"Yes."

"But she left. I heard her drive off in an old truck. I think half the county could hear it going down the long drive. Not sure she's ever heard of a muffler. I'm sure we would have heard her coming back."

"What if she walked back?" Ingram asked.

"I doubt it. I said she was an old lady, big emphasis on *old*. I doubt if she could walk very far in those old boots, especially the distance from the main road to the house.

"All right." He took a sip of coffee. "Did you notice anyone else out of the ordinary? A server brought in for the event, a suspicious character…" His voice trailed off and he waited for my answer.

"Oh, you mean like a rabid environmentalist who arrived with a double-barreled shotgun? Ah, no." Ingram didn't laugh, didn't even smile at my little joke. "Sorry, it's been a long night."

I got up and stepped around my sleeping dog. At least one of us was getting our beauty sleep. I took the lid off Simon's cookie jar and he was at my feet in a flash, smiling the way Labs do, panting for a goodie.

"There was a young man at the serving table, but I can't imagine he is your killer. He was a kid and paid absolutely no attention to what was happening in the meeting or what people were saying."

"Name?" I shook my head. "Okay, I'll get it from Dawkins." He made a note. "Anything else?"

I nodded slowly, thinking. "There was a man I saw talking to the young server."

"A stranger?"

"Yes, and strange."

"In what way?" Ingram asked, his eyes keen.

I looked down at Simon who had inhaled the two cookies I'd put on the floor. "You'd laugh if I told you."

"Try me."

Almost against my better judgment, I said, "He looked like an owner of an Italian restaurant I once knew."

Ingram scowled. "You're going to have to do a lot better than that description."

I shrugged. "I'm embarrassed to say he looked like an Italian stereotype."

"An Italian stallion?"

I chuckled. "Maybe when he was younger. Not now. Definitely, not now. He was older."

Ingram interrupted. "As old as your gatecrasher?"

"Oh, no. If he was old, she was ancient. He was bald, but vain."

"That doesn't make sense, sorry."

"Not vain like the men who do nasty comb-overs thinking we won't see the bare spot up there. He dyed the thin fringe of hair around his bald spot and his eyebrows dark black."

"Black is about as dark as you can get." It was his turn to chuckle.

"These eyebrows were thick and bushy and black-ety black, like he'd used shoe polish."

"Okay," the detective said slowly, drawing the word out. "I'll look for an old man with black eyebrows. That should narrow down the search."

"You should ask Dawkins about him. He knows him." I paused and looked down at my hands, shredding a paper napkin out of sheer nervousness. "Detective, who could have done this? It's too awful to think about."

"Sudden death always is, Abby. I can't give you a name, not yet, but I think it was a crime of passion."

I took in a quick breath. "Passion? Then it must have been his ex-wife Arabella. She must have been overcome with jealousy when she saw Alex and Lorraine together." My words were tumbling over themselves as my excitement grew. "Or it was his partner. When he saw his girlfriend put that scarf around her ex-husband's neck, well, let me tell you it made everyone who saw it uncomfortable. She was having an intimate moment, that's for sure. Maybe the partner saw it, the intimacy of it, and his rage erupted. He couldn't help himself. He found himself a gun and *Bang!*" I looked at Ingram, hoping, expecting him to shout his agreement and take off to arrest both of them.

Instead, he shook his head. "Or it could have been a different scenario. Remember that intimate scene with the scarf? Maybe someone else saw that, too and was consumed by jealousy and hurt."

The memory of a face wracked with the agony of heartache flashed in front of me.

Lorraine.

"This person went and took the gun, because she knew where it was kept..."

Lorraine.

"Went to the boathouse and waited until Alex came outside and sat down, because she knew where he liked to sit."

Lorraine.

"And let the anger and pain consume her. And took the shot."

No, I wanted to scream, but I knew...

There was a soft knock, the door opened and Ryan poked his head inside. I jumped up.

Without thinking, I ran into his arms. "Is it Lorraine? Is she back?"

"Yes, the police just brought her back. Dawkins, too. He wouldn't leave until she was released. I think that impressed the judge."

In a rush, I grabbed some cookies, dropped them on the floor for Simon and turned to the detective. "I have to go. I have to —" Tears choked away my words and I rushed out the door calling back to keep Simon in the house when they left. Halfway across the lawn, I turned back and was relieved to see that Ryan had a better idea. He'd put Simon on a leash and was taking him for a much-needed walk.

The rays of the morning sun were just touching the main house at Fair Winds. It was as if they were waiting for Lorraine to come home.

BLUE CRAB

Fearless, the Blue Crab is the iconic symbol of the Chesapeake Bay where it makes its home. Both the male and female are blue and green on top so when seen from above they blend into the underwater environment. They are white underneath so they blend with the sunlight. They molt or shed their shells as they grow. While the new shell hardens, they are defenseless.

The male spends the winter in deep mud found in the flooded ancient river bed of the Susquehanna. The female mates only once in her lifetime, but can fertilize her eggs at two different times. After mating, she migrates south to the mouth of the Bay to release up to two million eggs.

The Blue Crab needs thick underwater grasses to survive and reproduce, areas often harmed by dead zones, algae blooms and cloudy waters. Though rather ugly and menacing in appearance, its Latin name is *Callinectes sapidus* means *beautiful swimmer*

CHAPTER 8

The Family Silver pattern may be marked with a crest or armorial ornamentation. It is unique and representative of the Family and its position.

"The Butler's Guide to Fine Silver"
Mr. Hollister, 1898

I RAN into the foyer and skidded to a stop on the marble floor as Lorraine walked through the door. Dawkins was right behind her and closed the door silently. Her face, that sweet face that always gave me silent encouragement, was ashen, drained of all emotion. If her eyes closed and she lay down, I would have thought she was —no, I could not think of that. There had been too much death here already.

"Lorraine..." I said just above a whisper. But I didn't know what to say.

She held up her hand for me to stop. I did and watched as she walked past me. I glanced at Dawkins with a silent question, but he only dropped his head and shook it slowly. Together, we followed her down the hallway without saying a word. She paused at the French doors that lead to the terrace. I started to speak, but Dawkins touched my arm. We waited. It was her decision, not ours. With a jagged breath, she stepped through the door and stood in front of the blood-soaked white wicker chair. A single tear trailed down her cheek.

I held my breath. Any words I could say would be cheap. There was nothing I could do to penetrate her grief. I waited and didn't look away. I watched her. Not out of gruesome curiosity. I kept my eyes on her in case she turned toward me. I wanted her to see that I was willing to stand with her, no questions asked. Out of loyalty, out of love? It didn't matter and didn't need an analysis. As Gran liked to say, it was an *is*. A fact. A reality.

So, I stood and watched. Dawkins stood just inside the doorway. I could feel his eyes on me and somehow knew that he was watching us both. He had done his part by staying at the police station until she was free to come home. That his job, as he saw it, until she set foot on Fair Winds. Now, it was my turn.

A tiny cry escaped Lorraine's slightly-parted lips. I tensed, ready to reach out and grab her. But it wasn't necessary. She raised her shoulders, taking in a great breath of air, then let them sink back to their natural position. She turned her head and found me there. Slowly, she closed her eyes and opened them again. She conveyed so much in that single movement.

She shifted her gaze until she found Dawkins. "Thank you." And with those two simple words spoken with a rasp, the hush of the moment was broken.

Both Dawkins and I spoke at the same time, eager to help and offer comfort.

"Thank you," she said to Dawkins. "A tall glass of ice water sounds wonderful." He melted away to bring it.

She reached out and wrapped her fingers around my arm, both to offer reassurance and to gain a little support. "I'm not ready for bed, not yet. I just want to soak up the spirit of Fair

Winds for a little while. That's better than eight hours of sleep for me."

She staggered then righted herself. The happenings and storm of emotions had sucked out all her energy. I put my hand under her elbow and suggested we sit in the library, a place where we'd tackled so many problems before. A place where we could, if nothing else, sit to track the sun as it rose higher over the Miles River. She agreed with a small nod and we made our way slowly into the house. Away from the scene of sudden death.

She settled into her favorite chair by the fireplace with a clear view to the east. Dawkins appeared with a Waterford crystal pitcher filled with water, two crystal goblets and a small silver ice bucket, complete with ice tongs. Excessive? No, he had a purpose. He prepared her ice water with quiet decorum to remind her that the dirty place with puke green walls and the invasive stench of urine and worse—the place they caged people who committed violent crimes, one person against another—that was not her world. This was her world, here at Fair Winds, where it was normal for her to use crystal and sterling silver. *This* was her world.

While Lorraine drained her glass, Dawkins stole a look at me and without a word, he transferred the oversight of her well-being to me. I gave him a slight nod and he left the room.

I leaned forward. "More water?" I asked as I reached for the pitcher.

She groaned a little as she leaned her head back and closed her eyes, peace starting to smooth away the remnants of the horror from the night before. The shadows under her eyes were almost purple, her skin was blotchy and her eyes were rimmed red from crying.

We sat in silence, as two good friends can do, without the need of words. The companionship was enough.

"I don't want to talk about what happened right now, okay?" she asked, her voice hoarse.

"Of course," I said hurriedly. "Whatever you want to do or not do is fine."

"I've told my story so many times, to the police, your detective, the Chief. I'm so glad they believed me and let me come home." She shivered a little and pulled her robe close.

Funny, I hadn't noticed before. That wasn't what she had on for the meeting. She had come down the curving staircase in the foyer wearing a blue silk dress to the delight and appreciation of Alex, the man who now lay dead with his chest blown away. She'd returned to Fair Winds wearing her white summer robe that only occasionally appeared downstairs at breakfast. In fact, she wouldn't even wear it around the grounds.

As if she read my mind, she said, "They took my clothes."

"Who? Why?"

"The police. They took my clothes. Said it was standard procedure. Looking for gunshot residue." She brushed off the front of the robe though there was nothing there. "Dawkins had someone bring this robe. The white paper suit they offered me was awful." She shuddered. "At least, this is mine." She heaved a deep sigh. "I want to take a shower and lie down," sounding so tired, I was afraid she'd fall asleep before she made it to the bed.

I jumped up. "Of course, of course." I followed her slow steps as she led the way to the back stairway. I wanted to help, but I didn't touch her. With her last shreds of strength, she willed herself to be independent. "We can talk later," and added softly, "If you want to."

She nodded as she absently rubbed her eye and dragged herself up on the first step. In only a few hours, age had wrapped itself around my friend like a cloak. I'd never seen her use the bannister going up steps. She usually dashed or walked regally for effect. Now, she strained to pull herself up, one step at a time. Dawkins appeared next to me, watching, his jaw clenched, against… what? Tears? Rage?

Lorraine stopped about halfway up the staircase and swayed. Dawkins sprinted forward, but she held up her hand for him to stop. It was as if she was proving that she would survive, that she was still the woman she was yesterday or last week. Not a crumpled shell.

She took another step, then another. The look of concentration, determination, showed a hint of a smile at her progress. Then it fell away as she turned and looked down at me. "Abby, I'm so sorry. It's my fault you're involved."

"You didn't do anything to me," I said, wanting to reassure her. "This is —"

"Not just this..." She didn't speak the next word. It came more as a sigh. "Everything. Putting you in danger. Ever since I brought you here. Reggie at MEBA. The silver treasure hunt. You almost—"

"Stop. You've done nothing. I'm happy here at Fair Winds, happy here with you. I love my life. Now, go on upstairs and rest. I'll be here when you want me."

I lied. She had done one thing. She showed me how to go after what made me happy. In college, I got the brilliant idea to turn my back on what I truly loved and pick a practical major so I could support myself. It wasn't hard finding a job as a software developer. I tricked myself into thinking I satisfied my creativity by manipulating ones and zeros. When I came to Fair Winds, I was finally honest with myself and reveled in the work combining history, research and stories. And grateful to Lorraine.

True, sometimes my curiosity almost got me killed. Once. Twice. But I was still here, in one piece. And again, we were, facing the shock and sadness of a sudden death and the search for a killer. This time, it was too close to home. The spray of blood from the bullet that killed Alex had reached out and stained Lorraine.

Early the next morning, I settled in the breakfast room so I'd be there if—no, when Lorraine came downstairs. I didn't have to wait long when she dragged herself into the room with great effort, wearing a coral track suit, and sighed.

"What a waste," she declared. "It's funny how a person thinks of the smallest, most unimportant things sometimes."

"Did you remember something," I asked, hoping she remembered a detail that could help identify the killer.

"About last night?" She shook her head. "I was thinking about my dress, the one the police took. Alex likes… liked cornflower blue so I bought it to wear for the meeting to make him smile. He was nervous about what might happen, you know?"

And he was right, I thought.

"I could never wear it again. I don't even want it in my closet." Lorraine settled into a chair with a sigh. She looked at the warm apple walnut muffin on the plate for a moment, its sweet smell filling the room. She pushed it away and leaned her elbows on the table to hold herself upright.

"Well, I guess we should talk about what happened," she said, resigned.

I tried to hide the fact that I was brimming with questions. "Only if you feel like talking."

"Might as well. Fire away…" We both stifled a gasp at the horrible reference to what happened to Alex. "I mean," she said quickly. "I don't know where to start. Ask me questions."

I had no shortage of questions. They'd been swirling around in my head all night. *Where to start?*

"How did they treat you at the police station?" I bit back the words. There were so many things I wanted to know, but the questions smacked of being mundane and intrusive. She was home, that was all that mattered for now. "I would have…"

"Of course, you would have brought me a proper change of clothes, but I just needed something to wear at the station and for the ride home. Dawkins hoped you were getting some sleep." She looked down at her hands. "You know, he is incredibly loyal. He didn't leave me for a moment. After the Chief ordered the young patrolman to remove the cuffs, Dawkins made sure everyone treated me gently and with respect. I don't know what I would have done…" She raised her eyes and stared off in the distance for a moment. "Someone must have gotten that white robe off the hook in my bathroom. I think I'll throw it away, too."

"I hate the fact they treated you like a suspect."

She gave me a serious look. "Abby, it was my gun that—" She couldn't say the words. "It was my daddy's favorite. I keep it, kept it—" she corrected, "cabinet behind the door in the library. Come on, I'll show you."

We went into the library and I saw the narrow cabinet of a dark wood, with a tall glass door, designed to hold long guns. Some kind of plush beige fabric lined the inside to show off the rich wood stocks and blue-black metal gun barrels of the two guns stored inside. I didn't grow up with guns and never expected them to be kept so close at hand. I thought she'd keep any gun locked away somewhere out of the way.

"A gun cabinet, right here in the library where we sit and talk, where you work, where Simon likes to do his tricks for cookies?" I could hear the disbelief in my voice as the reality sunk in. "I thought you hated guns."

"I do," Lorraine said in a meek voice, so unlike her normal self.

"Then, pray tell, why did you have a loaded gun right here?" I wanted to yell at her. Who keeps a loaded gun in the house when she hated guns? I didn't grow up with guns. In fact, I'm afraid of them. To have one in the house was an invitation for disaster, according to the statistics... and they were right. If there wasn't a gun here... I wanted to scream. "Why did you have a loaded gun here in the house?"

"I'm my daddy's girl. A daughter of the Eastern Shore."

I shook my head in confusion. "I don't understand."

She sank into a deep, overstuffed chair by the fireplace, took a deep breath and sighed it out. "There's a saying here on the Shore and Daddy lived by it. He said, *If a gun isn't loaded, it's useless.*"

"Unless you want to shoot somebody," I countered.

"Or something. This is a rural area. What if an animal got into the house? Or...or faced off with one of the dogs or a person right here? A-a-nd it had white foam around its mouth? You have to act quickly. You don't need to be wasting time digging through those drawers in the cabinet looking for shells and loading the gun." She looked down as she folded her hands in her lap. "It was a rule in my Daddy's house to keep one gun loaded, in case. And it's been a rule here at Fair Winds since we moved in. So, every year, on Daddy's birthday, I remove the old shells from the shotgun and reload it with new ones. I do it out of love and respect for my father and everything he taught me. Guess I'm just an old softie."

I walked over to the gun cabinet and looked closer. There was an empty place for a third gun. I realized with a shudder that Ingram was right. It was easy for someone, anyone to remove the gun from the cabinet, sneak down to the boathouse and fire the fatal shot. "Do you keep the cabinet locked?"

"Of course, I may be sentimental, but I'm not stupid."

"So, how did somebody get into the cabinet and take the gun?"

Her shoulders sagged with sadness. "I have no idea."

It wasn't my intention to grind her down. That was enough for now. "Well," I announced as I uncurled my body from the chair and stood. "You old softie, I think you'd better haul yourself upstairs and get some more rest." I thanked the stars that she had slept in her own bed last night instead of a jail cell. "I'll walk upstairs with you."

Painfully, she hauled herself out of the chair and stretched. "I will, but I'm not quite ready to go up. Walk with me outside for a few minutes."

She guided us the long way around, avoiding the French doors to the terrace and the crime tape there. She held on to my arm and leaned on me as we moved across the lawn, like a young woman escorting her aging grandmother on a stroll. Yes, it was as if she had aged overnight. The old cliché could happen.

We stopped while she caught her breath and watched the late summer sun climb above the trees on the opposite shore. The days were getting shorter by slight increments as time moved toward the fall equinox. The cold blast of winter would be here soon. I just hoped Lorraine would be here, too. I soon realized that she wasn't watching the sun. She was staring at the boathouse.

"I wish I had never gone near the boathouse last night." She shook her head. "I was a fool. Boathouses are a magnet of bad luck for me." Still clinging to me, she patted my arm. "Do you remember the story of what happened to me the night of my 18th birthday party?" She didn't wait for a response and launched into the story that had given me the shivers the first time I'd heard it.

"The party was at Harraway Hall, Daddy's farm where I grew up. He'd built the boathouse to protect his Chris-Craft launch, a pretty wood boat, from the elements. People came from all over the Shore and the big cities on the East Coast—Washington, Baltimore, Philadelphia, even several from New York for the party. The boys looked so handsome in their white dinner jackets. All the girls wore long fancy dresses. We danced to a live band and had every kind of food you can imagine." A wistful smile touched her lips. "My little sister was the pretty one, not me. But that night was right out of a storybook."

The expression of enchanted happiness splintered, leaving behind an exhausted look of old hurt and humiliation. "It was a dream come true until it turned into a nightmare." Lorraine drew in a long breath. "A handsome young man from New York, a friend of a friend, charmed me in every way. I was thrilled when he suggested a walk in the moonlight down by the boathouse. When he put his arms around me, I thought he was going to kiss me." She shook her head with disgust.

"Oh no, nothing as romantic as that. He slammed me against the wall. His hands were everywhere. I begged him to stop. He ordered me to stop squirming. I tried to scream. He put his hand over my mouth. He pressed his body against me, trying to force me inside."

Without thinking, I gasped, even though I knew the outcome. It was still a frightening story to hear again.

She dropped her head. "That night, my old childhood friend, Evie, saved me. She body-slammed him right into the water. I'm not sure if the idiot knew how to swim." She looked at the Fair Winds boathouse. "And here we are again at a boathouse and I'm in trouble. Only this time, Evie isn't here to save me."

No, Evie had died in the kitchen, just inside the main house. Killed with the silver Angel Food cake server I'd sold Lorraine only a day earlier. Tragic, her murder triggered a series of events that brought me to Fair Winds to stand next to Lorraine today.

"Why were you down here after the meeting?" I asked.

"I wanted, needed to clear my head. That meeting was so contentious, not what I expected at all."

I felt fairly confident that she didn't expect Alex's ex-wife to show up with his business partner. It took a lot of nerve for that woman to walk into Fair Winds and make amorous moves on her ex with his winter scarf. It was just plain rude, but I didn't say a thing and just waited for Lorraine to continue.

"I walked down to the water. That's when I heard the shot. I thought it came from the boathouse which didn't make any sense. A gun shot was bad enough, but I've never kept firearms in the boathouse. Somebody screamed from the terrace. A woman, I think." There was a hitch in her voice. "I saw someone slumped in the white wicker chair. His chest was all bloody. It was Alex. I knew it was Alex. That's where he was when I went for my walk." She squeezed her lips together, fighting back the tears. "I didn't know what to do first—go to him or find out who had shot him? People were pouring out of the house. Somebody yelled to call an ambulance. I slipped out of my shoes and started running to the boathouse. I know it sounds hardhearted, not to go and help. But people were taking care of him. No one was concerned with the gunshot. It was the best I could do."

Her left eye narrowed as she peered at the boathouse and dock now cordoned off by garish yellow Police tape. "I went inside, but no one was there. As I turned to leave, I saw a shotgun laying on the floor. I went closer. I knew that gun, the silver scrollwork, the deep rich color and wood grain that shone from hours of loving care. The shotgun was my daddy's." She shrugged.

"I picked it up. It was automatic. It was his gun and it didn't belong there. I know now I shouldn't have touched it. When I touched the barrels, they were hot. This was the gun that fired the shot that hurt—"

"When I went back out on the dock, I think I was in shock. I was trying to put things together. What brought me out of my stupor was the man saying, Lorraine, what have you done? Just thinking about hearing those words gives me the chills. Because my heart froze in that moment. To think that somebody thought I'd shot—. I dropped the gun. The blast shook me to the core."

She removed her arm from mine and stood alone. "The rest you know."

"And now, everyone knows that you didn't have anything to do with what happened," I said with conviction.

She looked at me with a scowl. "What makes you think that?"

It was the last thing I expected her to say. "Isn't it obvious? That officer, the one who treated you like a criminal… I mean, did he have to make you kneel down and then clamp handcuffs on you?" I continued with all the confidence in the world. "When the Chief got here, he sure set him straight. Yes, he wanted to talk with you about what happened. They wanted to talk with everybody. Maybe you saw something that would be helpful in finding the k—" I swallowed the word. I was trying to make her feel better, not worse.

"You're right. It felt good to get those cuffs off my wrists. It felt like they were cutting into my skin." Absently, she rubbed the irritated skin. "It was humiliating to be treated like that, right here at Fair Winds, in front of all those people." She threw out her arms to the side and let them slap back against her body. "There's no way to remove that scene from their minds. I'm sure the whole county has heard one of several versions by now."

"Don't worry about that. No one will think you had anything to do with what happened." Lorraine started to slowly shake her head from side to side, but I continued, sure that I knew what I was saying. "Look, here you are at Fair Winds. You're not in some jail cell. The Chief brought you home himself. It's over for you. Now, they have to find— What? Why are you shaking your head?"

"It's not over for me," she said. A simple statement of fact.

"What do you mean? You are—"

"The Chief and your detective – what is his name?"

"Ingram," I replied, my optimism evaporating.

"Yes, that's right. The Chief and Detective Ingram have just started the investigation. They have to get the results back from the crime scene people, finish their interviews, look into Alex's life, maybe it was someone who felt slighted in a business deal. There are so many things they have to do."

"And they're doing what they need to do so they can make an arrest, arrest the right person." My certainty growing again.

Her face was filled with sadness. "The Chief told me not to leave the county. I'm to stay right here until his investigation is over."

That surprised me, and not in a good way. "Why? They can't think that you—"

"I may not have been in handcuffs when they took me to the St. Michaels police station, but we didn't just chat. Abby, they found gunshot residue on my hands. They found out that his ex-wife was here. I told them that Alex was... was more than a business acquaintance. More than a friend."

My suspicions were correct. But hearing her say it brought me no comfort. Alex was more than a friend. His ex-wife had invaded Fair Winds, but she was more than an ex. For years, she was the woman who shared his home, had his children, helped build his business. Now, she was an ex. Was his heart truly free to love Lorraine? I'd overheard angry words between them from the terrace. Lorraine was upset about that woman and, seeing them together, how they seemed to fall into an old pattern.

Did she have a right to be angry? Yes. Did she... No, it couldn't be.

Lorraine continued, flat and precise as she would when ordering supplies. "If no one confesses or if they can't make a case against someone else, they'll take all the evidence and their findings to the grand jury and..." she had to catch her breath. "And they may formally charge me with first degree murder."

I staggered from this news.

She appeared calm, but her voice quavered. "Now, if you'll excuse me. I just want some peace. You know how conflict upsets me." I think I'm ready to go upstairs and rest on a soft bed with smooth linens."

Instead of the hard surface with a scratchy blanket she saw in the cell at the station. The thought made me want to run away from the unfairness of it all. Instead I put out my trembling hand to help steady her.

"That won't be necessary. I can make it on my own."

I watched her climb the stairs with more strength than she'd shown earlier. That was good, but defiant attitude to do things alone bothered me. This was the time to gather support, circle the wagons, not go off on her own.

CHAPTER 9

Always keep a sharp eye on the pieces of the place setting. At first glance, they may appear to be of the same pattern. On close inspection, you may discover they are from different patterns and should not be used together.

"The Butler's Guide to Fine Silver"
Mr. Hollister, 1898

MY HEART JUMPED a little when I sensed a silent someone was standing next to me. "Dawkins, you have to stop sneaking around."

"I will tell you again, I do not *sneak around*." He said it as if the words tasted foul. "I am watching… to offer comfort, support and protection."

My head snapped around. "Protection? Do you think Lorraine is in danger?" Of course, a killer was still on the loose. Maybe Alex wasn't the real target. Was Lorraine…? Alex was sitting in her favorite chair. Could he have been shot by mistake? "Dawkins, do you think—"

"I do not know what to think. I only know that she is innocent. Someone murdered Mr. Alex. And there is a murderer lurking in the dark. I know that I must be vigilant and prepared. I must gather all intel – information that I can and be ready to strike, if necessary."

"Strike?" He was scaring me.

"I only meant that I may need to take action to protect Miss Lorraine and all here at Fair Winds. And I will do what is necessary. That's why I wanted a moment to talk to you about another threat we face."

I felt like I was going to swoon from everything coming at me: a shot, blood, murder, an arrest, a killer in the dark. "Don't we have enough to handle?"

"One would think that we are facing a staggering array of problems, but there is one more. I'm drawing you in, because I'm not sure that Miss Lorraine can manage what may need to be done."

I wanted to scream in frustration. "For once in your life, could you stop being obtuse? What are you talking about?"

He raised his chin. "The storm in the Atlantic."

"A hurricane?" I wanted to laugh with relief. "Is that all? I don't think we have to worry. We're not on the ocean. We're inland by any number of miles. If the storm does come here, it will probably only bring a ton of rain. We're quite safe here, Dawkins."

I turned to go back to the cottage, but Dawkins didn't move. He stood ramrod straight and continued to look ahead, staring at some invisible point. "With all due respect, you are from the West Coast. The weather conditions here in the East are quite different. Storms strengthen as they approach the East Coast and there is the matter of the possible storm surge." He pointed toward the river without moving his head. "You'll notice that we are not very high above sea level. If the storm pushes water up the Bay, the rivers will rise, including that one."

I fought down a chill. "Then in your position here at Fair Winds, I suggest you take all the precautions you think appropriate." I started walking toward the cottage. "But I reserve the right to say I-told-you-so, Chicken Little. Carry on, Dawkins." I'd always wanted to say that.

I burst into the little kitchen in my cottage with a famished Simon on my heels. I grabbed the scoop and sent kibble clattering into his bright red bowl imprinted with his name, a gift from Lorraine.

Lorraine. Her cool acceptance of a possible grand jury indictment rattled me to the core. She was always a fighter for what was right. And that wasn't right.

Or was it?

I'd heard her heated words triggered by hurt directed at Alex, the last words she'd ever speak to him. Did they come from jealousy, as Ingram said? Was the hurt enough to prompt her to go to the gun cabinet, take out her daddy's gun, sneak down to the boathouse and take aim at the defenseless man sitting on the terrace? She'd had the time if she sprinted through the shadows ringing the lawn.

No. She said she didn't do it. I had to believe her.

But there was no one else inside the boathouse. I didn't see anyone running away and I had a clear view.

STOP IT! I ordered myself. *This is Lorraine. If she said she didn't do it, she didn't fire that shot.*

If I, her friend, was having misgivings about her story, I couldn't imagine what other people were thinking. The best way to help my friend was not to let things spiral out of control until a grand jury of strangers decided *if* she should be charged. The best thing to do was to find out who pulled that trigger. And to do that, it was time to play a game, a game my Gran made up that saved my life.

When I was five, I stopped talking. It happened after, no, because of the accident. My parents and I were driving someplace and I was swaying back and forth to the beat of the windshield wipers. Suddenly, there were screeching sounds mixed with my mother's voice, shrill, and frightened. A terrible jolt. A crunch.

Her voice cut off. A tinkling of glass. I was too young to know exactly what happened. Other than the sounds that haunted my nightmares for a long time, I only remembered something raining down on my skin in little droplets that tickled. The police found me whimpering in the back seat of our mangled car, speckled with my mother's blood.

We were all victims of that crash. Dad was overwhelmed with guilt and grief. I drew a protective blanket of silence around me and stopped talking. I needed help, I overheard Gran telling him. I didn't understand why she kept saying they would lose me too, when I was sitting right there on the top step of the staircase. Finally, with a flood of tears and promises I didn't understand, Dad left me with Gran and Great Aunt Agnes, her sister. They shuttled me to endless doctor and therapy appointments, but it was the magnet game she created on the refrigerator door that drew my little mind out of the trauma.

It began with the magnet of an ice cream cone. I loved ice cream more than anything, but if I wanted some, I had to take the magnet out of the box she kept next to the fridge and put it on the door. It took a while for me to realize that something good would happen if I connected with the world again. Gran kept changing the rules. I could use the magnet, but I had to *say* please. Then I had to say *ice cream* and *please*. Soon, I was talking a mile a minute.

The magnets kept me linked to Gran, anchored in a good way. I kept the box of magnets and added to it over the years. I'd use them to remind myself of some of my favorite things, organize a crazy schedule or work my way through a tricky problem. Now, the magnets would help me clarify my thoughts and uncover a killer, the trickiest problem of all.

I opened the cabinet and pulled out the box of magnets. Armed with a cup of fresh coffee, I settled down in front of the refrigerator, ready to set up my own version of an incident board. I thought about my conversation with Ingram as I ran my fingers through the magnets in the box. Some were decades old, some almost brand-new. I hoped I had the right ones that would lead my thinking to the killer.

As much as I didn't want to do it, I sorted through the mess to find a magnet to represent Lorraine. After all, she was the one who had the possibility of a grand jury indictment hanging over her head. I had a choice between two magnets: A gavel to represent the indictment or two hearts interlocked in the old symbol of friendship. Stress was making my neck tense up. I rubbed the spot at the base of my skull as I forced myself to accept the fact that a magnet on the door represented my dear friend. It meant she might be a killer.

This was no time to relax. I had to keep going, to fill up the open space on the door and pinpoint some viable suspects for Ingram. He'd asked for my help, my insights, and I was going to deliver.

I started with the obvious name, the one person who had the most to gain as Alex's partner: Allen Barclay of Barclay Prestige Properties. Barclay was a respected name in the British financial world. Combining that old name with the words *Prestige Properties* was overkill and said more about the boss than the business. There was something about the man. Something in that first look the men exchanged when Allen walked into Fair Winds, late. But wait, there was something else. After Alex saw his ex-wife walk in the house, Alex flashed him a look filled with anger and what... betrayal? Yes. All was not well between those two men. I pulled out a magnet of a glittery palace and put it on the door.

And what about the ex-wife, Arabella. They were divorced, but it was obvious that there were emotions still simmering beneath the surface. What magnet would best represent her? I found a magnet with a diamond engagement ring in the bottom of the box, but it wasn't quite right. I searched again. How about a knife to symbolize cutting ties? Yes, that worked. As I put it next to the palace magnet, I felt a little thrill of anticipation. I wanted her to be the killer. But wishing didn't make it so. But a girl could hope.

Who else? There were a lot of people at the meeting who were angry about the possible impact of the new development on the environment? *Possible impact?* Some of them were convinced that the effects would range from detrimental to catastrophic. Violent acts by Greenpeace started playing in my head. Could eco-terrorism happen here on the Eastern Shore? I would hope they could talk through our differences. But a man had slumped in a chair last night with a mortal chest wound. Maybe we had already escalated beyond compromise. I had to be careful.

There was the man wearing a linen jacket and t-shirt who could go from polite to attack mode in nanoseconds. Jacob. Yes, he'd earned a place on my door, especially after what his wife said about the necessity of taking extreme positions, saying and doing things to the extreme to nudge people to change their position on issues. His wife, the woman whose head was so filled with *him* that there was little room for her own personality. She came across as an Earth Mother, ready to prove her commitment to a natural, organic way of life. Could he have persuaded her to do something extreme to prove her love for him? I chose a tree for him and a ball of yarn for her.

An ironic smile crept across my lips. Speaking of an eco-terrorist, that crazy woman who crashed the meeting certainly dressed the part. Who wears boots with a dress? A fashion model on the runway and an environmentalist. Was she a joke? Since Ingram had written down Mary Rose's name, I added a magnet of an old boot to my incident board.

There was another man who'd made a strong impression: The Don't-Touch-My-Bike man in the spandex shirt. In the face of Dawkins's polite reaction to his bike in the foyer, the man showed he had a short fuse. I found a tricycle magnet and added it to the door.

It seemed a laughable when I added a cookie magnet to the door to represent Stu, the cookie thief, who could have a heart attack at any moment. Did I really think he could have shot Alex? Probably not, but I had to consider him, which was more than Alex had done. Being ignored or dismissed as unimportant was deeply hurtful, more than we realized sometimes. Hurt feelings often lead to bad reactions.

Seeing this menagerie of magnets, it didn't hurt to be thorough. After all, there were a lot of people at the meeting. A bright orange-and-white clown fish lay on the top of the magnets. It would be perfect for the science kid who came with his teacher. I had to chuckle, the chances of finding a clown fish in the Chesapeake Bay were nil, but it was a fun idea. Except it wasn't a joke to add the kid to the suspect board. Could he have made the shot that killed Alex? Probably not, but if was helping the killer, no one would have noticed a kid wandering around. He could have slipped into the library, taken the gun and delivered it into the hands of the shooter. It didn't feel right, but I added the clown fish to the door.

Now, who else? I straightened up, my back starting to ache. There was the Italian with the bushy black eyebrows in the dining room. Who was he? I found an old magnet of Groucho Marx. And what about the young server who was sweating like it was a hot summer day during his police interview? Did he have a grudge against the developer? I added a champagne-bottle magnet. And there was the minister. I couldn't imagine that a man of the cloth would shoot another human being, but was his shy demeanor hiding the heart of a guilty man? I added a magnet with a cross on it. And what about the man with the beard who talked about recycle-reuse? Did he have an agenda that would save the land for the raccoons and deer or even turn it into a huge solar energy farm. I pulled out a Santa magnet and added the man to my suspect board.

What a cast of suspects! There were so many. How could I juggle them all? Then I remembered Dawkins advice: *Relax, watch and wait. The targets will show themselves.* The target had been Alex. And now, these people were the targets of my investigation. I had to be patient. I was confident the killer was there. It was just a matter of giving him or her time to emerge. The voice in my head cried, *You don't have time!* Lorraine would soon face a grand jury.

She was dealing with worry and grief. I could offer her comfort now, but the only true source of relief was identifying the killer. Dawkins was right. The target would show himself. Slip up. Make a mistake. I'd point it out to Detective Ingram so the process could grind the killer into dust.

I sat up with a jolt. *Wow! What nasty words. The American legal system didn't grind people into dust.* But the vindictive part of me wanted it to do just that. This killer had inflicted more than death on Alex. He had hurt Lorraine and that brought out the angry warrior in me.

"Simon, I think I'd better lay off the coffee." I refilled his water bowl, walked off the cramp in my leg and considered my door of suspects. Dr. Phillips, the librarian, was at the meeting, but I couldn't see him hotfooting around the property shooting people. What about the Nervous Nellie who drove him to the meeting? If someone handed her a gun, she would probably freeze like a statue or drop it on her foot. No, they were not likely suspects.

Who else?

A little wave of cold moved over my skin. Ryan. He loved the natural beauty of the Shore. He knew how to use a shotgun. He went out to help thin the deer population so they could survive. I closed my eyes, wishing this would all go away. I added another heart magnet. It made me ache to see the magnets representing people I cared about under suspicion.

Who else?

And, to be fair, there was one more that I had to add. A magnet to represent Dawkins. He had materialized near the dock when Lorraine emerged from the boathouse with the gun in her hand. His ability to silently appear always made me a little uneasy. He'd gotten to Lorraine so quickly. Where did he come from? Or did he just teleport in as usual? I pawed through the magnet box. There were several I could use: a broom, a napkin, a tray. They were appropriate symbols of his profession, but they really didn't capture the essence of the man. And then I saw it: a flying saucer. I broke out laughing. It was perfect. I hadn't known a lot of butlers in my life. I certainly didn't grow up with one, but there was something about Dawkins that didn't fit the stereotype. Maybe I was being unfair. Reluctantly, I put the little spaceship back in the box and snapped the broom magnet in its place.

I had work to do to sort through this crowd and find the real killer.

SNOWY EGRET

The name for this white graceful bird is drawn from the French word *aigrette* meaning little heron. Her yellow feet have earned her the nickname "Bird with the Yellow Slippers." While standing on one leg on the shoreline, she might trail a golden foot in the water to make lazy circles attracting her next meal.

Though a pair is mated, they do not recognize each other away from the nest. To avoid being attacked, the returning egret must perform an elaborate greeting ritual every time it goes home.

The white feathers of the Snowy Egret were highly prized by ladies of fashion in the late 19th Century. The coveted white plumes sold at a price of about $32 per ounce (almost $800 today) which was more than 125% of the price of gold at the time. Market demand almost drove this bird to extinction.

CHAPTER 10

The Assay Master presides over the testing of silver to determine the purity of a piece. Learn the assay office marks, such as the Lion for the London office and the Crown that marks Sheffield silver. Also be able to identify assay marks and the hallmarks of silversmiths.

"The Butler's Guide to Fine Silver"
Mr. Hollister, 1898

MY PHONE BUZZED and danced across the nightstand with some message. I just wanted to sleep. When my hand shot out to save it from crashing to the floor, the sunshine burned through my eyelids and shook my brain awake. Moments later, Simon flew off the bed and raced down the steps, barking like a maniac. There was no escape. I had to get up.

Somebody was pounding on my kitchen door. It was Dawkins. When I threw it open, words like *why can't you let me sleep?* and *Where's the fire?* stuck in my throat. He looked awful. His eyes were bloodshot and the lines on his face looked like a sculptor had carved them into his pasty skin.

"What's wrong?" I cried. "What's happened?" I wanted to grab the man by his lapels and shake him. Instead he made my world go haywire.

"Miss Abigail." His voice was like sandpaper rubbing against my ears. "I'm sorry to bother you, but the silver appraiser from New York is sitting in the living room. I've given him coffee. He spied the main piece of interest on the dining room table and is eager to begin. You might want to hurry."

Oh, if only I could sink into the floor and disappear. "I completely forgot."

"A murder in your own home will do that." A spark of Dawkins's wry humor was still alive.

"Stall him. I'll be right there." And I raced up the stairs to throw on some clothes.

Nerves – and a murder – had wiped his arrival from my brain. As curator of Lorraine's silver collection—pieces she'd inherited, collected and found in the attic—I'd declared the stately epergne was a major piece. My research suggested that it was an excellent example of silver from the Victorian Era and worthy of a museum's attention. Also, I feared the piece was seriously underinsured. Lorraine contacted a major antique auction house in New York and arranged for the appraiser to come. This was the first time I'd gone out on a limb about a piece of silver.

And now the moment of truth had arrived as I walked toward the living room and heard the man's deep, cultured voice declare quite specifically, "No, I do not care for yet another cup of coffee. I have had an elegant sufficiency, thank you. I arrive on time for my appointments. I don't appreciate—"

I plastered a broad smile on my face and walked in to face the man who could validate my find. "And you were right on time. I must apologize, I am the tardy one."

I almost giggled when I saw the man Central Casting would have sent as the perfect sophisticated, pompous art expert. He was a little shorter than most men and stood perfectly erect to make up for it. His flowing silver hair stopped just above his collar. His navy-blue suit, crisp white shirt and conservative blue and burgundy tie looked more appropriate for a chamber music recital than a trip to the Eastern Shore. But he was an authority on silver and had earned the right to look the part, even if it was uncomfortable.

He rose from the velvet-covered sofa holding a pale brown leather case that looked as soft as melting butter. "You can't be Mrs. Anderson." He shifted the case to his right hand so it wasn't free to greet me formally.

"No, I'm sorry. Mrs. Anderson is not available."

He raised his nose a little. "I normally meet with the owner of a silver piece I am appraising."

"My name is Abigail Strickland, in charge of her silver collections. I spoke with your assistant…?" He didn't react so I gave up trying to establish my credentials with him. "I'm delighted to meet you." I extended my hand, hoping to hide my annoyance at his snooty attitude. I needed his opinion more than his friendship. Reluctantly, he shifted his case and we shook hands. "I'm afraid we had an incident here last night that disrupted everyone's schedule. You have my deepest apologies. May I call you…?"

"Mr. Fuller."

Ah, so that was the way things would be. I too raised my chin a little to assume a more formal attitude and held out my right arm in a gesture towards the dining room. "May I show you the main piece that has brought you here?"

As we approached the piece, Mr. Fuller stopped and stared at the Murray Family Epergne, originally owned by Lorraine's mother. Almost two feet tall, it was an architectural achievement designed to be both the focal point of any gathering at the dining table and to serve several functions. For the sweet course of a formal meal, guests could help themselves to sugar-covered nuts, bonbons, and fruits from the small baskets hanging from ornate arms placed in multiple tiers on the center section. At the top of this epergne was a tall vase filled with Peace roses that were now limp from lack of water.

Seeing Mr. Fuller's look of intense interest that I read as appreciation, I felt a little rush of pride. No, I didn't own the piece, but it was my responsibility to see it was properly maintained and protected. My extensive research, comparing it to silver pieces at the Baltimore Museum of Art and other museum collections in Philadelphia and New York, had brought an important appraiser to Fair Winds.

"This piece has been in Mrs. Anderson's family for several generations. I suspect it dates back to the mid-1800's when the epergne was so popular." I was a little embarrassed to strut my knowledge in front of Mr. Fuller, but not enough to hide my satisfaction that my work was now paying off. "When my research suggested that the value of the piece was over $200,000, well, you can imagine, I thought we should get the opinion of an international expert like yourself."

The lines on his forehead deepened as he scowled. "Mr. Fuller? Is something wrong?" I asked hesitantly.

He didn't respond. Instead his fleshy lips disappeared under his ample silver mustache. He gave off a vibe of suspicion and disappointment. Had I made a mistake? No, I had done my due diligence. I took a step forward, but his hand shot out to stop me.

He turned to Dawkins who was standing silently to the side, ready to serve. "Would you move the piece down to this end of the table so I may inspect it?" It was more an order than a question.

Dawkins complied while Mr. Fuller placed his leather case on the highly-polished dining table. He opened it to reveal a well-organized set of tools of his trade. He took out a jeweler's loop to magnify tiny details and began a meticulous inspection of the piece. The silence was brittle, interrupted only by the man huffing a breath on the silver, which looked rude.

I just stood by and did nothing. I wanted to make this come out right for Lorraine, especially after everything that happened last night. I started to babble about the history of this epergne. Would it make a difference in his opinion of it? I hoped so.

"As I said, this epergne has been in Mrs. Anderson's family for well over a century. It was a wedding gift to her great-grandmother and is part of the Murray Silver Collection. If it is museum quality, as we suspect, Mrs. Anderson and I agree that it might be worthy of a donation to a fine collection. I believe it can be traced to the silversmith Thomas Pitts who was so famous for designing epergnes. I think you'll find his hallmark right—" I started to point.

The disapproving look on Mr. Fuller's face, in effect, slapped my hand away. Strange sounds were muffled by his moustache. He calmly returned his loupe to its place and closed the case. He cleared his throat and said in a superior tone, "I would understand and forgive the owner of such a piece making such a grievous mistake, but you..." Disdain dripped from the last word. Arrogantly, he looked down his nose at me. "You, a person who presents herself as an expert in silver, *you* should never have made such an egregious error."

I was stunned. "What do you mean?"

As if barely tolerating a question from an annoying child, he clasped his hands at his waist and sighed. "Where shall I begin?" With growing irritation, he raised his eyes to the ceiling. "Alright, you need information—correct information—so you can report to Mrs. Anderson..." He lowered his voice a little in disapproval. "who couldn't make time to meet with me personally. Let's begin with the hallmark you believe is associated with Thomas Pitts. It appears only on the base. It must appear on every part of the piece." He squinted at me. "You should know that. The hallmark must be on every piece that can be removed from the epergne." With that pronouncement, his nose wrinkled a little as he removed each basket of fine open-work, each caster, everything that could be taken away that added to the epergne's charm.

"*Your* job," he said with a sniff. "Your job was to inspect these hallmarks. If you had done your job, you would have seen that none of the hallmarks match it." He shrugged a shoulder as if to dismiss me. "I lost count at three or four different hallmarks. To be a genuine silver epergne, every…" The appraiser repeated the word in a high and mighty tone. "…*every* piece must be marked with the same hallmark. Even a beginner knows that."

I couldn't look at Dawkins, a witness to my humiliation. There was nothing I could do. My feet felt like they were nailed to the floor. I had to take this verbal flogging.

"Not only that," Mr. Fuller continued with great condescension. "You should have checked the construction of the piece itself." He leaned close and huffed a breath against the silver. "You do know how to frost the surface, don't you?" Numb, I shook my head. "Silver is generally cooler than human breath. By breathing on it at the place where the pieces were soldered together, the joining becomes apparent through the resulting condensation."

With a tight smile, he pointed to a place on the main column where a bracket was attached to hold a basket. Even without a loupe, I could see the rough connection and slight discoloration caused by the warmth of his breath, probably the only warm thing about him.

"You can see the joint only because the silver foil someone used to disguise it, rubbed off. Look here." He pointed to another joint where the foil was flaking off. "Any person who is knowledgeable about silver knows that silver becomes discolored when heat is applied. Someone tried to hide it and did a terrible job. You should have seen it."

And with that declaration, he shot his cuffs with flair and announced, "My work here is done. I trust that you will convey my findings to Mrs. Anderson."

I was dismissed.

"And now I will drive back over that awful bridge and catch the next train to the City." He meant, of course, New York, the only *city* that deserved the title.

I wanted to smack that supercilious grin off his face. It's what he deserved, this Mr. Fuller, the man so *full* of himself. But he turned and Dawkins escorted him to the door. That lame joke about his name almost brought a smile to my face as I stood staring at what I'd thought was a magnificent example of fine silver. I couldn't take a snide comment from Dawkins, the always-perfect butler. Not after the events of last night and almost no sleep.

He must have read my mind. "Miss Abigail, why don't you take some scones back to the cottage and get some rest. You'll find them cooling on the counter under a tea towel." And he slipped from the room.

Exhausted, I followed his instructions with gratitude.

I slept until the afternoon sun nudged me awake. I never closed the curtains on the west side of the cottage, because I was usually working or running around or sitting on the porch. But this day was different. Lack of sleep and the stress of seeing someone shot to death right in front of my eyes made it that way. At least, my sleep was restful, not troubled with terrifying images of a sailboat capsizing and tendrils of blood in the water. No, it was time to forget what had happened during the Governor's Cup Race. That disaster showed me that action was the best antidote for upset.

I swung my feet to the floor and Simon burst into a dance of "I'm so happy you're awake! Let's play!" And we played. He chased his ball around while I figured out what to do with the rest of the day. When he got stuck under the bed groping for the ball, I knew the time had come to accept that Simon was no longer a puppy and the area under the bed was now off-limits. So many things were changing. A little distance and some yummy comfort food at the Cove were just what I needed.

After my shower, Simon insisted on playing Tug of War with the towel. My firm *NO!* only energized him. It was my fault. I needed to stay on top of his training, but not right now. His place was in the kennel with the other dogs for companionship. On my way to the car, I spotted Lorraine through the breakfast room window, alone and looking forlorn. I couldn't walk away and leave her like that so I went inside and plopped down on a chair at the table.

"I don't know what's gotten into Simon. He's running riot. Barely listens to a word I say. And when I finally get him to pay attention to me, he cocks his head in that way he does..." I demonstrated the universal cute move that every puppy is born knowing how to do. "... and my heart melts. He's such a sweetie."

"A sweetie that can get out of control."

And that was it. Normally, the topic of dog training energized her. On such a pretty day, she would have rushed outside, called her dogs and put them through their tricks, all the while teaching me, training me. Instead she slumped in her chair with a sigh.

Dawkins saw it, too, as he stood silently in the doorway, his eyebrows knitted together with concern.

"At least there's something positive you can do about it." She raised her eyes that were becoming wet with unshed tears. "I have to prove I didn't do something. It's hard to prove a negative."

"Hard? Almost impossible."

"Why is that?" she asked in almost a childlike voice.

It was a big jump for me to go from wanting comfort food for lunch to the deep philosophical question of proving a negative. An echo of a college discussion drifted up out of the fog in my brain.

"If I remember correctly, it has to do with the burden of proof. Somebody says he didn't do something, but the best way to prove it is to show who did it."

And with that statement, I broke a promise I'd made to myself. After the terrifying and sad events connected to the Governor's Cup Sailboat Race, I'd resolved to stay away from anything out of the ordinary, any crime and certainly miles away from any murder. No, no more investigations. Maybe Detective Ingram and I would exchange holiday cards, but that was all.

But that was before murder invaded our home at Fair Winds, when someone hid in darkness and fired a bullet. This time, it struck too close. Grief haunted her. Anxiety consumed my friend.

Her daydreams were becoming nightmares. Desperately needed rest was elusive. Until the person, that coward who held that gun, was identified and in the hands of the detective, I knew what I had to do. Lorraine realized it, too, as fear sparked in those deep blue eyes. I didn't wait to have a discussion. I left for St. Michaels to see what I could find out.

CHAPTER 11

Unique silver serving pieces are designed for specific foods. For example, the Fried Oyster Lifter should only be used to serve this delicacy.

"The Butler's Guide to Fine Silver"
Mr. Hollister, 1898

I NEEDED COMFORT FOOD. And the place to get it was the Cove. I only wanted to slip into town, sit at the counter of the little restaurant at the back of the drug store, eat in peace and slip out again with no one really noticing.

As I headed to my Saab, I saw Alex's black Range Rover with his vanity plate, *Build*. I remembered how delighted he was when he drove it to Fair Winds to show off his new Velar First Edition. Lorraine almost swooned when she took her first ride with him. She said the interior screamed luxury: soft leather seats with a massage system built in and screens that reminded her of the Starship Enterprise. It was sitting just where Alex had parked it. No one had claimed it yet. I wondered...

I didn't want anyone to notice me around the car, but trying to tiptoe on the gravel was impossibly loud. The crunching noise reverberated in my ears. Surely, everyone heard it. I tiptoed faster. The doors were locked. I shaded my eyes and looked through the window. Did I really think I'd see something inside that might point to a killer? I started to walk away when I noticed a small piece of paper on the ground. It looked like a business card that might have fallen out of the car.

Xavier Pendergast
Attorney at Law
Specializing in Corporate Issues

Maybe it was Alex's attorney. Maybe not. I slipped it into my pocket to figure out later what possible significance it could have and went to my car. I needed to blow away the cobwebs in my head, so I put the top down on my Saab and I headed to St. Michaels.

It was during the Fall Into St. Michaels Festival when I'd made my first visit to this quaint town with charm, history and breathtaking vistas around almost every corner. Many visitors fall in love with it, but I had a special tour guide: Lorraine. She was born here, spent her childhood on her daddy's land and had a deep love for the Shore. Though she was educated in fine schools and traveled extensively, she always came home. During my first visit, she shared tidbits of folklore and historical events of the town as well as those of her family. Her father was a native son of the Eastern Shore, but had fallen desperately in love with a young debutante while attending a ball on the Western Shore. He'd captured her heart, then had to engage her imagination about the wonderful life and family she could have here as his wife. Once they'd overcome her family's patronizing attitude about the Shore, they'd married and her heart never regretted it.

Lorraine and her husband also set down deep roots here. This was the family's center. When Lorraine's younger sister died tragically, leaving a little boy, the family embraced him and raised him as the son they never had. Grown and eager to make his mark in business anywhere but the Shore, Reggie moved to Washington and started chasing his dream of owning a successful dotcom and software company. That's when I'd met him. His ideas were infectious. He was a born entrepreneur and I got caught up in his dreams. And then…

Those were memories that were best left in the past. Fortunately, the lunch rush at the Cove had come and gone so I didn't have to face well-meaning locals, eager for details about what had happened to Alex and the latest about Lorraine, now a murder suspect. As I sidled onto a stool at the counter, the waitress, Patti-with-an-I, according to her name badge, swooped up on the other side of the counter with the ever-present coffee pot.

"Hey, stranger," she said, as she filled a mug with the steamy brew.

"Hey, yourself! I haven't seen you in ages."

Patti cocked her hip in feigned exasperation. "That's not my fault. I've been here. Ha, where else would I be? You're the one who's been A-W-O-L." She said each letter with great emphasis.

I watched this woman with red hair and a cocky attitude to go with it put down the coffee and pick up her order book. She was the daughter of the cook, who was the granddaughter of the cook who started working at the Cove when she was 18. It was *the* place to come for light, flavorful pancakes soaked in warm maple syrup and that's why I had come.

Patti came back, licking her finger, to turn over a new page for my order. "You picked the right day to show up. Mom made a pot of lima bean soup with fresh limas from the farm this morning. It's an Eastern Shore delicacy, you know."

"And delicious." The raspy voice came from the woman on the other side of the U-shaped counter. When she looked up, I recognized her from Alex's meeting at Fair Winds, the night someone killed him. She wore the same fishing hat over her gray grizzled hair. Her lashes were short and stubby, but her eyes twinkled as if she knew a secret that she wouldn't share with just anyone. She had on a prim flowered-print that reminded me of the Villager dresses from the sixties and seventies I'd seen in the vintage stores. I wondered if the woman had on her black army boots laced up to her ankle. Not the normal choice of footwear when one is wearing a dress unless you're a hip teenager in London or on the runway in New York during Fashion Week. I suspected that her boots were not a fashion statement, but utilitarian.

"Lima beans?" I said hesitantly. "I'm afraid they aren't one of my favorites. I think I'll have—"

"You don't know what you're missing," said the woman in the fishing hat. "But that's okay. There'll be more for those of us who will appreciate it. Give my thanks to Miss Annie, will you, Patti?"

"Will do, Miss Mary Rose. It will really mean something to her coming from you."

As I ordered, I sneaked a peek at the woman, Miss Mary Rose, as she walked to the front of the store to pay her bill, clomping along in her scuffed black leather boots.

When Patti set my place, I leaned forward and asked quietly, "Who is that woman?"

Patti shot me a confused look. "Oh, you mean Miss Mary Rose?" And chuckled. "She's a little odd, I guess, but her roots run deep here. I think she's been here since the beginning, since there ever was a Bay. I'd swear the water of the Miles River runs in her veins instead of blood."

While Patti disappeared into the kitchen, my eyes wandered to the front of the store, curious to see if the woman in question was still there when there was a rush of breath that tickled my ear. That raspy voice spoke softly, the one that had gently scolded me for not eating the soup.

"If you want to know somebody, it's courteous to ask the person directly."

It was Mary Rose. She'd caught. I could feel the heat of a blush climbing up my cheeks. "Why should you listen to tittle-tattle, when you only have to ask the genuine article who is right here?"

I turned my head slowly, not sure what to say.

"We should have a nice chat. Come to my home tomorrow afternoon for High Tea, say four o'clock? We'll have a fine tea, not this swill they call coffee." She wrinkled her nose. "I have something you may find intriguing."

Did she know something about the murder? I shifted my body so I could question her, but she had an iron grip on the back of my seat so I couldn't swivel. "You are interested in silver, aren't you?"

I was so preoccupied with the murder that my primary job wasn't the first thing that came to mind. "Yes, of course. I—"

"Then come at four. Cross the St. Michaels River Bridge, take the first left to the end of the lane down toward the water. You'll see it…Willow Cottage."

Patti came up to the counter, watching Mary Rose slip away, and started drying the dry countertop. "She sure is a strange bird, isn't she? How do you know her?"

I shrugged. "I don't. She was at Fair Winds the night…"

Patti stopped all movement. "You mean she was there the night that man was shot dead?"

I cringed a little at hearing it stated so bluntly. "Yes, there were a lot of people there. That's what is making the job so hard for the police."

Patti's hand rubbed the cloth in tight circles on the counter again as her gossipy brain clicked into gear. "It's like what happened at the yacht club after that accident with the log canoe. My girlfriend works there and she told me that it was organized chaos. It didn't look like the police knew what to do first." She paused. "But I guess they did since it all worked out in the end." She put her hand on her hip. "My girlfriend makes better tips than I do, but they make her work till all hours, like that night. She didn't get home 'til three AM! I don't want to work that hard. I've got a life, you know."

She looked over her shoulder as if a silent bell had rung. "Your order's up." And sure enough, the plate holding my comfort food appeared from the kitchen.

She put the plate in front of me and I dove into it while she rambled from one subject to another. Fortunately for my digestion, she talked about people I didn't know so I only had to nod occasionally until another customer showed up.

I was lost in the pleasure of the wonderful flavors when Patti reappeared. "Did you see the newspaper?"

"No, and I don't think I want to see it. I came here to get away from all the turmoil, but thanks anyway."

She put the thin newspaper on the counter and started rifling through it. "I'm not talking about the article with all the gory details about the murder." She folded back the A section to the editorial page. "No, I'm talking about this." She pointed to the op-ed page, known because it was *opposite* the editorial page.

I took the paper and read. Jacob, the environmentalist, had written an opinion piece. It mirrored his attack on Alex with sentences like *Problems with the Chesapeake Bay caused by the debris fields are created by people like the developer of Chesapeake Haven.* It repeated his threat that until the developer answered important questions to everyone's satisfaction, *I guarantee the land defiler will meet a wall of resistance, a wall that will not yield.*

"Was this guy at the meeting?" Patti asked.

"He certainly was. He stood up and talked. At first, he sounded like he was just talking casually, but he must have prepared very carefully. This is what he said at the meeting, almost word for word."

I checked the date on the paper and was surprised to see his letter was printed the day *before* the meeting. Jacob had come with the adoring wife, as Gran liked to say, *loaded for bear.*

Patti wiped the already clean counter, a tactic I suspected she used while fishing for gossip. "From where I'm reading it, he doesn't sound casual. There's vinegar in those words."

"Do you know him?"

"Know him?" She turned up her nose. "No, not my type, hippie-looking and all. But he does come in here."

That surprised me a little bit. "Really?"

"Yes, really, but it's not for our cooking. You know we cook for the local crowd who loves their scrapple and butter and eggs."

She was right about that. I loved coming in for the company and the food, but I had to tiptoe around the menu choices to protect my arteries and waistline.

"He likes to come in for our ice cream. Cherry Vanilla is his favorite and you can't get that just anywhere."

I leaned closer. "What do you know about him?"

Her eyes narrowed and her voice tightened. "He cost me a friend. He came out here from the West Coast and married a local girl."

"Your friend?"

She nodded. "Maddie and I were close growing up. Our dads were best friends. Neither one of them had a son so they'd take us girls out with them to do things like we were boys."

"What did you do?"

"Around here, it means pulling crabs and hunting. One Christmas, Maddie and I both got shotguns, the ones scaled down for kids. It was fun in a crazy sort of way, but it all stopped when we were about thirteen. I was turning into a girlie-girl and Maddie's dad remarried and got himself a stepson. After that, the men did men-things together with the teenager." Patti made a face and rolled her eyes.

"Then what happened?" I asked.

"You know, the normal stuff. Maddie and I both got boy-crazy and somehow graduated from high school. Maddie got a job with one of the local non-profits and one day she called to tell me that her perfect guy walked into the office that day."

"It was Jacob?"

Patti's lower lip jutted out as she nodded sadly, still polishing the same spot on the counter. "After that, I didn't see her much. She was blinded by his brilliance or something. He looks like a hippie from the sixties to me. Born too late, I guess, but he's well educated. Speaks nice. Wowed her family and she liked the attention she hadn't got from her dad for a long time." She frowned. "I don't think he's into hippie stuff, like drugs or stuff like that."

"Why do you say that?" I asked.

"He always makes sense when he talks even though it's usually over my head. But he's never tipsy or out of it."

"Anything else?"

She folded her towel and shrugged. "He goes on and on about missing California—San Francisco, I think. Likes to talk about…" Patti raised her hands and made quotation marks in the air. "The environmental movement. He wants to make his mark, he says." She shook her head. "I don't get all that stuff about global warming and save the zebra something."

"What about the islands in the Chesapeake that are disappearing?"

She gave me a straight look. "It's terrible. I really feel for those people, but why it's happening, I don't know. It's way over my head." She picked up the cloth and put it next to the sink. "I'll make you some fresh coffee." And she disappeared into the kitchen.

I read through Jacob's article again. There was enough in it to keep Jacob on my door of suspects. No one would see that, but Ingram should see this letter. I sent him a text with a link to the paper's website. Then another thought hit me. I was right to add adoring Maddie to the door. According to Patti, she grew up hunting with her dad and knows her way around a shotgun. Could Jacob have talked her into taking a warning shot to scare off that big, bad developer? And then she got lucky and hit Alex dead center in the chest? I decided to keep that thought to myself for now.

The coffee was hot and fresh, so I treated myself to one more cup. The locals might like their fat and calories, but good coffee was a must for any restaurant on the Shore, if they wanted to keep the local trade coming in over the winter. I was savoring the flavor when my ears caught the word *hurricane* coming from people talking on the other side of a display case.

"...named the hurricane now. Zelma, I think it's kind of strange. Is that even a name?" A woman said with a Baltimore accent.

"Maybe they meant Selma?"

"Nope, it's Zelma with a Z. You know they used to always give the storms a woman's name? Finally, they started switching back and forth so we didn't always get the blame. Storms like Andrew devastated South Florida. A lot of my customers winter down there. Some of them got hurt really bad. At least that storm had a man's name."

"I don't think there's anything to worry about. Hurricanes don't hit St. Michaels." The woman was starting to cancel out the positive effects of my comfort food.

"Oh yeah? What about Isabel? She did some damage to the town, what with the flooding and all."

Great, my little respite was undone. Concern about the murder now had concern about a bad storm for company. I asked for my check.

CHAPTER 12

The Shell is an elegant design found at the terminal or end of the handle. Silversmiths sometimes combine it with the thread or bead border in their designs.

"The Butler's Guide to Fine Silver"
Mr. Hollister, 1898

I'D COME to the village of St. Michaels looking for a little relief from the tension at Fair Winds. And I'd found it. The comfort food at the Cove performed its magic again. I felt refreshed and stronger. Outside, the churning movement of the tourists swept me up. They hustled along the sidewalks, jostled people in their way, darted between the cars backed up by sheer volume. They only had eyes for the many different stores and restaurants along the main street and what they offered. It was almost Labor Day. The pace and hassles of normal life were about to ramp up, without the respite of summer fun. Desperate to milk these last days for all the distractions and purchases possible, they focused on dashing around. It all reminded me that I too had an urgent errand: find a killer.

Eager to get to my car, I walked around the corner and bumped into two people who were part of the nightmare: Alex's business partner, Allen and his ex-wife, Arabella. Or maybe this was an opportunity.

"Wait, you're that girl from Fair Winds, aren't you?" He squinted at me, not quite sure he'd made the right connection.

Arabella let out a theatrical sigh in exasperation. "Allen, I want to go."

He grabbed her elbow and held her in place. Seeing his interest in me, Arabella put me under her microscope and ran her eyes over me from my broken-in suede boat shoes to curly auburn hair. With a quiet sniff, she stared over my shoulder, probably at nothing. Two could play this game so, I did the same. The bright turquoise of her sundress would have brought out her eyes if they weren't hidden behind huge black sunglasses under a wide-brimmed straw hat. If she didn't want to enjoy the sunny weather, why did she go outside? On her feet, she wore espadrilles with a skyscraper heel that would cripple a normal person. But they were totally out of place here on the Shore where casual elegance and comfort ruled. Yes, she had definitely come over the Bay Bridge from the Western Shore, from another world to invade ours.

The partner interrupted our little girl game. "You are…?"

"Abby Strickland."

"Allen Barclay," he said with enthusiasm as he offered his hand. Did he think we would be best buddies? "I'm afraid we didn't have time to talk…" At least, he had the decency to lose the exuberance and drop his tone. "…after what happened. Terrible thing. I keep wondering if we hadn't been late…" His eyes flicked over at Arabella for a split second.

Arabella did a double-take then turned on him. "Oh, no…" Her voice went right up the scale with a warning. You're not going to blame me for—"

"No," he said carefully. He tried to ignore her, but she wouldn't evaporate. "I was just wondering if it would have made a difference."

She turned her head away so quickly, her long sheet of hair threatened to slap him in the face. I couldn't care. I was hung up on his comment that if they hadn't been late, would Alex have been sitting alone on the terrace? Would he have felt the need to retreat if things had been calm… if this man hadn't brought Alex's ex-wife who made things so tense? If they hadn't come at all, would Alex still be alive? Or maybe everything had happened according to plan? This business partner would get no comfort from me, especially if he could be the killer. "I really couldn't tell you, Mr. Barclay."

The way his shoulders hunched over, I wondered if he had read my mind. The lips of the ex-wife tightened a little, but that was the only reaction I could see.

"Mr. Barclay—"

"Allen. Please."

Now, he wanted to be best buddies. I didn't relish the idea, but I'd go along if it got me the answers I wanted. "Okay, Allen. You worked closely with Alex…."

"Yes, I did. In fact, some of our clients thought we were brothers. They always saw us together or I was always talking about something he'd said or vice versa. In fact, we were together so much, they'd get us confused." I looked at him, not understanding. "You know, Alex … Allen. Our names both start with an A. And we're both good-looking." He chuckled, but his little joke fell flat.

"Did he have any enemies?" I asked.

That question made his eyes go wide. "E-e-nemies? No! Everybody loved Alex. He was the kindest, gentlest man alive."

Arabella, who was listening to our every word, cocked her head a little toward Allen. I wished she would take off those big sunglasses so I could better read her reactions. But no such luck. Being this close to Arabella made me uncomfortable, like I was being eyed for dinner by a hungry cat. Bored, she looked away again and I relaxed a little.

"And he was always fair in business," Allen added.

"I'm sure he was, but sometimes people—"

"No, he was good. Always. I should know. I was his partner. I know you're trying to help, but enemies?" He shook his head.

Ever the salesman, he reached into his shirt pocket and took out a business card. "If there's anything I can do for you or your friend Lorraine, please don't hesitate to call me." He was calmer now, more comfortable doing what came naturally. "This is my card." He pointed to his name. "Allen Barclay. Allen, spelled the old English way. Barclay, of course, is an old English name so they go together."

"Yes, I know it. Are you related to Barclay's, the financial institution?"

"Ah, no, not directly," he stammered. "But I want you to know I'm here for you." He was about to hand me the card when he pulled it back, took out a pen and scribbled on it. Then he held it out so I could take it. "I wrote my cell phone number on the back." Call on me anytime."

Impatient, Arabella groaned softly. Finally, we could agree on something as I stifled a groan of my own. He acted as if I'd call him a friend. Not likely.

"Thank you, Allen." I slipped the card in my pocket, remembering too late that the ink might not be dry. Curious, I asked, "What are you two still doing in town?"

"We didn't want to miss an opportunity to have some absolutely fresh steamed crabs over at the Crab Claw. Do you know that you can see the watermen bring their bushels of fresh-caught crabs right up to the dock? The kitchen help plops them straight into the steam pots. I bet you could hear them screaming if you were there."

Arabella slapped his arm. "Stop it, Allen. Don't be vulgar."

"Oh, come on, you have to admit the crabmeat was succulent." Coming out of his mouth, *succulent* turned into something desiccated and disgusting. Yes, I knew the restaurant, Lorraine's favorite place for steamed crabs. It shouldn't have to serve these people. Why didn't they cross the bridge and get out of our lives?

Arabella was pouting. "I can't understand why you like getting your hands all dirty with that gunk on the shells. You'd think they'd clean the crabs and wash it off."

I bit my tongue. I didn't have to say anything, because Allen schooled her as he rolled his eyes. "Arabella, that's not gunk on the crabs. It's Old Bay Seasoning. It's traditional."

She shrugged one shoulder, dismissing his comment. "I don't understand why they season the shell. You don't eat that part, after all. And now you smell all fishy."

I couldn't stop myself from asking her, "Where do you prefer to have lunch?"

Her full lips lost their pout as she gave my question serious consideration. "The Inn at Perry Cabin, I think. Yes, I prefer white linen and fine table service instead of having Ellie Mae from the Beverly Hillbillies slinging crabs." She touched his hand. "Allen, do you think we could go there next time? I'm sure they have crab in some form on the menu."

I was ready to run away screaming to my car, but there still might be something to learn here. "Is that the only reason you're still here, crabs?" I said.

"Well, no." He shifted his feet as if to make a monumental announcement. "Actually, I've decided to go ahead with the *Chesapeake Haven* project." Quickly, he added, "In Alex's memory. It seems only fitting."

Fitting to make a boatload of money, I thought.

"There's still a lot of work to do," Arabella chimed in. "I'm helping Allen arrange another meeting with the locals to drum up support."

In horror, I looked at her, then at Allen. "At Fair Winds?"

"Oh no," she dismissed the idea. "We need a more appropriate place."

"Arabella!" Allen threw her a stern look then turned to me, his face filled with concern. "We wouldn't want to bother Lorraine with all the trouble and problems she's facing."

His familiar use of her name made my skin crawl. And I thought, *she wouldn't want to bother* with *you at all*, but kept the comment to myself.

Arabella smoothed her long jet-black hair and it rippled over her soft shoulder. "I don't know why we're wasting time with those backwater tree huggers. We own the land. We should be able to do with it what we want."

This seemed like as good a time as any to ask a question that was bugging me. I took a step back to give Allen lots of space—a trick I'd seen Ingram use so the suspect wouldn't feel threatened and might let a helpful piece of information slip out.

Trying to sound casual, I asked, "Do you know a Xavier Pendergast?"

Allen slipped his right hand into his pocket and looked up at the air above my head, thinking. "No," he said slowly. "I don't believe I do."

I got the crazy impression that he had shaken hands with the man at some point and didn't want to admit it.

His eyes dropped to my face. "Why do you ask?"

I gave him what felt like a tight, awkward smile. "Oh, somebody mentioned his name, that he has an office in Bethesda, close to Alex's offices. Your offices are there, too, aren't they? You two work ... worked closely together, didn't you?"

"Yes, we did." He raised his chin a little in a defensive move. "As a matter of fact, controlling interest of *Chesapeake Haven* comes to me. That's why this big meeting—"

With no warning, a woman with a head of tight white curls barreled into the center of our little group. Harriet, the local busybody, planted herself directly in front of me. "Oh, Abby," she wailed. It's so good to see you're alright." She ignored the develop-duo and started babbling. "That was quite an event I read about in the newspaper. We would have been there, if we had known."

Or been invited, I added silently. I glanced at Harriet's long-suffering husband Ben, standing on the periphery as usual.

Her face dropped into an exaggerated poor-baby expression. "But then we would have been there for such an awful... awful..." She couldn't seem to find the word so she moved right along to make her point. "But you know these activists. They get so excited sometimes that these things get out of control. Why, I hear they take over ships and even tie themselves to trees. Horrible people." She shrugged her skinny shoulders. "Anyway, I'm so sorry."

Why should I be the only one to suffer this woman's silly attention and her asinine comments? I should share the experience. "Harriet, I'd like you to meet the partner of the man who was killed."

Allen jumped in immediately. "I'm Allen Barclay." He flashed her a big smile, filled with blindingly white teeth. He introduced Arabella who looked away with a stony expression on her face. She could have been on a postage stamp celebrating boredom.

While Harriet prattled on, Arabella mentally escaped to another time and place and I had a chance to study her. I'd seen her before—not *her* but women like her—on summer and fall weekends, walking the streets of St. Michaels with her arm tucked snugly into the crook of a man's arm. He could be any age, but his persona said money. Arabella's sisters looked like they'd stepped out of some high fashion magazine wearing a well-constructed sundress or palazzo pants with wide, flappy legs. They paired their outfits with high-heeled shoes that threatened to twist an ankle on the uneven brick sidewalks. What did Alex ever see in this woman that they spent years together and raised a family? I suspected there was more here than what appeared on the surface.

Harriet's screechy voice penetrated my thoughts. "You poor man." She patted his arm and rolled her head sadly from side to side. "To lose a business colleague and a close friend..."

Harriet started to reach out to pat Arabella's arm. "You have our condolences, dear." But *Dear* pulled away just enough to avoid the old woman's touch.

Without even glancing in the direction of her husband, she said, "Doesn't she, Ben?" He nodded silently.

Harriet raised her chin to peer into Allen's eyes and said with conviction, "You're a good man, I can tell. To keep the victim's wife so close to you, to make sure she survives this terrible, terrible business."

As usual, Harriet got things all turned around. She would have had more fun if she knew the truth of the situation. I glanced at the man, wondering if he was going to burst out laughing. Instead, I saw something in this face. A slight tightening around his eyes, his eyebrows lowered. It was the look of a predator with his prey in sight. Suddenly, I felt protective of this nosy old lady. I waited, ready for Allen make his move.

He veiled his face in mock sadness. "Thank you, dear lady. You are very kind. You strike me as a sensitive person. I'm sure you'd like to help us make Alex's pet project a reality." He conjured up another business card, scribbled something on the back and handed it to Harriet. "Let this be my personal invitation to a meeting we're having soon. I hope you'll come."

Harriet absolutely glowed. "Oh, we'll be there, won't we dear?" she tittered as she turned to her husband. "Give him our card dear so that he can email us the time and place. See you soon." As she floated away on a cloud with Ben in tow, she muttered under her breath so I could hear. "Imagine that, his personal invitation."

It was a masterful performance. I was impressed at Allen Barclay's smooth moves in a sick sort of way. But the fact that these two were taking over Alex's dream project made me want to leave my lunch on the curb.

Arabella tugged on his arm, ever the aggravating spoiled child. "I want to go. I'm tired."

He patted her hand. "Thank you, Abby. See you soon." I swear he smirked as he walked her away. I wondered if I was looking at a murderer… or murderers.

I headed toward my car. Lots of crosswalks make it easy to navigate the main street in St. Michaels, as long as the drivers follow the rules. When a pedestrian stands at the curb, cars should stop. Cars *and* bikes, but some riders don't believe the rules apply to them. Just as I stepped down in front of the stopped cars, a fancy bike whizzed by me, so close I could feel the breeze. I stared at the fleeing rider, oblivious of the near collision. The neon green and orange stripes on the black spandex shirt stood out. I'd seen it before. The night of the meeting. Was it the same man who faced off with Dawkins about where to leave his bike? Could someone who ignored the rules on the street commit murder? The common denominator was arrogance. It could be a valuable observation or a ridiculous idea. I made a mental note to mention it to Ingram, just in case.

I threaded a path through the tourists, anxious to get back to my car and drive home. I almost lashed out when yet-another person bumped against me when I looked up to see Charlie's smiling face. A gentle port after a storm.

"Abby, you're brave to come to St. Michaels today. And it's my luck. Come and raise a glass with us at the St. Michaels Crab and Steak House." He nodded at two of his sailing buddies, being buffeted by the crowd. "We're going to watch the coverage of the hurricane building in the Atlantic and have a couple of Dark 'n Stormy's. Ya gotta come, Abby," Charlie urged.

I knew about the sailors love for a Dark 'n Stormy, a potent drink that combined a fine dark rum and a specific ginger beer. I'd also learned that even a weak version—in other words, not too dark—was enough to affect my ability to drive. I guess I'd never make a true sailor.

"I'm going to pass on the drink, Charlie, but I'll walk with you since my car is parked in that direction."

The big men made a great wedge and got us through the crowd to a side street in no time.

"Are you watching the storm, Abby?" Charlie asked.

"Isn't everybody?" one of his buddies chimed in.

"Yes, we're keeping an eye on it at Fair Winds. Dawkins thinks we'll be fine, but he's taking precautions. Always the Boy Scout, Be Prepared," I said with a laugh.

But Charlie wasn't laughing. "He's smart. This could be a bad one. Even so, it never hurts to have a lot of bottled water, packs of candles and batteries in the pantry. The forecasters should know more now that it's closer to the Gulf Stream. That's a game-changer."

"Why is that so important?" I had no idea. "There isn't a Gulf Stream along the West Coast."

"It's important in so many ways. When we race to Bermuda, it plays a crucial part in our calculations. It can move a slow boat to the lead or leave the leader dead in the water if the navigator makes the wrong call. And it can be the roughest part of the race. It can get so choppy that even seasoned sailors get violently seasick.

"The Gulf Stream moves like a warm river in the ocean without banks to contain it in one area." Charlie raised his hands to illustrate his lesson. "Down south around Florida, it can be as little as thirty miles wide while up here, it can be as much as eighty miles wide. It moves around all over the place. To find it, sailors put a wire or cord with a thermometer or sensor on the end to monitor any temperature change in the water."

"The water is that much warmer?" I asked.

"Oh yes, ocean temperatures rarely get over the low 70's. In the Gulf Stream, the temps can go over 80. When a storm hits, it sucks up all that thermal energy like a hungry man at a buffet."

I felt a little foolish since his buddies were nodding enthusiastically as Charlie explained the ocean phenomenon. "I had no idea. I'm from the West Coast. We really don't have hurricanes like you do."

One of the sailors with a windburned face jumped in. "That's right. There are only seven areas in the world that spawn hurricanes..."

"Or typhoons," the small guy in the back added.

Windburned face continued. "That's right and the eastern part of the Pacific Ocean around Seattle isn't one of them. It doesn't have the same kind of thermal energy to maintain or strengthen a hurricane. It's a true engine for severe storms."

"Sometimes, the only hope of preventing a strike," added one of Charlie's sailing buddies, "is a high-pressure system over land that holds off the storm and sends it back out to sea."

"That's why we're going to the Crab House to check on the storm's progress. Sure you won't come?" Charlie leaned forward a little, hopeful.

I was tempted. "Not this time, Charlie. I'd better get back. We're dealing with our own storm at Fair Winds."

Charlie's face fell. "That's right. I'm sorry, Abby. I'm an idiot. I forgot… got all caught up in the storm talk and—"

I reached out and touched his arm. "That's okay, Charlie. It's been a tough time for both of us. We'll have that drink another time."

"Promise?" The word spilled out all by itself. Honest reactions often did. He turned away, a little embarrassed.

"Absolutely," I said with more energy than I really had. "We'll do it after the storm passes.

"All the storms," added Charlie.

"It's a deal." I gave him a peck on the cheek and scooted off to my car, hoping neither the hurricane nor the murder investigation swamped our lives.

SEA NETTLES

As old as time, evidence of these creatures dates back to prehistoric times. Their soft, almost transparent bodies are almost 95% water. Sea Nettles have no brain, bones, heart or eyes, but they are attracted to light.

The umbrella-shaped dome undulates to move it around though it is usually cared by water currents. The dome shields graceful tentacles that trail below to attract and sting its prey. If a human comes in contact with a tentacle, the sting causes a rash, even if the sea nettle is out of the water.

Sea Nettles are phosphorescent. When the water around them is churned up by a boat propeller, they will glow in the dark, which is why they are sometimes mistaken for ghosts.

CHAPTER 13

The only spoon used for dessert is the dessert spoon, never the teaspoon. The dessert spoon has an oval bowl that is about twice the size as the teaspoon.

"The Butler's Guide to Fine Silver"
Mr. Hollister, 1898

As I drove to Fair Winds, I kept thinking that there was something almost slimy about Alex's partner and his ex-wife. I also wanted to tell Lorraine what they said about the project, that they were going ahead with it. They were going to follow her lead to persuade local people to support the idea, but without her cooperation or input. Somehow that move made it feel slimier, if that's a word. It certainly described my feelings.

Even though someone had fired a shot that ended a man's life here at Fair Winds, I felt safe and protected as I drove down the long driveway, home. A familiar car was parked in front of the main house. I was sure it was the unmarked car driven by Detective Ingram. Fair Winds' massive front door opened and

Dawkins showed the detective out. I was relieved to see Ingram was alone. He hadn't come to take Lorraine into custody again.

I pulled over and parked to pump him for the latest in the investigation. I had to quick-step my way to his car before he could slide behind the wheel and escape. I wouldn't be surprised if he was trying to escape. He'd said a time or two that I was meddling in his investigations. *Meddling!* I resented that. It was meddling, until he needed something from me. Well, I wasn't going to sit by and let the police figure out what happened. It was too dangerous. They'd already accused Lorraine once. Though the American Justice system is excellent, mistakes did happen and I wasn't willing to gamble with Lorraine's freedom.

"Hello, detective." I scurried between Ingram and the driver's side door. "What brings you to beautiful Fair Winds today? Do you have a lead?"

Ingram tried, but failed to hide his irritation at seeing me. I was right, he was trying to avoid me. "Fancy seeing you here, Abby."

I dropped the pretense of friendly banter. "I live here, remember?" He rocked back on his feet and waited. "Have you found anything new?" He was as silent as a sphinx. "I've been trying to look at certain aspects and I think—"

"Abby!" He snapped. "This is a murder investigation. I don't want you getting involved."

"I am involved," I shot back. "It happened right in front of me, remember? If you don't want me poking around, give me something."

He drew in a deep breath and held my eyes in a staring match. I wasn't going to gain anything this way. Unpredictable often worked with him, so, I winked. I barely caught the tiny jolt of surprise, but it worked. He crossed his arms and stood with his feet apart, as if he'd decided.

"I might as well tell you. You'll find out anyway as soon as you walk inside the house."

Did he want encouragement? Okay, I was happy to give it to him. "That's probably true, but I'd rather hear the news from you."

"We confirmed the gun we have killed Alex Conklin. It's a break action 12- gauge shotgun with side-by-side double barrels. And it belongs to Lorraine."

"I know that." It was a struggle to hide my exasperation. "Lorraine already told you that it was her daddy's shotgun. She told me that she keeps it out of nostalgia, not to shoot somebody." *Unless she must.*

"That may be true. But there's more evidence that puts her in a bad light. Her thumb print was found on the brass back of the shell."

"She admitted that she loaded the gun. How else would she press the shell into position?" I was ready to box the man's ears the way they did with difficult children in England.

"Abby, you have to stop trying to second-guess me and let me do my job." He looked away and blew out his cheeks with a big sigh. I don't know if he was upset with me or uncomfortable with where the evidence was taking him. He continued. "Today, the forensics expert took another look at the gun cabinet. Lorraine said she keeps it locked and hides the key in the drawer with the ammunition." He stopped again and shook his head. "Why are people so obvious?"

The man was exhausted and having trouble staying focused. "Go on."

"We'd found the key in the drawer, right where she said it would be. And that bothered me. I've told you, I believe this is a crime of passion. The ex-wife of a man she was interested in walks into Fair Winds and acts like the place is hers. I know a lot of women who would react like a match to a bomb if it happened to them." He scratched his thinning brown hair with a few gray hairs showing here and there. "If she was upset enough to grab the gun out of the cabinet to race outside to shoot him, why would she take the time to replace the key in its usual place?"

"Good point. I brought the forensics guy out here and he did a closer inspection." He ran his hand through his hair again.

I willed myself to stay calm. "And...?"

"He found scratches in and around the lock. Somebody opened the gun cabinet without the key."

I forced down my growing excitement. "Therefore, it probably wasn't Lorraine who opened the cabinet and took out the shotgun. She knew where the key was. She would have used it. This is a good thing, it helps prove Lorraine's innocence, right?"

He pursed his lips. "It seems so, but don't jump to any conclusions. She's still not out of the woods. Want me to explain how the evidence would implicate a devious woman—"

"Please don't."

"Or how it could implicate someone else in the house who was familiar with the location of the gun cabinet?"

"Speaking of someone in the house, remember the Italian guy? Watch his eyebrows. They're very expressive. They can signal a person is lying," I said, ready to throw suspicion on a stranger.

He threw his arms out at his sides. "Really, Abby? That's the best you can do?" He held up his hand. "I'm sorry. I haven't gotten much sleep."

"Okay, try this: the shooter could have been a guest here at Fair Winds at some point." I shrugged my left shoulder. "Anyone could know where she keeps her guns." I didn't add that I'd been at Fair Winds for a long time and had no idea the gun cabinet was in the library. Something was niggling at my brain. "What would someone use to jimmy the lock, detective?"

He thought for a moment. "Well, assuming he didn't have a lock pick, something narrow with a point."

"Something like a letter opener?" I said slowly and Ingram nodded. "There's a letter opener on her desk in the library. Would that work?" I felt the warmth of hope spread through me.

"Show me."

We charged up the front steps, blew through the door and tried not to run down the hallway. Dawkins raised an eyebrow as we passed him, but he remained silent. We burst into the library, found we were alone and closed the door. He went to the cabinet to inspect the lock while I dashed to her desk. "Yes, a letter opener might work," he said. "Do you have it?"

I pawed through her papers. "It's not here. It's always right here." I looked around on the floor. Nothing. I pulled open one drawer after another. Still nothing. "A letter opener can't just walk away." There was a note of desperation in my voice.

"Yes, it can," he said. "With a little help. Let's search the room again."

We walked around the library in opposite directions, checking every surface and the floor under each piece of furniture.

"I don't see it," he said, putting his hands in his pockets, losing enthusiasm for my idea. "It's not here."

Hope was fizzling out like a deflating balloon. "It has to be here." I insisted. "Why would the killer take the letter opener when he had the gun?" I dropped to my knees and looked under the desk, sofa and chairs again. I examined the Oriental rug to see if the object was lost in the pattern somehow. Nothing. Ingram picked up the trash basket by the desk and turned it upside down. Only a few papers fluttered out.

"Why are you looking there?"

"You'd be surprised what people do when they're stressed. It's normal to throw something away when you're done with it. But, at a crime scene, throwing something away doesn't mean it's gone. Maybe Lorraine used the letter opener instead of the key to make us think that someone else had taken the gun."

NO! I screamed silently. I took a deep breath to calm myself. Hysterics would only push Ingram away. "Or maybe that someone hid it in this room. There will be fingerprints." I launched myself at the sofa, pulling the pillows and cushions away. Nothing. Then I attacked the chair closest to the cabinet, sending the cushions to the floor. I froze.

There, in the space next to the armrest, was the silver letter opener with a slender blade that tapered to a sharp point that looked damaged. Ingram took two long steps to my side and stopped my hand from reaching for it.

"No! Step away, Abby. It's evidence." He pulled a latex glove and a plastic bag out of his coat pocket. His gloved hand picked up the object, slipped it into the bag. Safely sealed inside, we could now look at it closely.

"It's not really a letter opener," I said. "It's really a sterling silver game bird skewer. That's why the blade is almost a foot long. Lorraine likes it better than a regular letter opener, because she can slit open any size envelope with one flick." I pointed. "You can see the hallmarks. It's sterling, so it's not cheap."

Ingram frowned, creasing his forehead. "Really? It's so plain. I thought it was some modern opener from an office supply store."

"No, that's the beauty of English Georgian silver, especially the early pieces. They focused on the intended use of the piece, not a fancy pattern." I looked closely at the tip. "Sterling is relatively soft. The tip looks mangled from twisting in the lock."

"I'll take it back and see if they can lift any prints. Good work, Abby," Ingram said and rushed out.

I replaced the cushions and pillows and plopped down in the chair. Had I helped... or hurt Lorraine's case? It took me a few minutes of staring into space before I realized that I could be, should be, doing things. I dragged myself out of the chair and headed toward the back door, when I heard the TV in the breakfast room. Somebody was listening to the storm coverage. I peered around the doorway and saw the little man, the Italian, sitting at the table, his mouth open a little, his eyes glued to the TV screen.

Before I could slip away, he caught sight of me and jumped out of the chair. "*Saluti, Signorina Abigail.*"

The Italian greeting brought me up short. He not only looked the part, he spoke the language. I paused. No one had introduced us. He'd just appeared in the dining room to serve guests the night of the meeting, the night of the murder.

"Forgive me, but who are you?" I hoped I didn't sound rude.

"I'm afraid we haven't met." I don't know why, but I held out my hand. "I'm Abby Strickland, but I guess you know that."

He took my hand, but didn't shake it. He held it like a butterfly in mid-air, bowed his head and said softly, "*Si, Signorina. Tuo servo.* Your servant."

What a charmer. He had the speech and the manners that could mesmerize. With the household in such upset, bordering on emotional chaos, I thought it would be prudent to find out more.

"And your name?"

His chest puffed up with pride and he declared, "I am Norman Maggiordomo, Estate Manager and Butler of Palazzo dell'Angelo." Then his body sagged like a balloon losing air. He hunched forward. "*Former* Estate Manager and Butler of Palazzo dell'Angelo, for it is no more."

I wanted to ask why, but the poor man looked like he would burst into tears. I kept the focus on a more basic question. "What brings you to Fair Winds?"

"Me?" He put his hand flat to his chest and bowed his head. "For me, it is *famiglia*."

"Family?" I didn't know if I was more surprised or confused. "Are you related to Mrs. Andrews?"

He chuckled in a controlled way. "Oh no, no, no. The one I call family is, as you say, Dawkins."

CHAPTER 14

The after-dinner coffee spoon is used when a small cup of strong coffee is served after the meal to aid digestion.

"The Butler's Guide to Fine Silver"
Mr. Hollister, 1898

"Family? You're related to Dawkins?" I stammered.

"Si. Is it not obvious?"

No, it was not obvious. Norman was the stereotype of an Italian with ink black hair, flamboyant gestures and dramatic reactions, all the opposite of Dawkins. Then I realized they did have some things in common, like drifting silently through the house, paying attention to even the tiniest details of a party and, I guessed, after watching Norman serving the guests at the meeting, neither man tolerated a haphazard approach to *anything*. Finally, I'd found a source of information about Dawkins, if only I could get him to talk.

"Tell me, how are you related?"

"We are cousins." He perked up. "His *nonna*—ah, you say, grandmamma— and mine were sisters. To me, he is Carlino."

"Carlino?" I said with a note of disbelief. Funny, I'd never thought of Dawkins having a first name.

"'Scusa, but you do not know this name?"

"As a matter of fact, no. He's never shared it with me. We only ever call him Dawkins."

The man nodded. "Si, that is like him. Very private. But to his American family and friends, he is known as Charlie." Norman shuddered. "Carlino is a more manly name. In fact, that's what it means in Italian, manly." He tapped his impressive dark moustache. "A very appropriate name for my cousin."

"I think he's more of a ghost. One minute, he's not there, then he is! It can be unnerving."

"Si, that is like him. He has a way of blending into the background. He can appear without a sound."

Norman was referring to the man's most irritating habit, at least irritating to me. He had a habit of floating from one place to another without a sound. "Yes, he is very good at that."

"Si, it is an important skill for a maggiordomo. It is his responsibility to act for the owner of the estate and take charge of the household."

"He certainly manages everything here," I said, almost under my breath.

"That is his job." He cocked his head and inspected me. "Ah, I see. You are hurt that he is not a…" He paused and looked up at the ceiling. "I think you call it, a *pal?* Si, you are hurt because he is not your pal." He shook his head harshly. "No, no. It is not his job to be friends with the staff. He must keep them organized, praise their good work and control the details, the details *minuscolo*, so the *il capo*—the boss—she deals with the big picture."

I took a breath to respond, but stopped when he held up his index finger for me to wait.

"Every day, at every moment, he must hide his own ego. It is not important what he feels. His job is to create a comfortable, efficient world for others. *That* is the key to success in this job."

"It sounds like you speak from experience."

Again, he put his hand on his chest and inclined his head. "Si, I am maggiordomo in Italia for many years."

"Oh, then you're here to teach Dawkins a few things?" It was hard to suppress a smile at the thought of Dawkins being schooled. "A man of your experience must have something to share with him."

"No, no, *signorina*," he declared, as he swatted away the compliment like a mosquito. "There is nothing, no training that Norman can give his cousin, Carlino."

"I am confused. You are Italian, but Dawkins…"

Norman smiled. "*Si*, he is what you call an American boy." Norman made himself comfortable in the chair, ready, eager to talk. "Our family in Sicily talks of his grandmother's great love story. During World War II, his grandfather came to Italia to fight. Only nineteen, he thought he was…" Norman threw out his arms in a dramatic gesture. "A man of the world!" He laughed shyly. "That's what they say. One afternoon, he saw Maria a dark-haired, dark-eyed beauty and lost his heart." Norman shrugged. "Amore, when it blossoms, it cannot be denied. But alas, their love would be tested."

I felt like I was listening to the plot of an Italian opera. It was hard for me to accept cool, controlled Dawkins was the product of such an emotional story.

Norman continued. "Ours is a large Sicilian family, even then. Maria, she was only sixteen." Norman smoothed his large mustache and a serious tone entered his voice. "Italian families, we do not let our children fly free as birds like you Americans, especially not our daughters. It took months for the young man to finally meet her and when he did, even her father could see it was love. He decided they would have to wait until she was older. He wanted his bambina to grow into a woman, to know her own mind, to see if the *amore* was real."

Norman leaned across the table, lowered his voice to a whisper and tapped his nose. "I know, I know what he saw…a love that would not die." He leaned back and went on with his story. "The war ended and still she was too young. The young American vowed he would not go home without her."

"He taught her English under the watchful eye of her momma. In 1946, two days after her 18th birthday, they married and their love produced four children. The young soldier made a career in banking and taught his family the finer things in life. Maria and the children came to Italia to visit once, then twice a year."

"My cousin's father grew up to travel the world. He too had a happy marriage as they moved from place to place. He was, what you call, a career military man."

Norman smiled. "A little girl was born when my cousin was seven, a long time for a boy to be the only child. He told me stories about the things he would do with his papa, but his momma was treasured. Once a month, they celebrated Mother's Day. 'Why wait a whole year,' his papa would say, 'to show the woman you love that she is wonderful?'

Norman's shoulders sagged. "But this is not a story that ends in happiness. My uncle died when my cousin was only fifteen, old enough to feel the loss like a hole in his soul. My cousin lost direction. He went into the army like his papa after your high school. Once, he told me after too many glasses of grappa that it was his way of staying connected with his papa." His eyes, heavy with sadness, drifted down to his hands clasped on the table. "He said to me that he looked so much like his papa that his momma would see him and start crying… out of *dolore*. You call it grief."

To me, the word in Italian sounded more heart-wrenching than it did in English. My own memories of losing Gran were *dolore*. I was twenty-two when she succumbed to cancer. She was my grandmother, not a father who should have lived to see his son become a man. I could only begin to imagine how Dawkins felt.

"Where-re…" I had to start again, because I was afraid of the answer. "Where is his sister now?"

"Ah, she lives with her family someplace called the Yukon Territory. Her husband guides people through the wilderness." Norman held his hands up as if in defeat. "I don't know what that is. We have nothing like that in Italia. We are the cradle of civilization, you know."

I had to smother a giggle. Of course, he wouldn't know. He and his cousin had chosen a life that involved setting the table with the right forks, not elk, moose and bison in rugged country.

"Over a good wine this time, he admitted it was his fault that she ran away to a lifestyle, opposite of everything they had as children."

"Why would he think that?" I asked.

Norman sighed. "She was afraid something would happen to him in the army, something horrible. She couldn't bear the thought and pulled away. Oh, they talk. They are family, but they are not close. He hates visiting her where she lives. It's always cold and he hates the cold, a true Italian at heart. From time to time, he pays for her and her family to meet him for a vacation where it is warm, in the Caribbean or Mediterranean."

I remembered when Dawkins took a winter holiday and returned with a deep tan. He refused to share any details, except to say it was enjoyable. I figured that he had a lady friend somewhere and they had escaped the cold. I never thought he'd gone to spend time with family. "Is that why Dawkins has not married?"

Norman considered my question and then nodded. "Yes, I think that is true. To him, family means pain and grief, after what happened with his papa. He is happier serving and being part of a Family by Choice."

Dawkins appeared at the door, silently as usual. There was a flash of surprise in his eyes when he saw me talking with his cousin. But he didn't let on that it fazed him, as usual.

"Norman, please check the pantry for these items." He held out a sheet of paper. "We may have to secure additional supplies."

Norman rose and took the list. "Right away." Soundlessly, he drifted out of the room.

Dawkins moved to leave, but paused for a moment. That was so out of character for him. He always went from Point A to Point B, without hesitation. Did he want to ask about my conversation with his cousin? I didn't want to get the man into trouble so I brought it up.

"I was having a nice chat with Norman. He was telling me that you are cousins and a little bit about your background." Dawkins raised one eyebrow. "If you have a moment, it would be nice to talk about something else than…" I didn't want to use the word *murder*. "the trouble we're having. In fact, that's my first question. What do we call you?"

"Dawkins, of course." He was back to his sarcastic self.

"I mean, what is your title?"

"Did you watch the TV show *Downton Abbey*?" I nodded. "Think of me as Carson. That will do." He made it to the door when I stopped him.

"Wait, I'd like to know more. Where did you study?"

He stepped backwards into the room. "What brought on this interrogation?" There was steel in his voice and that surprised me.

Was there more to Dawkins than I thought? "This isn't an interrogation." "I'm just curious." He didn't respond. "Your cousin Norman said—"

His shoulders tensed. "What did he tell you?"

I was right to open this conversation to defuse any negative fallout from my conversation with Norman. "He told me that you are cousins and he was a majori…" I stumbled on the word.

"Maggiordomo of an Italian estate, yes" Dawkins confirmed.

"And he said that there was nothing he could teach you."

The comment turned the tables on Mr. Cool. His eyebrows shot up, then relaxed. I thought it pleased him that Norman had said that. "So, would you tell me a little about your training?"

He relaxed into his normal, rigid posture and I could see his eyes, the color of the blue ocean as a storm approaches. "If you really want to know... But why?"

"I do want to know," I confirmed. "We both live and work here at Fair Winds. We share everything from chocolate chip cookies to..." I couldn't say the word *murder,* but we both heard the word reverberate in our minds.

He began reluctantly. "Being a butler means being a good manager. It requires more knowledge than knowing which fork goes where or being a pretty face at the door. I studied at a professional butler's institute in London. They had an all-inclusive course of study. And if that is all..." He turned to walk through the doorway again.

"Like what?"

He paused. "I'm sorry?"

"An all-inclusive course of study that included...?"

He turned and sat down at the table. "I can see that your curiosity is more tenacious than Simon's. What do you want to know?"

I folded my hands on the table and asked, "What did you study?"

He sighed. "You will only laugh."

I shook my head. "No, I will not. Tell me."

He didn't look like he believed me, but he continued. "There were the obvious subjects such as bookkeeping and how to teach and motivate a staff. Of course, there were the standard courses about wine, mixology and apparel care. The school prided itself on preparing us to run a modern, vibrant household with efficiency, grace and style."

"What was your favorite course?" He had sparked my imagination. "Did they have specialized courses?"

He looked at me as if he was sitting across from a stranger, then answered. "Yes, there was one that I think you'd find extremely interesting. The Coffee Mastery Masterclass."

That was a surprise. "I know there're special techniques for roasting and brewing, but enough for a masterclass, really?"

"Those are important points, but there is much to the preparation and delivery of smooth, full-bodied blends of distinctive coffees. For example, one must learn to use a grinder to ensure the extraction that will deliver the full quality of taste. There are proper techniques for steaming and pouring the milk, as well. That's why we were trained in the art of coffee cupping."

Now, I wasn't sure if he was pulling my leg. His face didn't show a trace of emotion. There was no mischievous glint in his eye. Did the butler school teach him how to mask his emotions? He was waiting for my reaction. It wouldn't hurt to go along with his little game.

"Okay, I'll give. What is coffee cupping?"

He took a deep breath and explained. "It is the professional practice of tasting and identifying the aromas and flavors of brewed coffee. A barista, I mean a *true* barista, can judge a coffee by aroma, acidity, aftertaste and more. Those who are excellent at the practice can identify where the beans were grown. Think of it as high-level wine tasting for coffee."

I'd always loved coffee. This was news to me and excited me. "Could you do a coffee cupping for me sometime?"

A smile played at the corners of his mouth. "I would be delighted to try. It has been awhile since I have participated. I shall need some time to renew my knowledge. May I let you know when I am ready, hopefully after this terrible business we face is resolved successfully?"

"Yes. And thank you for reminding me that a good resolution will happen."

With a slight nod of his head, as a butler would say, he retired from the room. Somehow, I was not left with a calm feeling. Instead, I had the strange idea that Dawkins was being defensive. No, cautious. As if he was hiding something. And Norman knew what it was.

CHAPTER 15

Do not confuse the after-dinner coffee spoon with the demitasse spoon, which is only used if sugar is added.

"The Butler's Guide to Fine Silver"
Mr. Hollister, 1898

LATER, I looked down at the cold coffee at the bottom of my mug and felt a little disconnected. And a little guilty. I was sitting in a room filled with sunshine, surrounded by a view of nature's best, blithely talking about butler skills and coffee-cupping, while Lorraine was upstairs with a dark cloud looming over her. She needed rest. The horror of Alex's murder and the shock of being arrested for committing the crime and the false relief of returning home after posting bail… she was vulnerable and she knew it. The rest she needed eluded her. Fear about what could happen was her constant companion.

Lorraine didn't kill Alex. I couldn't accept the possibility that she did, but the evidence – the kind that would be presented to the grand jury – was piling up. Yes, she was trained to shoot. She wasn't afraid of guns. On the dock after the shot was fired, it was probably a natural reaction for her to pick up the shotgun. It was in the wrong place. It shouldn't be left out. When people reacted to seeing her with the gun, she dropped it immediately. Not the safest thing to do, but the natural reaction... of an innocent person.

Wasn't it?

And earlier on the terrace, wasn't it a natural reaction for her to lash out at Alex? I could see it in her face before she rushed away that she felt hurt, betrayed, when she realized Alex's ex-wife was making herself comfortable at Fair Winds.

Lorraine cared about him. What started as conversations about *Chesapeake Haven* grew into warm affection and I believe the feelings were mutual.

Lorraine became a widow many years ago when a drunk driver killed her husband and destroyed their vintage Thunderbird. One evening, we talked over a bottle of fine wine and she'd described her slow climb out of the caves of grief. She grew was comfortable in the role of Pillar of the Community. Oh, she had gentlemen friends, but they were *friends*, nothing more. Not until Alex. He was changing her life. His concept for a vibrant community, a place for people to find peace to grow, not just vegetate in retirement and wait for death, was thrilling. His passion and zest for life gave her the courage to trust and hope and accept his attention and caring.

I burned with indignation at Arabella and her attitude of entitlement. No wonder she was an *ex*-wife. I too would have felt betrayed when Alex allowed her to enter Fair Winds. Well, maybe that reaction was over the top, especially if she knew how to sell houses. But it probably hurt more when he chatted with the woman while they sipped Lorraine's fine single malt Scotch. Lorraine had lowered her defenses, bared her soul to that man, and then to have her feelings cast aside like an old grocery receipt must have hurt deeply. She thought he was honest and loyal, but if he could hurt her like that, what could he do to her beloved St. Michaels and the Eastern Shore? Was he a traitor?

Did she really have those thoughts and feelings that night? Did they battle what she believed in her mind and heart? She was a woman of action. So, how did she react? Did her emotions take control? Did Lorraine...? Could Lorraine...?

The news was filled with stories of good people doing bad things. But Lorraine grew up loved, was well educated and, above all, had a good heart.

She couldn't...

Why was I using logic to persuade myself that Lorraine hadn't murdered Alex? Didn't I truly believe she was innocent? Had I put this woman on a lofty pedestal? Had my loss of Gran and my deep, abiding need for *home* blinded me to Lorraine's true personality? Could Lorraine have fired...? Could she be a...?

NO! I wouldn't even allow my brain to form the word. She was not guilty. She did not end Alex's life. It was time for me to prove it. Not only to save her, but to save myself. If I was wrong, everything I believed in would collapse. A shot of energy ran through me. I needed to direct it into *proving* Lorraine's innocence. I had to prove a positive.

The weather was too wonderful to stay inside, so Simon and I went for a walk. It was a lazy summer day. The perfect time to walk barefoot in the cool, shaded grass. Perfect for others. It would be perfect for me again, someday, when Lorraine was home. Safe. To stay. To distract myself, I threw the ball Simon brought me from one of his hiding places and he chased it again and again and again. Until Dawkins walked out of the shadows, almost stopping my heart.

When I could breathe again, I said through clenched teeth, "Stop doing that. You do realize a murderer is still walking around."

"You are correct, Miss Abigail. I apologize. I will try to be more careful about my comings and goings around you..." And curiously, left the comment hanging for a moment. Was he being civil and respectful to me? Then said, "At least until the murderer is caught."

I wanted to rail at Dawkins for being so... frustrating, but I knew it wouldn't do any good. Rather than playing his little game, I jockeyed for another nugget of information, hoping to strike gold.

"Dawkins, why is Norman here in the United States? Why happened to the estate in Italy?"

"Ah, a sad story. Norman returned to Italy after completing his training and language courses in London. Using family connections, he entered the employ of a businessman, who owned Palazzo dell'Angelo, a little part of heaven on earth." He closed his eyes and I was jealous of what he was seeing in his mind's eye. Then the look faded and he dropped his head. "He had many, many years of a good life there, but the *signore*, he was in a bad business. You could say he dealt in death."

"What?! What does that mean?"

"He was purported to be an arms dealer." Dawkins let out a long sigh. "One day, his work caught up with him."

"Did his competition send an assassin, like in the movies?" I asked horrified, for the little man who looked like an Italian restaurant owner.

Dawkins chuckled a little. "No, nothing as exciting as that. Interpol swooped in one day and arrested him. They questioned poor Norman, but couldn't connect him to his *capo's* business dealings, so they let him go. When he returned to the palazzo, men watched while he packed his belongings then escorted him to the gate. Suddenly, the poor man was without a home, income or pension. His assets are frozen until the authorities finish their investigation. He called me, needing a place to stay. There was a time when I made the same kind of call. Years ago, he gave me a place to rest and pointed me down a new path. I just returned the favor, with Madam's permission, of course."

Simon raced over, sat and pawed Dawkins' leg. In response,

the man crouched down and scratched him behind his left ear in his favorite spot.

"Oh, don't encourage him," I complained. "I'm trying to train him so he'll stop these bad habits."

"I am sorry, Miss Abigail."

His actions betrayed what sounded like a sincere apology. Of course, I saw him slip Simon a treat. Oh, the man could be so frustrating.

"Oh," Dawkins said. "I'm glad you said, train. Norman wants to take a train to New York. I shall find him so we can make arrangements."

Norman—my source of information—was leaving?

Dawkins strode off like a man without a care in the world, our world, where a murderer was still lurking.

The sun seemed stuck overhead, sending its scorching rays down on the land and people making them both brown and unwilling to move. The calm water mirrored the blue sky and a few fluffy clouds. Close to the shoreline, the feathered bottoms of several ducks were up in the air as they fed on the plants and plankton floating by underwater. The world was ignoring the deadly uproar surging around me and those I thought I knew. I jumped a little when a man called out to me.

"It must be nice to have the time to enjoy this beautiful view," Ingram said as he walked across the lawn, tiredness pulling on each step. "Mind if I join you?"

"Not at all." *If you don't mind answering my questions.*

He fell into step with me and reached out for Simon's ball. With a smooth motion, he threw it farther than I could imagine, especially for a man not much taller than my own five feet, eight inches. And he was solid, probably a product of hours in the gym.

"Quarterback in high school," he explained shyly.

"That explains it," I muttered. "I thought you were going to explain where you are with the case?"

. . .

HE SIGHED and shook his head. "I feel like I'm at a Chinese restaurant with a huge menu. I can order from Column A, another from Column B." He put out his arms and let them drop. "I have so many suspects that I could mix and match a whole dinner."

"Talk it through," I suggested. "Maybe it will help."

"Alright, but no names."

I nodded and held my index finger to my lips.

"Funny," he said. "The menu of suspects is complicated. There were people still at Fair Winds when the shot was fired. Some of them were still in the living room and have given each other alibis. A man was in the dining room, foraging for more cookies. There's that man you said reminded you of an Italian waiter—"

"Restaurant owner," I corrected him. "Norman."

"Yes, that's the one. I talked to him and..." Ingram lowered his voice. "You were right about the eyebrows. Very expressive the way he waggles them up and down and all around."

We both gave a little laugh.

"What did Norman say about the cookie man?"

Ingram's own eyebrows went up for a moment. "Cookie man? Good one."

"I had to do think of a way to keep them straight."

He stopped and ignored Simon when he dropped the ball at his feet. "You know everyone who was there that night?"

"No, not even close. I'm using names like Cookie Man, Ex-Wife, Partner, that kind of thing."

"Good idea." He picked up the ball and hurled it. "We're still sifting through statements, trying to get a handle on who left the meeting, who stayed, and who left and came back."

"Gone to the restroom or gotten another drink?" I suggested.

"Yes, or someone who jimmied the cabinet lock, hid the gun and went away until it was the best time to strike."

"Could it have been someone who hid the gun, left the meeting, doubled back and took the shot?"

"See?" He lifted his hands to the sky and let them fall. "That's exactly what I'm talking about ... too many possibilities. At least, the officers matched the cars and trucks still parked in front to the people and made sure to get their statements."

"That's good," I said, with enthusiasm. The man looked like he could use all the encouragement he could get. Then, I kept quiet. I didn't bring up the fact that I'd found a business card by Alex's Range Rover. It probably wasn't helpful, but I'd broken the rules. I wouldn't say anything about it until I knew more. "Did your officers look beyond the parking area in front of the house?"

The homicide detective frowned. "What do you mean?"

"Fair Winds is a big place. Someone could have driven away and taken one of the side roads of the farm, parked and crept back to the boathouse."

Ingram stared off in the distance at nothing. He probably didn't appreciate that idea. "I'll check it out." He reached in his pocket for his keys.

I didn't want him to leave. I wanted to know more. "What about the investigation on the other side of the Bay Bridge?"

"You mean, Bethesda?" It was an upscale Maryland suburb of Washington, D.C. where Alex lived and had his main corporate offices. Ingram was cagey. "What about it?"

"I presume you have State Police interviewing people there, don't you?"

Ingram gave in. "You're right. So far, not much. There was some friction between the victim and his partner lately. Probably because of the ex-wife."

Or there could be some trouble with the business arrangements. I remembered the line on the lawyer's card, *Specializing in Corporate Issues.* I had to track down more about the attorney. I crossed my arms and smiled at him.

He frowned. "What?"

"You don't remember. That's how we met." He still looked confused. "You sent the State Police to my home in Northern Virginia to interrogate me about the silver cake breaker I'd sold to Lorraine."

"Interrogate?" His face brightened with the memory. "That's right. You were a suspect in one of my murder investigations."

"Not a serious suspect, but you were covering all your bases. Only, the detectives were so serious and scared me so much, I got in the car and came to the Shore."

"You went against orders to stay away," he pointed out. "As usual."

"Well, it all worked out. Look what happened. I got together with Lorraine, I uncovered some secrets..."

"Baited the killer and almost got yourself shot. Yes, I remember."

I shook my head so my curls bounced. "No, that's not the point. We've worked together since then, figuring out some complicated cases. We can do it again. You can do it again," I added quickly. I didn't want him to think that I thought of myself as police and freeze me out of his investigation. "You'll figure out this Chinese menu and prove Lorraine didn't do it." I called Simon. "And now, detective, I have an appointment."

CHAPTER 16

The Five O'Clock Tea Spoon harkens back to the era when tea was served at that time. It is slightly shorter than a teaspoon and slightly larger than an after-dinner coffee spoon. Be attentive that you do not confuse these pieces.

"The Butler's Guide to Fine Silver"
Mr. Hollister, 1898

I SPRINTED BACK to the cottage to make myself presentable for High Tea with Mary Rose. I'd heard that the old woman had been on the Shore forever. She knew everyone and what she knew might help lead me to the killer. Yes, Mary Rose might hold the clues I needed.

I zoomed down the sun-dappled roadway toward the Miles River Bridge. The shadows across the road were longer now. The days were getting shorter. It would soon be autumn. Time was running out for the green leaves and late seasonal flowers. Time might be running out for Lorraine, too.

I crossed over the modern bridge where an old ferry owned by a silversmith, used to work. Along the river, magnificent homes, that didn't look like much from the road, faced the water with imposing exteriors. Many dated back to the 18th and early 19th centuries when visitors arrived by boat, not by carriage. Thanks to Ryan and our little cruises, I'd seen them from the right perspective.

Now, I had to pay attention so I wouldn't miss her driveway.

When I turned in, a floral bouquet of scents settled around me like a cloud from the garden. I'm not sure what I expected when I agreed to visit an army boot-wearing elderly woman, but a neat cottage covered with gray weathered shingles was not it. Shutters, freshly painted federal blue, bordered large windows that winked in the sunlight, not a smudge of dirt marred the view. Graceful willow trees, rippling in the breeze, framed the cottage.

Passing under a white wooden arbor flanked with huge rose bushes, I found bees flitting from petal to petal and a dainty yellow-and-black butterfly landing like a whisper on a flower of vibrant pink. Small stepping stones led up to the front door. They were far too small for my feet. After taking a few steps, I realized that the stones were small by design. Unless one walked on tippy toes, it was impossible not to crush the green plants surrounding them and when I did, an explosion of scent reminded me of a chicken roasting in thyme. On such a tranquil afternoon, how could anyone believe a surging hurricane off the coast might disturb our weather and lifestyle? It wouldn't do any good to worry about it. The weather was going to do whatever it wanted.

On either side of the heavy front door painted white were two earthen pots of brilliant Mediterranean blue, planted with miniature trees heavy with small golden lemons. The scent was intoxicating.

I stepped forward and, as if I'd crossed an invisible line, muffled barking from inside the cottage made me pause. It was low and husky, not the sound of a lap dog.

The door opened and the little bit of a thing named Mary Rose said hello. Petite and delicate from advanced age, she wore a bright print dress with small red and blue flowers that looked freshly laundered and ironed. The leggings she often wore under her dress were nowhere to be seen, nor were the black leather boots. Today, she stood in a pair of flat sandals with gold straps. She gave the dog at her side a thumping pat on her back.

"She's better than a doorbell, my Sunny is. She's always hovering over me, protecting me and bringing a lot of happiness into my life." She waved her arm. "Come in, come in. She won't hurt you…" I took two steps forward and glanced down at the sweet Labrador retriever the color of sunshine leaning against Mary Rose's thigh. She stood quietly, protecting her mistress and offering a little support.

Mary Rose added with a smile, "She won't hurt you unless I say the *word*, then she'd tear you apart."

"When she was a puppy, she was always looking up, always checking out the clouds and the sun, even the moon. And she seems to watch over me always just like Mother Nature." She closed the door. "Glad you could come. As the British say, the kettle's on."

I was stunned to see the interior of the cottage. If I had to use one word to describe it, I'd say *delicate…* and cozy. It was in sharp contrast to the rough-around-the-edges person she projected to the world when she was out and about. Here, I'd stepped back to an earlier century, afraid I'd track even small bits of dirt on the gleaming golden oak floors. Antique furniture shone from loving attention.

An impressive stone fireplace stood ready to provide warmth when the fall temperatures took a dip. The walls were painted a delicate rose, except for one, papered with pink roses climbing a garden trellis, though the paper was fading and a little yellowed by the passage of time. Two bookcases with hardback books shared space with several framed black-and-white photos. With everything neat and in its place, the room felt comfortable and inviting. Then I realized one thing was missing: electronic screens. There was no sign of a computer, television or phone.

She must not have felt a need for such modern conveniences, since she lived so close to the land.

At the large bay window overlooking the river, lace curtains were pulled back in gentle swags to welcome the afternoon sun. There, two high-backed chairs covered in plush misty green velvet were set on either side of an antique walnut tea table. And on the table was a spectacular formal silver tea service. The large serving tray was polished to such a high finish that it mirrored the four graceful pieces sitting on it. Were a few pieces missing? No matter, few original antique sets were complete anymore due to loss, damage or plain carelessness. These pieces were in pristine condition. The pompous appraiser from New York would have wept with joy.

Mary Rose gestured to one of the chairs. "Won't you sit down and make yourself comfortable?" She caught me staring at the tea service. "Oh, that's right, you like working with sterling silver things."

"And this set is magnificent." I would have thought that I could come up with something more original to say, but the set truly took my breath away.

"Thank you," she said softly. "I'll just get the teapot from the kitchen."

Quickly, I counted the pieces again. A complete formal tea service usually had seven pieces. I hadn't made a mistake. There were only five here. There was the kettle for hot water on its stand. Not part of every tea service, it was a delightful surprise to see it on the enormous silver tray with its matching sugar bowl and milk pitcher. There was a round, almost chubby bowl with a smaller round opening. Again, it wasn't often that the waste bowl for used tea leaves or the dregs from the bottom of a cup was still part of a tea set. Some antique dealers preferred to split it off and sell it as a sweetmeats bowl. *Very inappropriate*, my Aunt Agnes would say. I wanted to inspect one of the pieces and check the hallmark, but that would have been rude. From where I sat, I tried to look for telltale signs of counterfeit work or alteration, in vain. This set was original.

She returned carrying the set's matching teapot. "Here we are. I hope you like Darjeeling. It's one of my favorites. Would you mind lighting the candle to keep the water in the kettle warm? The matches are on the side table."

The massive kettle was meant for hot water, not brewing tea. Once filled with hot water, it would sit on its stand over the lighted tea candle. After the first cups were served, it would be tipped forward to refill the teapot with hot water.

"I noticed that the coffee pot—"

"Isn't on the tray, I know. It takes up so much room and I never use it. Right now, it's doing double duty as a flower vase for some long-stemmed Black-Eyed Susans." She shrugged. "I know I shouldn't, but it makes more sense to use it than to store it inside some dark cabinet."

While I struck a match and lit the candlewick, she set the teapot on the tray and flipped over a little hourglass to time the brewing to perfection. We sat down to the table set with linen tea napkins, smaller than those used at lunch or dinner, that lay next to the bone china cups and saucers. An unusual silver cake stand —Edwardian, I guessed—was next to the tray. Its three tiers were not stacked one on top of the other but offset to make it easier to use the silver tongs to serve the sandwich triangles with the crusts cut off, delicate petit fours and custard tartlets.

"Please help yourself. There is Devonshire cream and jam for the scones, or you might prefer a piece of cake." Only her style of speech—relaxed with a little Southern drawl—reminded me that we were on the Eastern Shore. There was a gleam in her eyes that showed how much she was enjoying this. We both selected goodies for our bone china plates and, when the sand ran out in the hourglass, she asked, ""Shall I pour?"

I nodded, feeling transported to the living room of the house where I grew up. Gran believed that the English got it right when they created the tradition of afternoon tea, a time when the frantic pace of the modern world could pause for a few minutes. The delicious aroma of baking scones or tiny cakes spread through our house as I went to my room to change. When I was small, I would put on one of my tea dresses. Other little girls would call them party dresses, but I wore mine more often than when a birthday party invitation arrived. Gran and I didn't sit down to high tea every day, but she tried to do it once a week. The tradition began when I was little, so she gave me a china cup and saucer from a doll or child's tea set complete with a silver demitasse spoon. As I grew, so did my cup and saucer, until she trusted me with translucent bone china. When the tea had brewed, Gran would ask the question that began teatime. But when I was thirteen, she asked, "Would you like to pour?"

With those few words, we celebrated a rite of passage. She recognized that I was growing up. The connection we made over tea became a time when I could ask for advice, report eureka moments or just sit in companionable silence with her, sipping our tea, sipping from the font of love. During my teen years, the question morphed from "Shall I pour?" to "Who shall pour?" That simple question reminded me that I was no longer a child and by reaching for the teapot, I was accepting the responsibility of acting like an adult. Those times that I invited her to pour, it showed that I felt strong enough to share the honor.

Whenever I came home from college for a visit, I always tried to arrive at teatime so we could reconnect without the demands of studies, friends – life interfering. I no longer wore a tea dress, but I never wore jeans or a t-shirt. Respect for the tradition was still strong.

Then the day came when she lifted the teapot. Her hand shook so hard, she almost dropped it. Gently, I took it and poured our tea then I waited for the explanation I didn't want to hear. Being away at school for weeks on end, the shock of seeing her that day —her frail body, thinning hair, the life lines on her face now etched deeply in her ashen skin—the shock was terrifying. I watched her raise the delicate china cup to her cracked lips with both hands. Somehow, I kept myself from crying, and crying out. She had always made it a rule that there was no place for emotional outbursts or histrionics at teatime. It was not the time for a little girl to demand another piece of cake, a teenager to make disparaging comments or to test boundaries. And it was not the time to demand answers. Part of me would have been content to sit quietly forever and not hear about the cancer diagnosis, the advanced stage of the disease and the bleak prognosis. Teatime was for quiet conversation and acceptance. From that afternoon on, I poured until I could not make myself pour for just one.

Mary Rose brought me back to the present. "I saw you admiring my silver tea service. It's one of my most valued treasures. I use it almost every day."

"I'm so glad you invited me here today," I said. Your cottage and the silver set are lovely."

"And a surprise, I'd wager."

I felt my cheeks get hot. Had she read my mind?

She chuckled. "Oh, don't worry. Most people don't see this side of me. I wasn't raised in a household that shot meat for the table. I grew up at Willow Hall, like my mother before me, and her mother before her. Then I lived in New York and Philadelphia."

"That sounds exciting."

She gave a little shrug. "I suppose, only I wanted to be on the Eastern Shore more than anywhere else in the universe. My heart is part of the land and water here. Always has been. But before World War II, it wasn't proper for a young lady to pick up and live wherever she wanted. So, I did the next best thing. I escaped by marriage."

I guessed that Mary Rose was in her eighties and the world was very different when she was a young girl. "How did you manage to do that?"

Her lips twitched with a smile as she refilled the teapot with the hot water from the kettle. While we waited for the tea to steep, she told me the story.

"Every summer, I was allowed to come down to St. Michaels

to visit my mother's aunt. She had a small place just outside of town. I met up with the son of a family we knew who had a farm on the other side of the river. Their house wasn't as grand as Willow Hall, but they had managed to hold on to their land, something my father wasn't interested in doing. I made Clary fall in love with me. Oh, his given name was Clarence, but everyone called him Clary. We're big on nicknames around here."

She poured our tea and continued her story. "I knew my father would never let me marry. I was only 17 and he would have wanted someone more suitable." She said those last words with disdain. "That means someone with money." She sniffed and took a bite of a strawberry scone. "Well, Clary was 21, old enough to marry. So, I talked him into eloping to Elkton, Maryland, a little town north of here that's like the Las Vegas of the East if you want to get married quickly and without a fuss. It was done and consummated *again* by the time my father found out. I think he was secretly glad to be rid of his hellion as he liked to call me."

"It wasn't a term of endearment?"

"Far from it. I was a handful." She glanced toward the collection of photos on the mantel. "His mother was a blessing. She gave me a wedding present that meant the world to me, a chest filled with silver flatware in the Rose Stieff pattern. It had a lot more than forks and spoons we needed. Some pieces were missing, but I didn't care."

She glanced at the dining room with the table covered by an ironed creamy white damask cloth and a modest crystal chandelier hanging above. "I remember it like it happened yesterday. She was so uncomfortable, almost embarrassed. She apologized, because it was a very old pattern and so tarnished. She assumed there was no need for her to have it polished since I probably wouldn't want it." She turned back and looked triumphant. "But it was perfect, the same pattern my mother had. When I was little, we'd spend hours polishing the family silver together. Just the two of us. I didn't have to share Momma with anyone else. Happy memories." She sat up quickly. "Would you like to see it?"

I had seen many, many pieces of Rose Stieff that were part of the Fair Winds Silver Collection, but I was happy, eager to share this woman's joy in her own silver. "Yes, I'd love to see it."

We moved to the dining room and she retrieved an old wooden chest from the china cupboard. It no longer held tarnished silver pieces, rejected by other members of her husband's family. Mary Rose raised the lid and I blinked at the bright shine of the pieces inside. "It's beautiful, Mary Rose. You've polished it to perfection."

The pattern wasn't just bright and clean. It was done with care. Some of the tiny crevasses were allowed to darken against the gleaming portions to accentuate the texture of the repoussé pattern. That kind of care required patience. Dawkins certainly would be impressed and approve.

In a small voice, she expressed her pleasure. "Thank you. My mother taught me that caring for sterling silver is an act of love."

After spending several moments looking at the silver, Mary Rose lowered the lid and returned the silver chest to its rightful place. I was happy to share the old woman's memories, but I wanted her help to find a murderer.

"I'm afraid the candle has gone out." She touched the side of the water kettle. "And the water has gone cold. Shall I heat up some more?"

"No, thank you. I've had enough, thank you." I cleared my throat. It was time. "I wondered if you'd heard the latest about happened at Fair Winds."

"I know what I've read in the paper."

Mary Rose wasn't going to make this easy. "Do you know that Lorraine was arrested for the murder?"

Mary Rose nodded. "She brought that man to the Shore and into her home."

I was a little surprised by her reaction, so I said slowly, "Yes, yes she did. She is known for being a mediator. She was trying to bring people together to come up with a project that would benefit everyone, create jobs, build homes and parks that everyone could enjoy, bring some infrastructure…" I paused.

"I know what that is," she responded with an edge to her voice. "You mean upgrade the roads and bring in the last G technology for the internet and streaming. I don't live in the dark ages. I just don't choose to live my life on a screen."

"Of course. Well, you're exactly right, about everything." I looked down at my hands in my lap. "She didn't do it, you know."

"I know. I wouldn't have expected it of her. Lorraine is more of a peacemaker." She glanced out the window and added, "Not someone to resolve a situation by whatever means necessary. Even if it requires violence."

It was good to hear someone echo my innermost thoughts. "Since you've lived here almost all your life, you must know who most of the people were in the meeting. I don't mean to ask you to point a finger, but it would help if you could give me an idea…" It wasn't easy to ask someone to identify a person capable of murder. "Do you think there was someone in that room who could have fired the shot that killed Alex?"

She looked down into her teacup. At first, I thought I had offended her, that she wasn't going to answer my question. As I racked my brain to think of something to say, she looked up and smiled. "There were a number of people in that room who could have fired that shot. Hunting is a popular pastime in this area. Considering the deer population, it's a necessity." She took a sip of cold tea. "It takes time to become a good shot, to know that you'll hit the mark every time. People aren't willing to put in the time to practice anymore."

"Do you think there was someone there who was angry enough about the development to kill Alex?"

She glanced out the window. I began to think that her mind had wandered away the way it happens to old people, so I jumped a little when she finally spoke.

"People here on the Shore don't take kindly to change. Never have, probably never will. If a person wants change, it's best to move to a big city on the Western Shore. We don't like a fast pace here. We like thing the way they've always been. I knew some people who feel real strongly that way."

I was about to ask her for names, but she held up her hand. She wasn't finished.

"Yes, there are folks who feel that way around here, who will do want it takes to protect what they hold dear, but we all respect life. To take someone's life with violence," she shook her head and looked down at her hands in her lap. "I can't reconcile that someone would do that. Can't imagine the extreme... emotion it would take for someone to do that."

She stood abruptly. "Let's take a walk. All this talk about ugliness is upsetting me."

CHAPTER 17

The demitasse spoon, also known as a mocha spoon, is used to stir coffee that is made with an equal amount of hot chocolate and served in a demitasse cup.

"The Butler's Guide to Fine Silver"
Mr. Hollister, 1898

BEFORE I COULD APOLOGIZE for upsetting her, she had opened the front door and stepped outside. I noticed a weathered wood plaque with the name WILLOW COTTAGE chiseled into it. "Oh, is this the name of your house? I love the way people here give their homes a name."

"I grew up over there." She pointed across the river and down a little way. "When Clary and I got married, his parents gave us this house and land, I named it after the Hall where I was born and raised. My husband wasn't an ambitious man. He was content with who he was and he loved me. He was happy for us to spend our lives here on the Shore, which was fine with me. He was the third son in his family, so he wouldn't inherit much. Nevertheless, his parents were good people. They gave us several acres of land, carved it off one side of their farm, as a wedding present. Its access to water meant he could work as a waterman and we'd never starve. Between pulling crabs, tonging for oysters, fishing for Rockfish and the crops we grew, we were set. Our needs weren't great. We were happy here."

She set off for the dock and I followed. It was a breathtaking scene of natural beauty. The breeze was picking up and blowing out of the south, whipping in my face.

"Ah, Mother Nature is trying to get your attention. She doesn't like to be taken for granted. She unpredictable, almost fickle. She likes to keep us on our toes. After all, she is a woman and as all men know, a woman can change her mind and act up at any moment. And she is our mother trying to train us to be better residents of this planet. Everything we need to know is all around us. Do we pay attention? She shook her head hard. "Do we heed her warnings…about the health of the Bay? About our misuse of the land? About a monster storm headed our way?"

"So, this wind is the beginning of the hurricane coming in?" I said, repositioning my head to let the shifting breeze keep my hair out of my face.

She gave me a sidelong look. "You haven't been in a hurricane, have you? Bet you've only seen one on television." She flung the question like an accusation.

"Well, no, I grew up on the West Coast and we really didn't have any storms like that." I thought for a moment, again feeling like I had to defend myself. "But I have been here for several nor'easters. Those are impressive storms."

Mary Rose chuckled. "A nor'easter, even a bad one, is a walk in the park compared to a hurricane, even a Category One. It is one of the most destructive forces on the planet."

"What about a tornado?" I remembered how people, filled with anxiety, watched the skies in the Midwest whenever there was an alert.

"If one touches down, it causes a lot of damage. But it's down, it's up, and it's over. People are impressed when a funnel is a mile wide. A hurricane can be hundreds of miles across. Superstorm Sandy was one of the largest hurricanes to spin up in the Atlantic. They say it was 1,000 miles across at one point. When she made landfall, the storm covered the East Coast of North America from Georgia to far up the coast of Canada."

She waved her hand around in the open air. "This little breeze, this is nothing in comparison to what is coming." Mary Rose must have taken pity on me, the woman she'd invited to tea, because she softened her voice. "Don't you worry. People around here know what to do and they'll make sure you're safe."

"We didn't have to deal with this kind of storm when I was growing up in Seattle."

A disapproving note of suspicion was in her voice. "So, you think this is a bad place to be?"

"No, no, not at all," I countered quickly. "It's just that we had other kinds of natural events."

"Like...?"

"Well, the West Coast is famous for earthquakes, of course. Fault lines run everywhere. There's one right inside the city limits."

"You say that with pride?" Mary Rose huffed softly. "Arrogant people build cities on fault lines. They are tempting fate and Mother Nature," she said, with a note of disapproval.

"I guess the same is true about people," I said.

She closed her right eye, not in a friendly wink. She was considering what I said. So, I took the idea a step further. "We need to heed the warnings we send out to each other." I got no reaction.

The old woman, face permanently tanned by the sun, just looked at me with her sparkling green eyes filled with intelligence. I suspected I'd lose a debate about man's arrogance in a confrontation with nature, but I wasn't ready to concede, not yet. "People are careful around volcanoes. Did you know there are five active ones in the state of Washington?"

"People were killed during the big eruption of Mt. St. Helens. People didn't listen when the scientists said *Stay Away!* Arrogance again."

I sputtered. Before I could say anything in the defense of my hometown, my home coast, she brought up the devastating wildfires. "People need to pay attention to those fires and figure out why they're happening."

At last I could show I was well-informed about something in the natural world. "There are several factors at work there. A major one is the drought, and another is the buildup of brush and —" She didn't give me the chance to finish.

"It is an act of Mother Nature saying that things are not right in her forests," she said with a conviction I couldn't dispute.

My side of the argument was getting weaker. "We're trying to be smart about a possible tsunami." I was surprised when she conceded the point.

Her head nodded a little and said in a considered tone, "Yes, an early warning system would be good to alert the people…" followed by her zinger. "…who are crowded all along the coast and will maim and kill each other while they're clawing a path of escape from the oncoming water. Yes, an early warning system that people would heed is a good idea."

"I don't see a lot of people evacuating here."

"It's not time," she shot back.

"We have ice storms… and windstorms. They're not classified as hurricanes, but wind gusts can get up to 80 MPH."

"Child's play compared to what is coming here."

"Everyone at Fair Winds is a little on edge. The TV is on constantly. The forecasters are talking about it 24/7. It's never been easier to keep up on the latest information." *And to live in almost a constant state of anxiety,* I added silently. Everyone else acted calm and confident. I didn't want my concern to show, afraid that people might tease me about it *forever.*

"The forecasters, yes," she said with a little chuckle. "They serve a purpose, but they use numbers and squiggly lines to determine what's going to happen. You don't need that." She raised her arms to the heavens in a dramatic way. "The signs are all around us. You only have to take the time to read them. Mother Nature is telling us everything we need to know."

She came and stood next to me and gazed out over the water. "There's one clear sign that a storm is coming. Watch for Leucothea. She will dance out there."

"Who?"

She smiled, as if she was talking about an old friend. "Leucothea, a sweet Greek sea goddess, the goddess of spindrift."

"You mean the white foam that flies off the tops of waves? I guess the Greeks had a goddess for everything, even foam."

"I don't think you'll have to wait very long before you see her dancing on the waves right here in the Miles River. She'll look like a ballerina wearing an airy tutu, doing pirouettes in the wind. When Leucothea dances, a storm is coming."

After all the scientific talk on television between the meteorologists, it was refreshing to hear a romantic version of a storm's approach. I looked at Mary Rose with fresh eyes. When she'd walked into Fair Winds wearing a stained dress, black leather boots and gloves, her gray hair sticking out from under a tan canvas hat the night of the meeting – the night Alex died – I got the impression of an uneducated, homeless person living rough. Mary Rose was anything but homeless. She was comfortable on the land with its delicate flowers and in her cottage, delicate linens and fine silver. I marveled at how people can get the wrong impression about someone. It seemed that my lessons were not over.

"Look down in the water," she instructed. "What do you see?"

Just below our feet were a multitude of jellyfish floating around. Graceful. Fragile.

Mary Rose said, "People believe those sea nettles are worthless creatures. I guess they are, because they don't do anything that is obvious. They float around and make being in the water a pain, literally. If you brush one of those tentacles, you're stung with poison."

I jerked back. *Poison.* I glanced back at the graceful creatures, unsettled. "Not like those deadly ones," I said, inching along the dock toward land.

The old woman chuckled. "No, they won't kill you, but they can sure make life miserable. You'll get a rash, is all. Sprinkle some meat tenderizer on it, grit your teeth and you'll be fine." She crouched down to get a closer look at them suspended just below the surface, rhythmically opening and closing their domed-shaped bodies. "They're older than time." She put her hands on her hips. "There is something magical about them."

"Yes, their elegant movements are mesmerizing." I looked at her when she didn't respond to see a stunned look on her face. "What?"

"Those are fancy words for a creature with no brain, no bones, heart or eyes."

"But the magic?"

"The magic happens at night. If the water is churned up by something like a boat propeller, they become phosphorescent. They glow in the dark. Check it out the next time you're in a boat at night. Look over the stern and you'll see quite the light show in the wake."

I looked down in the water again, almost wishing it was dark and I was on a boat.

"I have to warn you. Somebody seeing their light might think they're seeing a ghost." She chortled quietly. "Mother Nature sure can confuse a person when she wants to."

We walked down the dock together toward her garden. "I love fresh flowers in summer, but I'm afraid I must have an orange thumb. Plants don't seem to like me." Fortunately, Fair Winds has beautiful gardens and the staff to care for them."

"Enjoying Mother Nature's beauty is a gift and only requires some time and attention." She ran her palm over white cone-shaped flowers. "Take these Limelight Hydrangeas. They need almost no assistance to grow into these stately bushes."

I pointed to the arbor over the walkway to her cottage. "Those pink roses gave me a wonderful welcome with their heavenly fragrance."

"That's the America Climbing Rose. The double blooms look and smell like a rose should." She walked over to a lush rose bush and picked a pink rose with a profusion of petals. "You must take this with you as a memento of your visit to my home. It is the Mary Rose."

"The Mary Rose rose. How appropriate. Did your parents name you after it?"

Her skin blushed a delicate pink. "No, my mother was so delighted to have a baby girl that she picked this old English heirloom rose to celebrate. It was named after a flagship of King Henry VIII. Momma figured that if a king could give such a gentle name to a strong ship of war, it would be a good reminder to me to appreciate beauty and to know I'm responsible for my own survival and all that is important to me."

She caressed the petals. "She planted them all around Willow Hall. When my father sold the estate, the new owners ripped them out. I tiptoed around the property one night and salvaged some of the bushes and brought them here. These roses are from the original bushes my mother had planted."

Yes, this woman was like her roses, strong, bowed by life, but not broken.

We walked back to my car and that's when my breath caught at seeing a small field of bright yellow-orange Black-Eyed Susans. How had I missed them on my way in?

"Oh! How beautiful to see a field of these bright flowers. They are the Maryland State Flower, aren't they?"

Mary Rose didn't do a good job hiding her impatience. "Yes, I suppose, but that's not why I seeded them here. Once, there was a grand field growing wild at Willow Hall. They bloom at the end of summer when they don't have to compete with all the showy flowers that rush to bloom as the weather warms up. That was my Field of Magic. I planted this one when the new owners …" The words dripped with scorn. "… plowed it under to put in that swimming pool."

"How sad. But at least you have this field."

A slow smile spread over her wrinkled face. "Yes. I was only a little thing, maybe four years old, when my mother had a fairy dress made for me. It was the lightest pink chiffon you can imagine. It felt like acres and acres of fabric when I wore it, like being on a pink cloud. I could float around, go anywhere I wanted. All I had to do was run through my Field of Magic, the Black-eyed Susans. Momma made a crown of flowers and a wand wrapped in pink silk ribbons and I reigned over the animals and birds. Squirrels came up to me for the nuts and seeds I *borrowed* from the kitchen. Butterflies fluttered by sometimes and if I stayed very, very still, one would land on me." She paused, not seeing me, but the butterflies and friends from her childhood.

She shook herself back to reality and turned to me. "Would you like to see it?" I wasn't sure what she meant. "Not the field, it's gone, but I still own a small patch of Willow Hall. Would you like to see it sometime?"

I imagined that this was a rare invitation I couldn't pass up. "Yes, I'd like that. When—"

She held her hand up. "Enough planning. We have to watch the weather. I fear Mother Nature is about to throw a raucous party and we're all invited, whether we like it or not. I'll have to let you know."

After we said good-bye, I roared down the open road to the Miles River Bridge. It was glorious. What did they say about the Saab? *Born From Jets.* When the turbo kicked in, it did feel like takeoff. Gran would have loved this car. She'd special-ordered it, but by the time it arrived, she was too sick to drive it. At least we took a few rides with the top down, before…

Who would have thought an *old* lady would pick a car with so much power? The first time I activated the Sport Drive, I almost lost control of the car. When I drove across country to Washington for my new job, I learned a lot about the car and, by the time I'd crossed the Rockies, I could whip around other cars like a ghost. Why, oh WHY did they cease production?!

Now, it was taking me back to Fair Winds and the reality of a murder a little too fast. I had to be honest with myself that visiting Willow Cottage had been a nice respite from the worry, grieving and upset. I wasn't quite ready to return. I came up with the perfect excuse to run into town: the library. Lorraine said that Simon needed to learn his manners now that he was growing into a big boy. All I knew about training was what she'd taught me. If I got some books about obedience, it would give us something to talk about, something other than the silver fake sitting in the dining room... or murder.

CHAPTER 18

Avoid polishing a silver piece called a Turkish wedding or puzzle ring. It is made by fitting many bands together and was once given to the wife to indicate her faithfulness. If removed from the finger, the bands fall apart and it is difficult to reconstruct them into a single unit.

"The Butler's Guide to Fine Silver"
Mr. Hollister, 1898

As I HURRIED along the sidewalk, I saw Allen and Arabella walking toward me. Why, oh why, did I keep running into them? It felt so uncomfortable, but it was too late for me to make a quick detour. They'd seen me. I wondered if they wanted to avoid me as much as I wanted to duck away. Then the situation went from bad to worse. Dealing with them both was awkward enough, but Allen was turning away.

"I forgot my portfolio," he said to Arabella. "Wait here, I'll be right back." And he dashed off in the direction they'd come, leaving Arabella alone.

Our chance meeting might be a golden opportunity for me to find out more information about these two, if I could face the tiger. I sucked up my courage and walked right up to her.

"With all the upset, I haven't had a chance to express my condolences to you. I know you and Alex were divorced, but still…"

Arabella's eyes grew wide in surprise. Could those have been the first kind words she'd heard since coming to the Shore. I was surprised at how sincere I sounded then realized I wanted to honor the fact she and Alex were once in love, had married and made a home and a family. Even though their marriage had ended and they hadn't appeared to be on the friendliest terms, it was the right thing to do. I stood quietly. I wouldn't be surprised if she walked away in a huff. That seemed to be her trademark, to take offense easily. I watched her turquoise eyes narrow in suspicion, then relax. She had made her decision.

"Thank you. That's very nice." Her voice was deep and smoky, sensual, now that she'd dropped her antagonistic attitude. "If I still wore his wedding band, everyone would be falling all over themselves to be nice to me."

Her eyes strayed to some point over my shoulder. I didn't dare turn around, didn't want to break the moment. But she wasn't looking at anything but her memories.

"We were together for years. They were good years, until he was more married to the business than he was to me. Sure, I had a big house, nice cars, the Black American Express Card, but he was never around." Her shoulders slouched a little. "I wasn't willing to give up on our marriage. That's why I got my real estate license." She paused with a little harumph. "I thought he'd notice me again if we worked together, but no… I was losing him." She took a step back and held out her arms. "Look at me! *I* was losing him to a bunch of buildings?" She dropped her arms in frustration. "I tried everything, even thought if I made him jealous…" Her voice trailed off. "How was I to know he'd divorce me?" A hard look flashed in those remarkable eyes. "Everyone is treating me like a wicked witch. It's not fair." Her lower lip quivered for a moment then her chin rose in defiance. "But I can handle that."

I'd always been curious about what went on behind the scenes of a relationship, things that other people never got to see, except in candid moments like this. I guess it came from trying to understand why my father basically gave me to Gran and walked away when I was five.

Softly, I asked, "When is the funeral?"

My question caught her off guard. Her mouth opened, but no words came out. She looked away as if searching for something anchor her and tried again. "I'm not sure. They have—" She swallowed, then continued. "His body is in Baltimore with the medical examiner, I think. As if they can't tell why he died." She was trying to cover her emotions with snide comments. "His chest is gone, shredded. He worked so hard to develop those muscles." A tiny smile touched the corners of her mouth. "He built a room on our house, so we didn't have to waste time going to a gym. We worked out right at home, together."

She reached her hand up to her head and ran her fingers through that impossibly-shiny ebony hair. Her eyes were glistening with unshed tears. She was grieving, not for a friend, but for a true love. Then she flipped her hair over her shoulder and something inside her hardened.

"How should I know when the funeral is? You do remember that I'm the *ex*?"

"Somebody must be making the arrangements." I hoped it sounded like a question.

She didn't answer right away. She brought her hands together and rubbed them while a mess of emotions marched across her face. With a huff, she responded, "Our daughter, Erin. She won't let me do a thing, say a thing. I swear if she tells me one more time that this was *her daddy,* I will scream. She's never forgiven me. She still believes Alex's side of the story."

This gorgeous woman brushed an invisible bug off her shoulder with an air of defiance that it was more important than her ex-husband's funeral or her daughter. Her timing was perfect. She had tightened down her defenses as Allen returned.

"Sorry about that. We can go in now." Allen slipped his arm around her waist and propelled Arabella to the library's front door. "See you at the meeting, Abby," he called out over his shoulder.

I watched as they entered the library, but I made no move to follow them. Yes, I had come for books about dog training, but I couldn't even bring myself to walk in their wake. I didn't like how they'd acted at Fair Winds that deadly night. Their cavalier attitude toward Lorraine sickened me. And the way they'd treated Alex in the last moments of his life… it was so wrong.

Somebody killed Alex. Could one of them have pulled the trigger? I fought the urge to dismiss Arabella as the shooter. No, I would not be taken in by what seemed like genuine emotions she'd shown me for a few moments. She could raise and lower that tough façade without hesitation. I'd wager she could do anything she wanted if she wanted it enough. And Allen was busy moving the project forward according to his vision of *Let's get this done.* He couldn't set it aside for a few days until after the funeral for his business partner? Wasn't he with his partner's ex-wife, the woman who was still in love with Alex? The man had no respect for boundaries. He too could do anything, *anything* to get what he wanted.

No, I wanted nothing to do with either one of them. If people saw me following them into the library, they might get the impression that we were together. No, I'd come back for the books another day. Simon would just have to wait.

I laughed at myself as I got back in my car. I'd come to the library to avoid an uncomfortable conversation with Lorraine at Fair Winds and ran into two vipers. No, I'd take Lorraine and Fair Winds any day. I took a couple of back streets to avoid traffic and headed home.

I went straight to the main house to tell Lorraine about the appraiser's opinion of the epergne. I just wanted to get it done, but when I walked in the kitchen door, I found Mrs. Clark and Dawkins standing in the doorway to the breakfast room, eyes glued on the television.

"... and it picked up energy as it crossed the warm waters of the Gulf Stream," the weatherman said.

Just as Charlie and his friends predicted.

"You're wasting your time, Mr. Dawkins." Mrs. Clark chortled.

Dawkins turned to her as I'd seen him do so many times. She couldn't seem to accept that he wanted to be addressed by his last name alone. *It's just Dawkins.* She insisted on adding *Mr.* to his name. This time, he paused then turned back to the TV screen. Maybe he realized there were more important issues to face and this one was a losing battle.

Mrs. Clark didn't notice. "If you're worrying about this storm hitting St. Michaels, you're worrying for nothing. I will admit we've had some high water and a few trees blown down in the past, but some damage from Mother Nature is to be expected. This storm will bypass us." She folded her arms with certainty.

I'd been watching the screen over his shoulder and had to say something. "But it's showing a cone. Those are the places that could be affected by the storm and we're right on the edge."

"The cone, the cone... everyone worries about the cone." She threw her hands up. "It will be fine, mark my words."

I left the two of them hashing out the particulars of the storm. If they wanted to spend their time debating something that the experts couldn't figure out, fine. There was something I had to do which far more difficult.

In the dining room, I faced the epergne, my nemesis. What I'd thought was a magnificent piece of silver had foiled my first real attempt to be recognized as an up-and-coming silver expert. Foiled by some silver foil. The little joke didn't diminish the fact that I was mad at myself and my feelings were hurt. Mr. Fuller didn't have to be so harsh. I'd spent a lot of time on research and inspection. Obviously, not enough. There was no one else to blame, but myself. The person who had committed the fraud in the first place had left lots of breadcrumbs for me to discover that the piece was a fraud. I'd missed them. The only thing I could do was to learn from my mistake so it never happened again. And the place to start was with the hallmarks.

I removed all the baskets, everything that could be taken away from the main column. It held the major clue that should have shown me the epergne was masquerading as something it wasn't. Disgusted with myself, I grabbed the silver piece with too much force and it began to tip, all two feet of metal, aimed right at my head. I couldn't control it. I cringed from the blow… that never happened.

I opened my eyes to see Dawkins setting the piece safely on its feet. Silently, he spread a pad on the tabletop and laid the silver on its side. "Now, it is safe for you to conduct your inspection." And he silently left the room.

Speechless, I straightened up, shaking my head in awe. The man not only knew where to be and when, but he had the reflexes of a magician.

"He is amazing, my cousin." Norman stood in the archway to the foyer.

"Did you see that?"

"I did." Norman shrugged. "I am not surprised. The Army Rangers, they trained him well."

"Dawkins, a Ranger?" My father was a Navy man. I knew about elite military forces.

"Si, what is the slogan? 'Anywhere in the world in 18 hours, ready to serve.'" He smiled, pleased that he remembered. "Carlino was a natural, so proud to wear their Tan Beret. What did he tell me?" Norman looked up at the ceiling as if all the answer was written there. "He learned marksmanship, physical training, small-unit tactics and mobility and…" He shook his head. "I don't remember, all the skills he mastered, but I do know that to him, it was all about the success of the Ranger mission." He dropped his eyes. "But to me, it was about control... control of himself, of the circumstances, control of everything. He believed he could bend any situation to stop bad things from happening."

"But no one can do that."

"*I* know that." He shrugged again. "But there was no way to persuade him."

I couldn't believe it. An Army Ranger. No wonder he could move like a shadow. No wonder he had to know what was happening everywhere at Fair Winds. "But what is he doing here, working as a butler? This job is about as far as you can get from what a Ranger does." *Unless we needed protection from a murderer*, I added silently.

"Ah, then you know, the skills he has. The tests he had to survive. The challenges he had to meet..." Norman shuddered. "I don't know how he did it. Have you ever seen him running, sprinting, push-ups, pull-ups, sit-ups? I get exhausted just watching him. My dear cousin knows how to eliminate an enemy from far away," Norman formed his hand into the shape of a gun, brought it up to his eye and squinted as if taking aim. "with one shot." Norman's finger pulled the trigger of his hand gun.

"You talk so calmly about killing a person." I felt myself recoiling.

Norman looked at me as his bushy black eyebrows shot straight up. "Of course. There are bad men in this world. Verrrry bad men." His Italian accent with the rolled *R* stretched out the word. "If you do not kill, they kill you," he jerked up. "Or me!" He shook his head quickly. "But we will be safe. Carlino knows about those people and what to do without being told."

"What do you mean?" I pulled out a chair from the table and sank into it.

"The Rangers, they taught him how to watch. He can tell a liar, a fake, a violent man by watching. Yes, he reads the person like a book!"

How many times had I seen Dawkins silently watching someone? I realized Lorraine knew of his skill and used it whenever the estate hired new people or interviewed contractors and vendors. Dawkins told her to trust this one, avoid that one. She noted how often he was right.

"Where did he serve, do you know?"

Norman held up his hands to ward off my questions. "Everywhere, nowhere. It's all secret, what you call classified."

"Did he go on missions?"

Norman cleared his throat with a soft rumble. "I only know of one. It was his last." Norman glanced at the door to be sure no one was listening and lowered his voice. "There was a very bad man there. The Americans could not get information for a successful drone strike. They sent Carlino in to find him. You know he speaks Arabic and Farsi like a native?"

I shook my head. I'd overheard him speaking Spanish and French on occasion. I assumed that some proficiency in some foreign languages was part of his job, but those languages…? The thought of him working in the violent areas where those language were spoken sent a shiver through me. To be constantly surrounded by lethal threats was more than I could imagine.

"He told me the story of how he went in alone and lived with a host family near the target's house. From there, he monitored the man's movements. It took many days and nights of observation to identify the signs that the man would soon visit that house. When Carlino was certain of the pattern, he planned the assault. The odds were against another drone strike so, a small team was sent in. On the appointed day, he told his host family to stay inside. No one should leave." Norman took a deep breath. "Everyone obeyed, except one. A young boy, who was like my cousin's shadow, following his hero everywhere."

A child? I thought Dawkins didn't like kids. Or had one touched his heart? Norman's voice was soft, so I had to lean closer to hear his words.

"When the team assaulted the house, gunfire broke out. The target came out of the door my cousin was covering and the bad man escaped. My cousin didn't take the shot. He never even raised his gun. His eyes were transfixed by the small body that lay sprawled on the stones, leaking blood."

"Don't tell me." My voice cracked.

"I am afraid it is true. Unknown to everyone, the little boy had followed his hero to the scene of the assault and was caught in the crossfire. Bullets mangled the child's body. Dear Carlino described how he gently gathered the boy in his arms and watched as the light went out of the boy's eyes." Norman wiped a tear from his eye. "The boy was collateral damage. While the American team fought to escape with their lives, Carlino carried the boy's body to his father." Norman sadly shook his head. "He believed the team missed their target because he did not take the shot. He declared to me that it was his fault. He'd put the whole team at risk while gunfire poured out of every window and from around dark corners. He said they buried his soul with the boy."

I was amazed that the Dawkins I knew was the same man who held a dying child. "How did he survive? What did he do to save himself?"

Norman took a deep breath and let it out slowly. "He was beaten. He tried to leave the Army, but they made it hard for him. They had invested so much in the man. He was their war machine. They wanted to treat him for… PTSD, is that right?"

"Post-Traumatic Stress Disorder," I nodded. "Many suffer from it."

"He refused. It was as if he didn't want to get better. He only wanted to take off his uniform, put the tan beret he respected on a shelf. He said he didn't deserve it anymore. He wanted to close that chapter of his life. He also stopped using his name *Charlie*. It reminded him of what happened. Finally, they let him go. And then he was truly lost. He had no goals. No direction. Then something happened."

"Oh no, did someone else die?"

Norman had a sweet look on his face. "No, what happened was good. The way our old auntie tells it, and you do know that Sicilian women are very wise. She said that his grandmother Maria whispered to him to go to the family. Not the one in America. His true *famiglia* in Sicily. There, she promised he could rest and find himself again."

"Does he believe in that…"

Norman raised one bushy black eyebrow and looked at me. I hesitated to say the word mumbo-jumbo which is what I was thinking. Dawkins didn't seem like a man who believed in superstition. I said nothing and the little man relaxed.

"He did the right thing. He came to Sicily and the old aunties attended to him. They said he was out of balance and they went to work, doing the mystical things they do. They held up a mirror for him to see who he truly was inside." The little Italian man stood tall. "When he was better, ready to face the world again, they sent him to me."

That was a surprise. "To you?"

"Yes." He dragged out the word to emphasize that it was the most logical thing for the aunties to do. "While he was in Sicily, the women determined that all the killing and hostility had sucked the life force out of his body. Not everyone grows up with the consideration and love for others that his father taught him. All of that had been trained out of him. He needed to be nurtured. He needed beauty around him to counteract all the ugliness he had seen. So, they sent him to me."

"But weren't you working on an estate?"

"Si, I was in charge, the Maggiordomo, of an estate on the mainland. It was bellissimo! While he was with me, he found he liked the regimen of the lifestyle, the beauty and the calmness. He liked taking care of people while always having a small degree of separation so he could not get too close to caring." Norman folded his hands over his round belly. "I remember the day he said he wanted to train for a position like mine. I was proud and I was frightened that he would fail."

I viewed at the little man with new appreciation. "It must take a special kind of person to do what you do."

"Si, it does, but I worried for nothing. My cousin, he does not fail."

RIVER OTTER

You might not know that there is a River Otter is nearby because this incredibly shy creature loves to play. If you spot one swimming, then it disappears, she may not surface again for many long minutes. When she's not swimming, she loves to slide across the ice or in the mud of the riverbank. An excellent housekeeper, she gives birth and raises her young on her own.

She is very talkative using whistles, buzzing sounds, chuckles, chirps and growls, but when she's frightened, she'll let loose a ear-splitting scream that can be heard more than a mile away over water.

The water quality around her home directly affects her health and well-being.

CHAPTER 19

Poets claim there is always a silver lining within storm clouds. It is your job to squelch any unpleasantness that may upset the House.

"The Butler's Guide to Fine Silver"
Mr. Hollister, 1898

AFTER INSPECTING THE EPERGNE, now seeing all the signs that it was a fake, and trying to digest the information that Dawkins had been in special ops and suffered a severe trauma, I needed some fresh air to clear my head. A little dog training would help clear my head. If I had any hope of getting Simon to pay attention to my directives, I needed those dog training treats Lorraine kept in the butler's pantry, Dawkins domain. I didn't want to bother the man for something I could find easily. If I could just slip in with being caught red-handed… But it was not to happen. He caught me with my hand in the cookie jar, literally.

"There you are, Miss Abigail.

"Here I am, Dawkins. What's up?" I tried to act cool, but felt guilty as can be.

"I've been looking for you everywhere."

"Obviously, not everywhere." I had to keep up my normal banter, what was normal before I learned about his Ranger training and what happened to him in the Middle East or he would suspect something.

"And I called your cell phone...."

"The battery is dead."

He squinted at me here in his pantry. "And why are you here?"

I tried to look innocent. "I need to work on Simon's training. Everyone says he's getting out of control and I need some treats for positive reinforcement." My voice went a little higher. "What is it you want, Dawkins?"

"Did you see the phone message I left for you on the kitchen counter?" I shook my head. "I thought it was rather odd that she called on the estate's landline. She said she didn't have your cell number." He dismissed the occurrence with a wave of his hand. "Of course, I was happy to take down the details."

"Who was she? Do you remember her name?"

"She only gave her first name. The message is next to the coffee machine, an appropriate place to get your attention."

I made my way past Dawkins and into the kitchen. There, in flowing script, was the name Mary Rose.

Dawkins followed me. "She would not leave a telephone number, but the message was quite clear. She was calling to confirm the excursion the two of you discussed over tea."

Excursion? I racked my brain, trying to remember. Was she referring to a trip to Willow Hall?

"And," Dawkins continued. "She said she would meet you here at Fair Winds..." He glanced at the kitchen clock. "... in about twenty minutes, if I'm not mistaken."

In the next breath, the doorbell chimed.

"Oh dear, I believe she's early." Dawkins went off to answer the door and I was close on his heels. I didn't want her to be intimidated. Then I remembered how she'd taken over control of the community meeting the other night and I stopped stressing. This was one woman who could handle herself.

As he greeted her, I moved past him gingerly. "Thank you, Dawkins. I've got this." He moved away silently as I turned to Mary Rose who stood primly on the top step in a summer cotton dress with a bit of a poufy slip under the skirt. This must be a dressy occasion, because she was wearing duck shoes, not her black boots.

"I'm sorry," I said. "I just got your message and—"

"That's fine. Your man did well on the phone though I think he was a little annoyed, because I wouldn't leave my number. Do you have the time now to go to Willow Hall? You said you would." Her eyes shone with expectation, while she bit her lower lip, bracing for disappointment.

Well, I thought, *I wanted a distraction and this certainly qualified.* "Yes, I'd be happy to join you," I said and closed the door behind me.

I followed as she marched down the front steps. "Are you driving?" I asked, a little unsure about the idea since I wondered what was holding her ancient truck together. More than a few rust spots spread over its body.

"Heavens no! I'm not going to have a classy girl like you get up in my truck." Her watery eyes of pale blue filled with longing as they strayed to the front of the main house of Fair Winds. Its snowy white façade and tall columns gleamed as it caught the rays of the afternoon sun. "I was a classy girl once, too. I lived in a grand home like this one, you know."

I remembered my surprise when I entered this old woman's cottage of comfortable elegance. There was more to her story and I hoped she would share it.

She went on. "Back then, I would have never stepped inside a truck like mine. Times change... and time changes people. Can't do anything about that. The only constant is Mother Nature."

Once again, the Eastern Shore had put an interesting

personality in my path. I was willing—no, eager—to find out more about her and see her childhood home, Willow Hall.

"Get your car and follow me," she snapped. "I don't have all day,"

Okay then...I ran back to the kitchen, got my keys and caught up with her at the head of the drive. Her truck engine sounded like it would wake the dead.

She called out the truck's window, "Follow me." And we raced up Route 33. Her truck had a lot of well-oiled power under that rusty hood.

As I paid attention to keeping up with her, her last comment kept pushing at me. *The only constant is Mother Nature.* Mary Rose was always quick with pronouncements in her well-ordered world. This time, I felt like I needed to push back a little, later when we weren't exceeding the speed limit.

Up ahead was a bike rider in a familiar black shirt with orange and neon green stripes. I recognized the man who was still on my refrigerator's suspect board. I slowed down a little to get a better look. His bulging leg muscles were pumping away. He was so focused on his riding that he didn't give a thought to a car coming up behind him and his oh-so-special bike. I had to admit it looked pretty special with its sleek design, hefty tires and a complicated gear mechanism on the rear wheel. A neon green swath on the bike matched the one on his shirt. The brand name *Cannondale* in silver decorated the slanted bar. I could barely make out his face under the—

I slammed on my brakes! Mary Rose was turning right just before the Oak Creek Bridge. The bicyclist threaded his way between us and went on up the road. I figured that guy was oblivious, too self-centered to steal a gun and shoot someone, unless the victim stole his bike. He had to come off my suspect board.

I parked by the tiny Newcomb post office, next to Mary Rose's truck and before I put the car in park, she jumped into the Saab's passenger seat with a bunch of sunflowers in her hand.

"You can drive from here," she ordered. "I'll show you where to go." And we were off.

Now, I had the chance to push back about her comment. I braced for a whirlwind reaction as I asked, "You said that the only constant is Mother Nature. But nature is changing all the time."

"Of course, she is. That's part of her beauty. She brings us hope for the future. Take the seasons around here. You can see the change, not like Florida where it's hot and hotter. Here, summer is glorious and in winter, you're shivering from the cold. Your garden is bleak, but you know spring is coming. It always does. Mother Nature doesn't lie to you and she won't lead you astray. She won't leave you with a promise unfulfilled."

"What about the storms, like the hurricane bearing down on us right now? It could bring sudden, even catastrophic changes. Lorraine told me how scared people were when Hurricane Sandy was expected to hit this region."

"Yes, but she slipped by and hit farther north."

"And devastated areas of New Jersey," I countered.

"Maybe some natural changes had to happen up there, to correct what man had done." Mary Rose looked up at the trees and blue sky with wisps of clouds. "Sure, she kicks up a fuss sometimes." She had an almost beatific look on her face. "Have you ever smelled the air the morning after a major storm? Ever seen the sky, such an aching blue? And the light, it's so clear and pure." She paused lost in her memory. Then she turned to face me. "Well, have you?" she barked.

"No, I grew up on the West Coast, remember? I wonder if the violence and fear a hurricane brings is worth that morning-after experience you describe?"

"What do you know? Have you lived through a life-changing trauma in the dark, hoping for a morning after? I have. And I know that if I rely on Mother Nature, the world will be alright again."

"How can you be so sure?" Her attitude brought out the challenge.

"It's simple. You never have to second-guess Mother Nature. She doesn't have a hidden agenda, like people. People can tell you one thing, then do another, no matter who it hurts. It's folly to depend on them. People!" I swear, if this woman chewed tobacco, she would have spit it out right there in utter disgust.

"No, there's no question," she declared. "You'll live better following what Mother Nature tells you. She is all about survival, no matter what life hands you." She stretched out her arm in across my face and pointed. "Turn left here."

I almost missed the road, because it really wasn't a road at all. It was more of a path of oyster shells just wide enough for my car. I maneuvered the Saab and listened to the crunching of shells under the tires. "Where are we?"

"Willow Hall. It belonged to my momma's family for generations. It's where she grew up and where I was born. Beautiful things filled the huge main house and there were gardens and fresh vegetables, even fig and peach trees. There was staff to take care of it all. My momma was the last living child of her aging parents. They flitted between Baltimore, Washington, Philadelphia and New York City during her debutante years. My father swept her off her feet. He was The Man About Town in New York City who could do no wrong, even though he gambled and drank too much, but, as he liked to say, he changed his ways when he met his princess.

"They moved to the Shore and lived here in the main house. She was a young bride when she inherited the farm, the estate, call it whatever you want." Her face hardened. "Of course, this isn't the main drive. This is the only way I can visit what's left of my family's land. It's where the dead stay, my ancestors, the foundation of who I am."

CHAPTER 20

Jewellery made of sterling silver comes in contact with the oils of the skin as well as materials such as wool. This contact can cause the piece to tarnish and requires more careful attention than the silver pieces used in the dining room.

"The Butler's Guide to Fine Silver"
Mr. Hollister, 1898

MARY ROSE TOLD me to park in the middle of the path and we headed down toward the water. The tall pines, a blend of muted greens and browns, towered over us in a protective embrace. The oak and maple trees were not yet ready for the riot of color that fall would bring as the last hurrah of the season. A few wispy clouds drifted across the clear azure blue sky as the sun dipped behind the tops of the trees to play peekaboo through the leaves. It was hard to believe a major storm could be coming.

My foot slipped on the loose shells and I stepped over to the grass that was slick with the condensation of the high humidity. "Oh, watch your step!" I said without thinking.

She turned and put her hands on her hips. "Who are you talking to?" Her tone was mocking. She raised one boot. "Why do you think I wear these? They got great tread and a steel shank inside. I'm not going anywhere, while you'll slip-slide around in those boat shoes." She turned back toward our destination. "*You* watch where you're going. I don't want to be picking you up and carrying you back to the car."

I followed her, determined not to appear silly to her, and gestured at the group of headstones. "Is that the graveyard?"

"No, that's not the graveyard." There was a little sneer in her voice. "A graveyard has to be next to a church. There's no church around here. My granddaddy wouldn't have it. Said nature built the best church to bring him close to the Lord. Better than anything man could devise."

"So, this is a cemetery?"

"That's right. The Willow Hall cemetery is filled with my people. I'm the last one, except for my brother Luke's family, but I don't think they'll end up here. Even though somebody else owns Willow Hall, this is ancestral land and tells our story. Nobody has the right to dismantle this part of our history."

Clutching a bouquet of fresh sunflowers, she walked down the path of half-buried oyster shells, she said, "This was once a dirt path, fine for a horse-drawn hearse to bring a casket down for burial. Granddaddy laid down oyster shells to keep it from getting muddy and rutted."

I bent down and picked up one of the shells. "Oyster shells?"

"Same thing they use to serve up the oysters on the half shell in the fancy restaurants that kowtow to tourists."

"But it's illegal to use them for a path now, isn't it?" I asked, as I inspected the shell. It was irregular in shape, rough on one side, but the underside was iridescent, except at the spot where the oyster clung to its shell until it was ripped away.

"Yes, that's why the path is disappearing. Nobody wants to pave it and it doesn't seem right to lay down a bunch of white stones with the oyster shells."

She stopped for a moment with her fists on her hips and stared off in the distance, not focused on anything I could see.

"There used to be mountains of white shells all over the Shore, gleaming in the sun. When I was little, my father used to take me down to the Tilghman Island Packing Company when they were in full swing. It wasn't a business. It was a family, all working together. Mostly women with their hair all done up, makeup on, looking pretty. I wanted to work there. It was like a big family. My father said no, said I didn't need another family. He had other plans for me." She pointed at my feet. "Watch your step!'"

I sidestepped the hole in front of me and hurried after her where the weeds were working hard to swallow the last white shells winking in the afternoon sunlight.

"Are you sure we're not trespassing on private property?" I asked. If this was Fair Winds, Lorraine wouldn't appreciate strangers tromping across the grounds.

"No, no, this belongs to my family. I have a right to be here," she snapped.

Ahead, there was a flat area of land, a private island of memories surrounded by an old-fashioned wrought iron fence with splotches of rust here and there. Small rose bushes stood on either side of the creaky gate.

The cemetery was compact. One only had to read the names on the stone markers lined up neatly to know that a family was buried within the fence under the sheltering boughs of the maple trees above. There was a feeling of safety here, of being part of a world that was gone. This place contained memories of people related by blood and marriage. The headstones marked dreams that came true and those that did not. It almost felt like home, a home for the ages.

She swung the gate open on its squeaky hinges and walked onto what to her was sacred ground. "My grandparents, their parents, a couple of great uncles, three great aunts..." Her arm swept the enclosure. "...are here. But there are more here."

"What do you mean?"

"Oh," she snickered. "This place is more crowded than you think."

I looked at the ten headstones with large areas of grass in between. It didn't look crowded at all.

She cracked a smile. "In fact, you could be standing on the bones of one of my ancestors right now." I looked down at my feet in fear that I had offended someone long gone, but there was no sign of a grave. "Don't worry. It's hard to walk around here without stepping on somebody. Back a hundred years and more, not everybody's grave was marked with a headstone. Back in the 1800's, they were a superstitious bunch. Some people believed that if you placed a gravestone for someone, you'd be the next to die. That's why there are so many unmarked graves. It's not a problem really. They found a place for my brother Luke ten years ago." She lowered her voice as if delivering a secret. "You know, men don't hold up as well as women." She glanced around the enclosure. "It will be up to the undertaker to make a spot for me here next to Momma. This is where I want to be."

She knelt down next to a headstone and placed the sunflowers in two marble urns. Their cheery faces defied the sadness, the grief and the menace of the coming storm. Then she gently caressed the name Mary Elizabeth carved into the once-white marble stone now marred by lichen. "And this was the one who made and molded me, my Momma. She wanted me. Always said I was part of her."

I stood silently, out of respect. I noticed a very small blank marker with no name nestled close to her mother's plot.

When she roused from her memories, I asked, "What is that?"

Mary Rose's face clouded. She stepped over the small marker and pulled away some weeds that threatened to overwhelm it. "This is the marker for a baby that didn't get a chance to be born."

I mulled those words over in my head. "I'm sorry, what does that mean?"

She spoke in a whisper. "It means that I killed this child before he was born."

Was I standing calmly in a cemetery with a homicidal maniac? Did she just add Alex to her list of victims? As my chest tightened, Mary Rose told the story of the baby not born.

"Momma and I had a tea party on the terrace of Willow Hall."

"Did you put something in the tea?" I asked, not sure I wanted to hear the answer,

She spun around and glared at me. "Are you crazy? I was a child having a tea party with her mother... with pretend tea! I would never hurt her." She glanced at her mother's headstone. "Momma and Father told us that there was a little brother or sister coming to join our family. They were so happy." She paused and her face clouded with the sad memory. "During our tea party, she was smiling and laughing one minute, and the next, she was bent over, screaming." She looked away. "Later, Nanny said the Lord needed the baby more than our family did. For a long time, I thought my tea had made Momma sick..." She twisted her mouth a little. "You see, I really didn't want the baby to come."

I felt like an idiot, thinking this old woman could be a killer. I was more upset about Alex's murder than I realized. I took a deep breath. "Isn't that a normal reaction when there's a new baby on the way? I don't have any firsthand knowledge, but the family adjusts. The parents make the older child feel loved, right?"

Her head whipped around in my direction. "You know nothing. No firsthand knowledge," she grumbled. "Well, I do. When my little brother Luke was born when I was five, everyone said life would be the same. There would just be a new person to share it. Well, Luke didn't share. Those people were wrong."

Mary Rose sank to the ground by her mother's grave. "I was the only child, the golden child, for five glorious years before he was born. From the moment I was out of diapers, my daddy took me everywhere, like old watermen take their dogs everywhere they go."

She sighed again. "Father said the baby was coming five years after I was born and that was good luck. I believed him until Luke arrived."

I asked, "That's a superstition, right?"

Mary Rose narrowed her eyes and I silently vowed to stop interrupting.

"Not a superstition. A sign of bad times, for me. When Luke was out of diapers, Father took him everywhere and left me at home. At first, I was devastated, but Momma stepped in and we did many things together. We tended the garden, arranged the flowers, helped in the vegetable patch, pulled crabs from the dock. It was Momma who taught me how to eat off the land. She really taught me how to survive and overcome disappointment."

A broad smile spread over the old woman's face. "And she taught me the finer social graces: how to be respectful, entertain, and how to make a house into a home. That's when we spent many hours polishing the family silver together."

"Happy memories." I breathed, thinking of my own childhood with Gran, polishing silver, enjoying tea parties with real tea, attempting to master crocheting. I felt a wave of warmth.

Mary Rose looked up at the tall trees all around us. "When I come to this place, I can hear her singing in the breeze. It's the lullaby she always sang to me." I listened to the rustle of the leaves as she remembered until she dropped her head and looked at the stone.

"But it didn't last." She reached over to a clump of weeds and started tearing them away to reveal another small stone for a baby, except this one had a name chiseled into it...Joshua. "I was twelve when she became pregnant again. Father was concerned because it was seven years since Luke was born and the number seven was a bad luck number for him. You must remember, my father loved gambling before he married Momma. She was sickly right from the beginning of the pregnancy. When she went into labor, it was horrible. It wasn't long before both she and the baby died. I used to bring her flowers from our garden, so many, they covered the whole mound."

"What about your father?'

"He sat in the dining room, where we had so many happy

times under the crystal chandelier, and drank himself into a stupor. He told the relations not to come to Willow Hall, that he had a shotgun and wanted us to be left alone." She brushed a little dirt off her hands. "Sure, we had food to eat and clothes to wear. The staff took care of us, but there was no one could comfort us, except Father and he was lost, until one night." She drew in a ragged breath as she remembered.

"There was a storm. Lightning flashes made monstrous shadows on the walls. Thunderclaps shook the house. Luke and I were terrified. We scrambled from our beds and ran to our parents' bedroom, but Father wasn't there. He was downstairs, standing at a window, lightning and thunder crashing right over our heads. All he did was stare out at the cemetery."

A tear trailed down the crinkled lines of the woman's face. "Luke screamed, *DADDY!* I can still hear the panic in his voice. By some miracle, it broke Father's connection to my mother's grave. He gathered us in his arms and the next day, everything changed." Mary Rose breathed out a long sigh, as if all the air was leaving her body. "Before I realized what was happening, he sold the land and the house with everything in it."

"Everything?"

"We left with only our clothes and some toys. On that horrible day, I saw he'd left the family pictures and a small oil painting of my mother in the living room. I grabbed the portrait and a picture of Momma and me. He left the family silver, too."

"Your mother's silver?"

The elderly woman slowly nodded. "All gone to strangers." She raised her face and her earth-brown eyes twinkled. "But I remembered the name of the pattern, Rose Stieff, and how I used my grandmother's magnifying glass to pick out the individual roses."

My heart broke for this woman. I knew how much the silver at Fair Winds meant to Lorraine. She'd never consider leaving it to strangers. It was important enough to her that I worked to organize it all, the collection that included her own, her mother's silver and that of her two great aunts who'd never had children. At least Mary Rose had found a caring woman in her mother-in-law who gave her the very special wedding present, the silver chest she'd shown me.

But that wasn't the end of the heartbreak in the young life of Mary Rose. As we looked at the cemetery, she went on with her story. "I have to be honest. My father was a boozer, a gambler and a spendthrift. He didn't care that he was tearing me away from the one home in the world that I loved more than anything."

She heaved a sigh and spoke to the headstone. "I'm sorry, Momma, I know you loved him, but he was weak. He couldn't protect his children, because he was too busy taking care of himself."

Mary Rose bent over and yanked out a few more offending weeds letting their roots dangle in the air. She was clearly in pain, even now. I could sympathize. A daughter's relationship with her father was often complicated. Mary Rose was a daughter who had to grow up too fast. She had lost her mother, the center of her world, then she lost her home because no one was listening. It's a terrible thing to feel invisible.

The old woman continued her story. "We were hustled to New York and moved into a fine hotel that felt like a prison. Here at home, I could go outside, run and play whenever I wanted." She paused and looked down at her hands clasped at her waist. "And I could sit in the cemetery and talk to my mother. But New York City was loud and dirty. Father said I had to stay inside the hotel. Luke obeyed, but I felt caged.

"One day, I escaped. I looked up at the small slice of sky high above my head that looked like it was held up by the skyscrapers. I ran singing down the sidewalk where people rushed everywhere. They didn't feel the breeze. They didn't smell the sweet flowers in the window boxes. They didn't notice me.

"I wanted more than anything to come home to the Eastern Shore. I wanted to fly." Her voice became soft. "I remember leaping off the curb to take off." She paused at the memory. "There was a screech of tires. Then blackness. When I opened my eyes, people stood over me, crying out for an ambulance. One woman with a bright red hat asked if I was dead. It might have been better," she murmured.

"Father came to the hospital, cried like the night Momma died, then yelled about what a stupid girl I was. When I got better, he sent me to a boarding school in Connecticut."

I couldn't imagine such a free spirit caged in a boarding school. "I bet you hated it."

Her skin took on a pink hue from the raw anger she still felt. "You have no idea! The school had walls all around and they kept the gates locked."

She brushed a few early leaves from her mother's headstone. "I just wanted to come home. "I was always in trouble with the school mistress. Then the Day of Reckoning came! I was standing in that woman's office filled with the sour smell of lilies past their prime. They were stuffed into a crystal vase she claimed came from Tiffany's. That was the day she went too far. She said my mother didn't know how to raise a lady. I can still hear me screaming at her. 'You don't know anything about my mother!' I picked up the crystal vase from the corner of her massive desk and flung it against the wall with all my might. It broke into a thousand pieces." Her face beamed with pride.

"I bet there was a stiff price to pay after that."

She shrugged. "Not right away. Of course, I had to leave the school. Father shipped me to his great aunt in Philadelphia. He said he preferred living only with Luke, his good boy! During the summers, I was allowed to spend time with my mother's cousins on the Shore. Father apologized for *dumping his hellion* on them. They couldn't understand, because I was polite and helpful and attentive. Of course, I was. As far as I was concerned, I was home."

"So, your father let you live here on the Shore?"

"Oh no, he was not doing well at the gambling tables. He went through Momma's fortune. Money was tight and he was afraid the family would want money to keep me. Shows how much he knew." She cocked her head to the side, considering a private thought. "But I have to give him credit. He added something to the Willow Hall deed so this cemetery would always be ours. It meant I could visit Momma..." Mary Rose glanced away then continued. "Her grave, anytime I wished."

She squinted at the reflection coming off the river. "I've always known this is where I belong. This is where I'm going to stay. I've got a lawyer who will make sure this is where I'll be. And not dug up for some shopping center."

I had to ask her something. Maybe she didn't realize she know something important. "Do you know if there was anybody in that meeting who feels like you do about the land?" *Somebody who feels strongly and is willing to commit murder*, I added silently.

Mary Rose put her hands on her hips. "You mean, do I know who shot that man?" She acted insulted that I'd asked. I tried to smooth things over, but she didn't really give me a chance. "I have no idea who wanted to hurt him. I didn't see anything. I left before the meeting was over. Had better things, more important things, to do." She went back to pulling weeds. "I don't understand people anymore. Can't even count on people to do what they promise they'll do. Remember that mouse of a woman who was saying what the developer wanted to do was all right?" She flung her arm out in the direction of the Willow Hall main house. "She lives up there. She's supposed to keep the grass cut, but she lets the staff get away with only getting as close as those big mowers let them. It's me, I'm the one who mows around the stones. She doesn't know how to keep her own promises. How's she going to take care of the Shore?"

She slammed the clump of weeds she held in her hand to the ground. "Look, I'm sure they're probably good people, the ones in the meeting, even the ones who live in my house. They just need to be reminded to do the right thing so the Shore can stay like this so the young ones who come after me will have something to love."

She stood silently for several moments, taking in the whole

scene—the cemetery, her mother's stone, the tiny markers, the rusting fence, the river down below, the tall trees rustling in the air above.

"And I'll be here, watching." Then she turned to me and announced, "It's time for you to go on. I have things to do."

"What?" That was an abrupt switch. "I drove us here, remember? I'll give you a ride back to your truck," I said, turning toward the gate. I was ready to get back to the land of the living.

"No, you go on." She started tugging weeds out of the dry ground, then straightened up. "Look, you're a nice kid. Thoughtful and all. I've been getting around this land since way before you were born. I can do it now."

I'd offered, insisted, but she did have a point. I wasn't going to sweep her up in my arms and carry her back to the car. "Okay, if you're sure?"

"I'm sure," she said, with a sharp nod of her head. "And Abby, thank you."

I nodded and started the trek up the hill. The humid air of the late afternoon enticed clouds of mosquitoes that whirled around me in a frenzy. I slapped at my bare arms and legs trying to deny the females the blood meal they needed for their eggs. I pushed myself to hurry back to the refuge of my car.

CHAPTER 21

Be sure there is a reputable reference book about silver marks, hallmarks and assay marks in your library of information. Do not allow it to collect dust. Use it to confirm that the Family's collection contains only genuine pieces.

"The Butler's Guide to Fine Silver"
Mr. Hollister, 1898

As I drove down the road, my body was itchy and my brain was buzzing. So many stories. The heat made the air throb. I felt listless, but had no time lie down. I was no closer to finding out who murdered Alex and, right now, that was the priority. There was a potential lead sitting in my purse. It was the business card of one Mr. Xavier Pendergast, Attorney at Law. Who was this man and why was his card sitting on the ground next to Alex's Range Rover? Sure, it might have nothing to do with the murder victim. Maybe it wasn't his, but I knew just the person to help me find out. Instead of heading to Fair Winds to tell Lorraine about the counterfeit silver piece sitting on her dining room table, I picked up my phone and called Dr. Rupert Phillips, the librarian.

As usual, the delightful gentleman with the welcoming smile was in his library, wearing a tailored business suit. While we waited for his housekeeper to deliver coffee and cookies as promised, we talked about the one other thing—other than murder—that was on everyone's lips: the storm.

"They say the storm is moving over the Gulf Stream and gaining in strength," I said, sneaking a peek at the clear blue sky through one of the tall library windows.

My Font-of-Knowledge smiled knowingly. "Yes, it's sucking up the warmth and water from the mighty river flowing within the great Atlantic."

"A river within an ocean?"

"Yes, the Gulf Stream is a gigantic source of energy surging past the East Coast of the U.S. and Canada at a rate of eight billion gallons a minute up then across the northern top of the ocean to the British Isles. It is reported that it generates as much energy as several nuclear power plants. Someday, I hope scientists can find a way to harness that power for *good* instead of it just fueling destructive storms."

It wasn't long before we settled back with our coffee and he asked what brought me to his home. I cringed inwardly at the thought of his disapproving lecture that I knew I deserved, but I told him the truth about the business card.

He listened, but his white eyebrows rose then he frowned as he looked at me over the top of his glasses. "Abby, Abby, you don't need me to tell you …" He paused and I couldn't seem to meet his gaze. "No, I can see that you know you should have been honest with your police detective right when you found it." I took a deep breath and I caught a flicker of a smile at the corners of his mouth. "That being said, I can always count on you to come up with something interesting. Show me the card."

After examining it for several minutes, he picked up the phone and a mumbled conversation ensued, followed by a long stretch of listening, interrupted by *I see, That's interesting.* He hung up and his face shone with triumph. And waited. He enjoyed teasing me and this was one of those moments or my punishment for hiding the card.

Finally, I couldn't stand it anymore and blurted out, "Well? Who did you call? What did you find out?"

"All good questions easily answered. I had the man's listing checked in Martindale Hubbell and—"

"Martin—who?"

"Martindale-Hubbell is a directory of lawyers and law firms. It's been around since the Civil War. It's a wealth of information." He held up the card. "Our lawyer has a listing and a high rating that shows he's well-respected in his profession. He specializes in conflict resolution in the corporate world."

I sat forward on my chair. "Do you think that he was *resolving* an issue between Alex and his partner, Allen?"

"It's possible." Dr. Phillips tapped an index finger on his lips, his favorite pose when he was thinking.

I rushed on. "But I asked Allen if he knew the name Xavier Pendergast—which is kind of memorable in its own right—and Allen said he didn't know him. Was he lying?"

"That's also possible. Or he didn't know about him yet, because Mr. Pendergast was still gathering information and hadn't opened a dialogue yet with the other party in the dispute."

I had one more idea. "Or Allen found out what Alex was doing, bypassed all legal help and *took care of the situation* himself."

"All possibilities, but..." He sighed. "And I'm afraid this is where we bump into a wall."

"But that's won't stop you." It was my turn to tease, but I was halfway serious. "You told me that a librarian doesn't know everything, but he knows how to find out, even if he's retired from the Library of Congress. So, you know how we can get on the other side of that wall." He wasn't smiling. "You do know this is important. It could be the one thing that helps uncover the killer."

"I know." He shook his head and took off his glasses. "But I'm afraid there's nothing I can do. The wall we're up against is the one of attorney-client privilege. I suggest you talk to your detective friend. He'll know how to proceed."

It was not what I wanted to hear and I fretted all the way back to Fair Winds. Ingram would explode when I told him about the card and how I found it. When he heard how long I'd held on to it — I didn't want to think about it. He wouldn't consider *I forgot about it* or *I got distracted* as an excuse. I had to pick the right moment and hope the possibilities the card opened up would help balance out his anger.

My brain was still spinning when I walked into the main house at Fair Winds. I couldn't put it off any longer. I had to tell Lorraine about the appraiser's visit and the disaster he exposed. Now.

The house was quiet, almost empty. No Dawkins. No Lorraine. No activity in the kitchen. I went down the hallway toward the library even though she felt uncomfortable using that room. Alex was fatally shot on the other side of its French doors. It was too close, too soon. But I heard voices coming from there. Had she decided it was time to reclaim her inner sanctum? One of the voices made me stop. Detective Ingram.

I used to think of him as a friend. But ever since he arrested Lorraine on suspicion of murder, just seeing him made me react and not in a good way. Even without the pressure of telling him about the card. Why was he here? Was he arresting Lorraine again? It was Lorraine's voice that kept me from breaking into a run and bursting into the room. Her tone alerted me to be calm, thoughtful and finesse the situation.

I took a deep breath and walked into the room. "Hello, detective, what brings you here today?" I gave him a smile that carried the warning to be kind to Lorraine. I sat down next to her on the sofa, patted her hand and waited for his response.

The detective seemed a little tongue-tied, so Lorraine jumped in with an explanation. "The detective has come up with an idea that might catch the real killer."

"That's terrific!" I had to tamp down my excitement over what that meant. He was focused on arresting the killer and it wasn't Lorraine.

She began the explanation. "It's really a novel idea. I mean it, an idea out of a real novel or, I should say, a series of mystery stories by Agatha Christie."

Ingram explained. "I'm going to call a little meeting, a gathering of suspects, so to speak, and apply pressure."

"Like Hercule Poirot, Agatha Christie's detective?" I glanced at Lorraine. "Yes, I do read the occasional detective story." I turned my attention back to Ingram. "Isn't that a little dramatic?"

Ingram cleared his throat. "I don't usually go in for the dramatic approach. I prefer making my case based on the evidence, but I believe this case is based on emotion. And where there is emotion, a dramatic approach might bring a confession. That would wrap up this case quickly."

Then this horror would be over for Lorraine. No more nightmares, no more worry about the grand jury or a trial. I patted her hand again. "Okay, what can I do?"

"Listen to his plan and do what you can to support it," Lorraine said and we both turned our attention back to the detective.

"As I was saying, I want to bring together the suspects here—"

This plan was starting off badly. "Here?" I looked at Lorraine in disbelief. "You want him to recreate …" There was no other way to say it. "…recreate the murder?"

She cringed.

Ingram jumped in. "No, not at all." He glanced at Lorraine. "Being in the place where it happened will help people react to what we know, jog someone's memory and, with any luck, unmask the killer right there. I need to know who was in the room? Who left early? Who was seen in another part of the house or on the property where they didn't belong? *That's* the information I want."

"Agatha Christie's famous detective brought the suspects together to announce the name of the killer." I added little French accent to my words. "The little gray cells have whispered to me and now, I, Hercule Poirot, shall reveal the name of the killer." I cleared my throat of the strain and continued in my normal voice. "He has the meeting so everyone can tell him how brilliant he is, not continue the investigation."

"Well, I'm not Poirot."

Lorraine jumped in with another thought. "In order for that to work, you have to get everyone, including the killer, into the same room." She shivered. "I think this killer is smart. He may smell a trap and not show up."

"That would tell us something, too." He glanced out the window, as if looking for an answer.

I suggested in a voice barely above a murmur. "What if the meeting wasn't tied to the murder, but to *Chesapeake Haven*, which I think it is, the killer might be lured if he thought something important would happen, even something that could lead to a decision."

"That just might work. I believe this was a crime of passion tied to the development of the land. The shooter didn't bring a gun. Something happened in the meeting to tip the killer over the edge. I think the killer cares very much about the land and the environmental impact on it."

"The killer might even have a connection to that particular piece of land," Lorraine suggested.

"A family connection." He nodded. "Bad blood."

I shrugged. "Or none of those things and we're missing something."

Ingram grinned. "I can't promise you, but I believe we have the motive and now, we just have to connect the motive to the right person."

Always the organizer, Lorraine reached for paper and a pen. "Let's make a list. I'm ready now that I'm not at the top."

I was tempted to take them over to my kitchen and sit them down in front of my fridge and the suspect board on it, but no, it was my secret.

Ingram gave me a quick nod. "Abby, why don't you start."

"Well, not in any order of importance, there's Mary Rose. She made a dramatic entrance. She's eccentric, even a little scary."

"Scary?" Ingram chimed in. "Definitely. I'd hate to run into her in a dark wood, but I think she's harmless."

"She could be a dead shot."

Ingram chuckled. "Yes, when she's shooting squirrels and raccoons. I can't see her hunting down and shooting a human being." He shook his head a little. "No, this case requires a killer like... like the partner... or the ex-wife."

The corners of Lorraine's mouth twitched at that idea.

"It looks so easy when they solve a murder on TV," I said with longing.

"Yes, it does." He stood up slowly, the strain and lack of sleep were showing. "I'm going to keep my eye on those two. Sometimes, truth is stranger than fiction."

"I heard someone say that sometimes truth is too much reality for fiction."

"Amen to that. I'd better start setting the trap," he said, moving toward the door.

"Wait, how are you going to do that?" I wanted to know.

"You'll see" he said with a wink. With a little nod toward Lorraine, he left.

"I think—"

Lorraine held up a hand to stop me. "It's up to the police to manage this, not us, Abby. We will attend, of course, but it's the detective's meeting." She put her hands on the sofa cushion, getting ready to push herself up when I had to stop her. It was time to tell her the bad news.

"I need to talk to you about Mr. Fuller."

She chuckled a little, in the way she did before Alex died. "How is the pompous appraiser from New York? What happened? Did he faint dead away from the beauty of our epergne?"

"Not exactly. You know I did a lot of research, comparing it to other pieces and—"

"Abby, stop. Just tell me what happened."

All the air seemed to escape from my body as it sagged. It was with a heavy heart that I admitted, "It's counterfeit."

"Counterfeit?" Lorraine said slowly in disbelief.

I nodded. "A fake. I should have seen it, Mr. Fuller was happy to point out."

She sat back against the pillows. "Okay, now give me the details, please."

"He saw it almost immediately. He took the piece apart, searching out all the hallmarks that were on each separate piece."

"Shouldn't they have all been the same?"

"They weren't. The little baskets that I really like all match. They all have a hallmark in the same place which was a good sign. The only problem is that the hallmarks on the baskets don't match the hallmark on the main piece."

"Is that the only evidence he offered you that the piece was counterfeit?"

I shook my head slowly. "No, that was only the beginning. Piece by piece, he took the epergne apart. He showed me all the little places where parts from other pieces had been soldered into place. Then the new joints were covered with silver foil. He said it was part of my job to breathe on all those joints."

"Breathe on them? Why?"

"My breath would have caused heat and condensation..." I wanted to crawl into a corner and hide. "Lorraine, I'm so sorry—" I felt hot tears prick my eyes.

She threw her arms around me. "Oh Abby, don't apologize. It would've been nice to have such a major find pulled from the attic. It would've been considered a *discovery* in the world of silver, but think of the insurance." She threw her head back and gasped. "I would have had to find a museum to accept it as a donation and you know how complicated that can be. Keeping a piece of silver valued at $200,000 or more here at Fair Winds would've made us all very nervous." She leaned closer and said softly, "I don't think Dawkins would've appreciated that additional responsibility. You know how seriously he takes our safety and privacy. You probably saved him from developing an ulcer, but he doesn't have to know the details."

"I'm afraid he already does." I wanted to whimper at the memory of the humiliation I felt.

"Oh dear, what did he say?"

"Nothing. It's like it never happened."

She smiled. "He can be nice like that." She sat back against the sofa pillows. "I like the idea of keeping that piece here at Fair Winds. It looks rather regal on the dining room table when we entertain and nobody has to know its true value."

I appreciated her kindness, but I still felt responsible. "I'm sorry I made the mistake. I got your hopes up. You brought that appraiser down from New York and wasted his time."

"Oh please! He was doing his job. I'm sure he will do a lot of moaning and groaning when he gets back to The City." It only took a moment for the humor to affect both of us and we burst out laughing.

When we caught our breath, I ventured a thought. "The epergne might not be the only thing here at Fair Winds that might not belong." She raised her eyebrows, curious. "Well, I've been wondering about Dawkins who seems so strange and now his cousin…"

Oh, why had I started down this road?

"Go on."

I let out a little moan. "Should I assume that you know the details about these two men?"

Lorraine took a deep breath. "I know what I need to know and that's enough. The two men are assets, no matter what happened in their past." And then her face fell. "Considering what is going on, it's a comfort having additional protection. In comparison to facing a grand jury on a charge of murder, these other things are nothing."

CHAPTER 22

A locket is a small case designed to hold a valued remembrance of someone dear to one's heart.

> "The Butler's Guide to Fine Silver"
> Mr. Hollister, 1898

IN THE MURKY GRAY LIGHT, when the earth is holding its breath for a new day to begin, the sound of one cricket cracked the silence with a single note. Like a morning alarm clock, his note shook me out of my deep sleep. I wasn't the only one. His note woke one bird who sang out a short trill of a question, *Is anybody there?* The air hung heavy with humidity, waiting for a response. A chorus of bird song twittered through my open window.

Why didn't I close it, I thought as I turned over and covered my ears with the pillow?

Mary Rose was right. Mother Nature is demanding ... and a little fickle.

The pillow didn't help. Whether I could truly hear the birdsong or imagined it, it didn't matter. I couldn't get comfortable, because another thought was chirping in my brain. Betrayal. An insidious feeling eating away at the very fabric of my being. I was the one. I betrayed my friend Lorraine when she needed me most. Not in the times of entertaining or researching silver. It was in the moment when she was threatened and I stood back, paralyzed by ... what? Fear? Confusion? Was it uncertainty, or the worst of all reactions, hesitancy to get involved? I didn't have the answer. I don't think I was even trying to figure out what happened. But it was sticking with me like the shadow attached to my feet. It went everywhere with me, the feeling of inadequacy. She wouldn't have betrayed me that way if I'd been in trouble. I knew I let her down and I needed to learn why.

But tossing and getting tangled up in the bed covers wasn't the answer. I gave up and swung my feet to the floor to face the day and whatever dragons it would bring. It's a good thing I got moving when I did so I was ready when the text from Ingram hit my phone.

WE'RE HERE

He'd arranged yet another visit to Fair Winds, only this time he was bringing someone with him, a witness.

Whenever he was working a case, he always kept the statements in his briefcase that was never far from him. He read and reviewed them time and again, because he never knew when he'd find a nugget. And this time, he had. It was in the statement given by Edward, the teenager attending the meeting with his teacher the night of the murder:

"I went exploring and saw something, someone come out
of the boathouse and go into the water."

Ingram said it sounded a little farfetched, but he needed something to break this case. This might be that something. He'd arranged to bring the boy to Fair Winds to go over what he saw.

And Ingram wanted me to help. This was my cue to appear at the front door.

But Ingram met me without the boy as I approached the front drive. "Abby, he's nervous. We need to take it slow, make him comfortable. Can we do that?"

I'd seen the detective take charge of a crime scene, order officers around, even face down a killer. I'd never seen him nervous like this. I touched his arm. "I'll do whatever it takes. Remember, he might lead us to the real killer." I walked past him to the main door. "Detective, where is the boy?"

He rushed up next to me. "He was right here. I just came to talk with you for a minute." His eyes darted around the area as he turned this way and that. Anxious, the man was edging toward panic.

"It's okay, don't worry. We'll find him. Nothing will happen to him," I said, willing myself not to think that a man was shot to death here days earlier and the killer was still at large.

I walked slowly to the other side of the house with Ingram on my heels. No sign of Edward.

"Only my boss knows that we may have an eyewitness. You don't think—"

I smiled with relief as I saw some movement by a lush rhododendron. "Don't worry, detective. He's in good hands. Or, should I say, good paws." Edward was down on his knees giving Simon a tummy rub.

I got down on the ground with them. "Hey, Edward. I'm Abby. I see you've made a new friend."

When he looked up, his cheeks were red, but his smile was filled with joy. "Isn't he beautiful?" He almost swallowed the words. "Do you know his name?"

"Yes, I do. Simon is my roommate."

"That's so cool." Simon licked the boy's cheek, just missing his glasses, eager to reclaim his undivided attention. "I love dogs. I like dogs better than people. Cats, too. And birds."

"Wow, that's cool." I wasn't sure what to say. I'd never spent time with teenage boys, except when I was a teenager and then they made me self-conscious.

"It's easier to understand animals than people," Edward said. "Teachers want us to follow the news. I hate it. Why are people so mean? Animals are easy. They don't have those hidden agenda things." Simon closed his eyes and moaned in delight, which made the boy grin. "Someday, I want to be a biologist, maybe even a vet. Yeah, that would be good." He looked me square in the eye. "And I can do it, too. I know how to study really hard and get good grades."

That was it! He'd given me the opening. "Edward, do you think you could help me study something right now? It's kinda hard, but I bet you can do it." His hand on Simon's tummy slowed to a stop. "It's really important," I added.

The boy looked at me with chestnut brown eyes filled with worry.

"It will be you, me and Simon, okay? Detective Ingram can come, too."

Edward looked back at Simon, who licked his hand and jumped to his feet.

"Okay. If he's ready, so am I." Edward said, as he stood up.

Ingram and I exchanged looks of relief as we walked down toward the boathouse. I thought Ingram would lead the gentle interview, but from behind the boy's back, he motioned me to take over.

"So, the policeman brought you here to meet Simon and tell us a story. Remember when you came to Fair Winds with your teacher?"

Edward nodded. "Mr. Franklin."

"That's right. You sat in the big room during the meeting, but when it was over, what did you do?"

"You want the truth?"

I tried not to show concern. "Yes, Edward. That would be good."

"I was bored." He glanced at me, unsure how I would react. I nodded for him to continue. "Everybody was standing around," he complained a little. "They were talking over my head, I mean it, they were talking over my head. I'm kinda short, you know, so it's easy for them to do that, but I still think it's kinda rude." He took a deep breath. "I went outside through the doors to the patio and went exploring. I wasn't going to hurt anything, honest."

I smiled. "Of course, you wouldn't. Where did you go? Can you show me?"

"Sure." He took a couple of steps then turned back to me. "You're nice. You can call me Eddie." And he headed off to the trees and down toward the water.

Ingram came up beside me and whispered, "You're doing great. Keep it up."

I hurried down to the place where the boy was waiting with Simon.

"I'm not sure," he said. "It was dark. I think I was here when I heard the shot…" He caught his lip between his teeth and looked out over the rolling green lawn.

I was sure he wasn't seeing the sun glinting off the river. He was reliving what he'd felt that night in the dark, just as I'd been doing ever since it happened. I put my hand on his shoulder. "Eddie, it's okay. People were running around, yelling. It was scary. I know because I was standing over there." I pointed in the direction of my cottage. "I know what I saw from that side, but I couldn't see this side of the boathouse. What did you see?"

I could feel Ingram's anticipation. This was the answer he needed.

In a small voice, Eddie said, "I saw somebody come out of the boathouse, there." He pointed at the door on this side.

Ingram lunged forward in his excitement, then stepped back. The boy had seen the shooter.

"Could you tell who it was?" Eddie shook his head. "Was it a man?" Eddie shrugged. "Was it a woman?"

He shrugged again. "It was a person, but I couldn't really see him or her."

Now, I was confused and ready to have the professional take over, but Ingram shook his head and motioned for me to continue.

"You saw a person, but you couldn't tell if it was a man or woman?"

"Let's say it was a man," Eddie said matter-of-factly. The young scientist was tackling the problem. "I saw his shadow on the boathouse wall. I guess he was between one of the spotlights and the building. I saw him come out of the door and run along the wall."

"Toward the land?"

"No, toward the water."

I was really confused now. "Where did he go?"

"He disappeared."

"Disappeared?" I turned my head to examine the area around the boathouse. "Where?"

"I guess he went in the water. Yeah, 'cause his shadow got shorter and shorter then *poof!* He was gone."

"Did you hear a splash?"

Eddied shook his head. He was stroking Simon's back, losing interest in the shadow man.

I tried one more time. "Could you tell how big this man was, Eddie?"

"Nope, his shadow almost went up to the edge of the roof, but no one is that tall. The light was at the right angle to cast his shadow that way." His knowledge of science was showing and it helped, but only a little bit.

I crossed my fingers as I asked one more question. "Did you see this shadow man again?"

"No, he was gone. Does Simon like to play ball?"

I found a ball so they could play while Ingram and I talked.

"I'm sorry, I did my best."

"You did great. You proved that someone left the boathouse just after the shot was fired." Ingram was eager to follow up on this new information.

"Someone other than Lorraine," I said with satisfaction and relief. "But you don't have a description or anything to go on."

"Oh yes, I do. The killer had a boat."

"I know it's called a boathouse, but Lorraine doesn't keep a boat there."

Ingram settled back and stared at the boathouse built over the water. "Then the killer isn't a thief. He must have brought it with him."

"But everyone came to the meeting by car or truck. You saw how packed the drive was. And if he came by boat to escape after killing Alex, wouldn't he have also brought his own gun? Wouldn't we have heard the boat engine?"

"Not likely with all the screaming and yelling. Of course, he could have rowed away." The man tugged on his ear. "I don't know all the details yet, but we're closer to the truth than we were." He called out to Eddie that it was time to go.

The boy ran up to me, all arms and legs. He was at that gawky age when he might trip over his own feet. "Can I come back and play with Simon sometime? He's such a great dog."

I promised we'd work something out and watched them walk away, the man seeking answers and the boy who'd seen a killer.

After Ingram and the boy witness left, I was ready for some of Dawkins exquisite cold press coffee over ice. I was looking forward to the coffee cupping ceremony Dawkins had promised me, especially since it would happen after the murder investigation was over and Lorraine would be safe. During my coffee preparations, I heard the TV in the room across the hall and wandered in to hear the latest. Norman sat at the table, his eyes glued to the screen.

The odd little man looked at me. "Miss Abigail, what is this thing, *hurricane*? We don't have it in my country."

Hmmm, how to describe what could be a devastating, even life-threatening storm without scaring the man to death. "Think of it as a giant whirlwind." My left hand made a spinning motion. "Only it's hundreds of miles... kilometers wide and, if it's strong enough, the winds can drive a piece of wood through a brick wall."

The blood drained out of the poor man's face and he shrank back in his chair.

"But it's still a long distance away. And it might stay out at sea. We'll probably only get a heavy rainstorm. Don't worry about it. We'll be fine."

The color was coming back to his face slowly when the TV announcer's latest pronouncement caught our attention. "Well, folks. It's now official. The National Hurricane Center has declared he weather system we've been tracking for days is a Category 3 hurricane. To repeat, Hurricane Zelma is now a Category 3."

The camera shot changed to a man standing in front of a weather map featuring the newly-upgraded storm. "What's remarkable is that this system has gone from a weather disturbance to a depression to a tropical storm to a hurricane to a Category 3 hurricane in a very short time." He stopped abruptly, forgetting about the millions of people listening to his every word, and touched his earpiece. "I've just been informed that this storm is showing a change in direction."

The weatherman, swooping his arm this way and that, explained the weather phenomenon, again. Why do weather people act like it's the end of the world? Hurricanes, tornadoes, thunderstorms are happening all over the globe. There's nothing we can do about them, except get out of the way. Did they have to frighten people to get them to be safe?

Well, I was frightened, but I wasn't going to run unless someone I trusted said it was time to run. Then we'd all run together. This wasn't my area of expertise. Frankly, after the debacle with Mr. Fuller, I wasn't sure that silver was my area. And I couldn't come up with anything to help the detective. Yes, for now, I'd follow the crowd. For now, I had other things to do and I headed for the door.

"'Scusa, you are not watching?" The Italian man said. "They say this storm, she may come here."

I looked up at the TV again. The cone of impact covered most of the southeastern United States, including the mid-Atlantic area where we were.

I tried to sound confident and unconcerned. "No, it's still too early to tell anything."

"Ah, so it won't come here?" Norman was so hopeful.

"People tell me that hurricanes don't hit St. Michaels."

Silently, Dawkins appeared in the doorway. He stood head and shoulders over both of us, almost painfully erect, commanding attention in a very quiet way. He always wore a suit, always. He rejected the casual look of slacks and a polo shirt, even one emblazoned with the Fair Winds name. "Miss Abigail, Norman, is there any further news about the storm?"

I gave him the gist of what the forecasters were repeating over and over again. "I hope we don't have anything to worry about, Dawkins."

"No, you have nothing to worry about at all, Miss Abigail. Fair Winds shall be prepared."

He knitted his eyebrows together as he spoke to Norman. "Please check the pantry and storage for the standard emergency items: candles, water bottles that need to be filled, batteries..." The two men exchanged looks. "Yes, of course. You know the drill."

As Norman rose from his chair, Dawkins challenged him. "Is there something going on here I should know?"

Norman grinned at me. "See? I tell you. The man misses nothing."

Dawkins face clouded and his stormy eyes drilled holes into his cousin. Emphasizing each word, he asked, "What did you tell her?"

My muscles tensed, reacting to the sudden change in atmosphere. Dawkins stare didn't seem to faze Norman. He returned his cousin's look with a genial smile. "Things about you." The smile melted away. "Things you should have told them."

Dawkins raised his chin a little. "Those who need to know, do." His eyes shifted to me for a split second then bore into Norman again. "And you have no place—"

Norman shot to his feet and held his hands clenched and fists close to his sides. "It is my place to know about you. We share blood. There is no greater bond."

"It is not your place to speak—"

Norman raised his chin in defiance, a mirror image of his cousin's stance. "It is right for them to know. These people treat you like family. You return that feeling, but you do not tell them about yourself. You keep it locked away. That is not right. Either they are family by choice or you are nothing more than an employee."

Norman stomped to the doorway and faced off with Dawkins, though he had to bend his head way back to look him in the eye. "And I do not believe you are nothing to them." He slapped his palm flat on his chest. "You are family to me." Then he pointed at me. "And you are family to them. You must not hide. You do not hide from family. And now, I go."

He walked away, leaving me with his angry cousin who slowly turned his eyes to me, almost afraid of what he'd see there. I crossed my arms.

"He's right, you know. You and I are the same. We are part of the Fair Winds *family*. Lorraine, you and me."

His eyes narrowed. His shoulders tensed. "What did he tell you?" He shot back like an arrow.

"Nothing really, just that he was your inspiration for the work you do today. He's rather proud of that."

"What else did he tell you?" Intense anxiety rolled off his body.

This wasn't the time or place to talk about the Rangers. I needed to deflect his concern. "He told me you studied in London to become a butler." I pulled out a chair and casually sat down. "Since you studied in London, you must have had your pick of opportunities in England, Europe, anywhere around the world. How did you end up here?"

He stared at me, not moving a muscle. Literally. I wasn't sure he was even breathing. Was it another sign of his elite forces training, being able to blend in and lose his humanity? I had plenty of time. I could *outwait* him, but I hoped that his concern about the storm would cut short our confrontation. But that wasn't to be.

He spoke, the words coming from his mouth, but his lips and jaw barely moved. "I wanted to come home."

Home? To Fair Winds?

He dropped his eyes and his chest drew in a deep breath. "I was tired of things foreign; the accents, different cultures. I wanted a cheesesteak and fries."

Still confused, I asked, "But why here?"

He raised his eyes and gazed at the scene around us. "I didn't want the competition of New York, the egos of Los Angeles, the snobbery of Chicago or the Southern backstabbing of Texas money. I wanted what I found ..." He spread his arms and opened his hands. "...here."

I still wasn't satisfied. "But the Eastern Shore and Fair Winds is far off the beaten track. Was it an agency that found the position for you?"

He gave his head a little shake as his back straightened. Dawkins was reemerging. "I was referred by..." He paused, then sighed a little. "... a friend."

I cocked my head with the silent question. *A friend?*

He spoke the name barely above a whisper. "Ryan."

Now, my questions flooded out like a broken dam. "Ryan?! Was he a Ranger, too?" Seeing his look of surprise, I spoke quickly. "Yes, yes, I know. Tell me, how do you know Ryan?"

"It's his story to tell."

"He hasn't told me much of anything so you win the prize. *You* get to tell me everything."

He bowed his head in appreciation. "You are truly formidable, Miss Abigail, when you want to be."

I didn't take the bait. I wasn't going to let him hijack the conversation. "Answer my question, Charlie Dawkins."

He knew he was caught and conceded. "We met while I was a Ranger. My employer and Ryan's father had mutual interests. My employer was a customer."

The United States government—the Pentagon—bought something from Ryan's father? I remembered the $600 toilet seats bought by the military years ago, but that foolish buying had stopped. *What else did they have in common?*

"Was it software? Did the government buy software from Ryan's family company?"

Slowly, Dawkins shook his head as if I, the child, had disappointed him.

What else could it be? Uniforms? Mess kits? But it was something Ryan didn't want to discuss. I thought Lorraine had said Ryan had inherited his father's holdings after the man disappeared? Didn't Ryan himself disappear for months on end because the company needed him? What was so important that he wanted to keep the business a secret? Then it became clear to me and I met the former Ranger's steel-gray eyes.

"Yes, Miss Abigail, you may say the word."

It was more of a disbelieving breath than a statement. "Weapons."

"Yes, Miss Abigail, quite a selection of them actually, delivered anywhere, at any time we needed them."

I gripped the table to keep myself upright. I'd fallen in love with an arms dealer.

Dawkins continued as if we were chatting about a grocery list. "I contacted Ryan for help finding this place or someplace like it. I called on an old friend for help in changing my life, the way he had."

"And Norman, is he part of this, too?"

Dawkins chuckled quietly. "Ah, poor Norman. He worked for

someone also in the business, but his capo cut corners, squeezed every Euro out of every deal… and then some. He is not a good man. He is living on a beach somewhere, waiting, wondering when the black helicopters will appear on the horizon. Even with the trouble, Norman is better off." He frowned a little then understanding what I was thinking smoothed out the lines on his face. "No, Miss Abigail, Ryan would never conduct business in such a fashion. Rest assured, he would never put anyone in his sphere in peril."

In his sphere? Was I in his sphere? Was Alex part of his shady world or was he threatening to expose Ryan to the friends in his sphere? Was I surrounded by killers? Did Ryan bring murder to Fair Winds?

BALD EAGLE

In normal flight, the Bald Eagle can travel about 30 miles an hour, but can dive on prey at a speed of 100 miles an hour. The term *eagle eye* is an appropriate, term because this bird has better vision than people, a wider range of vision and can see ultraviolet light.

The Bald Eagle mates for life. It is difficult to tell the male and female apart because the plumage is basically the same. The key is the size of the bird: the female is 25% larger than her mate.

The Bald Eagle, found only in North America, has made a spectacular recovery from the ravages caused by the insecticide DDT used to kill mosquitoes and other agricultural pests. As the chemical moved up the food chain, the eggs laid by the Bald Eagle broke because DDT made the shells too thin. When DDT was banned in 1972, only 471 Bald Eagle pairs were found in the continental United States. Today, there are about 2,000 in the Chesapeake Bay region alone.

CHAPTER 23

A carving set includes a meat fork, a sharp knife and a knife sharpener. They should be in the same pattern.

> "The Butler's Guide to Fine Silver"
> Mr. Hollister, 1898

I wasn't sure what to do with the information about Ryan. Did I feel better *not knowing* about what was going on, why he had disappeared from my life for months on end without a word? Or did I feel better knowing? I wasn't sure. The only constant in my life, the one person I could depend on, was Lorraine. I did the one thing that made sense to me. I went upstairs and found her in the sitting room off her bedroom, just looking at the Miles River flowing quietly by Fair Winds.

"Hi!" My attempt at sounding upbeat fell with a thud in the quiet room.

She motioned me to sit down and the smiles we'd plastered on our faces slipped away. We sat in silence until Lorraine said, "It's such a waste. He was such a good man."

I wanted to talk about Ryan, but I knew it was Alex who was in her thoughts. "He was kind and warm and funny." She took in a quick breath. "He cared, he cared so much about people and the place he wanted so much to create." A slow smile spread over her face and crinkled the area around her eyes with delight as she relived a memory. "He used to tell me to change out of my designer shoes and put on boots. We'd drive to the Haven in that high-tech vehicle of his and we'd walk. We must have walked every square inch of his property while he described what he saw, his vision for the property and the life the people would live there. He had such hope for the project, so much respect for the land and everything around it. And he had the confidence that he could make it all happen."

Her smile and delight evaporated. "I wonder if that's what made someone mad, his confidence. It wasn't arrogance, Abby. It was a certainty, a commitment that he would do whatever it took to make *Chesapeake Haven* happen the right way." She turned her head and stared out the window while a single heartbreaking tear trickled down her cheek.

"I know you're sad Lorraine." I couldn't control the quiver in my voice. The last thing she needed was for me to turn into a crying blob. I swallowed and began again. "I would take this pain away from you if I could. Do you remember what Alex always said? He even said it to his partner and *her* that last night. He said, 'You'll only find the best here at Fair Winds.' Do you remember that? It should give you some comfort knowing that he thought *you* were the best."

Just when I thought she would erupt in a torrent of tears, a different emotion boiled up. Her relaxed fingers coiled into a fist and her eyes went hard. Anger.

"Somebody made a big mistake aiming that shotgun—my gun—at him. That person did more than take a life. That person insulted me." Her fist thumped softly on her thigh with almost every word. "It was an invasion of my home. An abuse of my possessions. Nobody comes into Fair Winds and does that." Her fist thumped again, harder.

"But the joke is on that person, the killer." As she spoke, her fist uncurled. "Alex wasn't the enemy, *The Developer*. Yes, he was involved in real estate for years. He built small and medium projects. Yes, a couple of them were huge. He told me that those experiences were good preparation for what he wanted to do here on the Shore. Yes, his vision was to build, but in a way to make the homes and hotel and conference center *part* of the landscape. He didn't want to bulldoze the land the way most developers do. He wanted to slide the buildings in between the trees. He knew it was going to make the construction costs soar. It's not the most economical way to build new structures, but he was willing to do it. He believed it was important, because this wasn't just a big piece of land to him. It was someplace special."

A smile teased at her lips. "He spent so many hours at the library. The stacks of books he'd carry out and on my card!" The smile broke free. "Finally, the librarian suggested he get his own card. He was approaching the limit of fifty books and she thought I should be able to borrow a book for myself, perhaps a good mystery set here in the area." The smile faded slowly. "He kept asking me to identify the people and organizations that cared about the Bay region, who could guide him as he planned the development. I almost felt like a social secretary as I made calls and set up appointments. It wasn't just fun spending time with him. It was exciting to see him in action."

She slowly shook her head as she remembered. "One day, he was like a little boy going on and on about how it was important to protect the osprey and..." A nervous giggle escaped. "And when he spent time with an expert about oysters and the oyster beds... well, his enthusiasm was infectious."

Her body bent over under the weight of grief. "They have no idea what an advocate they lost. I suppose, intellectually, I can understand why people were suspicious of him. He was the dreaded *developer*." She paused and tilted her head, thinking. "I don't understand why Dawkins was always watching him. Do you think he was suspicious of him? He, of all people, should have seen he was a good person. Alex was always willing to listen, consider and, if necessary, make a change.

"I love the Shore, Abby. You know that." Her blue eyes met mine. "But I was born here. The Shore is in my blood. But Alex..." Her eyes dropped to her lap. "I watched Alex fall in love and it was a marvelous thing to see." Struggling to maintain control, she grabbed her knee and dug her fingers into the skin. Tears welled up and teetered on the edge of her lashes. "He was like the blue crab that sheds its shell in order to grow. But like the crab in that growth process, he was vulnerable and defenseless—right here in my home where we should all be safe. But he wasn't." The tears welled up in her eyes, but she fought through them.

In that moment, I knew my suspicions were correct. "He was falling in love with everything he found here. I hope that brings you some measure of comfort."

Lorraine nodded as she raised a tissue to her eyes, losing the battle with her tears. "It does. And I am inspired by him. He faced resistance, but he never gave up. But a man like that doesn't always win." The emotion overwhelmed her and she started shaking. "When someone killed him, he was like the crab, when it's caught and cooked and turns from an iridescent blue to blood red. Whoever pulled that trigger hurt the Shore and hurt..." The word *me* was lost in a torrent of wrenching sobs.

I put my arms around my friend and she let me hold her, rock her, while her heart broke. This cry had been coming for a long time...born of the loss, the grief of losing a newfound love, the anger at being falsely accused of a crime Lorraine could never commit. Add the fear that a grand jury could take away her freedom and it was natural that she broke down as if her heart was breaking. I felt sure it was.

At one point, I saw Dawkins standing stoically watching over us, not out of morbid curiosity, but from anguish he could not share. Was he reliving those moments when he carried a little boy's body to his father? I wanted to reach to him as well. Grief is a little easier when it is shared. As if he read my mind, he stepped away silently.

After a long time of gut-wrenching sobs, Lorraine calmed. There were no more tears for now. I led her into her bedroom. There on the nightstand was a small crystal glass filled with what looked like brandy. Lorraine had been denied the company of Alex, but she still had the guardian watching over her, anticipating her needs and fulfilling the ones he could.

I tiptoed out of Lorraine's room after she drained the glass of amber liquid, slid between the sheets and fell into an exhausted sleep.

I'd suspected that her feelings for Alex went deeper than she admitted. She always spoke highly of him as an ethical businessman and visionary, but never uttered a word about her feelings for him as a woman. I'd seen them together, having fun, enjoying each other's company as they had long conversations about her beloved St. Michaels and the Eastern Shore. There were the moments when their hands touched or he put his arm around her back to usher her through a door. I noticed the electricity. There was a growing bond between them, a bond based on trust, a bond that someone had destroyed right in her own home. Now, the house was quiet as if Fair Winds itself was mourning. Lorraine would need its spirit to recover and move on the way she always had after a tragedy. This was the source of her strength.

By nature, I am not a violent person, but, at that moment, I could have throttled the shooter with my bare hands... if I only knew who it was.

CHAPTER 24

Different carving sets are designed to serve different types of meats. The fowl or game carving set is thinner and smaller to allow easy separation of the various cuts, such as the thigh meat from the breast meat.

"The Butler's Guide to Fine Silver"
Mr. Hollister, 1898

I COULD HAVE USED a small glass of brandy myself. My own emotions were wrung dry. But this was not the time to rest. It was time to go back to the cottage, to my kitchen, hopefully to find answers among the magnets on my refrigerator door.

I brewed a pot of fresh coffee and sat cross-legged in front of the fridge with a steaming mug. The vast array of magnets stared back at me: black boot, broom, a tree. More than ten in all! The real shooter was hiding in the crowd.

The first thing I did was consider the tricycle magnet for the biker. His own private world consumed all his attention. He barely noticed what was going on around him, unless it was a car or truck on the road, and even then... I took away his magnet.

The rest of the magnets waited, almost taunting me, daring me to move them around. The answer was there, I was sure of it. I just couldn't see it, yet.

Detective Ingram always asked, *Who benefits?* He did say this was a crime of passion, unbridled emotion. Did those emotions get out of control turning that person into a killer? Ingram had told me that there were warning signs that could lead to murder, if someone chose to see them.

There were the interviews with neighbors of a sexual predator or murderer who said he was such a nice man. Then they started remembering things, things they now chose to see, and the alarm bells started ringing. *The signs are always there,* Ingram said. That's why he would constantly sift through the evidence and statements looking for them. How did someone react to a word or statement? How did a person react to someone's name or describe him? Was that person really saying, *You hurt my feelings or you hurt someone I love?* Was that person saying, *You've crossed my boundaries and invaded my space.* If those warnings were ignored, emotions could escalate and cause someone to cross the person and commit the ultimate crime? Where were the warning signs?

Simon tried to crawl into my lap the way he did when he was a puppy, but my lap wasn't big enough for his hefty seventy pounds. Instead, he ended up putting his head on my knee and my hand went right to his favorite spot behind his ear. He snuffled with contentment.

"Simon, I don't know why I think I can do something with this case. I didn't know these people until a few days ago. I don't even remember seeing them on the street. And now, I think I can spot the warning signs that led to Alex's murder? Talk about arrogance." He licked my hand. The tickle made me laugh. "Okay, okay, I took a shower this morning."

The diversion allowed another thought to surface. Ingram probably didn't know these people either. I wasn't hurting anyone, thinking about relationships while in the privacy of my kitchen with my best buddy. It wouldn't hurt a soul. So, I freed my thoughts and they ran every which way.

There was the tree magnet. Maybe I should have given pompous Jacob a megaphone magnet instead of the tree. He was bombastic when he got revved up. And he had a curious philosophy. Whenever two or more people were within earshot, he'd start saying things to get a rise out of them. But he never got crazy. How did his wife Maddie put it? 'Jacob says you have to take something to the extreme to force people out of their comfort zone to get them closer to your position.' It sounded a little risky to me. Treat some people like that and they dig in and refuse to listen to your side. But Maddie was convinced that Jacob would do whatever it took to sway people over to his way of thinking. That alone made him a strong suspect.

Right next to his tree magnet was the ball-of-yarn magnet I'd chosen to represent his wife. Maddie gave the impression of being an Earth Mother with her natural-fibers clothing and long hair showing the first signs of gray. She didn't hide them, because, as she liked to say, Jacob likes things natural. It was obvious she adored him. Would she do *anything* for him? I remembered my conversation with old Patti at the Cove. She'd said Maddie knew how to handle a gun. Would she fire a warning shot to scare Alex? Was this a sad case of foolishness gone wrong? I envisioned the petite woman who dressed in nondescript clothing so she could blend into the surroundings, so she didn't distract from her husband. Her husband. Did Maddie try to make the shot to impress her husband? That sounded farfetched. But people did things when they were in love or felt diminished. It was possible. I positioned Maddie's ball-of-yarn magnet in the middle of the collection.

A little shudder went through my body. Was I surrounded by killers the same way that Maddie's magnet was surrounded by other suspects?

That thought was triggered by Ryan's magnet. A heart. *Ha! That was a poor choice*, I thought. It hurt to think that I was so wrong about him. There were so many wonderful hours we'd spent together—talking, really getting to know each other. I thought we were building a bond, something special. I knew I should talk to him, but it's true, actions do speak louder than words. The hurt I felt was still raw from the time he disappeared without a good-bye and not a word for months. How could he believe I wouldn't understand? After all, he's not his father. Just because he sold guns didn't make Ryan a purveyor of war and death, too. I shouldn't paint the son with the same brush as his father. Being related to someone didn't make the child a *chip off the old block*.

I truly believed I wasn't my father's daughter. I wouldn't have abandoned my child to live with her grandmother and gone to sea, too far away for a comforting hug. He kept his distance, communicating only by Skype and email. I could read a little bit, but I couldn't type out messages to him, let alone describe my emotions. I was only five years old. Love doesn't track through cyberspace when you're that age.

No, we are not our fathers.

But Ryan chose to hide from me for months and months. He'd lost the benefit of the doubt. *Do I trust him anymore?* That question brought me up short. I didn't have an answer. Not now. Should I take his magnet off the door?

Simon moved and raised his chocolaty-brown eyes to mine. Their soulful look gave me his answer. "I'm sorry, Simon. I can't. I know more about him than you do. I have to trust *my* gut feeling this time." I left the heart magnet in play on the suspect board.

Next to it was the broom magnet that represented Dawkins. The idea of using a broom magnet to represent a good butler was silly, especially a man like Dawkins. I toyed with the idea of exchanging it for a gun, if I even had one in my box of magnets. Yes, he probably still had the skills to make that one clean shot that blew apart Alex's chest, but would he do it? This crime was one of passion, emotion, I reminded myself. I used to think Dawkins didn't feel anything, not until his cousin Norman revealed his true background and what had brought him to Fair Winds. Could I ever make a joke about his chilly, efficient exterior again, knowing that deep feelings bubbled underneath? I tapped my finger against my chin. Could one of those emotions be jealousy? I remembered Lorraine's comment about Dawkins always watching Alex. Surely, his training would have reeled in his emotions. But was Dawkins jealous of the attention Lorraine lavished on Alex and their growing attachment? Did seeing Alex's ex-wife saunter into Fair Winds, acting like she was the lady of the manor make him angry enough to punish Alex?

There was another person who made it hard to believe that she could commit murder. I looked at Mary Rose's black boot on my door of suspicion. How could I think this woman could commit murder? She respected life and Mother Nature. She loved the finer things like afternoon tea. Sure, she was a little rough around the edges. Okay, a lot rough. I couldn't think of a lady who would carry a big Swiss Army knife on her belt unless she was on safari, but life had knocked Mary Rose around. She wanted to be ready to handle whatever it threw at her. Yes, she'd fight back, but commit murder? No. I moved her magnet to the side.

And, of course, there were two other suspects who could have acted separately or together. Either way, they both stood to benefit, Allen, his business partner, and Arabella, the gorgeous ex-wife. They had a variety of motives that ran from money and control to the age-old competition for the lady and the lady's wish to strike back at the man who spurned her.

"Yes, we have quite an array of suspects, Simon."

CHAPTER 25

Inspect every item of silver in your care for minute signs of damage. Do this on a regular schedule. Pitting or severe tarnish and discoloration are signs of pending destruction.

"The Butler's Guide to Fine Silver"
Mr. Hollister, 1898

I NEEDED to talk to Ingram. There were two sets of suspects that I wanted to make sure were on his radar. I sent him a text and grabbed my car keys so I was ready to meet him. But I didn't need them. The detective was going over the scene of the crime again. I headed to the main house and flew around the corner toward the terrace. Instead of running into the detective, I ran straight into Ryan's strong chest. I'd bottled up all the anger and hurt I felt since I learned the truth about him. The collision popped the cork. All I wanted to do was strike out at him for deceiving me.

"I know, I know it all." The accusation in my voice was sharp and it brought him up short. I'd always thought his quiet composure was a strong personality trait. Now, I wasn't so sure.

Wouldn't great self-control under fire be an asset to an arms dealer? Wasn't Rudyard Kipling who wrote that one must keep his head when all around you are losing theirs? That would be especially true when dangerous people were holding guns. And this calm man who kept his head thought I was an idiot. My resentment at being left in the dark bubbled over. "I know all about you. I know what you don't want me to know."

And, true to form, he maintained his cool. "And what would that be?"

"I know you hang out with killers." I waited for a look of shock to cross his face, but there was nothing. No, Dawkins wouldn't have lied. He'd told me the truth. "You could have been honest about your family business. Instead you've been slinking around, being secretive about what you really do for a living."

"I wasn't keeping it a secret. I just never talked about it." He was showing so little emotion that we could have been talking about going grocery shopping.

"That's what I mean. You've been keeping it a secret that you have family connections to the arms-dealing world. I don't like spending my time with somebody who keeps secrets, big secrets like that. I've had enough of that in my life already and I'm not interested in playing that game anymore." I turned to walk away, but he caught my arm and stopped me.

"Abby, I wasn't being secretive." I opened my mouth to disagree again when he added, "I was embarrassed." He looked around. "C-c-could we go someplace that's a little more private and talk. Please?"

Desperation strained his voice. I nodded and pressed my lips together as we walked. The light shimmered in the heat waves rising above the grass. When we stopped, I relaxed my lips and felt the prickle of blood.

"This is better. Thank you." Ryan continued. "I was never proud of what my father did for a living." I glanced out at the river. "I was never proud of him as a man, now that I think about it."

"But he was your father," I insisted.

"Yes, biologically. And that was enough to earn my respect and love?" He shook his head slowly. "He never came to one of my soccer games or watched me compete in a regatta. He was never at one of my birthday parties, but always sent a huge gift so all the other kids were impressed. He never got it that having him there would have been the best present in the world for me. Time and again, he had an excuse that he had to be out of town for work."

The vein in his neck throbbed. "Do you know that growing up, I had everything I wanted, but no idea what the man did for a living. My mother always said he was a businessman. That sounded good. Many of my friends' fathers were businessmen. But it took years for me to find out about his business and who he was." Ryan put his hands in his pockets and seemed to gather his thoughts.

"When I graduated from high school, he suddenly realized he had a son. I was thrilled when he told me that I was old enough now to go with him on a business trip." Ryan tried to mask his hurt and disappointment, but I could still see it there in his eyes, in his hunched shoulders after all these years.

"So, did you go with your father somewhere?" I asked, forcing the question through pursed lips. I wasn't sure if I wanted to know the answer or any more about this man.

He looked down at his hands clamped in front of him. "Yes, I did go with him on that trip. It was one I will never forget."

"Did you go someplace exotic?"

"If you call central Africa exotic, yes. We flew over on his private jet and for a teenager that was cool. After we landed in the chaos of an African international airport, we switched to a smaller plane with big engines. As we skipped over the treetops, I was glued to the window, seeing a giraffe nibbling on a tree and a small herd of elephants at a waterhole."

"That's amazing. Did you think your dad was a zoologist or preservationist?"

Ryan glanced up at the sky and gave his head a little shake.

"No, but I soon realized that you could call him a preservationist. He was all about preserving... and building his wealth. That day, I found out what my father really did for a living. We landed on a grassy strip in the middle of the jungle. It was scary coming in over the treetops and bumpy as hell. To this day, I always close my eyes during approach and landing, whether I'm flying commercial or private. Once we were on the ground, we taxied around to an area where there were several battered jeeps parked.

"The plane stopped and the crew lowered the stairs to the ground. I remember so clearly my father saying to me, 'Come on, son. It's time for you to start learning the family business. He took my hand and I literally followed in his footsteps down the aisle to the gangway.

"When I took my first step outside, it was as if I walked into a solid wall of sweltering heat. The pungent smell of rot assaulted my nose. I remember staggering from the effect, but my father ordered me to come and stand at his side. Men, with skin the color of ebony and wearing some kind of military uniform came towards us. At first, I thought this was a welcoming committee. Maybe we were going to meet a jungle king. Maybe my father was on a diplomatic mission."

"It must have been exciting for a young boy," I said.

"Only it was nothing like that. When they were within ten feet of us, the men planted their feet on the scorched earth, brought out their guns and held them across their chests. We were there to meet jungle guerrilla soldiers."

"What happened then?" I asked breathlessly.

"I'm not sure I remember, but it probably was the same thing that happened every time he made a delivery. The customers only had eyes for our cargo. They grabbed the crates from the belly of the plane and hauled them out onto the grass in the blistering sun and broke them open to inspect the merchandise. I didn't know it then, but I know now that we were delivering Kalashnikov's."

A little gasp escaped me. "Rifles? Guns!" *So, it was true. Deep inside, I'd hoped Dawkins was lying.*

Ryan dropped his eyes. "Yes, guns. My father was an international arms dealer." Ryan looked away, not wanting to meet my eyes.

I looked away, as well. I wasn't that surprised to hear confirmation that Ryan's father was an arms dealer, but the news that his customers included guerrilla soldiers and rebels made me stagger. I'd seen those people, dressed all in black and carrying guns, in the news and movies based on actual events. I was not ready for such stunning information. I'm not sure I ever would be. My world lurched with the realization that the man I was growing to love was connected to such a business.

Then Ryan turned his face to me, his eyes narrowed into slits. "But you said you knew. How did you find out?"

I couldn't walk away. I couldn't lie. "I learned about Dawkins experience in the military. He told me how you two became friends and how you introduced him to Lorraine." Ryan's face relaxed, but his blue eyes darkened into the color of night. I didn't know how I was going to reconcile all this, but Ryan story wasn't over.

"That day in the jungle, sweat was pouring off me. I don't know if it was from the heat or fear. I felt like I was in a thriller movie, but when it's really happening, it's not exciting. I was terrified and just wanted to get back on the plane and go home. I turned, but my father caught my arm before I could run up the stairs. 'Stay here,' he ordered. 'I don't want you to miss the best part.'"

My mind raced. What was the best part? An African princess? An execution to test their new weapons?

"After inspecting the merchandise we'd brought, their leader motioned a soldier to drive a Jeep over to us. There were two small cases stacked on the back. It was my father's turn to inspect the delivery."

In a meek voice, I asked "Was it money?"

Ryan shrugged a little. "Not the kind of money that you put in your wallet. I've since learned that they were bearer bonds. I will never forget the smile on his face that day. It was not a smile I'd ever seen before. In a nursery rhyme, you might say he smiled like the cat who caught the canary, but in this case, the cat was a leopard and the canary was a great deal of money. That smile frightened me, but I soon learned there was more to come."

"What happened?"

"He looked the guerrilla leader in the eye, challenging the man who held a powerful gun. It would only take a small move and he could have sliced us to ribbons with its bullets. And no one in the world would know, because no one knew where we were. I held my breath when my father said, 'I believe you have something else for me.' It felt like forever for the interpreter to translate that simple sentence. We all stood there like statues. Nobody moved. Nobody dared.

"I couldn't breathe as I watched the leader slowly raise his right hand and at a snail's pace reached into his shirt pocket. I wanted to yell, he's gonna shoot us! But I couldn't get my mouth to work. That was a good thing, because the man pulled something out of his pocket, something that fit in his fist. When he held it out to my father and opened his hand, there was a small sapphire blue bag sitting on his palm. Then, in slow motion, he tilted his hand and the bag dropped. Everyone lurched as if to catch it, but it dangled safely from his finger by its drawstring.

"And then the leader did the scariest thing of all. He threw back his head, opened his mouth so his white teeth flashed against his dark skin... and he laughed. A sharp, mocking laugh. No one moved as the ugly sound rang out in that godforsaken jungle.

"Then without warning, with a flick of his wrist he sent that pouch sailing through the air at my father. I don't know how he did it. My father had nerves of steel. Without blinking, he caught the pouch in midair, spread the opening and spilled some of the contents into the palm of his hand. I'll never forget how they glittered in the sun."

"Diamonds," I breathed.

Ryan nodded. "Yep, big flawless diamonds. And he said to me,

'This is why we came, son.' Then with no fanfare at all, he signaled one of the crew to transfer the bearer bond cases into the cargo hold of the plane. We followed and settled into our seats while the pilot started up the propellers and we took off. I don't think I said more than ten words on the flight back to his plane or on the trip home."

I could understand. I too, couldn't think of anything to say.

He grabbed my hand and turned me toward the river. "Come on, let's walk." And we did, each lost in their own thoughts.

I could feel my brows squeezing together in disbelief as I wrestled with the new revelation that Ryan's family business didn't just sell guns, it was involved with African guerrilla soldiers. What did a light-haired white boy look like to those dark-skinned men and boys in the jungle whose life was all about struggle and death? I never imagined I'd be this close to such violence. It was hard to take in. I remembered reading about child soldiers used in African conflicts, but I never finished the article because the horror was too much to imagine. Childhood was too precious to be stolen.

I glanced up at Ryan. Now that he was back on the Shore from his months-long business trip, his skin was taking on that natural healthy glow that came from being in the sun and on the water. The sun was lightening his hair again. His profile was strong, clearly defined. It was the face of a man who knew who he was and what he wanted. The number one impression I'd always had of Ryan, once I got past his drop-dead good looks, was confidence. Now, he looked unsettled and hurt. No, it was more than that. It was the look of an injured animal. This man had just revealed a secret he'd kept carefully hidden from everyone for a long time.

I knew I needed, no, wanted to say something, but I was overwhelmed by what I'd learned and lost for words. And the words I needed had to be right.

Ryan stopped, his eyes still downcast. I needed those words fast. As I opened my mouth, Detective Ingram hailed me from the terrace. "Abby, Abby!" He jogged across the grass toward us. "You're just the person I need." As he joined us, he said, "Ryan, good to see you."

Ryan gave him a curt nod and stomped away. Ingram gave me a quizzical look. "I'm sorry, did I interrupt a lover's tiff?"

I stayed quiet as Ingram eyed me, looking for clues to why I was upset. I didn't want to lay out my love life for Ingram's study and analysis. I certainly didn't want to tell the detective about Ryan's connection to guns and arms sales. It wouldn't help anything to make Ryan a suspect in the detective's eyes.

Finally, he gave up. "Okay then, let's change the subject. I wanted to remind you to attend the meeting with the new developers."

I was annoyed... with myself. I'd forgotten that Allen and Arabella were losing no time in turning the concept of *Chesapeake Haven* on the drawing board into a brick-and-asphalt reality. They'd made changes. I suspected Alex would not have approved, but Alex was gone. Allen was hot to get the homes built so Arabella could sell them. Only then could they start raking in the gold and move on. They didn't strike me as people who would put down roots on the Shore.

"Abby?" Ingram brought me back from the morass of my thoughts. "You're up to your ears in this case and I want your interpretation of what goes on." He hesitated, then asked the one thing he had on his mind. "Abby, who do you think killed Alex?"

"I suppose you just mentioned the best suspects, the new developers. Didn't they have the most to gain? Taking over a multi-million-dollar development sounds like a strong motive to me."

He reached into his pocket and pulled out his notebook. "And you might be interested to learn that one of those developers..." He referred to his notes. "Mr. Allen Barclay isn't who he says he is."

Ingram had my full attention. And he noticed. With a satisfied grin, he continued. "Yes, I thought you'd find that interesting. He has a Polish last name with lots of *c's* and *z's* and *k's* so I can't pronounce it for you, but I'm going to go out on a limb here and say that putting his real name and the words *Prestige Properties* wouldn't have the same panache for attracting clients."

And I thought I was done with surprises for the day. "I'm shocked. How did you…" Of course, he'd run a check on the main suspects and unearthed this tidbit. "And he's so proud of his name. He gave me his business card the other day. Pointed out that Allen was spelled the old English way to go with his last name, Barclay, an old English name famous in financial circles. He said something that was a little strange, that the two names went well together. I thought he was complimenting his parents on choosing a good name for him, but I guess he was proud of himself for concocting a great alias. Is he a criminal?"

Ingram took a step back. "Whoa, that's a big leap. A man can change his name if he does it legally and the court had no problem with the name Allen Barclay." He lowered his voice. "And to answer your question, other than a few parking tickets, he's clean."

"Maybe." I wasn't willing to give either Allen or Arabella a Get-Out-of-Jail-Free card just yet.

"So, you still think they had something to do with the murder?"

"Maybe," I said again.

He sighed. "I agree, but I was really trying to whittle down the big pool of suspects. I think this meeting coming up is going to be important and will tell us a lot. What do you think?"

I shrugged. "I don't know what to think." Then silently I added, *Except I'm surrounded by killers.*

CHAPTER 26

Never allow tarnish or polish residue to remain after polishing a silver paper knife. When it is used to cut the folds of a printed book or monograph, it should make a smooth cut and never leave any stain or trace behind as this would mar the printed matter permanently.

> "The Butler's Guide to Fine Silver"
> Mr. Hollister, 1898

THE TIME for the meeting with the new developers had crept up on me and I had to hurry. I did have time to notice that a rather dramatic change was happening over my head. Storm clouds in shades that ran from slate to ivory were beginning to clutter the sky. The only saving grace about Zelma the hurricane as that she was weakening to a Category 2. Some thin, wispy white clouds in the distance gave me a little hope that the storm might pass us by.

I was late arriving at the library in St. Michaels and, to make matters worse, I had to park blocks away. This event had captured a lot of attention and motivated a lot of people to show up. I made my way down the library's long corridor used as an art gallery, but on this evening, I didn't take time to look at the work of the local artists. I claimed a chair close to the door and looked around the room to get the lay-of-the-land, so to speak, before the meeting started.

People were milling around, chatting and filling paper coffee cups. Jacob was tucked into a corner, chatting with a young woman who was twirling lock of long blonde hair around her finger. The gentle blush on her cheeks suggested they were not talking about the salinity of the Chesapeake Bay.

There was one person sitting alone in the sea of folding chairs. It was the minister and he looked uncomfortable, sitting with his arms crossed in a way to protect his chest and cradle his chin in one hand. As I went over to say hello, I noticed several seats in the front row were taped with pieces of paper, the word *RESERVED* printed on them. I wondered VIPs were coming then turned my attention back to the minister who looked like he could use a friend. I had ruled him out as a suspect and he probably didn't have any useful information about the killer's identity, but I could stop for a few minutes.

"Hello," I said, and he almost jumped out of the chair. I started to apologize for shocking him, but decided it would be better to ignore his reaction.

When he caught his breath, he eked out the word, Hello.

I tried to put him at ease. "I remember you from the meeting at Fair Winds. I'm glad to see you here tonight." Not that I was, but I couldn't think of anything better to say.

He brightened. "Yes, I was there. But I'm afraid tempers might get out of hand tonight. I came to see if I could do something to inspire calm. That's one way of doing the Lord's work—promoting peace."

I nodded in agreement though I thought this quiet, painfully shy man in a black suit and clerical collar might be rolled over by the stronger personalities now gathering in the room. I excused myself when I saw the wife of the eco-terrorist, at least that's how I thought of him.

"Hello, again. Maddie, isn't it?" She beamed. This must have been one of the few times someone had noticed her since she always seemed to be standing in her husband's shadow. "I see you made it to this meeting."

"Oh yes, Jacob thinks it's very important for us to be here tonight." She glanced around the room, her head nodding slightly. I was surprised this woman didn't live her life being constantly seasick considering how much she moved her head during a short conversation. "He's been talking to a lot of the people who are coming tonight. Raising awareness, that sort of thing. Jacob thinks that they'll find a way to stop this project. In fact, more and more people are coming around to his way of thinking, just as Jacob said they would. We're going to have a little impromptu dinner, a pitch-in, a pot luck dinner, but it won't be as formal as that sounds." She cast her eyes down and rocked a little, like a shy child. "I'll have the last summer vegetables out of our garden on the table. Jacob likes everything natural." She looked up, her brown eyes almost pleading. "Would you like to come?"

I had the strange feeling that I would be the only guest *she* invited. Maybe ever. I felt sorry for her. I couldn't imagine how she felt being treated like the *little woman* by her husband, as if we were living in the early 20th century.

"Ah," I stammered as her fresh shiny face waited for an answer," I said, hoping that my response was vague enough. "It all depends—"

Interrupting, she put her hand on my arm. "Oh, I do hope you'll come. We... Jacob could use your help. There is so much work to be done."

This issue of a large real estate development wasn't going away anytime soon and it would probably keep the people here on the Shore in an uproar long after Ingram identified the killer. People would be concerned with clearing land, building houses, paving streets. I was so focused on finding Alex's killer that I'd lost the perspective of the Big Picture. I couldn't get rid of that nagging feeling that the two issues—the development and the murder—were linked.

We were missing something. With a little sigh, I hoped that we discovered what that something was before I had to go to Maddie's little dinner soirée.

"I'll let you know," I repeated and pointed to the front of the room, toward Allen and Arabella. "It looks like they're getting ready to start. I'd better get back to my seat." I didn't want to get swallowed up by the sea of chattering people. I might not get back to my excellent vantage point close to the door.

Maddie grabbed my arm with an iron grip. "Tell me, you don't think it will come to violence again, do you? You don't think someone else will be shot?" Maddie stopped nodding long enough to scan the room madly. "I have to find Jacob. I have to make sure he's all right."

Jacob's wife was frightened, but of what? Another shooting? Or that her husband might do something awful? I watched as she rushed away. In the opposite direction of where I'd seen her husband. I didn't stop her. I didn't want to encourage another act of violence. If Maddie had taken the shot that killed Alex, even if it was only supposed to be a warning shot, I suspected that she could shoot someone dead on purpose, if she was motivated. I'd spotted Jacob in the corner talking to a young woman who projected herself. I assumed that Maddie wouldn't be pleased to see him with a young woman, their heads together, whispering. I felt sorry for Maddie who had probably spent her life chasing after him. But this was no time to feel sorry for a wronged wife. I was on the lookout for a killer.

"Pssst, Abby. Over here."

I turned to see Charlie threading his way through a group of chatting people, trying to make his way to me.

"Hi," I said, feeling sorry I couldn't put more enthusiasm into my greeting.

He gave me a worried look and even though he'd guessed the answer, he asked me, "How are you doing?"

I shrugged. "I don't know. This whole thing has taken its toll."

"I'm not surprised. To have a murder committed in your own home." He shook his head with regret. "And to have your close friend accused of the crime. It was tough on me when somebody died while I was doing the sport I love, but ... well, I can't imagine." He reached out, paused then put his hand on my shoulder. "Is there anything I can do for you?"

I wanted to scream, *Yes! Find the killer! That's the only way to end this nightmare.* Instead, I shook my head. "I'll be okay. It will just take a little time, that's all."

He gave me a serious look. "Just remember to keep an eye on the weather."

"I am, but I saw some white wispy clouds on my drive into town. Maybe the storm is going to bypass us."

"Were they thin, wispy like feathers?" I nodded and he frowned.

"They are a sure sign that a storm is coming. They are at the higher elevations and made of ice crystals."

"Come on, Charlie. Ice crystals? It's August."

"You're going to have to trust me on this, since we don't have time for a weather lesson. Weather observers during World War II watched for those clouds and flashed storm warnings to the convoys crossing the North Atlantic."

I felt a curtain of gloom settle over me. Charlie must have seen it, because his face brightened. "This might cheer you up. I saw Tiffani the other day. You do remember her? She—"

I grabbed his arm. "She didn't relapse, did she? Tell me she's alright?" Tiffani was the young girl who loved racing log canoes, the majestic sailboats only found on the Chesapeake Bay. She'd fallen victim to opioid addiction after knee surgery. I'd heard her cry for help and got her into rehab. She'd been clean for a while, but there was always the possibility of something terrible happening.

Now, he had a silly grin on his face. "Far from it! She's been invited to enter some prestigious art competition in New York and she has a teaching job at an art school in Philly that will let her get her master's. I don't know all the details, but she was downright giddy with excitement. She said that she wanted to tell you herself, but she has to move and be ready to start, like yesterday. I was supposed to let you know and that she'll see us both at Christmas."

I bit my lip. This was not the time or place, but I wanted to cry. Tears of joy. I wanted—

"Hello, Charlie," Lorraine said. "Abby, do you have a seat?" I nodded. "Good and don't forget, afterwards, we're… you know."

I looked at Charlie. "I have to…"

"Yeah, I understand," he said. "I just wanted to let you know about our friend."

"I appreciate it. More than you know."

"I thought it might help. And Abby, if you need to talk or want to have a drink or…" He wiggled his eyebrows and grinned. "Or take a hair-raising drive along the back roads in my Jeep, just let me know."

I promised I would.

Alone again, I surveyed the room, before I made my way to my seat in the back. Everyone was milling around, chatting and checking out who was there. A rustling noise swept the room and people looked up to watch several people file in and take the reserved seats in the front row.

I leaned over to an older woman near me. "Do you know who they are? Some faces look familiar."

"They should. A couple of them are on the County Council and there are a few St. Michaels Town Commissioners."

Allen had certainly been busy. Had these people made up their minds before public hearings were held? "Are they in favor of the project?" I asked her.

She shrugged. "Who knows? Once they win an election, they

stop listening to us and follow their own agendas. They talk a good game *until* the votes are counted. Then if we don't like the direction they're taking, they say "Take us to court!" She harrumphed.

Someone accidently bumped into me. It was the lady friend of Dr. Phillips who was so distraught the night of the shooting. She squinted at me. "I know you. You were *there*. Oh dear, I do hope they find the killer. I've never been accused or suspected of anything in my life." She stumbled away, terribly unnerved. She was one person who would never take a pen or printer paper home from the library. The stress would probably kill her.

She wasn't the only one who was out of sorts. Everyone in the room seemed to be *off*. It must have been the tension of seeing familiar faces, familiar from the night of the shooting. Everyone was on edge knowing that there might be a killer in the room, maybe sitting in the next chair. It could be anyone.

As if on cue, the din in the room quieted down and my favorite suspects made their entrance. Alex's business partner Allen entered the room with a swagger, Arabella on his arm like a prize heifer. The thought made me chuckle, just enough to attract attention, so I covered it with a cough.

I caught a glimpse of a cap of snowy white curls and swallowed a groan. Busybody Harriet was in attendance. She might be a well-meaning elderly woman who had too much time on her hands, but she loved gossip, craved to be in the middle of things and often made the most outrageous comments. Too often. I don't think she planned to say any of those malicious or hurtful things that just tumbled out of her mouth. As usual, I felt sorry for her dutiful husband, Ben, following along behind her. The man never got anything into a conversation, except *Yes, dear.*

I recognized the bearded man who endorsed the concept of Recycle, Reuse at the first meeting. He passed close enough for me to overhear his comment to someone. "This place is more appropriate for our meeting than that fancy estate house on the river. Did she think she'd impress us into submission?" he declared.

The man didn't know it, but he'd just moved up on to my list of suspects. We should keep an eye on him.

Dawkins materialized out of the crowd and stepped closer so he could deliver a message only I could hear. "The most important part of this meeting is not the details about the proposed development. It's the process. So, be watchful, especially for anger turning destructive."

"Great! So, only Alex was shot at the last meeting. With Allen and his tiger in charge, there should be dead bodies all over the floor."

A rare smile touched Dawkins' lips.

Lorraine appeared. "I saw you two over here, plotting."

"Us?" I gave her an exaggerated innocent look.

She looked over the room that was rapidly filling up and leaned closer. "It's a shame. Situations like this make people so competitive." Her eyes narrowed. "Especially that one."

I followed her glare and watched Arabella march into the room, enough steps behind Allen to make an entrance on her own without making him feel upstaged. Her black hair hung like a waterfall straight down her back. Her turquoise eyes shone from under the black fringe of bangs framing her stunning face.

Staring at Arabella, I tried to look unimpressed, but I wasn't. She knew how to play the situation. She was the diversionary tactic. Men would fantasize about her. Women would hate her... or want to be her. Either way, the people in the room would be distracted from the real business at hand and Allen could do his thing. I realized that the devil might wear Prada, but tonight, she was wearing a short, soft leather skirt and a rich-red silk blouse that fluttered over her ample breasts. Yes, the men, even the rabid environmentalists, would love to have their nature take its course with her.

Lorraine's voice drew me out of my revelry. "These people made a grave mistake when they killed Alex and now they'll pay for it." She was relishing this moment and that threw me a little. It was out of character for Lorraine to delight in someone's suffering. I looked around the room and it was apparent that these people were going to suffer at the hands of the tyrannical duo of Allen and his lady friend Arabella. It was only a question of how bad the damage would be.

CHAPTER 27

The paper knife must never be used to remove the seal from correspondence. Its dull blade is too thick and will damage the paper. An erasing knife with its small, sharp blade is designed for this task. Be sure the appropriate implements are always at the ready.

"The Butler's Guide to Fine Silver"
Mr. Hollister, 1898

PEOPLE WERE eager to jam into the library's meeting room. The air crackled with expectation. It was clear that the polite, courteous atmosphere that surrounded the first meeting at Fair Winds was absent here. As Allen and Arabella made their way through the crowd to the podium, I think they sensed the attitude shift, too. Instead of easing the undercurrent of tension, they barely hid their contempt for these *backwater tree-huggers,* as Arabella called them that day on the streets of St. Michaels. Even though Allen had gently chastised her, it was obvious that he agreed.. They had concocted an excellent act of good cop/bad cop to advance their moneymaking interests.

It was sad that the local people weren't just battling the developers, they were quarreling with each other. They were the ones who should have been motivated to come to some kind of an understanding, because they saw each other every day. As each side dug in, the whole situation might end up in court, then who knows what would happen. Would a judge or a jury be able to broker a deal everyone could tolerate or would they just force something to happen? A vision had disintegrated to ashes and now the two people at the front were whipping them up to blind everyone. I had to agree with Lorraine. These people would only do the minimum. The community was better off with Alex.

As Allen droned on about selling points and Arabella clicked slide after slide of their presentation, the tension in the room was growing until Stu, the cookie monster, heaved himself up and made an announcement.

"Folks, let me summarize this for you. They want to drop this piece of suburbia right in the middle of our beautiful Eastern Shore and life here will never be the same."

I was surprised at his about-face on this issue. I'd seen him ask Alex for a job supporting the project. Now, he was rabblerousing for its destruction. Guess he shouldn't have been ignored.

A young man shot up. "He's right." He pointed an accusing finger at Allen. "You have no right to destroy my family's legacy."

Another man bellowed from the back of the room, "You're just going to add to the debris from the dam."

Allen chuckled. "I assure you, sir, we have nothing to do with the Conowingo Dam. That's up north."

"Yeah, but all that asphalt is non-permeable and the runoff with the fertilizers and pesticides will be horrendous," the man countered.

Allen didn't have a comeback and he was rapidly losing control of the meeting.

A bearded man raised his hand, but didn't wait to be recognized. "We need to repurpose things instead of taking them to the dump and it'll save energy when building something new."

There was a smattering of applause in the room and he looked surprised and rather pleased with himself as he sat down.

The comments kept coming. When the young Mayan woman from the first meeting raised her hand and stood, Arabella did her best to look right through her. But Allen called on her as if she was a lifeline. "Yes, pretty lady."

She was taken aback by his sexist approach, but got tough. "At the first meeting, at that pretty house, I asked your partner, the poor man who was shot..." The room gasped. No one had mentioned the murder. "I asked if there would be jobs for men like my husband and brothers. He said there would, but he isn't here, so I ask you the same question." She remained standing, waiting for an answer.

Allen looked to Arabella who shrugged her shoulders and looked away as if she'd rather be shopping. "I suppose there will be" he said. "We are in favor of minority hiring, of course. You must understand, I'm not quite as hands-on as my partner Alex was. The men in your family will have to talk to the foreman on the site. I can't make any promises. Next question." He searched the room, hoping for a puffball question.

Instead, Jacob, the man committed to the environment, jumped to his feet. His question was not for Allen. It was for the people in the room. "Are you going to let them distract you from the real problem here? Yes, it's too bad that a man died, but think of all the trees that this development will kill. And the forest animals who will lose their homes. The waters of the Chesapeake are polluted, *poisoned,* by uncontrolled building, thoughtless land use and the spread of chemicals on the land." He glared at Allen and Arabella then thrust out his arm, pointing at them. "They are the real criminals here!"

Allen shot back, "Who are you?" He was ready for a fight.

Jacob spun around, turning his back on Allen, shrugged out of his jacket and turned around again. The bright yellow and red ink on his t-shirt blared out his message:

FOILED SILVER

System change, not climate change
-- Karl Marx

HE HELD his arms out at his sides and turned around slowly so everyone in the room could see the message. The blood-soaked fist of defiance made people squirm, along with the Communist quote. I almost blurted out the words, *I was right!* The man was an eco-terrorist. At least a Marxist. Both Dawkins and Ryan tensed, ready to act, but Jacob wasn't done.

Bathed in the prideful gaze of his wife, Maddie, he declared, "You want to know who I am? I am an Earth Warrior who must do what must be done to take care of this planet. That's who and what I am. And I'll do everything I can to stop you and this big moneymaking scheme. You are hereby warned."

Jacob jerked his head toward the door and his wife Maddie leapt to her feet and followed him out of the meeting room. I shifted my gaze to Ingram in time to catch him making a note and stuffing it into his pocket.

The meeting got raucous. Tempers flared and the temperature in the room skyrocketed. I felt little trickles of sweat from under my arms. People stood. Hands flew around to dramatize points. Gestures were aimed at the duo at the front table, but also at others in the audience. Opposition had reared its ugly head and some people didn't appreciate it. Well, too bad for them.

Through the melee, a head of white curls bobbed toward me on their way to the door. It was Harriet supported by Ben. They were jostled by the growing anger of others, younger and more engaged in the debate. I helped clear a path for them out of the room.

"Are you leaving?" I asked with surprise. I'd never known Harriet to walk away from a cornucopia of gossip. Something must be wrong.

Harriet was fanning herself. "Oh, my goodness, this is more than I can take. And my knee is killing me."

"It's the low pressure from the storm coming in," her husband said to reassure her.

"I know, I can always tell in my bones when it's going to rain, but Ben, dear, please take me home."

His hands were all aflutter around her to support her aging body, protect her from the riled-up people close by and stay upright himself. "Of course, dear. Right away, dear. Come along now."

In true Harriet-style, I heard a long, melodramatic sigh that went right down the scale. I helped maintain a path for them to the door while he half carried her away. I was glad they had escaped. There was no need for a fall or broken hip. Yes, things were getting heated. A couple of uniformed police officers were on their feet, exchanging looks. One spoke into the radio mike on his shoulder.

Allen and Annabella had their heads together at the front table, ignoring the hostile commotion in front of them. Allen shook his head. Arabella made a fist and slammed it down on the table to make her point. He caved and closed his eyes for a moment in resignation and stepped up to the table.

"Ladies and gentlemen," he called out to the room. Everyone ignored him. He reached down and took off his Italian loafer and banged the heel on the table. The sharp raps got people's attention long enough for them to pause and look at him.

"Thank you. I want to let you know that we'll have all the plans and presentation materials available for your review at the construction trailer at the property site."

Someone called out. "What about the engineering studies?"

It sounded like someone knew the right questions to ask to trip up this arrogant man and his proposal.

"Do you have permits?" The question was heard over the noise and the room calmed down a little to listen.

Allen gave a little nod and the room exploded.

"Wait!" Someone called out. "When did that happen?"

Arabella shot him a coquettish look. "Today. We're moving forward." And with that, the vixen threw fuel on the fire.

People roared in loud outrage. Officers arrived and waded into the crowd to defuse some of the more volatile confrontations. The police chief appeared in the art gallery outside the door. At least he had taken this meeting seriously. Two of his officers moved to the front of the room as the developers scooped up their papers, grabbed their charts then the uniformed officers escorted them from the room.

I scurried out of the crowded and highly-charged atmosphere and took up a position in the art gallery, barely out of the way of the people in heated debate leaving the meeting room.

Mary Rose was one of the first to explode from the crowd. Distracted and muttering to herself, she almost missed my hello. She looked at me, but my face didn't seem to register right away.

"It's me. Abby." She was agitated and I wanted to help. I reached out to, I don't know, steady her or something. "Are you okay? Do you need—"

She pulled away like an angry child about to throw a tantrum. "I don't need your help." She glanced back at the meeting room. "This bunch is worse than that other man. Well, I'm done with the lot of them. Don't need them. Never have. Never will." And she blasted out the door into the fading twilight.

I had the urge to follow her, but the crowd between me and the door made that impossible. One man stood gazing at some paintings on display, letting people stream around him. He looked like the consummate creative, a man of delicate physique wearing a flowered top, three beaded bracelets on one wrist and rugged leather sandals. But I don't think he really saw the paintings. He was oblivious to the turmoil surging around him as he stood bouncing his fist over his lips. I took a step closer to overhear what he was saying to his wife.

"Where will I paint? If they destroy that area of the river, what will I paint? We shall have to move," he moaned as his beautifully-coiffed wife led him away.

Everyone had personal concerns as well as public ones.

"Abby!" I heard Lorraine's voice, but couldn't see her in the crowd. "Go to the house."

Detective Ingram caught up with us in the parking lot. Lorraine turned and figuratively shot a barb right between his eyes.

"I hope you are no longer thinking it was me who pulled the trigger," she proclaimed. "After this meeting, I assume you realize that you have a vast selection of suspects in your murder investigation."

That comment brought Ingram up short. "Is that all you have to say?"

"No. I hope you don't underestimate the power of greed. You saw its face in that room. And you're still expected to come to Fair Winds to discuss the suspects. We'll see you there shortly." She turned and climbed into Ryan's truck.

CHAPTER 28

The letter opener is a modern desk accessory. The blade tip is more pointed than a paper knife so it can slide neatly under the flap of the envelope. Use care, the narrow long blade is sharp to separate or cut the paper of the gummed flap.

"The Butler's Guide to Fine Silver"
Mr. Hollister, 1898

BACK AT FAIR WINDS, Dawkins led us into the breakfast room, away from the living room packed with memories stirred up by the events of an hour ago. Tonight's meeting about *Chesapeake Haven* couldn't have been more different than the one held here at Fair Winds. People reacted with raw emotion. There was almost no civility and a distinct lack of respect. Instead of a conversation and exchange of information, it turned into a competition to see who could be more obnoxious. I wanted desperately to slip over to my cottage and curl up with Simon. His only agenda, hidden or otherwise, was love and cookies and chasing a ball. I craved that simplicity, but I'd promised to give Ingram my impressions of the meeting, even though I didn't think I could add much. With that in mind, I settled into a chair with a cup of decaf and an oatmeal cookie.

Once we were all present, Ingram launched into a recap of the meeting. He brought up the dramatic surprise of the evening: Jacob.

"That's one I'd put at the top of your list, detective," announced Dawkins.

"Would you call him one of your targets?" I asked, remembering our conversation that first night. But Dawkins didn't remember what he'd said and did a double-take. "You told me not to consider *everybody* as a suspect, but to wait until people made themselves stand out, that they were our targets."

Out of the corner of my eye, I saw a shudder run through Lorraine's tired body. It was the word *target*. I quickly rephrased my point. "Those are the people that are the real suspects."

"Yes, Abby, the suspects are rising and stepping into our crosshairs," Dawkins agreed.

Ingram chimed in. "I like that guy, Jacob, for making trouble and maybe more. We'll keep an eye on him."

Lorraine spoke up. "He was so polite in the beginning."

"But he's been ramping up the rhetoric," Ryan pointed out.

"Did you see his t-shirt?" Now, it was my turn to shudder. The quote by Karl Marx was a shock, but the blood dripping off the fist would give me nightmares again.

Discussion about other possible suspects went around the table and finally petered out. We all had Alex's partner and ex-wife on our lists. There were a few other ideas, but nothing that really moved the investigation forward. It was time for Ingram to spring his idea. With a tiny nod from Lorraine, he did.

"I know that not every murder is solved, but I will tell you right now, I'm going to do whatever it takes to close this case and put the killer behind bars." He took a breath and said in a soft voice. "I made a promise and I'm going to keep it." He glanced at Lorraine.

Lorraine helped the man who was hesitating. "Detective, what do you want to do and what can we do to help?"

He licked his lips and launched into his idea. "I want to hold another meeting as I said. I want to do it the way Poirot does it at the end of a case, a recap of the situation, the motives, the secrets I've uncovered, everything."

I closed my eyes and let the voice and comments roll around me.

"*Another* meeting?"

"That's too dramatic for me," Ryan said.

"What do you hope to accomplish?" Lorraine asked.

"It will only be a repeat of tonight."

"The killer will think this is a big joke and probably go to Florida for the winter."

The laughter made Ingram lose his patience. "Listen to me!" We all fell silent. Ingram took a quick breath to suppress his irritation. "I assure you that I'm not trying to be dramatic and we are not living in a novel. A man is dead, and I believe the person who shot and killed him will be in the room. I'm trying to shorten this investigation by flushing him out."

"Don't forget, detective," said Dawkins. "It could be a woman."

Ingram's eyes strayed in Lorraine's direction.

"No, somebody else. Not Lorraine." Dawkins continued with practiced authority. "I'm just suggesting that you not discount the possibility that the shooter could have been a woman, a woman taking aim out of anger."

"Go on." This was one thing I really liked about Ingram. He was always willing to listen, even to impossibly outrageous ideas. "You could be on to something."

"People think a violent act born of anger or passion is committed by a man. I get it. We're all macho and tough. Can't take an insult or a slight. But a survey done by *Esquire* magazine and NBC showed that women are angry more often than men."

"I think I read something like that in *Elle* magazine. I was surprised. I—" The detective was staring at me with a quizzical look on his face. "What? I do read, you know." How ironic. We're standing here, talking about anger, and this man had managed to ignite mine.

"No, it isn't that." Ingram shook his head. "I suspect that you do a lot of reading when you're researching the silver."

I nodded. "I do, so why the funny look on your face." There was no teasing tone in my voice.

He gave his head a quick shake as if he was clearing the cobwebs from his mind. "I just didn't have you pegged as reading *Elle*. I'm sorry."

"You should be. I may not be a girly-girl, but a woman wants to keep up on fashion trends, even when she lives on the Eastern Shore." He cringed a little, so I knew my barb had hit the mark. "And I like reading the articles."

"And speaking of articles and studies," Dawkins said quickly to smooth out the awkward direction our conversation had taken. "The experts say that what they call 'self-silencing' anger—when someone keeps it all bottled up inside—can lead to depression, anxiety, eating disorders, self-harm, even suicide."

"So, the advice of Let It Roll Off isn't the right attitude?" Ingram asked.

"I think they're saying that getting really angry at all is a bad idea for a lot of reasons."

Ingram considered that for a minute then said, "I'm convinced this was a crime of passion. The killer didn't come prepared with a weapon and a plan to kill the victim."

I listened as he mulled over the emotional side of this crime. The way he worked things out fascinated me.

"No, this was a crime that was almost spontaneous. I'm convinced that the person who took that shot and killed Alex was in the living room at some point during that first meeting."

A chill ran through me as I thought that I was there, right there, when it was all happening. I didn't realize, no one could know that within an hour, one person in that room would be dead at the hands of someone else sitting in the same room.

"Something triggered the reaction. Anger flipped the switch that sent the killer to Lorraine's gun cabinet to get a gun and take the shot."

"You certainly have enough suspects. That big room was full." I said.

The detective arrived at the bottom line. "I, we, have to figure out who was angry and who left the meeting."

"If only we knew who was in the room before the shot and who left." Growing frustration tightened my throat. "There was no sign-in sheet which would've made this so much easier." I plopped down in the chair, not sure what to do with myself. "But there's one thing we know for sure. Whoever killed Alex was one fantastic shot."

"It was a once-in-a-lifetime shot," Norman added.

"It had to have been fifty yards," Dawkins said in awe.

I voiced a thought that had been floating around the back of my mind. "Maybe the shooter wasn't trying to kill him? Maybe the shooter was only trying to scare him?"

Norman added," And got lucky?"

"I'm not sure killing someone by mistake is lucky," Dawkins mumbled.

We all sat in silence, troubled by our own thoughts. I suspected that Dawkins was thinking about the little boy in Iraq who was considered collateral damage. But I couldn't think about that now. I had to think about this bullet and what would have happened if it had hit the house instead of shattering Alex's heart and Lorraine's life. If only…

"Yes, I think we can narrow down the list of suspects and watch the reactions very carefully at this meeting I'm proposing. Lorraine has agreed to have it here."

"My choice is *Allen*," The name dripped with all the disgust I could give it. "He doesn't strike me as a consensus builder if it gets in the way of his brick-and-mortar building. And that bit of arm candy he brought with him doesn't help."

"Now, now, Abby. Cattiness doesn't become you." He reacted

before I could say a word in my own defense. "I hope it makes you feel better that she is high on my list of suspects."

"Why?" I said, through a satisfied smile.

"When a husband dies and the wife is around, even an ex-wife, she's the first person to consider. More often than not, it's the spouse."

"And she's not very nice," I mumbled.

"I heard that," Ingram said, with a frown. I tried to look contrite. His face relaxed as he added, "But I happen to think you're right."

Lorraine and I exchanged tight smiles.

Dawkins added, "Detective, you must agree that this could be a dangerous move. I assume you will have officers present."

"What do you mean?" Lorraine said, her voice strained with worry.

"I mean," Dawkins continued, "A cornered animal can become vicious. This person has already killed once. If this person feels threatened, he or she could lash out."

"That's why I'll have officers, both men and women, in plainclothes blending into the group. They'll be ready to head off any trouble before it can happen."

"Well, I guess you know what's best to bring this situation to a close." She started to push herself out of her chair.

Ingram said rapidly, "There's one more thing." He said the next words as if he was tiptoeing over eggshells. "And I'd like to have the meeting here."

Around the table, eyes grew wide. There were quick gasps. Dawkins looked down and shook his head.

"Agatha Christie always had her detective return to the scene of the crime with all the suspects."

Ryan bellowed with a laugh. "That might work on TV, but this is real life." He added almost under his breath. "This is getting stranger by the minute."

"I know, but the place can take people back to that night, nudge their memories," he said with conviction. "We may find out who left the room. Once we know that, we've got our killer."

The grumbling about such a bad idea began again, but was silenced when Lorraine spoke.

"He has a point. I'm a big Agatha Christie fan and, yes, I know this isn't make-believe, but her stories worked, because they were based on good ideas and good techniques." She searched Ingram's face. "Do you really think this will give you the break you need?" Ingram nodded. "Then we'll do it. You get everybody to come and we'll open the door to Fair Winds." She pushed herself out of the chair. "Now, if you'll excuse me. I need to go to bed before I fall down."

As people filed out of the room, Ingram went to Lorraine and quietly thanked her for opening her home again and giving him the chance to flush out the guilty person. In my book, the man had the sensitivity and compassion of a gentleman. That's probably part of what made him a great investigator.

I slipped out and found Simon curled up by the kitchen door, waiting for me. We walked out, both of us too sleepy to play. Frogs croaked. Wavelets slapped weakly at the riprap along the shoreline. Fireflies danced across the heat-worn grass to join the bug cotillion going on among the leaves of a nearby tree. Without using any electricity, nature put on a show of winking lights to mesmerize and make mere humans believe in fairies.

Abruptly, Simon stopped, raised his head and looked off into the shadows. I followed his gaze. A tall man emerged. I couldn't tell. Ryan? Simon was barking and streaked past me. Was he protecting me? From what? Was he in danger? My feet moved faster. Simon stopped barking abruptly. I couldn't sacrifice my dog just to save myself. I had to make sure he was all right.

The man in the shadows crouched down by an exuberant Simon. He was in heaven, wiggling on his back in the grass, soaking up the joy of an enthusiastic tummy rub given by his friend, Ryan.

I couldn't walk away, leaving Simon there. I just stood and

watched. My mind was a blank. Ryan must have felt my eyes on him. His hand stopped stroking the happy pup and raised his head slowly. I didn't want his gaze to meet mine. In defense, I squeezed my eyelids shut. If I couldn't run, at least I could hide my feelings, but I could feel the betrayal of my tears running down my face. I wanted to get to the cottage, go in and lock the door, barricade myself inside, to keep my heart safe. But I needed Simon with me.

A rustle of steps on the dry grass. A puff of damp breath on my leg. Simon had come back to me. There is nothing more genuine than a dog's love. Simon, the one male I could depend on. I breathed a small sigh of relief and opened my eyes. Simon sat at my feet with that Labrador retriever smile, panting, tail wagging furiously. Then that tail was slamming against Ryan's ankles.

The man I thought I once knew, took my hand and cradled it in his large one that was softer than I'd ever known it to be. Before he disappeared for months, he worked with boats and their rough lines. But he hadn't handled a line for a long time until recently. The weathered parts of his palms had gone soft. He wasn't holding my hand in a romantic way. It was more like he was holding on to a lifeline.

"What do you think of Detective Ingram's plan?" he asked.

I was willing to avoid the real issue between us. "It's farfetched if you ask me, trying to catch a killer based on a tactic used by a mystery writer decades ago." I was babbling. I was tired and had no idea why Ryan had waited for me in the shadows. I clamped my mouth closed. The sky was cloudy, blocking the moon, so I couldn't see his face as he spoke, but his voice was weak, unsure. Out of character for this man.

"I didn't know Alex, except to say hello and comment on the weather, but his murder has really gotten under my defenses. I think it's because it happened right in front of you, Abby. Right here at Fair Winds, a place of safety and sanctuary." He paused for a moment and looked down as we walked. "And because he was killed with a gun."

And with those simple words, the details of his story growing up and his family business came crashing back to me. I was appalled at my instant reaction to it all: revulsion. I had to fight down the urge to pull my hand away.

My rational self lectured, *That's not who this man is. He's kind and generous and thoughtful. And sells guns for the sole purpose of killing people,* my conscious screamed. I stole a glance at Ryan to see if he sensed my turmoil, but he was calmly surveying the sky as a building bank of clouds drifted across the face of the moon.

Then in the dusky twilight, Simon romped around. He'd probably been stalking the smell of Bunny or Squirrel. I needed him now. "Simon! Come!" I needed the comfort he always brought me and he was a good excuse to pull my hand from Ryan's clasp.

As the husky Lab ran out of the shadows, I braced myself for the lunging jump that had become part of his inappropriate behavior recently. I was shocked and delighted to see him skid to a stop and sit at my feet. His wagging tail wiggled his entire body. I knelt down and threw my arms around his neck. "Oh, what a good boy! Such a good boy." And he loved it. The puppy in him took over and he slathered my face with his wet tongue then rolled on his back for a belly rub.

Ryan watched our ritual in silence. Happy barking by the main house alerted Simon that someone must be giving out the evening treats. Even I couldn't compete with that. He twisted himself onto his feet and took off.

Ryan reached down, put his hand under my elbow and helped me up. He held out his open hand to me and, for the first time, I didn't want to touch it. A little gust of wind saved me. It whipped my hair into my eyes. I used two hands to tame the curls. I knew that Simon and Mother Nature were not going to continue to save me from what was becoming an awkward situation. I had to say or do something.

I stole another glance at Ryan and decided now was the time. "Remember when you were telling me about the first business trip you took with your father?" I could sense Ryan's body tense. "What happened when you got home?"

He shrugged. "What always happened, my father had someplace else to be. So, when we landed in New York, the driver met the plane and hustled me into the car while my father flew off to someplace, to do business I no longer wanted to know about. On the drive home, I resolved to ask my mother if she knew what he did for a living, but, when I arrived, she fluttered around me like a bird. It wasn't necessary for me to ask the question. She knew. She'd always known. She was willing to accept it, because of the advantages and trappings the money brought to our lives. I knew I had to deal with that at some point, but first I had to deal with me."

Simon appeared out of the shadows again, but he was dragging. The day had finally caught up with him and he was worn out. Ryan reached out to give him a pat, but Simon accepted only the briefest one and settled in to walk along next to me. Once again, this dog gauged the atmosphere of the situation and reacted accordingly. I shouldn't have been surprised, because he had done it so many times before.

"How did you do that?" I wanted to get the rest of the story out if I could, kind of like ripping a bandage off a cut.

Ryan sighed and put his hands in his pants pockets. "Mom and I let the distractions of my preparations for going to college consume us. When I arrived, I went straight to the registrar's office and asked them to add a name change to my records. I fed them a story about the court papers were being processed, but from that moment on, I was known as Henry Ryan Black."

"Henry?"

He smiled. "Yeah, that's why I laughed when we first met. Do you remember? It was during Tilghman Island Day and you called me Hank."

"Actually, I said Hunk." I could feel my cheeks warming and knew they were turning bright red. It was worth it, because that admission made him relax.

He stopped and looked at me with a goofy grin. "Really? I thought you said Hank which was my nickname. I like that." He winked at me then his face grew serious again. "I needed a new identity. I stopped using my father's surname and took my mother's maiden name. I wanted to put as much distance between us as I could." He shrugged. "And it worked for a number of years. But it was as if I betrayed myself. I started as a liberal arts major and tried all kinds of possible courses of study, but there was only one that really fired my imagination. Business. As much as I wanted to have a different career, this apple didn't fall very far from the tree. I postponed the inevitable as long as I could. After I earned my MBA, I was eager to put everything I'd learned into practice. On the day I picked up my diploma, he appeared after the ceremony as my mother and I were leaving. I'd succeeded avoiding him over the past years, but now, I had to make a choice.

"I knew this moment would come and I guess unconsciously I had prepared for it. I could've walked away. Instead I walked up to him. We didn't exchange one word. He held out his hand, a key dangling from a chain, the same way as the pouch of diamonds had hung from the soldier's fist so many years before. I knew it was the key to his office. I couldn't ignore what he was doing anymore. I could only change things from the inside. I took the key and walked away."

My heart fell. The man I'd grown to trust chose to become a merchant of death for the world. But he said he wanted to change things. How? He reached for my hand. I pulled away. Could I be like his mother and just accept what they did for a living? I removed the barrette and shook out my hair to free my curls. But when I shook my head, I was really saying no.

And something inside me fractured.

"I get it, you had to take care of the family business—"

"Stop that! Stop calling it the family business. It isn't, not anymore. My father is dead. My mother went before he did, I'm convinced because she loved the wrong man and the stress of that love finally killed her. So, there's no family. And the family business that he created isn't what it used to be. In fact, if he could he would be rolling over in his grave if he could see what I've done to his precious company. But will never know if he's doing that, because I have no idea where his grave might be in this world, if he even has one. All we know is he flew off one last time to a destination unknown and never returned." It was an ironic smile on Ryan's face and it wasn't pretty. "In fact, for all I know, he's sitting on a beach somewhere, surrounded by a bevy of beauties each with a big fat diamond around her neck. I don't know and I don't care. What I care about is standing in front of me. And for some reason I can't break through this wall you have put up between us."

I jammed my fists on my hips and stood right in front of him. "Me? I put up a wall between us? I think you have misidentified the builder here. I wasn't the one who took off without a word. I wasn't the one who let months and months and months go by without a word, not even an email or text or two. We live in a world of constant connection and social media. That something that doesn't just happen. You had to work at it. You had to work to push me away, to push me out of your life. And now I think I know why you did that. Something special, something intriguing must've happened with your company and with your network of people all over the world. Maybe there is a little more fascination with what's happening in you that you inherited from your father than you realize."

I took a step closer to him, almost wondering why he wasn't showing burn marks from my smoldering anger. "You were the one who went away. You were the one who made the choice to wall me up from your life. You made a decision to keep your dirty little secret. Maybe you were blinded by the glitz and glamour of jetting around the world, but in the language of the corporate world, the bottom line is that you chose your families business that is all yours now over any relationship that we might have had."

I was determined to walk away. I took a couple of steps, but then I realized I wasn't done. I turned back slowly and raised my eyes to meet his. In a soft voice, I tied the ribbons on what might've been. "You made the decision, Ryan. You shut me out. And I'm not sure I can ever forgive you for that."

The look of regret on his face tore at my heart. But this shouldn't be happening. It never had to happen this way. But when I felt the stinging pain of tears in my eyes, I turned and rushed away. I would not let him see me cry.

"Fine! I'll just crawl back under a rock which is where you think I belong." He turned his back to me and took long strides across the grass to leave quickly.

I couldn't bear to watch him leave. But I couldn't call out to stop him. I turned my face to the river, a quiet, constant element in my world here on the Eastern Shore. The sky was achingly bright as the gentle breeze pushed light, fluffy clouds high above. That same breeze tried to dry the tears rolling down my face and falling unchecked to the grass under my feet.

My eyes were drawn to a light streaming into the growing darkness from the open kitchen door. A figure stood there. It was Dawkins. At first, his silent presence made me feel uncomfortable, as if he was spying on me. But over his time here at Fair Winds, I'd learned that he wasn't spying, but watching over me, protecting me. After what happened on the terrace and the death of Alex, his presence was a comfort. He took a step back, so the light fell on his face. There was a sad smile there, an expression filled with regret as if he had heard every word that Ryan had spoken and the reactions they had triggered in my mind and heart. Silently, Dawkins closed the door.

OSPREY

The Osprey flies to South America for summer there then back in the spring to Chesapeake Bay to mate and raise a family. It averages 170 miles per day. During the day, he flies over land, but prefers to cross water at night.

When in flight, his brown back doesn't stand out against the land or water below. His white underside blends with the sky. Dark feathers around his golden eyes help reduce glare from the sun. His keen peer deep into the water so he can circle as high as 130 feet then dive on a fish and emerge with it in his talons. He'll keep its head pointed forward so it's easier for him to fly. After eating, he'll fly dragging his feet in the water to clean them before returning to the nest.

Before the ban on DDT and PCBs, the chemicals built up in the fish the Osprey ate, making the shells of the eggs so thin, they were crushed when the bird settled to incubate them.

CHAPTER 29

Do not be surprised when a small silver case often worn on a chain is unusually weighty. This pendant may be masquerading as a piece of jewelry with a secret inside: an iron key to a small chest kept hidden for a private reason.

"The Butler's Guide to Fine Silver"
Mr. Hollister, 1898

THE DAY and hour had almost arrived for the meeting, the meeting to catch a killer. Ingram had asked us to gather a little early for a briefing. As I wandered over to the main house, the high humidity gave the air body and substance that made it a little hard to breathe. It felt like a piece of wet lace clogging my nose and making my lungs heavy. Grateful for the cool air inside, I eased into a chair in the breakfast room to watch the latest storm news. I sat like a moron, eyes on the screen, but not really engaged.

Ryan walked in quietly, ready for Ingram's meeting, and

looked up at the TV. "It looks like she's throwing off some squalls. What are the experts saying now?"

"Handmaidens preparing the way for the main event," Dawkins said casually.

"Why, Dawkins, I didn't know you had a romantic streak?" I said.

"Just something else for you to learn about me," and he cruised out the door.

"I thought you were going to miss the meeting," I said.

"No, I want to be here, but I had to secure my boats first."

I looked up out the window. I'd given up the hope that the storm wouldn't affect us. The cloud cover of pewter with strains of charcoal was solid now and felt so low, I almost wanted to duck. The winds were picking up and making whitecaps on the river.

"The storm isn't going to be here for hours," I said with a little dread in my voice. I couldn't pretend anymore that it wasn't coming.

"I didn't want to wait. I had to make sure my boats are tied up to handle any rise in the water level."

"It's not even raining yet." As if the storm gods heard me, thunder growled in the distance. Ryan alerted to the sound like a hunting dog.

"We have to be ready for a storm surge and the high tides. Tomorrow night, we'll have a full moon."

"And that could make things worse." Ryan raised his eyebrows and looked at me in surprise. "Hey, I've been paying attention," I said. A full moon always makes the high tide higher. If the hurricane pushes the water up the Bay, the moon will make the wall of water even higher. But it doesn't happen all at once, does it?"

"No, it starts as a swell, a long bulge in the water. The faster the wind, the more the bulge builds. If there's lots of open water, the swell will be even higher."

I felt a little shudder as the hurricane threat was becoming real. "The beaches along the Atlantic could get hit hard."

"That must be why there's an evacuation order."

I breathed a little sigh of relief. "I'm glad we're inland with very little open water." He cocked his head to the side and gave me a look. "What, what did I say?"

""You haven't got it quite right. Even if a storm stays off the coast or makes landfall in Virginia or even North Carolina, the counterclockwise circulation can push the water up the Bay and considering the Chesapeake Bay is about 200 miles long…"

I took a breath. "That's a long way…"

"…to build a wall of water."

I was picturing the Bay region in my mind. "And that water has to go someplace."

"…like up the rivers and creeks…."

"Then it would flood the land." My skin went cold.

"If that happens, I don't think we'll get as much water as Annapolis and the areas on the Western Shore, because the winds will be blowing to the West, pushing more water that way. But you have to take into account the heavy rains."

I grimaced. "You're right, when Hurricane Florence came ashore in North Carolina, she was only rated a Category One. But the flooding went on for days and many inland areas were affected, because the rains were biblical."

"Timing is important. If the storm arrives at high tide, it's all a recipe for disaster."

Mentally, I crossed my fingers. "Could it be that those dire projections are pessimistic?"

"No, I'm afraid not. When Hurricane Isabel hit St. Michaels years ago. The storm surge was only about three feet, but that was enough to put eight inches in the lobby of the hotel across the harbor. It flooded the first floor of the Crab Claw and put the land around the Chesapeake Bay Maritime Museum under eight inches of water. The staff and friends of the St. Michaels Crab and Steak House stacked things three feet off the floor, but the water came up 3 ½ feet inside. Boats left in the water were banged around by the wind and waves. Those that weren't tied right, slammed into pilings making holes in their fiberglass hulls. Lines snapped. That kind of water can even put some pilings underwater so some lines floated up and off, releasing the boats to the mercy of the storm. Floating free, they did all kinds of damage both on the water and up on land."

"Maybe they should have hauled all the boats," I suggested.

"Many did. The wind was a problem too. During Isabel, seventeen hundred-foot trees came down in town. Storm sewers backed up. It took 24 hours for the water to recede. That was enough time for things floating in the water to crash into buildings and cars. Enough time for snakes to swim up on dry land, far away from their natural habitats. Our worst scenario is a storm surge of 8 to 10 feet during high tide." He sighed. "And that's why I had to secure my boats. We live in a beautiful place, Abby, but we're vulnerable as—"

Dawkins came back. "Detective Ingram is here and wants a little chat before the *suspects* arrive." He looked at Ryan as if I'd disappeared. "Are we ready for any eventuality?"

Ryan took a deep breath as his hand strayed to his belt and nodded. "You?"

"In more than one way, my friend. More than one way."

What was happening right in front of me? Were these men armed? It wasn't out of the question considering their backgrounds, but this was Fair Winds. Not some jungle or mountain pass in Afghanistan.

But a man had been shot – assassinated – right outside the window on the terrace. There was a murderer on the loose. It would be prudent to be prepared, especially when he was expected to attend the meeting in the living room.

I looked at these two men. I lived here on the estate with one and thought I was falling in love with the other. But neither was the man I thought I knew. I looked at Dawkins, always so proper, organized and calm... and a trained killer. My eyes flicked back to

Ryan—smart, sophisticated... and intimately familiar with the dark world of arms sales to guerillas and insurgents.

Who were these men who lived by a different code I didn't know? Who was an ally? Who could I trust? Dizzy, I pulled myself out of the chair and staggered from the room.

Detective Ingram met us in the hallway. Dawkins didn't waste a moment to confirm that everything was in place.

"You do have officers present, just in case, detective?" Dawkins' eyes narrowed, drilling into the man as we stood in the hall.

My new understanding of Dawkins' background allowed me to see his military training kicking in. Only a trained operative would think this way. I was having trouble reconciling that a person who fretted about the proper placement of a sterling silver fork could also evaluate a possible life-threatening situation. *Hunt or be hunted. Kill or be killed.* Those words from our talk came to mind. Unsettling, yes. But a relief, as well. We had someone who would protect us if the killer became a threat.

Ingram pursed his lips. It was obvious that he didn't know Dawkins' background and the butler was clearly getting under the detective's skin. "Everything is under control, I assure you, sir. Now, if we could get this meeting underway..." He moved to lead the way, but stopped when Dawkins added, "*Signore* Norman is covering the door and seating your guests in the living room."

Ingram turned to Dawkins and narrowed his eyes. "Guests? There are no guests. There's a killer among the sheep and it's time to make an arrest." And with that pronouncement, the detective marched away to face the group.

The beautifully-decorated living room designed for fine entertaining was teeming with murder suspects. Men and women milled around, talking in low undertones so it wasn't possible to hear anyone clearly. I wanted to call out, "Will the real killer please stand up!" but, of course, that request would send everyone scurrying for a seat or the door. No, we'd have to wait for Ingram's plan to play out.

Each person in our little group who knew what was supposed to happen headed off in a different direction. Ingram moved to the front of the group. The detective had called this meeting to flush out the killer, which meant that he no longer believed that Lorraine had fired the shot. Even so, my friend was still skittish as she tucked herself into the corner of a wing chair at the far end of the room. I glimpsed Norman standing at the edge of the foyer where he could seat any latecomers.

I took up a position in the doorway out to the hall, close to the silver closet. Somehow, it seemed appropriate. I didn't want to take a seat with the group facing Ingram. I wanted to watch the faces of the suspects as he laid out his evidence.

Ryan slipped up next to me. "Aren't you going in and sit down?"

"No, I think I'll watch from here."

Dawkins stepped up to Ryan and lowered his voice. "Be alert." Ryan nodded and Dawkins moved away.

It all happened in a fluid motion. Innocuous, unremarkable. Until it hit me what he was really asking... and what Ryan's answer meant. Yes, he was armed and ready.

I tried to take a deep breath to cover my uneasy reaction, but it was impossible.

Ryan touched my shoulder. "Don't worry. Everything will be fine." His deep, Mediterranean blue eyes were clear and filled with confidence.

I was glad he was on our side, but still worried about what could happen. I turned to the group and plastered a tight smile on my lips. I didn't want anyone to read our intent and be forewarned. I looked around the room and ticked off the people represented by the magnets on my refrigerator.

Of course, Lorraine, Dawkins and Ryan were there. They were part of the original grouping, because of their proximity to the shooting. Lorraine was no longer a possibility, not that I ever believed she could kill someone. It would be ironic if either Ryan or Dawkins was the killer. I knew Dawkins had the skill and assumed Ryan did as well. But I didn't want it to be either one. They were to much a part of Fair Winds. Murder would destroy its spirit.

Norman, the Italian cousin, was fussing around the periphery, looking for something to do. As people arrived, they were confused. Fair Winds always offered the ultimate in hospitality, but today there were no signs of entertaining, no beverages, no nibbles, no flowers anywhere to be seen. Stu, the cookie thief, entered dressed in a lime green polo shirt and pastel plaid shorts that should never have left his closet, let alone escaped out the front door. He tried to slip into the dining room, looking for goodies, but Norman steered him back into the living room. Jacob walked in acting as if it was his meeting and his venue, with his wife, Maddie following in his wake. Geraldine stepped into the room hanging on to the arm of Dr. Phillips like a drowning woman. Lorraine had told him that it wasn't necessary for him to attend, but I suspected that the man didn't want to miss a thing. He had made his contribution and he would want to see the scenario play out.

Wearing a rose-print dress with leggings underneath, Mary Rose entered quietly instead of making another dramatic appearance. Again, a pair of black leather gloves was tucked primly over the thin belt around her waist. She came and stood next to me so we could both watch the people entering the large foyer and making their way to the living room.

I said, "I'm a little surprised to see you here." She harrumphed. "After the meeting at the library, you said you were done with all this."

She pursed her lips and nodded her head once. "You're right, I did, but I heard there's going to be a big announcement, some revelation. Maybe they're going to throw in the towel and give up on *Chesapeake Haven*. Wouldn't that be a hoot?" She glanced over at me. There was a hint of a smile on her chapped lips, but her eyes had lost the gleam I'd seen that day over the tea table at her house. She appeared tired in a way that a good-night's sleep wouldn't cure. Her voice had even more of a rasp than usual.

"Are you okay?"

"Oh, will you stop asking me that?" she snapped. "I'm as okay as any eighty-two-year-old woman can be. I wish people would just leave me alone." And she walked away to the living room, almost in a huff.

There was a little commotion at the front door and, late as usual, Allen breezed in with a tight grasp on Arabella's hand, almost dragging her along. When Allen paused under the archway to the living room, Arabella tried to yank her hand away, but he yanked back and led her to a small settee in the center of the room.

Which one was the killer? It would be so much easier if a flashing sign appeared over the murderer's head. The funny thought made me relax a little as Detective Ingram called the meeting to order.

"Ladies and gentlemen," the detective began. "If you'll please settle down and find a seat, we'll try to complete our business quickly so you can get home before the storm hits."

Ingram took a moment to survey the group then asked that questions be held until the end of his presentation. Geraldine fidgeted. Did she really think that people believed she could shoot a man dead at 50 yards? The recoil would have shattered her spindly body that hadn't been in a gym since high school. Stu searched his pockets, but came up empty except for a linty piece of candy. The man was out of cookies. He sat back and laced his fingers over his ample belly.

"It is my understanding," Ingram stated, "that all of you were present the other night, a fateful night, when Mr. Alex Conklin was gunned down while sitting on the terrace here at Fair Winds."

When Ingram use the phrase gunned down, there was a general shuffling sound in the room. As one would expect, direct language like that would make the ordinary citizen very uncomfortable.

Ingram waited for the people to settle down then he continued. "We have been receiving a number of telephone calls at State Police as well as the St. Michaels Police Department asking for information and updates about the case. I thought it might be easier and as a service to those who were present that night to invite you to hear the information in person that we have gathered thus far. As you know..."

Ingram droned on describing that evening, how people were welcomed at the door, offered refreshments and sat in this room to hear the victim's presentation.

Stu raised his hand. Ingram repeated that he would be happy to entertain any questions after—

"But I just wanted to say that the chocolate chip cookies you served that night..." At which point he turned toward Lorraine. "Those were the best I've ever had. They must have been made right here at Fair Winds. In fact, if—"

Ingram interrupted. "Thank you, sir. I'm sure Mrs. Andrews and the staff here at Fair Winds appreciate your comments. However, we are here to discuss the tragic event that took place that night. You all were very cooperative in giving your statements. Many of you have delivered additional information and now we believe—"

Stu was not to be denied. He rumbled to his feet. "Now, wait just a minute!" he demanded in a voice that might have rattled the china. "Are you saying that the person who killed that developer fellow is here? In this room?"

Just about everyone in the room gasped. One woman jumped up and headed toward the front door. There, she was met by Norman who tried to escort her back into the room, but several others were also anxious to escape. Pandemonium grew.

"LADIES AND GENTLEMEN!" thundered Ingram. "Please, take your seats!"

Dawkins and Norman did their best to block the doorways out of the living room. Lorraine, as if awakened from a stupor, rose to help calm the situation.

"Friends, please." She tried again, raising her voice over the chaotic chatter. "Friends, please." Several faces turned toward her and the room settled a little. "Thank you. No one knows better than I do how upsetting this situation is." She took a quick breath and pushed past the emotion growing in her voice. "What happened that night was wrong, not the discussion about a possible new neighborhood, but the taking of a precious life. What alarms me … and the reason why I've opened my home to you again… is the fact that the murderer is still at large. We can't allow that person to go unpunished. We are not safe until the detective makes an arrest. So, please, I ask that you listen quietly to what he has to say."

She sat down and made a point to direct her undivided attention to Ingram. Others in the room followed her example and soon, the detective had an alert audience.

"Thank you. Now—" Ingram was interrupted again.

"Why are you talking about the murder?" a man shouted out from the back of the room.

People jumped to their feet and the accusations started flying.

"Yeah, we were told to come here today, because a decision about the development was in the works."

"You lured us here under false pretenses."

"It's your job to catch the shooter, not put us all in danger."

The tension in the room ramped up. I could spot the officers in plainclothes. They were the ones who appeared calm while their eyes darted from one speaker to another. I suspected this never happened to Agatha Christie's little Belgian detective.

People began to stand. All were dressed as I would have expected: men in polo shirts, women in blouses or tank tops. Even though some were wind-blown, everyone's hair was clean and well-cut. Even though they were angry, even frightened, even though they raised their voices, they kept their words under control. They didn't cross the line. Not the way someone else had done the night of the first meeting about *Chesapeake Haven* held in this room. Someone who had stood out from everyone else.

I felt my body go rigid. It wasn't because Ryan touched my arm and said, "Abby, let's…"

"Give me a second." I squeezed my eyes shut and visualized the magnets on my refrigerator door. I could see all the magnets in the center of the door, magnets for the people who had motive and opportunity, some more obvious than others, but all who were capable of pulling the trigger. In the beginning, there were a lot of magnets on my suspect door. Over the last days and hours, I'd carefully considered many of those people and some I'd moved to the side, no longer under suspicion. But I'd made a mistake.

Ryan's eyes searched my face. "What's wrong, Abby?"

I breathed. "I know who killed Alex."

CHAPTER 30

Do not be surprised when a small silver case often worn on a chain is unusually weighty. This pendant may be masquerading as a piece of jewelry with a secret inside: an iron key to a small chest kept hidden for a private reason.

"The Butler's Guide to Fine Silver"
Mr. Hollister, 1898

I HAD TO BE SURE. I turned away from him and dove into room full of people on their feet, moving around, to longer content to sit down, listen calmly and perhaps become a target. I wormed my way through the crowd to place where Ingram was being lectured by three people, all talking at once. I grabbed his arm and made him turn to face me.

"Not now, Abby." His skin was gray from the strain of the situation.

"Yes, now! I have to know," "Did a short, little old lady give you a statement the night of the murder?" He looked confused. "She had on a print dress buttoned up the front, wearing dark leggings and black leather boots? You would remember her. Think, please."

He glanced down to the floor for a moment.

"Was she here that night? Did you see her?" I wanted to shake the man who was being so deliberate.

He raised his eyes to meet mine and ever so slowly shook his head "I don't remember anyone like that. You're right, I would've remembered. Are you sure she was here?"

Stu, the cookie fiend, shoved his way in front of me. "Detective, I may have relevant…"

I turned away, sure I was right. I would never forget her grand entrance. I turned away, struggling with what I now knew to be true. How could I reconcile the idea that a woman so dedicated to nature and beautiful things commit such a violent act? Then I remembered what she'd said when we were talking about the rose in front of her cottage. She'd said her mother taught her about beauty and how to be responsible for her own survival and all that was important to her. Alex was the face of the worst threat she could imagine: the destruction of her beloved Eastern Shore.

Ryan had made his way through the crowd. "Abby, are you all right?" Lines of worry creased his forehead.

I shook my head slowly. "I was wrong. I got it so wrong." I could feel the tears pricking my eyelids

Ryan put his hands on my shoulders. "Abby, tell me."

"I can't, not now. I have to find her before the others do." I turned and surveyed the room of people dashing about, wildly gesturing at each other and talking at the top of their voices. It was chaos. I rose up on my toes to get a better view, but still all the bodies and flailing arms were in the way.

I pulled on Ryan's arm. "You're tall. Can you see her?"

"See who? Abby, you—"

"Just tell me, Ryan, do you see Mary Rose?" It was an eternity before he answered.

"No, I don't see her anywhere." His voice caught. "Abby, did she—"

I couldn't stop to answer his questions. She was gone and I had to find her. I dashed out to the hallway and Ryan was not far behind. I stopped when I realized that she couldn't have gotten past Norman at the front door or Dawkins at the other end of the hall. But I knew she wasn't in the house. "She must've gone out the French doors."

I started back to the living room when Ryan took my arm. "Abby, honey, you're not making any sense. Please tell me. Please let me help you."

I looked into his eyes and saw, not a man involved with guns and death, a man haunted by the past. Could he once again be my ally and support?

Rushing up to us, Lorraine ended the moment as her eyes bore into mine. "Abby, tell me what's going on," she demanded. "I saw you sprint into action. Tell me."

"It was Mary Rose. She killed Alex. And now she's running. I have to find her."

Lorraine caught my arm. "Wait, the storm is coming. It's not safe for you to be out there in your convertible. Let the police—"

"No! She'll never surrender. Something terrible will happen. They'll hurt her. Or worse. She'll fight back. It won't end well."

Her eyes searched mine and I saw the moment she made the decision. "I'm going with you."

"Lorraine, you two can't—" Ryan barked.

"Oh, yes, we can," she said in that voice that defied argument. "Abby, let's go."

"You're coming with me?" I felt almost weak with relief.

"I may kill her when I see her, but you're not going alone. Come on." She grabbed my hand and we ran out to the garage. "We'll take my car."

It was a good choice. Her four-door sedan was big and heavy and had a hardtop. As we headed out, I asked Lorraine to drive slowly while I scanned the vehicles parked in the front of the house and along the drive looking for a beat-up old truck.

"I don't see any open spaces." I shielded my eyes and tried to see down the long tree-shaded drive. "I don't see anyone driving away."

Lorraine slowed. "She's probably still here. What does she drive?"

"A beat-up old truck."

"Like an old F-150?" She asked, cruising past the vehicles.

"No, this truck is so old that you'd have no idea what make or model it is." I almost wanted to laugh, a laugh born of nerves. "That place over there on the grass where people parked in a crazy mess, let me check there.."

I threw open the door and ran around the vehicles, hoping to find Mary Rose crouched down, hiding. But neither the truck nor the woman was in sight.

Lorraine now stood by her car, fists on her hips, surveying the area. "I don't see her. Should I get some help to look for her?"

"No," I called out. "She's gone." I didn't know how I knew, but I was certain I was right. And then it all became clear. *Is that how she did it? Is that how she escaped on the night of the murder? Is that how she got away now? Her little boat didn't look solid enough to cross the river with the storm coming in. Mary Rose would know that.* And then I knew where she was going. She wasn't going to cross the river. She only needed to hug the shoreline to get to her destination.

"Get in the car and drive. We have to catch up with her before Ingram calls out the troops."

Lorraine was about to argue, took one look at my face and silently got back in the car. As I ran back to the passenger door, I heard a familiar bark.

Simon.

He must have gotten out of the kennel, made his way through the house and got out through one of the doors. Not a surprise with all the chaos and strangers around. If I left him running loose, those people driving away might run him down. I couldn't take the chance.

"Simon!" I called, hoping he could hear me over the dull roar of the wind from the horizon.

"Get him in the back seat." A twinge of fear was in Lorraine's voice.

"Simon! SIMON! Come here!" A black streak raced across the drive and a panting black Lab sat at my feet. Maybe the training was paying off. "Up, Simon. UP!" He jumped into the back seat and we sped up to the St. Michaels Road where I pointed her toward Willow Hall.

Thankfully, there was no traffic as Lorraine made the turn on what felt like two tires. In the side mirror, I could see Simon standing with his head out the window, facing into the wind, his nose twitching a mile a minute.

The Oak Creek Bridge lay ahead. It was short, but gave a panoramic view of the Miles River.

"Slow down on the bridge. Maybe I can see if she..." My voice trailed off. *If she was...what? Running to Willow Cottage or Willow Hall?* This was the moment to make a decision. THE decision. If I saw her heading to one place, did I tell Lorraine to go there? Or misdirect her to the other to let Mary Rose escape? If we caught up with her, maybe we could talk her into surrendering. If we let her go... no, the police would confront her eventually and there might be a very ugly ending. But first, I had to see her on the water. I strained against my seatbelt and searched.

The light was fading even though it was still early afternoon. The blue-gray clouds hung so heavy, they unfolded down to the water almost obscuring the far shoreline. Then, an air current tore a hole in the cloud cover like an invisible hand and revealed a sunlit tower of pearl-white clouds against an azure blue sky. Even though the storm clouds threatened to envelop the earth, there was still hope. It was such a stark contrast that I glanced to my right and yes, the angry dark clouds were still roiling toward us. In the moment it took to look away and then back again, the tear in the clouds had closed. Hope had disappeared, just like Mary Rose. As if our fate and hers were sealed.

A sense of certainty lay over me like a blanket as we flew up the road. Trees blocked my view of the river. The decision was out of my hands. Either Mary Rose had escaped or she had gone to Willow Hall where we would confront her. Now, I could only hope for the best outcome.

"Up there, Lorraine. That little service road on the left. Do you see it? Turn in there." I grabbed the dashboard to brace myself for the turn. "But slow down! It's only a path of oyster shells." No stranger to the ways of the Shore, Lorraine slowed down almost immediately and took the turn carefully. We drove down the narrow path. Majestic pines loomed high over us, their branches thrashing around as if they were trying to take flight and escape.

"Yes, this is the place. Stop here," I almost shouted, trying to see the little family cemetery, but it was lost in the growing gloom. "Wait here. You'll be safe." Lorraine started to contradict me, but I held up my hand. She quieted, turned off the engine and reached back to scratch that special spot behind Simon's ear to keep him quiet. I got out of the car and closed the door.

Sound bombarded me. Winds roared in the pines high above sending down a shower of brown needles. Tree trunks creaked with an ominous threat. No longer singing a mother's lullaby, they wailed and screamed, crushing my confidence and sending fear through me like a tidal wave. My lungs ached for air, but breath lodged in my throat, squeezed there by that fear. My muscles froze as I fought a desperate impulse to run, run away. After what seemed like an eternity, my body reacted and I gasped, taking in huge gulps of air.

Not far away, the river was wilder than I'd ever seen it… angry. Angry at what was happening, angry at what was coming.

Now, there was only the storm and Mary Rose while Leucothea danced the tarantella to celebrate Mother Nature's force.

I stepped along the grassy edge of the oyster shell path leading down toward the water and the family of headstones surrounded by a rusting wrought iron fence. A low rumble of thunder from the east caught me off-guard and rattled my nerves, but not my resolve. Angry charcoal-gray clouds driven by the growling wind flew by. The long, drooping branches of the willow trees whipped around, lashing at everything, even themselves. The river heralded the storm's arrival. As Mary Rose predicted, Leucothea, the Greek sea goddess of spindrift, danced madly atop the growing waves.

I looked to the cemetery. There was no one there. Had I gotten it wrong? Had Mary Rose run her little boat through the growing whitecaps to her beloved Willow Cottage? The boat looked flimsy to me, but she had sworn it was sturdy. Maybe it was sturdy enough to face the wrath of the on-coming storm.

High above, thunder rolled. I had to find Mary Rose for her own safety and ours. Surrounded by these trees that reached into the turbulent sky, the possibility of a lightning strike was growing. They could split and crash to the ground. A burst of warm, moist breath hit my hand. Simon stood next to me, alert and brave. I looked behind me and saw that Lorraine was not far behind. For our own protection, I had to act fast.

My eyes searched the cemetery again. I was so sure Mary Rose would come here, but there was no sign... Then I saw it.

There was something on the ground. A bit of cloth flapping in the wind.

"Simon, stay close." Together, we moved toward to the iron gate left open. Next to it, the rose bushes had sacrificed their last petals of the season to the storm. But Simon didn't wait. He rushed through the gate. Then he paused and whimpered. I moved inside the little cemetery and almost tripped over the tiny marble marker set for the baby who didn't have a chance to be born.

I stood quietly next to Simon who looked up at me with his golden-brown eyes, filled with sadness and confusion. Then together, we watched the hem of a rose-print dress fluttering in the wind. Her beige canvas hat with a broad brim had fallen to the side, threatening to take off. That was the only movement around the old woman's body.

Mary Rose had collapsed on top of a grave. Her head lay next to a marble vase filled with sunflowers. The name on the headstone was Mary Elizabeth. Her mother.

With a deep sigh, Simon crept forward, sank to the ground and laid his head next to her hand. On the other side, a slight movement caught my eye. A terrapin turtle with a diamond pattern on its greenish shell moved on to the back of her hand as if Mother Nature was welcoming her spirit.

I went and knelt to touch the woman's hand, but I knew. Only her body was here now. Her spirit couldn't face the changes coming to the Shore. She couldn't tolerate what she thought of as destruction to the land and waters she loved. And I felt sure that she was having trouble living with the fact that she had taken a human life. She'd come here for forgiveness, to the source of the greatest love she had ever known.

"Is she…" Lorraine asked softly as she walked up next to me.

I could only nod. Tears choked off the words.

The roaring winds paused just long enough for us to hear Ryan calling out. It was a relief that we were not alone. With a flash, lightning cracked almost right over our heads. Waves of thunder pounded above. Ryan cringed and stared at the churning clouds. Blood drained from his face, eyes wide with fear. Helpless, I watched as he forced himself to stand straight and move one step then another down the hill, faster and faster, to the cemetery.

"Abby! Lorraine!" Each word was separated by a gulp of air. "Come!" He motioned wildly for us. "The storm. It's bad!" We've got to go."

"We can't just leave her here!" I cried. I looked back at the aged body, determined not to leave.

The wind screamed and the skies opened. Then raindrops, fat and heavy, pelted us. Ryan's hand closed around my arm, his strength flowing into my body, and lifted me to my feet. "It's okay. I'll make it okay. You two, get to the car. I have a tarp in the truck. I'll cover her. You call for help."

I reached in my pocket and took out my phone. Immediately, raindrops smacked into the screen so it wouldn't read my touch.

Lorraine hunched her body close to mine to make a little cave for it. After I wiped the wetness away, I made the call.

It seemed like only minutes before the ambulance and the police drove their units carefully down the oyster shell path. They ordered us to take shelter in a safe place since the storm was growing stronger. They promised to take care of things at the cemetery and contact us after the worst of the storm had passed.

Followed by Ryan, like a guardian angel, Lorraine drove us back to Fair Winds in silence, two, no three, drenched and grieving spirits. I couldn't leave out the quiet pup in the back seat. As I stretched out my hand to comfort him, the salt of my tears mixed with the raindrops on my cheeks.

OYSTER

More than a delicacy, the Oyster is vital to the health and well-being of the Chesapeake Bay as it filters particles out of the water leaving it cleaner. Naturally, it lives on the bottom of the Bay and its rivers. The Oyster must move about fifty gallons of water through its body every day to take in enough food to survive.

Unlike the Blue Crab, this creature does not molt. The rough shell with a smooth interior grows with the creature. It is common for an oyster to begin life as a male then become a female by the age of two.

The Oyster is suffering from excess nutrients that run off the land into the Bay leading to the growth of algae blooms. Sediment can suffocate the Oyster as well as other shellfish.

CHAPTER 31

The silver porringer is a bowl designed with one handle to assist in the feeding of a child, providing nourishment in the sick room or caring for an invalid member of the Family. Be attentive for tarnish and wear on the handle for it is often held by a bare hand.

"The Butler's Guide to Fine Silver"
Mr. Hollister, 1898

BACK SAFE AT FAIR WINDS, we didn't have time to think about what had happened. The storm was bearing down on the Eastern Shore. When Ryan knew there was nothing more he could do for us, he was anxious to go home to deal with the storm there.

As I walked him to the door, I thanked him for all that he had done for Lorraine, Mary Rose … and me. "I'm so glad you followed us. I don't know what we would have done—"

He put his finger against my lips. "Sh-h-h, it's over."

I raised my eyes to his. I hoped he could see how much his actions meant to me, to all of us. "You were very brave out there."

"Not really." He dropped his eyes, but not before I caught a flicker of disgust.

"Yes, really," I insisted.

"I don't deal well with loud noises, especially thunder. You don't need to know about the times my father insisted I travel with him except the one when our plane was attacked in the middle of the jungle. They were lobbing grenades and homemade bombs at us. Obviously, we got out okay, but loud noises still give me nightmares." He raised his eyebrows in surrender and sighed. "There will be plenty of loud noises tonight."

I reached for him as he leaned forward and kissed the top of my head. "Be safe, Abby."

Standing in the doorway, I watched him drive away.

Before retreating into the safety of the house, I stopped. It was quiet. The tree branches were still. The rain had stopped. I stepped outside. A single raindrop clung to a trembling leaf of a shrub, then tumbled into the void below. Was it over? Had the hurricane shifted away from us?

I stepped down to the grass and relief washed over me. I had this mad urge to spin around like a little girl with my arms thrown out wide. Then I heard it and it sent shards of ice through me.

It began as a low growl from deep in the throat of a monster. It grew quickly to a roar. But still, it was a sound only. Nothing around me moved. The sound grew and grew till it burst its bonds and its rage slapped the trees. An invisible hand whipped high tree branches around the house and along the drive. The attack burst across the ground. The rigid fingers of the wind tore away my barrette and turned my curls into slender switches lashing my face. Then its full force slammed into my body, forcing me backward. I struggled to keep my balance.

Simon barked from the doorway, calling me inside. It wasn't easy to climb the steps with the wind pushing me this way and that. I lunged for the door jamb, grabbed it tightly and pulled myself inside. But my fight with the storm wasn't over. The wind fought hard to stop me from closing the door. Even with my full weight against it, I was losing the battle. Suddenly, a thud next to me sent the door into place.

"Lock it!" ordered Dawkins and he rushed away.

I threw the deadbolt with great relief, then sank to the floor to hug Simon. "You're always there when I need help, my sweet boy." And he left me hold him in a tight hug until my heart stopped racing.

Dawkins thought it was safer for us all to spend the night in the main house. I joined our little hurricane party in the kitchen where Dawkins was putting together a fruit and cheese platter, but no one was really hungry. I was more interested in what was happening outside so I wandered into the breakfast room and stood at the big windows overlooking the river.

At first, it looked like a regular rainstorm, but before I could think that it didn't seem so bad, things changed. The rain came down harder, pounding the leaves of the plants just on the other side of the glass. The wind buffeted the trees and stirred up the water even more.

Lorraine massaged her forehead. "I'm getting a headache. I think I'll go upstairs and lie down."

Dawkins zipped out of the room and was back in a flash. "Here, take these two aspirin," and he handed her a glass of water. "Now, let's all go into the living room so you can lie down."

"I'm perfectly capable to go up to my room," she said with a little snarl.

"Yes, you are, but it would be prudent to go to the living room to ride out this storm. I've made preparations." He held out his arm to encourage her, but she shot back, looking at the television screen. "I want to watch the reports."

And at that moment, the signal failed.

Dawkins tried to hide pleasure at the cooperation of circumstances. "Since the cable is out now, perhaps you'd like to go to the living room where I have a weather radio and another with the local station dialed in."

With a huff, she stood, took a step and reeled. She fell back into the chair.

I rushed to her. "What's wrong?"

"I feel a little dizzy, that's all." Her voice quavered.

"A sign of all the stress you've been under," I reassured her.

Dawkins cleared his throat. "Perhaps, or it could be a sign that the barometric pressure is falling. It affects our blood pressure, too." He went and stood next to Lorraine. "Now, Ma'am, if you'd lean over and put your head down, I think you'll feel better."

"I don't need your help," she snapped, as she forced herself to her feet. "I'm not an invalid." Holding on to the chairs, table and doorjamb, she left the room.

Dawkins said softly, "Some people are more affected by a storm and pressure changes than others.

That's why she's getting a headache, I imagine. Are you feeling alright?"

I nodded, but I was a little taken aback by Lorraine's snippy attitude. "I can see that. But why didn't you want her to go upstairs?"

"The second floor is a dangerous part of the house. It's too close to the roof. If something comes crashing down, she'll be vulnerable. This way, she has the whole second floor between her and injury, or worse."

I remembered a story about a mother being killed by a falling tree branch in her own home during a storm. Her baby was in the next room and untouched. My quick glance out the window was well-timed. A wind gust moved the curtain of rain so I could see that the river was rising. It was over the riprap and moving up the lawn, drowning the grass. Then the pelting rain blinded my view again. I reached for the top of Simon's head and we followed Dawkins down the hall.

All of a sudden, his cell phone shrieked with an alert. He checked the screen. "It's a tornado-watch alert from Talbot County Emergency Services. I'm not surprised. We'll be fine. It's only a watch."

Dawkins had transformed the elegant living room into a dorm. All the draperies were pulled tight over the windows. Comforters and pillows were stacked around the large room so we could nest in comfort. There were water pitchers, an ice bucket, nibbles and candles. I thought I caught sight of a first aid kit. Truly, Dawkins had thought of everything.

The wind kept building until it started to howl. It grew loud, so we had to raise our voices to hear each other. Dawkins' phone kept dinging with alerts.

Lorraine was testy and snapped, "Will you please turn that thing off?" She bit her lip. "I'm sorry. The wind is so loud. If there is a tornado, they say it sounds like a freight train. I don't think we'd hear it. This is so frightening."

She was right.

I spread a comforter over one of the sofas and had to call Simon to come. He'd stopped at the archway of the foyer. The dogs were never allowed in this room. On the command, *Come*, he barreled to me, jumped on the cushions and curled as much of his body into my lap as he could.

"Dawkins, what about the other dogs?" Fear riddled her voice.

"Not to worry. They are fine. Two of the single guys volunteered to give up somebody's hurricane party to stay with them."

"Oh, thank goodness," she sighed. "You will—"

"Yes, I'll thank them for their effort."

Outside, the wind screamed. Inside, the house around us creaked a little. Before long, Simon was snoring and the rest of us were yawning. Another effect of the low barometric pressure. It wasn't long before my eyes closed and I fell into a dreamless sleep.

CHAPTER 32

When sterling silver is properly polished, it will brightly reflect light which adds to the elegance and ambiance of a candle-lit dining room.

"The Butler's Guide to Fine Silver"
Mr. Hollister, 1898

I THINK it was the quiet that woke me. I threw off the light sheet Dawkins must have spread over me, went to the window and pulled back the drapery. The sun was strong and clear casting neatly defined shadows across the green grass, lush from all the rain. After a quick shower in my cottage and went outside to experience the aftermath of the storm.

The air was scrubbed clean in a way I'd never experienced. The sky was a dome of azure blue. As if painted by Leonardo da Vinci's brush in a palette of white, gray and blue, a swath of clouds flowed like a river across the face of the sky. They must be what was left of the bands they talked about when the storm was organized and deadly, before it slammed against the land and shredded itself to pieces. The clouds were dragged along to some unknown destination, perhaps out to sea where they would be lost to most human eyes. There, they would disintegrate, reform, perhaps gather moisture and begin again. Or be torn apart by the winds like a writer tears a sheet of prose that is no longer worthy or needed.

It was quiet now, almost silent compared to the roar of the wind and beating of the rain just hours earlier. A light rustling of dying leaves came from the tops of the trees. The pines seemed to whistle. The birds chirped to celebrate their survival. In the distance, I could faintly hear the chiming of the bells at the stone church in St. Michaels, a rare occurrence at this distance. Maybe they were ringing, thankful that the storm was not worse and that the Shore had dodged another bullet and avoided a direct hit.

Yes, the Shore was lucky. And it was different. Was it the subtle tang of salt in the air? Was it the vistas of water, earth and sky? Was it a different set of priorities people chose so that competition to get rich wasn't the reason for being? Here, just looking around, one could feel rich in ways that cost nothing.

An osprey flew overhead to the Number 7 mark where the river split. I'd seen the babies grow ever stronger in the heat of summer. They all would be leaving soon, flying south thousands of miles to South America to winter in those warmer climes.

A subtle movement by the shoreline caught my eye. I had to look closely to make out the gray-blue feathers of the Blue Heron, patiently waiting for his next meal. Yes, patience. That was something else I was learning here on the Shore. My ambition hadn't disappeared, I thought ruefully, as I remembered the epergne fiasco. The Shore still had a lot to offer and a lot to teach me.

And there was Ryan. These last days had taught me that the phrase *Things can turn on a dime* was true. I never would have guessed why he was always so evasive when I asked what he did for a living or about his background.

And there was Dawkins with his secrets. Thinking of that little boy dying in his arms broke my heart all over again. I could understand why he would construct a strong, unflinching façade to keep others at bay. For him, it was the only way to survive and move on with his life. It was amazing that he'd found a way to help others, protect others, by surrounding himself with beauty. I suspected that the day I saw him painting again would be the sign that his recovery had taken a giant step toward making him whole.

And he wasn't the only one. Lorraine had her own road to travel. It would be easy for her to lose her way in the grieving process. As a child mourning my mother, I'd lost my voice. But like Gran, Lorraine's friends and her little Fair Winds family would help. And the Shore would work its magic, too. It always would.

I felt invigorated as I headed to the main house and some of Dawkins's cold press coffee. I found Lorraine in the breakfast room, reading the local paper, something she hadn't done since that fateful night when Alex was shot.

"Good morning, everyone," I said. "Isn't it a beautiful day?"

Lorraine raised her head and gazed out the window. "Yes, yes, it is. The air and the light are always different after a major storm. It almost makes it worth the damage, but not quite."

"No, nothing would be worth that, but it would be nice to have weather like this more often." I settled into my chair. "Oh well, the storm is gone and it's back to—"

"Oh no," Lorraine interrupted. "The effects of the hurricane are not over yet."

I perked up. Now that the damaging winds and rains were over, I wondered what else we could expect. I scanned the skies and the land. My eyes followed the river as far as I could see. "I don't see any storm clouds or flooding."

"No, thankfully, that danger is past, but now we have a new threat."

"Really, where?" I eagerly looked out the window and searched the landscape.

"Everywhere," Lorraine sighed. "We'll see how good a job we've done, in about two weeks,"

Somehow, that sounded ominous. "I'm sorry, I'm confused. What are you talking about?"

Dawkins appeared in the doorway and announced, "I want to report that I've consulted with the farm manager. He has started the remedial work. I have the gardening staff and landscape service scouring the areas around the house."

I sat up straight. Did I miss something? "Did Fair Winds suffer damage? I can help."

Dawkins smiled his funny little smile that he usually saved for the pups. Lorraine reached over and patted my hand. "It's okay, dear. We're taking precautions."

I looked at them both and asked again, "What are you talking about?"

Together, Lorraine and Dawkins answered my question. "Mosquitoes."

"Waves of them," she added.

Dawkins provided the detail. "Last night's storm alone dropped almost eight inches of rain. Places that normally thrive with a little rainfall were inundated. Now, there is standing water everywhere."

"The females that bit us over the past few weeks needed our blood to lay their eggs. They've been waiting for water to hatch and grow." Unconsciously, she scratched her arm. "They got a great gift from Zelma. Now, we must spill out the standing water from birdbaths and pots, drain away water anywhere we can…"

"Or they might grow so large and massive, they might carry someone away."

I didn't know how to react. Dawkins had made a joke. I started to laugh, but swallowed it. This wasn't a laughing matter to them. Considering stories about mosquito-borne viruses, fortunately few in our area, I realized that prevention was serious business. "I'm happy to help in any way I can." I looked toward the kitchen. "Is that what Norman is doing, helping out with the water?"

Dawkins and Lorraine exchanged looks then he explained. "No, my cousin has left Fair Winds." He glanced at his watch. "In fact, he should be boarding his flight shortly."

"Oh, is he going back to Italy?" I asked.

Dawkins chuckled. "No, Miss Abigail, but almost. He is going to a situation that is infinitely better than what he had or would have found here in the States. He told me to say *addio* and *in bocca al lupo*. Good-bye and good luck."

"Don't tease her, Dawkins. She knows the background. Give her the details," Lorraine scolded lightly.

Dawkins face flushed a little pink. "Yes, ma'am. Pardon the expression, but my cousin felt like a fish out of water here. I'd hoped to find him a position locally, but he was able to uncover an opportunity on his own. He will be working for a retired art dealer who travels a great deal and only occasionally resides at his property in the Alps. Norman hates the cold, but they assured him that there are many fireplaces, an unlimited source of wood and a staff to tend them. It will feel more like retirement to him than work. He will have his paints and time to use them."

"Oh, so the artistic gene runs in the family?" I said.

His skin started to turn pink again as he nodded.

"So, you returned the favor," I said.

"The what?" he asked.

"Years ago, when you needed to catch your breath and figure out what you wanted to do, your cousin gave you a place to land. And now, you've returned the favor."

Dawkins considered what I said for a moment, then nodded. "Yes, I hadn't thought of it in that way, but you are correct."

Lorraine added. "That's what family does." She winked at me then scooped up the paper. "As much as I'd love to sit here and chat—" Her face drained when she saw Detective Ingram standing in the doorway.

"I'm sorry to barge in on you. I guess you didn't hear the door bell, so I came in through the kitchen. I hope you don't mind. I wanted to deliver the good news in person." We all held our breath. "There's still a lot of paperwork to do, but I can assure you that your nightmare is over. You will not have to face the grand jury."

Ryan burst through the door and we all looked up in surprise. He too looked surprised by the smiling faces around the table.

"What's going on?" he asked as I questioned what he was doing in the Fair Winds breakfast room.

He looked to Dawkins. "He called me. I saw the detective's car outside. Is it...?" His voice trailed off.

Lorraine beamed at him. "Not to worry, dear friend. Everything is all right. It's over now. Coffee?"

We all sat around the table for a while, laughing and enjoying each other's company. It was the time for a nervous release of tension. It was almost as relaxing as a visit to a spa. Almost. It wasn't long before I felt the sadness, my grief for the old woman. I quietly moved out of the room and went directly outside for a deep breath of the air cleaned by the storm. People said that the air was fresher because of all the ions the storm generated. I didn't want to understand the science. I just wanted to enjoy it. I needed some quiet time. Just like Sunny, Mary Rose's dog, curled in a tight ball in the shade, alone. I guess we both needed time to process the loss of good people. That's why when I heard the kitchen door open, I didn't feel that little thrill at seeing Ryan.

"Want some company?" he asked.

I didn't trust myself to say the right thing so I started ambling across the grass, looking at the river flowing by Fair Winds, a little browner from the runoff from the storm, a little chunkier with the random tree limb or debris.

"You're a million miles away," Ryan observed. "I'd like it if you were right here for a while."

Without moving my gaze, I responded. "Not a million miles. Just up the river a bit."

"At Willow Hall?"

"And Willow Cottage, yes. It's too bad what parents do to their children."

I noticed in the silence that Ryan was now looking wistfully at the river and I waited. Was his mind full of the memory of his own father and how he'd built up his family's wealth? Was he aching for the times they could have spent playing catch, when his father could have come to watch his school games or see him win a science fair or a Junior Achievement ribbon? Was he wondering if his father would approve, maybe even be proud of how he was using that money today? I couldn't read his mind. I wasn't sure anymore if I wanted to.

Simon broke the silence by romping up to us and tossing his red ball at Ryan's legs. He didn't respond in that instant, but he soon looked down and smiled. "I guess the point is to do for those you care about in the moment." He picked up the ball and threw in a high arc over the rolling lawn of Fair Winds to the ecstatic yips from my dog. I wished I felt the same.

CHAPTER 33

Care of an openwork silver trellis flower vase requires patience and meticulous attention. All flakes and fragments of polish must be carefully removed with a soft cloth. The glass liner must be washed and dried thoroughly before it is reinserted in the vase.

"The Butler's Guide to Fine Silver"
Mr. Hollister, 1898

"Thank you for coming with me today, Abby," Lorraine said in a quiet, reverent voice.

I followed my friend to the squeaky gate in the wrought iron fence surrounding the family cemetery at Willow Hall. Only it didn't squeak anymore. It swung open smoothly on its hinges. She took a few steps inside the area and stopped in front of a new white marble headstone for Mary Rose placed next to the one for her mother Mary Elizabeth.

"I'm confused," I said softly. "How did this—"

"I made it happen," she said simply. "The undertaker had a little trouble figuring out the placement. They used some kind of ground-sensing equipment. It cost extra, but I thought it was a safer, more respectful way to go then to have his men come out with their little digging machine or shovels and poke around until they found an empty spot."

"Mary Rose said there were many more family members interred here than there are stones."

"She was right. I guess it's a good thing that her family has, well, died out. Her brother had two children and they have families."

"So, they may want to ..." I let the thought trail off.

"No, I don't think so. The undertaker contacted them. Her brother took after their father. He was more interested in gambling and booze than in his children. They have chosen to be with their mother or with their spouses. This little cemetery has seen its last funeral."

I stood close to Lorraine. "Why?" The word was as soft as the seed puffball of a dandelion.

"I don't know. I guess families—"

I touched her arm. "No, I meant why did you do this?"

She took a deep breath and let it out slowly. "I didn't plan on things ending this way. I wanted to hold on to my anger and hurt. I heard that her body was languishing at the funeral home. She was a forgotten part of the new generations of her husband's family and, as I said, the bonds with her brother's family dissolved away a long time ago."

Tears crept into her voice. "What she did was wrong." She took a moment to master her emotions and then she turned to me. "I kept thinking about something you said."

I was confused. I never said that Lorraine should see to the final resting place for the woman who had murdered the man she loved. I couldn't do that. Yes, the Jewish tradition teaches that a person should do a good deed for someone, a mitzvah, in a way that the recipient cannot repay the act. Making sure that a person is buried properly is an ultimate mitzvah, because there is no way the person can reciprocate. But arranging the funeral and setting the headstone for a killer— that was more than I could imagine.

"What did I say?"

"You said that, after spending time with Mary Rose, you thought that this was a woman who walked hand-in-hand with Mother Nature. That's why so many new people come here to visit, to buy second homes and eventually retire." Lorraine looked out over the water and sighed. "They say that's why the old ways are dying out."

"What do you mean?"

"The local men used to make a good income from working the water, pulling crabs, tonging oysters and all. They could afford a good life for themselves and their families, but the people coming to the Shore now have different priorities. They prefer sitting in a restaurant or on a dock to enjoy the fruits of the water."

"But the local people are still here."

"Oh yes, but they are different from the Come-here's. The locals are committed. No, connected to the Shore as if the Bay water runs through their veins instead of blood." She glanced back at the little cemetery with its new stone. "In a weird way, it makes sense that Mary Rose would react the way she did. But I can't seem to take that final step to forgive her though."

"But you did all this for her," I said with a note of surprise.

"Yes, yes, I did, because it was the right thing to do. It's not a sign of forgiveness. I don't know if I'll ever be able to do that, which somehow brings me no comfort."

She sighed again. "And there was something else. You said that you thought that she might have just wanted to scare away the developer, let him know that the opposition to *Chesapeake Haven* was unbending and could get violent." There was that little hitch in her voice again, threatening to release the tears. But Lorraine was determined to finish. "And that she just got lucky with her shot."

"Or very unlucky."

Lorraine nodded her head a little bit. "Her loyalty to the land was more important to her than exploring the possibility of change."

Lorraine said as she stepped up to Mary Elizabeth's headstone and placed some of the sunflowers there that we'd cut from the place Mary Rose called her magic field by Willow Cottage. "But this was the right thing to do."

She turned and held out the rest of the flowers to me. I took them and placed them in the matching vases at the headstone carved with the words, Mary Rose, Beloved Daughter.

"She was certainly a character," Lorraine said with an ironic laugh. "You don't meet many people like her in a lifetime,"

"You're right about that. It seems that her parents gave her an appropriate name."

"Mary?" Lorraine gave me a quizzical look. "It makes me think of the Holy Mother."

"In Hebrew, Mary means *bitter* and Rose means *beauty with thorns*. She was a thorny character, not letting people get close to her."

"She let her bitterness at what happened to her when she was young eat her alive," Lorraine said thoughtfully. "She probably felt that it was happening all over again. That the development of *Chesapeake Haven* was taking the land away from someone's family."

"And from Mother Nature," I added. "She felt betrayed by people throughout her life and probably had every right to be bitter, but she found beauty everywhere she looked."

"She must have felt that Alex was just another in a long line of people who tried to spoil her life. But that doesn't excuse what she did," Lorraine declared.

"No, there is no way to excuse her, but she thought she was doing the right thing, for herself and everyone else."

"I think she acted rashly, and she certainly left the project up in the air in ways I don't think she could've anticipated. I believe the development was a good idea, especially the way Alex had envisioned it."

"Now, what's going to happen?" I asked with a sigh.

"Throwing it into the courts to decide is a waste of time and money. If Mary Rose had just given Alex a chance…" She cleared her throat. "It's a terrible thing to feel ignored, to feel that what was important to her didn't matter. It mattered to Alex. I hope now she can rest in peace."

We stood for a few more minutes, each lost in our own thoughts. Then we turned and walked through the gate and closed it securely. A breeze caressed my cheeks and I looked up to the tops of the tall trees. The aging leaves were rustling. Did I hear the sound of a lullaby or were the emotions playing tricks on my mind?

Lorraine put her arm through mine. "Come on, Abby. It's time to go home." And we headed up the oyster shell path.

"Speaking of home," I said. "That day that we found her, I'm so glad we went over to Mary Rose's Willow Cottage to get Sunny."

"That was a bit of a harrowing drive. Reminded me of your first visit to St. Michaels and we got caught in that horrendous thunderstorm."

"Oh, don't remind me. Storms on the Eastern Shore can be very impressive. But I'm glad we went that day. I couldn't imagine leaving Mary Rose's dog in that house by herself during the storm, all alone now that her beloved owner was never coming home. Thank you for taking her in, making her part of your kennel."

"Again, it was the right thing to do." Her face darkened for a moment. "Though I'm a little worried about Sunny. She misses her owner." Then she perked up. "The dogs are thrilled. The more the merrier." Talking about dogs always put a smile on Lorraine's face.

As we walked toward the car, I felt a sense of peace, almost. There was one more thing that I felt needed to be said. "That night, the night that—"

Lorraine stopped and faced me. "Yes?"

"They took you to the car and…"

"I remember."

"I was standing by the car. I wanted to ride with you. I wanted to talk to you, but the officer wouldn't let me get close. I couldn't see you through the tinted windows. I wanted… I tried." Now, it was my turn to choke back the tears from that night. "He asked me if I was related to you." Lorraine listened. "I didn't know what to say. I froze. And he ordered me to leave."

She waited. I think she sensed I had to tell her everything. To put it into words.

"I didn't know what to say then." My voice grew strong. "But I know the answer now."

"And the answer is?"

"We are not a family by blood. We are a family by choice. By love."

TWO DOGS, ONE HEART

To the readers of the series, the name Cody is familiar, the black Labrador retriever who appears in the author photo on the back cover of my early books. Sadly, he was diagnosed with Cushing's Disease and, after several months of wearing gloves to give him a pill I couldn't touch, I called the vet *to come*. They say our animal buddies let us know *when it's time* and Cody did. Dr. Coughlan made a difficult moment almost bearable. Since Cody always loved to see him, there was no fear, just delight and relief. Cody and I went through a lot together and I couldn't imagine having another dog.

But life had other plans... as seen in the picture on the back cover. This yellow Labrador went through a lot before his arrival here. Found wandering around a park, he went to the Greenbelt Maryland Animal Shelter, more than an hour away from my home. Howard, the director, told me they thought the owner would appear, because the dog was in excellent condition with a loving personality. But that didn't happen.

People fell in love with him so he was adopted...and returned in less than 24 hours! "I can't control this dog!" the woman said. Then he was adopted again. Four hours later, another woman called emergency number, "You have to take this dog back!" Yes, they'd take him back, but the shelter was closed until morning. This person admitted that she "stuffed him into a small crate overnight." (Maybe that's why we're having crate-training problems now.) The Animal Control Officer/Shelter Coordinator Howard Stanback was shocked so he took him home for the long Thanksgiving weekend to see what was going on with this mild-mannered dog. He saw no difficult behavior, even with an indignant Yorkie around. Then real trouble started. When he returned to his place at the shelter, the dog showed anxiety by chewing on his tail. Howard suggested this dog only after he grilled me about the home environment, my temperament, etc. Meanwhile, the tail became infected and the vet had to amputate part of it. I showed up the next day.

He moved in and had a somewhat quiet night. The next morning, this calm, sweet dog handled the planned arrival of family and friends for a day of the Christmas in St. Michaels Festival like he'd been part of us for years. Then the infection spread. Drs. Coughlan and Christie went to work. Three weeks, seven vet visits and lots of pills later, the dog is alive, well and still has his tail!

This dog's name is Leo, short for Leonides, the brave Spartan king who turned back the Turks in Greece. Remember the movie *300*? It's appropriate because of my Spartan heritage and the bravery this dog has shown.

Now, Leo has claimed his place next to my writing desk. His antics are already inspiring blogs which I'll post at www.SusanReiss.com. And yes, he is the basis of the new character, Sunny.

ACKNOWLEDGEMENTS

*Y*es, it takes a village to write a book! Many thanks to...

HELEN HERMAN at Blue Crab Coffee in St. Michaels who introduced me to cold-press coffee which makes a heavenly iced beverage for a scorching hot summer day. It's now a favorite that Abby and I share. And many thanks to the baristas there who always keep my cup full of piping hot tea.

The Police Chief and officers of the St. Michaels Police Department. Corporal Ben Taylor shared his expertise about firearms and police procedure and the Eastern Shore axiom, "An unloaded gun is useless."

Anne Bartlett and John Jelich made suggestions to create Mary Rose's garden surrounding Willow Cottage. Anne is a well-known landscape architect on the Eastern Shore.

Leslie, a unique woman who loves grammar! She keeps me on my toes as we debate the proper use of commas, hyphens and compound adjectives. Any mistakes in this story are mine.

Beth Shortall, a transplant to the Shore, who has a keen eye for interesting character traits and names and is always a great source of encouragement!

The staff at the St. Michaels Library: you always meet the challenge posed by my research questions with enthusiasm and determination. And Mary, the volunteer in the Maryland Room, who came up with this great title!

Roy Myers who served St. Michaels as a town commissioner and a member of various boards and commissions. His study of the effects of climate change on our low-lying village make us aware of what's happening so we can talk about how to protect our way of life.

Steve Friedberg and his family who care for an old cemetery on private property next to a creek off the Miles River. It was the inspiration for Mary Rose's family cemetery. There, I found the small stone marker carved with a sleeping dog next to a woman's grave, a perpetual sign of love that was too beautiful for this writer to pass up.

And to my family, you are my source of love and support and always in my heart.

"NAME THE CHARACTER" RAFFLE

We held the raffle to benefit the St. Michaels Library, a branch of the Talbot County Free Library. The winner was Pat Rogers, a resident of Easton.

She chose the name Edward Stephen in honor of her son struck down by disease in his youth. Hearing Eddie's story, I decided to create a special character who plays an important role in this story. We'll be seeing more of Eddie in a coming book.

All proceeds from the raffle are going to the purchase of new DVDs and books on CD. Thanks to everyone who participated!

Silver Mystery Series
Set in Saint Michaels

FIRST BOOK

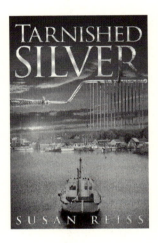

When software developer Abby Strickland receives an unexpected inheritance sterling silver, her world turns upside down. The police arrive when her special cake server becomes a murder weapon. With blood on the family silver, she sets out to find the real killer. Lured to the crime scene in Saint Michaels, a sailing destination on the Chesapeake Bay, Abby finds a different way of life filled with quirky characters, boat races,
a handsome guy.

And a tangled web of wealth, greed and family secrets.

Silver Mystery Series
Set in Saint Michaels

SECOND BOOK

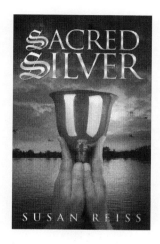

Sterling silver expert Abby Strickland wants to spend the holidays curled up with her books and her puppy, Simon. When an antique chalice disappears from a local church with a puzzle of clues left in its place, she is drawn into a dangerous treasure hunt. Along the way, she learns about things that people do for love… and some they shouldn't.
Can she navigate the maze of secret desires
in time to save the spirit of the season…and a life?

Silver Mystery Series
Set in Saint Michaels

THIRD BOOK

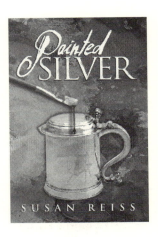

Accidental sleuth Abby Strickland goes to the Plein Air Art Festival where gifted artists compete for big prizes and fame. Elite art collectors eagerly search for their next acquisitions. Tension between rivals runs high as all are drawn into a net of creative envy, greed… and murder.

It's a charming summer event…
until somebody screams!

Silver Mystery Series
Set in Saint Michaels

FOURTH BOOK

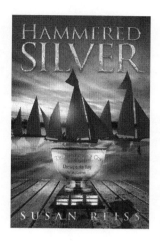

The discovery of an engraved bowl draws sterling silver expert Abby Strickland into a world where nothing is what it seems... where majestic sailboats unique to the Chesapeake Bay are called log canoes... hammered doesn't mean drunk... close friends become fierce competitors in the race for the coveted Governor's Cup Trophy.

Does the story of a century-old murder stay in the past or lead to blood and chaos in the water right in front of Abby's eyes? Was it an accident or was it revenge? Does the color purple lead to the killer or to a secret that puts Abby in danger?

Made in the USA
Middletown, DE
23 March 2019